I0585458

A PENNY FOR
YOUR THOUGHTS

Creative Texts Publishers products are available at special discounts for bulk purchase for sale promotions, premiums, fund-raising, and educational needs. For details, write Creative Texts Publishers, PO Box 50, Barto, PA 19504, or visit www.creativetexts.com

A PENNY FOR YOUR THOUGHTS
By Jerry D. Young
Published by Creative Texts Publishers
PO Box 50
Barto, PA 19504
www.creativetexts.com

The following is a work of fiction. Any resemblance to actual names, persons, businesses, and incidents is strictly coincidental. Locations are used only in the general sense and do not represent the real place in actuality.

ISBN: 978-0-692-12566-3

A PENNY FOR YOUR THOUGHTS

JERRY D. YOUNG

Chapter One

-

The shock that Horatio Billings received immediately upon entering his office when he returned from his two-week business trip was only the first he would receive that day. And those shocks came fast and furious.

"Uh... Hello?" Horatio said when he saw the long copper hair of a female stranger sitting at the reception desk in his modest attorney's office.

The woman spun the desk chair around, the copper hair catching the sunlight from the window, causing it to shimmer. Despite the pixie face surrounded by the hair, Horatio's eyes were suddenly looking around the reception area. "What happened here? Who are you? Where is Kimmy?"

"Oh. Hi. Hm... Where to start..." The woman's soft tones brought Horatio's eyes back to her. But he could not see her eyes. They were studiously locked on the surface of the desk.

A desk that, Horatio noticed, was devoid of any of the mess it had held when he had departed two weeks previously. And the old wood gleamed with a shine like he had never seen.

The woman's eyes cut up, under her long lashes, but dropped back down immediately. "I should explain..."

"Uh... Yeah? That would be nice. Just who are you and why are you in my office, sitting behind my receptionist's desk?" Horatio asked, his voice rising slightly by the end of the question. He stood with hands on his hips, all six feet two of hard muscled body quivering with impatience.

"I'm Penny. I am... well... sort of filling in... for a while..."

Sudden alarm shot through Horatio and he paled. The gasp that escaped him brought the woman's eyes up to his face. Horatio felt his eyes widen slightly. The woman's eyes were an astounding shade of green. Clearer and purer than emerald even. They put him in mind of a tsavorite gemstone he had seen on the very trip from which he had just returned.

He shook off the shock of seeing those eyes in that pixie face and quickly asked, "Is Kimmy okay? Did something happen to her? Tell me!"

The woman lifted her hands, palms forward. "She's fine. She's fine," her eyes on Horatio's more emerald green eyes. But her eyes dropped quickly. "Physically anyway."

Horatio could barely hear the words; they were so soft and low.

"Physically? What does that mean? Physically?" Horatio found himself leaning forward, his hands on the desk.

His shadow cut across the desk and the woman looked up and a faint gasp escaped her naturally soft red lips as they formed a tiny *O*.

Horatio noted that she did not scoot the chair back in fright, but just met his gaze for a moment before dropping her eyes again. Horatio quickly stood up and took a step back. He had learned from the past that his size and demeanor could intimidate people, even when he did not intend to. When he did want to, it was quite an advantage.

He took a deep breath. "Let's start this over. What is your name again?"

"Penny. Penny Arcade." Her voice trailed off as she looked at Horatio again, holding out her right hand. When his left eyebrow lifted in curiosity, she put her right hand down and clasped her left with it, on top of the desk.

Her eyes cut down, but immediately back up, fascinated by the look on his face. It came out without thinking. Which did not surprise her at all as soon as she said it. "How do you do that? That eyebrow thing?"

Horatio looked stunned. "Eyebrow thing? What are you talking about?" He was totally at a loss.

Penny lifted her eyebrows but lifted her right hand and pushed down her right one. "Like this. Just your left eyebrow went up. I've never seen anyone that could do that before."

Both of Horatio's eyebrows went up with that.

"Okay. So, it isn't a droopy eye or anything," Penny said, sounding pleased. "That is good."

"Penny. Penny Arcade," Horatio said, taking a half a step forward, his voice going lower, and in what sounded even to himself like an ominous tone," continued, "How is Kimmy?"

"She's kinda angry. Well... Truthfully, she's very angry."

"Angry? About what?" Horatio asked. The fact that Kimmy was angry did not surprise him all that much, but why Penny knew was beyond him.

"Her houseboat sank." There was the tiniest pause, but Horatio noticed it. "For one thing."

"For one thing? That mansion on a boat sank? How?"

Horatio thought Penny might giggle at his reference to Kimmy's houseboat as a mansion on a boat. But she did not. Her eyes dropped again.

"It is... was... a humongous thing, wasn't it? Two stories and a roof deck, and what... one hundred feet long?" Penny asked, taking a quick peek at Horatio.

"Hundred twenty. Twenty-four wide." Horatio closed his eyes and shook his head. "Kimmy would be more than angry. She'd be furious. Do you have any idea what happened?"

Horatio saw Penny wince, and her shoulders slump, her eyes not on the desk any longer, but on her lap, where her hands seemed to be wringing together, though he could only see where her forearms went below his line of sight.

"Penny?" Horatio questioned, his voice firm.

"Well... She thinks I kind of sank it..."

"You kinda sank Kimmy's houseboat?" His voice was at least three octaves higher now. "How the bloody... How could you have possibly sunk that battleship?"

At least his voice had dropped lower again. Penny was thankful for that. "I... uh... Sank probably is not the correct word, actually," Penny's voice was soft. But she was a stickler for the truth. Sort of.

Horatio let out a relieved sigh. "Thank God. What? It just settled down, there at the dock?" Even as he said it, he was already sure that was not what Penny had meant.

"No..." The word was rather drawn out. "When the bass boat ran into it..." her words faded away.

This time Penny's eyes stayed on Horatio's ever more incredulous widening ones. "Uh... The bass boat hit it going pretty fast... Full throttle, actually... That pointed bow punched a hole... a really big hole... in the side of the houseboat hull almost right in the middle. The bass boat kind of disintegrated and left a hole that went under the waterline.

"The houseboat hull began to fill pretty quick and listed, throwing Kimmy and... and someone else on the top deck into the water, and then the thing turned turtle and settled on its sun roof and support arches. I am sorry. So sorry."

Penny had finished in a rush, and her eyes went back down to the top of the desk. But her hands were still on her lap. Horatio was sure he had seen tears bead on her lashes.

"Lord! She must have been livid! Wait! You said she went into the water? She can't swim!"

"No. I know," Penny replied promptly. "When she did not come up immediately, I went under the water and felt around until I found her. When I got her to the surface she was able to take a breath okay. And then she started screaming. Kinda in general at first.

"Then at the guy. He had waded ashore and took off running. Kind of funny actually. Running down the marina naked. Oops."

The touch of a smile that had formed on Penny's lips for a scant moment disappeared as quickly as it had appeared.

"Naked man?" Horatio asked, unable to take that fact in quite yet.

Penny had both her lips sucked in, her teeth biting on them. She nodded and took a quick look up at Horatio. Quickly she went on with the tale. "I got Kimmy to shore. I had some of my things on the dock and that included the big skirt and peasant blouse I sometimes wear on research trips in one of my bags. I got her dressed before anyone else showed up. It was kinda short on her and tight, but... anyway, she was dressed when people started to show up."

It suddenly hit Horatio like a blow. "Wait. Kimmy was naked, too? With a naked guy?"

Again, the double lip bite. Penny nodded. "Fortunately, they were on the top deck going at... Uh... At least they were on the top deck and were thrown clear so they were not trapped in the houseboat when it turned turtle."

Now quick nervous glances brought Penny's eyes up to Horatio's face. His eyes had a distant look in them. He looked hurt. Quickly she said, "I'm sure..."

"What else happened?" Horatio asked, cutting her off.

"The guy driving the bass boat was already headed up to the marina office to get help. Fortunately, he'd been wearing the seat belt and PFD when he hit the houseboat and did not get hurt. He was able to get on the dock.

"Then... Uh... well... when Kimmy got a good look at the houseboat... and then me in the lights from the dock lights... she sort of lost it, then. She assumed I was driving the bass boat I guess. You know. With me being wet and all..."

Horatio's eyes went to Penny's hand when it rose to touch her left cheek and rubbed it gently. When he looked closely, he could see the now faint marks on her face, despite the light makeup that Penny had tried to cover them with.

"She hit you?" Horatio gasped out. "Kimmy hit you?" He was just as angry at the fact that he was not surprised when Penny nodded as he was that Penny had, indeed, nodded.

But Penny was already saying, "Not with her fist, of course. She just slapped me." Then more softly, hand still on her cheek. "A couple of times. She just lost control. It could happen to anyone."

Horatio noted the slight protest. "Kimmy has a temper, all right." Horatio stepped up to the desk. "Wait! You weren't driving the boat that hit the house boat?"

Penny shook her head.

"What happened then?"

"The marina people grabbed her and hurried her off, and the fire department showed up, and then the police. I explained what happened and when they were distracted by Kimmy up on the parking lot I sneaked back into the water and recovered what I could of my stuff and took off. The bow wave of the bass boat, and then the house boat turning turtle washed some of my stuff off the dock and into the water."

It suddenly struck Horatio that Penny had mentioned the dock lights. And she had snuck back into the water. His eyes widened again and he nearly shouted, "This was at night? You were in that freezing water, at night? With all that stuff that had to be there after the houseboat went over and the bass boat?"

"Uh... Well... Yes. I had to get it before the fuel caught... uh..." Penny saw the concern flash in Horatio's eyes, and then the anger. "It was no big deal," she quickly said. "I see really well at night, and I'm a very good swimmer."

Horatio's face went pale. Alarmingly pale. Penny jumped up from the chair. "You okay? You want a glass of water?" The concern on her face and in her voice cut through Horatio's shock. And then he noticed that she had stood up. It was kind of hard to tell, since her head was not all that much higher than it was when she was sitting down.

He leaned forward and looked over the desk. There was a thick pillow on the seat of the chair. Horatio cut his eyes over to Penny and saw her turn red. "How tall are you?" he asked.

She straightened to stand as tall as she could. Horatio looked over the desk again, this time at Penny's feet. She had on remarkably tall heels. "Without your heels?" His eyes went to her face. The red was fading from it, but there was still color in her cheeks, and a stubborn look on her face.

"Four nine... almost." Her eyes dropped again. The *"almost"* was barely audible.

Horatio closed his eyes and sighed. He opened them and saw the concerned look still on Penny's face. "I'm fine. I do not need any water."

Penny slowly sat back down as Horatio looked around the office. His gaze snapped back to Penny and she winced. "Okay. Kimmy is okay, at least. And angry. Still does not explain why Kimmy is not here, and you are, and what transformed this office." Horatio decided he would think about and deal with a naked Kimmy and naked guy that was not him on her houseboat. In private.

With a deep sigh, Penny spoke again, "Well... since I guess I distracted the guy in the bass boat, it was sort of my fault... And... And I overheard Kimmy telling someone named Maddy, that had come to pick her up at the marina, that your office would just have to stay closed until you got back because there was no way she was going to go to work with what had happened…"

Horatio blanched. Kimmy was his paralegal as well as girlfriend. He had scheduled clients in for the time he was gone, for Kimmy to work with to get things ready for action.

Penny saw the reaction. "It's okay," she said reassuringly. "I came in the next morning… Saturday and found the appointment calendar and read up on the files after I found them and… and… well… Got all the appointments taken care of, and new appointments set for the next few days so you can get back on track with everything."

Again, Penny's words had been fast and furious as she completed her statement.

Horatio knew he must have looked livid. Because he was. "You can't do that! That is confidential information! And you cannot give legal advice! Even Kimmy can't give legal advice! Only an attorney can do what you did! I could get disbarred!" His shoulders slumped.

"It's okay! Really!" Penny said, standing again, looking at Horatio again, sincerity in her eyes. "I've worked as a paralegal before. I know the rules. I am just acting as a temp until you straighten things out with Kimmy."

The last sentence was again a soft one, with it being obvious to Horatio that Penny was feeling sorry for him about Kimmy and the naked guy.

Horatio began to breathe again. "You're a paralegal?"

"Well, for the moment. Just for this situation. I don't really like the work and decided to pursue something else after I got my degree and worked for a while."

Horatio loved being an attorney. He could not fathom anyone with legal training to not love doing it. His disbelief showed when he asked, "You don't like being a paralegal?"

"Oh, it was all right. I thought about going ahead and becoming an attorney, but it just isn't for me. There are some other things I want to do."

Her earnest words convinced him. But it was still hard to accept. He decided to get back to the subject at hand. "How did you get in here? I have serious doubts that Kimmy would have given you the code, considering."

"Um… The… Uh… The back door was unlocked when I checked. I thought a cleaning crew might be here and I could get in when they weren't looking."

Horatio was shaking his head. "Cleaning crew comes in Wednesday nights. Kimmy left the door unlocked again?"

"She'd done it before? It really surprised me that it was unlocked and no one was here." Penny said. "I thought I would have to pick..." She shut up quickly. Horatio seemed not to have caught the last part.

With a sigh Horatio flopped back into one of the chairs facing the reception desk. "Yeah." He ran a hand through his auburn hair. "Bone of contention. She has problems with responsibility."

Horatio cut his eyes quickly to Penny. He was not about to get into his relationship with Kimmy with Penny. It was none of her business. Suddenly he calmed himself down. Penny had not brought it up. He had.

When the phone rang, and Penny picked it up, Horatio took a quick look at his watch. It was just after nine. He refocused his attention on Penny. She was talking to one of his clients. His left eyebrow lifted again, as he listened to Penny's side of the conversation.

She had responded with Harry Peterson's name right after her initial greeting on the phone. He was rather impressed as Penny obviously answered some questions Peterson had about his case. From what she was saying, she obviously knew the legalese, and he had a feeling that she was giving correct answers to the questions.

When she hung up a couple of minutes later and saw Horatio watching her, color rose in her cheeks again, but she said, "You have an appointment in twenty minutes. The file and my notes are on your desk. You want some coffee while you get up to speed?"

"Um... Yes. Please." But Horatio gave Penny what he hoped was a hard look. "But this discussion is not over. And do not think for a minute that you will be working here any longer than it takes me to find out what happened with Kimmy and she comes back to work."

"Of course," Penny said, standing again to head for the small employee break room down the hall past the restrooms.

Before she took a step, though, she looked over at Horatio again. "You know, you might want to call the police. I know this looks very bad. It would not hurt my feelings or anything if you wanted to go through legal steps... It is just... Well... I can call and have them send out a detective for you to talk to... And to questions me, of course... And..."

Horatio had watched, amazed at her suggestion. And notice how fast she was talking when her voice trailed off. He sighed. There was just something about the woman that made him feel like he could trust her.

He had good people reading skills, developed working with clients. Everything he was hearing, seeing, and feeling told him to trust her. At least long enough to get to the bottom of things himself, first.

Besides, the thought coming to him suddenly, he really did not want to bring Detective Logan into it. The man was a menace and would dearly love to give Horatio a hard time. And complicate everything as much as possible.

"No," Horatio said. "That is not necessary. But you and I are going to hash all of this out, just as soon as we get a break."

Penny nodded, and headed toward the break room, as Horatio entered his office. When Penny returned a moment later with the cup of coffee on the saucer with two chocolate chip cookies she found Horatio standing in the doorway of his office.

"You did this?" he asked when Penny cleared her throat hesitatingly.

"Um... I kind of had a hard time finding things. I organized everything so I could find it more quickly."

Horatio turned his head to look at her, but then turned back around and stepped into the office, headed for the chair behind his desk. He continued to look around.

Like the reception area, his office had been transformed from a messy, disorganized near disaster area, to a sleek, professional looking attorney's office with everything clean, polished, shining, and looking like everything had a place and everything was in its place. Horatio picked up the file and read the set of sticky notes attached to the outside cover.

Horatio cut his eyes up to Penny as she placed the saucer with cup and cookies on the desk, near his right hand. He went back to reading the notes. They were all in line with what he had been thinking about for this case before he had left.

The phone rang then and Penny hurried back out to the reception desk to answer it. Horatio was too busy the rest of the day to think about anything but work. He ate the lunch that Penny set on his desk thankfully, while he went through the next file for his first appointment in the afternoon.

He could not believe the amount of work he accomplished. Before he had gone on the business trip, he would not have been able to complete the morning's appointments, using the entire day, much less those in the morning and four more during the afternoon. And he had even eaten lunch.

At four o'clock, not long after his last appointment for the day had left, and he was getting things ready for the next day, based on the appointment calendar that Penny had provided, Penny showed up in the door to his office.

"I guess I'd better get my stuff out of the way and let you have your life back." She turned to go.

"Wait. Penny." Horatio stood and moved toward the reception area. Penny was bending over to get her purse from beneath the huge U-shaped reception desk and counter.

He could not help it when his eyes traveled from the black heels on Penny's feet, up the length of her legs to the hem of the dress that rose up high on her thighs, to her trim waist as she straightened, and then when she turned the small bust in the modest bodice of the dress, and finally her pixie face, framed with copper hair. And those deep tsavorite green eyes.

"Look. Until I get things straightened out with Kimmy... Or get a new paralegal, would you hang around and help me out for a few days?"

"Of course. I didn't mean clean out here. I meant at the... Oops." Penny's eyes and voice both dropped.

"Penny?" Horatio asked softly. "Oops what?"

Penny heaved a deep sigh and looked up at Horatio again. "There's a bit more to the story..."

"Oh, really?" Horatio asked, not a bit surprised at the revelation, he realized.

"Um... Yes. I'm afraid so." Suddenly she was rushing through the explanation.

Horatio decided it was a nervous habit of hers. To say anything she did not really want to say, quickly. Get it all out in a hurry.

"I just got into town and wanted to get my research done, and then all that happened and I didn't have a place to live and since Kimmy said she wasn't going to open the office and I had to take care of that and then found Kimmy was staying with her father and not at your place and I needed a place to live and your house was going to be empty for a while..."

Her words finally slowed down and trailed off. Horatio could not help it. He flushed, his fists balled up onto his hips and he stared at Penny for long moments before he bellowed, "You are living in my house?"

Eye's down, Penny nodded. Very slightly, but it was enough for Horatio to know it was a fact. "I do not believe this! How did you get in my house? I know I did not leave any door in it unlocked. And Kimmy doesn't even have a key. I have the only keys!"

"Not really..." Penny said softly. "There is the one in the rock keeper..."

Horatio's eyes narrowed. He remembered having bought the hidden key keeper that was made to look like just one more stone among many that lined the flower beds along the walk up from the sidewalk to his porch. "You found that key?"

Penny shrugged slightly. "Actually, it was kind of obvious."

Horatio nearly choked. "Obvious? That stinking rock cost me forty dollars! It blends in with that rock border like one of the native rocks!"

Penny was shaking her head. "Uh. The shape and placement kind of gives it away."

"That is just great! All this time and I thought that place was secure when I was gone." Horatio sighed and shook his head again. Then he remembered what the primary discussion was about.

"You moved into my house?" He knew his voice was rising again and tried to calm himself down again.

There was that biting of her lips again. Horatio could not seem to take his eyes off them. She nodded. But then quickly said. "It will only take me a few minutes to get things moved out and loaded up. But... perhaps you should call the pol..."

Horatio managed to keep from shouting, but it was a strong, "NO. We do not need the police." Then he frowned. "But moving out would probably be a good idea. I have to say I am more than a bit... uncomfortable... about anyone being in my home..."

"It is an intrusion. I know. I am sorry. I just..." Penny said, her words fading. She quickly started through what Horatio realized was a well thought out office shutdown for the night procedure.

The back door was locked, office equipment shut down, bathroom checked for paper and toiletries, the coffee pot turned off, coffee supplies checked, small refrigerator checked, and an organized reorder list marked. Penny set the alarm system and then hurried out the front door of the small office building.

Horatio was a bit befuddled by the tiny woman exiting his free-standing strip mall office building. The list of shocks that had started when he walked in, followed by one after another. And one more was added when Horatio walked toward his new Chevy Impala, while he watched Penny head for whatever she was driving.

That was when the shock occurred. She did not get into any sub compact car. Not a hybrid. Not a crossover SUV. He was more than a little surprised when it looked like she was headed for a Suburban parked at the corner of the next freestanding office building in the mall. What shocked him was that she walked right past it and stopped at the vehicle next to it.

He knew he was staring, mouth wide open, his chin almost on the ground, when the diminutive woman opened the left side saddle bag of a tricked-out Harley Davidson trike. At first Horatio thought it was trike, but then he noticed that it was a two-wheel conversion unit, flanking the rear drive wheel of an obviously custom Harley bike. A very big bike. Made even larger with the conversion.

Penny took out a set of brown motorcycle leathers, tall leather boots, and a helmet from the saddlebag and proceeded to put them on as Horatio hurried over.

She still had her back to him when she leaned over slightly to pull the brown leather pants on over her feet, hiking the back of her dress up probably more than she realized, causing Horatio to let out a squeaking breath at the sight of her trim, firm thighs before the pants were up to her waist and she was fastening them under the dress.

Penny whirled around at the sound and looked up at Horatio's face. "You okay? You look... a bit strange..."

"I'm... I'm fine." He knew it was probably more than a bit insulting when he asked Penny, as she shrugged into the heavy leather jacket, "You're going to ride this?"

But she did not bat an eye. She was putting on the boots. She just said, "Yep. This is my day ride. I'll meet you at the house?" she asked as she put her heels in the saddle bag. It came out more like a question than statement. She had her helmet on before Horatio could gather enough wits about him to nod.

Her helmeted head nodded in return, and she climbed onto the left side running board, threw her right leg over the seat, curling the leg behind to clear the backrest, and sat down on the low-slung seat. A scant moment later and the bike roared to life.

"Geez!" Horatio muttered as he ran toward the Impala, watching over his shoulder as Penny ran three gears, accelerating quickly toward the mall exit on the bike. She was long gone on the street by the time he bumped into the Impala's rear end, recovered, ran around, and got in.

Horatio started the car and headed out after Penny. It was not until he turned onto his street that he saw her again. She was already parked to one side of the driveway, the bike facing the street, standing there, waiting for him, without the jacket, but with the dress still covering the leather pants.

Her hands clasped in front of her, eyes down, Penny told Horatio when he approached, "I will get the trailer loaded with most of my stuff. I'll have to get the truck to get the rest. I'll get it from storage and bring it tomorrow."

She looked at him, twisting her head slightly sideways and tilting it as Horatio hurried past her, "I should have stopped here first..." Horatio was saying.

Penny already had the key she had been using in her hand to give to him when he whirled around after opening the door and stepping inside. He had got a good look around the living room before he spun around.

"Oh," he said, taking the key absently. He pretty much glared at her. "You cleaned this place up, too!" It was an accusation.

Her delicate look shoulders shrugged slightly. "Just picked up a little..."

Horatio stalked off toward the hallway leading toward the bedrooms. Penny was still standing just inside the door when he marched back into the living room and on into the kitchen. When he did not come right back out, Penny edged that way, meeting him at the doorway just as he was coming back.

Penny managed to stop, but Horatio did not, bowling Penny over so hard she landed on her rump and rolled backwards, feet and legs flying upward as she "Oomphed" loudly.

"Dang it!" Horatio muttered. More loudly he said, "I'm sorry." He reached down and essentially picked her up with one hand and stood her on her feet.

"Wow. You're even stronger than you look!"

A look of concern was on Horatio's face now when Penny looked up from the bulging muscles of his right arm to his face. "Are you all right? Did I hurt you? Did the fall hurt you?"

"Naw," Penny said, shrugging the incident away. "I managed to control the landing okay. No harm, no foul. I'll get my stuff." She spun on her heel and headed for the bedrooms.

"Wait a minute," Horatio said, carefully controlling his voice now. He touched her arm gently, making sure not to grab it. As upset as he was he knew he could easily bruise her tanned arm without meaning to.

Again, her head was down, her eyes on the floor.

"Look at me." Again, Horatio controlled his voice, both timber and tone.

Penny looked up hesitatingly. "Yes?"

"Picked up a little? This house is spotless. Laundry done, tub and toilet scrubbed to a shine, the kitchen is spotless. And the fridge is stocked with enough food to last a week."

"Uh... You didn't look in the pantry, did you?" Penny asked, managing to keep her eyes on Horatio's face.

Horatio blinked once, spun, and went back into the kitchen. Penny heard the pantry cabinet door open gently, but close rather firmly. When Horatio returned he gave her another look, which she met. "Enough food for a month! For a baseball team!"

Penny shrugged again. Horatio was beginning to wish she would not do that. Every time she did his eyes would drop to her bust. There was not much of it, but it was very... jiggly. He was pretty sure she was not wearing a bra, but that the dress had a shelf bra built in.

He lifted his eyes hastily. Penny did not seem to have noticed the direction his eyes had gone. "A good pantry is just a good idea. Never know when something might happen and you might not be able to restock expeditiously."

There went the left eyebrow again, Penny noted, when Horatio repeated the word.

"Expeditiously?"

"Un-huh. Like if the stores do not get their JIT deliveries for some reason."

Again, Horatio repeated a word. "JIT?"

"You know. Just in time?"

"Just in time for what?" Horatio asked, truly and completely baffled.

"Just in time so the shelves don't go empty."

Horatio was shaking his head. "I have absolutely no clue what you are talking about. But that can wait. Are you going to tell me why you decided to move into my house in my absence?"

Horatio, though he was the one facing the door, was the one that nearly jumped out of his skin when the loud, angry words, "I would like to know that, as well," came from the doorway. Out of an obviously angry Kimmy.

Horatio heard the sad sigh, and then the "Uh-oh," from Penny as she slowly turned toward Kimmy, who was marching toward the two of them, murder in her eyes.

Quickly deciding that while discretion might be the better part of valor, Horatio stepped between the rapidly approaching Kimmy and the steadfastly standing Penny anyway.

"Calm down, Kimmy. I am sure there is a reasonable explanation for Penny covering at the office... And staying here..."

Kimmy's angry gaze cut from the sliver of Penny's face she could see behind Horatio's broad shoulders, to Horatio's face. The high-pitched voice went even higher. "She has been at the office? I did not open the office at all for the past two weeks!" she nearly screamed.

"Uh. Yes. I know," Horatio said, trying for a calm tone, though her admission stung him and annoyed him more than a little. He carefully put his hands on her shoulders when she got close enough and was trying to get around him to Penny.

"Is she the one that changed…" Kimmy quickly closed her mouth.

"I will get to the bottom of this," Horatio said. "Just calm down and we will hear Penny out."

A low, but firm, "I will tell you. I'm not going to tell her," came from behind Horatio.

Horatio winced when Kimmy's screech hurt his ears. Kimmy tried to push past Horatio again, but even her tall, firm body did not even budge him.

"Calm down, Kimmy. This is not helping. I will find out what this is all about. Just give Penny and me a few minutes."

"You are not going to be alone with that… that… pipsqueak!"

Horatio closed his eyes for a moment when he heard Penny mutter, "Sticks and stones…" and then fall silent behind him. It had been like a mantra. One she had probably learned as soon as it became obvious she was not going to get any taller than she was, Horatio decided.

"Now, just go sit down in the living room and I will take Penny into the kitchen and get to the bottom of this."

Kimmy stamped her foot. But Horatio was glad to know that she relaxed slightly and began to draw away. But as she looked around at the living room she was screeching again. "You hired a cleaning lady while I was gone! I have been trying to get you to do that for ages! And you do it while I am gone? Who did you get? You better have hired…"

Her eyes suddenly narrowing when Horatio started to turn and look at Penny, she screeched again, "She did this? She cleaned your house? Why? What, are you sleeping with her, too?"

Kimmy gasped at the look that was suddenly in Horatio's eyes. His eyes cut to Penny, who was now standing slightly away from Horatio, though still essentially behind him. "You told him something!" Kimmy looked at Horatio again. "She's lying! I am telling you she is lying! Who are you going to believe? That little shrimp of a tramp or me, your girlfriend of three years?"

"I only told him about the office being closed," Penny said quietly. "None of the other… Aw, shucks. Oops." Penny sighed, and then muttered, "I have to learn to just keep my mouth shut completely."

Horatio's eyes quickly went back to Kimmy. He saw her pale to whiteness under her deep tan, and a look of panic show up in her eyes. "You will not believe her, Horatio! Do not believe anything she says! She's out to get me for some reason. She sank my houseboat, for crying out loud! On purpose!"

There was color back in her cheeks, Horatio saw, but she was still pale otherwise. And staring daggers at Penny.

"Perhaps you better go and let me deal with Penny. On my own terms. We'll discuss whatever we need to discuss. Later. Sometime later."

Kimmy looked at Horatio's stony face and decided it might be better to regroup, come up with a new story, and a new plan, and try again after Horatio got rid of the woman. Which she knew he would. He wanted her, Kimmy, not some little nobody. There was nothing the woman could say that would change Horatio's mind about her.

She could not have heard much, if anything of that conversation with Maddy at the marina, beyond the not opening the office. She had been yelling at that point, she remembered. And there was no way she could know any of the rest. Kimmy spun on her heel and marched out of the house.

Horatio looked around. Penny was watching him, a guarded look on her face. He sighed, closed his eyes, and then took a deep, calming breath. "Okay. Penny. Please, sit down. Will you go over the whole thing again for me? I am having a hard time getting my head around all of this..."

Horatio shook his head. Penny could see that he was truly confused. *"And no wonder,"* she thought to herself.

So, Penny went over to the sofa and sat down, putting her hands together in her lap as she waited for Horatio to take the chair near the end of the sofa where she sat. Then, without prompting from Horatio, she repeated what she had told him that morning.

Penny did not repeat the part about Kimmy and the guy on the top deck of the houseboat being naked.

"Wait a minute," Horatio finally broke in, having listened right up to the point when Penny mentioned that she was assuming some responsibility for the accident because she had distracted the guy in the bass boat. "How can any of this be your fault? What do you mean you distracted the guy in the bass boat?"

Horatio saw Penny wince. "Well... you see... I changed out of my wet suit in my boat, out on the lake after I got out of the water after I had dived..." Penny saw the look on Horatio's face.

"You were diving in the lake?"

Penny nodded. "Looking for signs of... well... that doesn't matter. When I checked for other boats before I dove, and put out the dive marker, there wasn't anyone anywhere around. I guess I didn't look close enough when I got back in the boat. That bass boat was really compact and not very tall.

"I was a bit cold, so I stripped out of the wet suit and dried off before I put on my clothes." Penny sighed. "I guess the guy in the bass boat had stopped and backed off quite a ways when he saw my dive marker.

"When I was dressed I heard the bass boat engine roar, and then finally saw the boat. He was coming right at me. That is when I figured out that he must have been curious because I think he probably had his binoculars on me when I came out of the water."

Horatio noticed that though she had turned pink, and even red a couple of times during her explanation, she did neither when she admitted that someone had probably been watching her change from her wet suit to her other clothes. She just went blithely on.

"I didn't really want to have to explain what was going on, nor talk to some guy that had just seen me change clothes right out in the open, so I headed for the marina before he got close."

Penny cut her eyes over to Horatio when he said, "Some of those bass boats are fast."

Penny nodded. "Yeah. I know. But I'd rented one that just happens to be faster. A lot faster, I guess. Because I was already at the dock and tied up when he came barreling in at full throttle, looking for me, I think. He saw me and didn't see the houseboat. It was already past twilight."

"So that makes it your fault? That doesn't make any sense," Horatio said. "It was his fault." Horatio suddenly went silent. "Where was the houseboat, exactly?"

Penny sighed. "At the dock just beyond the fueling dock."

"Kimmy knows she is not supposed to tie up there at night!" Horatio had his elbows on his knees. He put his head in his hands and groaned. "She's been warned and warned about blocking the entrance to the rest of the marina with that thing. She likes to be close to the marina club house."

Penny stayed silent. But then Horatio lifted his head and said, "Please continue."

"Not really much left," Penny said. "The authorities took everyone's statement that was there. I... loaded up my stuff and..." Penny dropped her eyes and fell silent.

"And?" Horatio prompted.

"It... well... it kind of gets complicated from there..." Penny said softly.

"Actually, I think you left out a couple of things that you mentioned this morning. Care to go over those?" Horatio asked. His voice was not loud, or even demanding sounding, but Penny heard the plea in it.

"Do I really have to?" she asked, a wince visible on her face as she looked at Horatio as she spoke.

"Please?" Horatio asked softly.

Penny sighed. "Okay. I... uh... heard Kimmy talking to her friend... Maddy... I heard her say... words to the effect that she wasn't going to be going to your office until you got back, because of all that had happened. I heard the word attorney in the conversation somewhere. Not sure exactly what part. I was a little... disconcerted about some of what she was saying."

Penny met Horatio's eyes and held them for a long time with her own. "I'm sorry," she said softly.

"Please. I need to know. And you know I need to, I suspect." Horatio's voice was just as soft.

After a moment, Penny nodded. She dropped her eyes and continued, quietly. "Kimmy said... again, she was screaming wordlessly and then sobbing and then yelling... And then whispering to Maddy.

"I was kinda out of the way, sitting on a bench sort of behind one of those big pillar trash containers... But close enough to hear most of it. It was a little difficult to make out part of it... So maybe I am misinterpreting some of it..." Penny gave Horatio a hopeful look.

But when he did not give her any indication of any kind, she took a breath and continued. "There was something about moving up a timetable. Something about some accounts and some money transfers."

Penny fell silent for long moments. She looked at Horatio again, but he was still silent. "Something... Something about, since she didn't have a ring yet... She was going to have to do it the hard way."

At that, Penny heard Horatio groan. She looked over. He had his head in his hands again. "I should have listened to Andy," she heard Horatio mutter.

He lifted his head and looked at Penny. "Go on."

"That's about it. I just got a bad feeling about things..." This time Penny sighed deeply. "I have a bit of the Irish in me... I'm... well... I'm fey. Some, anyway. I get these... feelings... premonitions... things I can't explain. I have found that if I don't act on them... I usually regret it. So, I did.

"I asked around, just before I left, kind of casually, and found out Kimmy is your girlfriend, and who you are. So, I went down to your office... Like I said, the back door was unlocked. So, I went in, found your home address, and came here.

"I needed a place to stay... I'd gone out on the boat to do my research as soon as I got into town that morning, and had not made any arrangements, since I wasn't planning on staying. So, I looked around, found the key keeper, and came in."

Horatio was studying Penny now. He saw the slightly pleading look on her face when she said, "I just couldn't leave and let things happen. You are an attorney. You have responsibilities to people. People would have been hurt if your office wasn't kept open. You would have been hurt... I just couldn't allow that to happen."

Penny fell silent, and Horatio did not speak, either. Penny finally said, "I better get my stuff and get going. You will want to get this figured out... on your own."

Horatio stood up when Penny did. He glanced at his watch. "It is well past dinner time. I am starving. And where are you going to go? You can't be moving this late in the evening."

"Not a problem," Penny assured Horatio. "I'll just stay in the truck for a few days, until I decide where to go from here."

"I am not going to let you sleep in your truck!" Horatio said.

"It isn't a big deal," Penny said, trying to reassure him. "I do it all the time. I'm set up for it."

"No."

Penny saw the sudden stubborn look on Horatio's face. One similar to the one she had seen when Horatio had told Kimmy to leave and that he would deal with things with her later.

"Really," Penny said. "I..."

But Horatio cut her off. "No. We are going out to dinner. And then we are going to get some sleep so I can think about this some more. You'll stay here. I can sleep in the guest room."

"Uh... Not on your life," Penny said. Horatio shot her a quick look. "I'm staying in the guest room," Penny quickly continued. "I haven't been sleeping in your... in the master suite. I just cleaned it up some. I've been sleeping in the guest room."

"Oh..." Horatio did not know quite what to say. It appeared that Penny was not arguing about staying the night, just which room she would be staying in.

"And," Penny added, "We don't need to go out. I can fix something for supper. I have some things already prepared that just need to be heated up."

"Oh really?" asked Horatio.

Penny nodded firmly.

"In that case…" Horatio said, pausing, "We are going out to eat."

"But…" Penny tried to protest.

"No buts. Let's go. I am hungry."

Penny frowned. Horatio took an impatient step toward the front door, looking at her.

"Well, at least let me get out of my leathers. I'm getting warm in them, anyway."

Penny looked at Horatio curiously when he made a strange sound and turned away quickly. She shook her head and ignored it, headed toward the guest bedroom to take off the leather pants, get another pair of shoes, and get a suitable jacket for the evening.

Horatio was waiting by the open door when Penny returned, in another pair of heels, sans the leather pants, but with a jacket that complimented the dress.

Penny stepped outside and Horatio locked the door, shaking the knob to make sure it was secure. Without thinking about it, Horatio put his palm on Penny's back, just above her waist to guide her to the Impala. Penny either did not notice or decided not to comment on the fact.

Horatio handed Penny into the passenger seat of the Impala, keeping his eyes well away from the hem of her skirt when it started to slide up her thighs. He hurried around to the driver's side and climbed inside the car and started it.

He looked at Penny's Harley. "Will the bike be okay?"

"Oh, sure," Penny said. "Great security system on it. Plus a few surprises."

Horatio cut a quick look over at Penny but decided not to ask exactly what she meant. He had a feeling he might not want to know.

Without asking Penny her opinion, Horatio drove to the nearby Red Lobster restaurant and parked. The parking lot was already full, but Penny decided suggesting going back to Horatio's so she could fix a dinner for them probably was not a good idea.

Horatio took the annunciator after the hostess put them down on the wait list and guided Penny to the bar. Most of those waiting were standing around outside or in the lobby and the bar had a couple of empty barstools.

When Horatio headed for them Penny touched his arm. "Can we get one of the tall tables? I don't do too well on stools at a bar."

Horatio looked down at Penny and immediately grasped the situation. With her stature, sitting at the bar would probably be a bit uncomfortable for her.

Changing directions, Horatio quickly claimed the last tall table before the couple headed for it could get there. The guy glared at Horatio, but he ignored it. Horatio gulped and cut his eyes away when Penny hopped up onto the tall chair. He wondered if Penny ever wore a bra.

Horatio leaned over and asked Penny over the noise of the others talking, "What do you want to drink?"

"That's okay," Penny said. But she saw the stubborn look in Horatio's eyes again. "Okay. Sure. See if they can make a peach iced tea, heavy on the peach syrup, with a half shot of a good light rum." She cut her eyes up to Horatio. "If that's okay. I don't like cheap alcohols. They always give me a headache."

"I'll see what I can do," Horatio said.

Penny checked her Smartphone while Horatio was at the bar. She put it away when he returned a few minutes later with their drinks. "Nice," she said when she took a sip from the glass Horatio placed in front of her. She noted that it looked like he had ordered one for himself, too.

She smiled when he took a sip of his drink and looked surprised. "Not bad," he admitted. "Never occurred to me."

"Just the one, though," Penny said. "Plain peach tea with dinner. I limit myself strictly. I'm a lightweight around alcohol."

Horatio opened his mouth but shut it quickly. He caught the look of appreciation in Penny's eyes when he did not make fun of her size, even given the opening she had given him.

"Yeah. Well, it pays to keep one's wits about one. This will be my limit, as well. Driving and all that."

Penny nodded and took another sip of the drink. It was getting louder as more people crowded into the restaurant as the temperature began to drop outside.

They sat companionably, not even trying to talk, just sipping the drinks slowly as they waited for the annunciator on the table to light up and sound off.

It was not as long as they thought it would be, and Horatio quickly guided Penny behind the hostess toward their booth, again with his hand lightly on her lower back.

It was much quieter inside the restaurant proper, thankfully. Although Penny was dreading the additional conversation she expected Horatio would want to have now that it was quiet enough to talk.

And the booth they were in was isolated enough so they could talk, and not be overheard, as long as they kept their voices down. Which Penny was sure she could do. She was not as sure about Horatio being able to do the same thing.

Horatio waited until they had placed their orders before he gave Penny a long look and then said, "I think you better tell me a little more about what you have been doing at the office. From what you finally told me what you overheard Kimmy said, there could be some things that I might have to take care of."

Horatio's hands were clasped together on the table and Penny reached for them to place her hand on his but realized what she was doing just before she touched him. Horatio watched as she pulled her hand back and clasped hers together, also on the table.

"I'm really sorry," Penny said quietly. "I didn't know what else to do. Everything I was seeing and hearing convinced me you are a good guy. I couldn't let what Kimmy was planning... seeming to be planning... anyway, I took some steps to protect some of your assets."

"You have been into my financial accounts?" Horatio asked, his voice vibrating with the effort to keep his voice low and even. "How did you even find them, much less access them?"

Penny was impressed with his control at the moment. She cut her eyes down, but nodded, and then said, "I... Um... I have some pretty good computer skills," Penny explained. "I accessed your laptop when you went on-line the next morning..."

Penny glanced up at Horatio. The look on his face varied from impressed, to incredulous, to annoyed, and then to angered all in the span of a second or so.

His voice boomed for the first word, but then he paused and quietened it for the rest. "You hacked my computer? Remotely?"

Penny nodded again. "Uh... Yeah... I did. Found your password file and copied it to my system. After that it was easy to find and get into the accounts."

"That file was a hidden file. And password protected. And all the various other files and accounts were both coded and had coded passwords. How could you possibly have accessed them? And easily?"

Horatio was having a difficult time accepting the fact that Penny could have done it. And it surprised him more that he was thinking that was more important than the fact that she had been into his financial accounts. And other personal files. He felt himself pale and then color at the thought. He then asked before Penny could speak, "Did someone help you?"

Penny shook her head quickly. "Oh, no. I would never let someone get access to another person's information!"

"You did it all yourself?"

Penny could tell that Horatio was struggling with the idea. She looked at him earnestly. "Well... you see... I'm... Well, I'm pretty smart. And I have a wide range of interests and got curious one time about computer systems and logic and computer security. So, I studied up some and taught myself how to do it. I never really intended to actually use the knowledge... I just wanted to know how."

"Okay," Horatio said in acceptance that she had actually successfully hacked his computer. "So, you did it. Exactly what did you do with the information?" Horatio suddenly realized he would believe whatever she told him. He trusted her to tell him the truth. And he had no clue why.

Horatio saw Penny brighten slightly as she spoke again. "Not much, actually. I just moved the accounts and changed the access passwords. I also changed the security questions and answers."

Her next words were rather chiding. "You used the same ones on everything. That is kind of risky."

"Yeah. I have been meaning to do better with that... Wait. Why did you move them? Why not just change the access codes and passwords? And why change the security questions?"

Penny did not reply as their meals were brought to the table. She had picked up her fork but did not move to eat. Instead she sighed again and said, "I couldn't be sure just how much influence and access Kimmy might have at the institutions where the accounts were.

"Or just how much you two might have shared about the kind of things you used for the security questions.

"I was pretty sure she probably knew your birthday, and some of the other personal information that are usually in those standard security questions. Especially if she had made a point of finding out, since she was planning..."

Penny stopped. She cut her eyes over to Horatio. He was not eating either. He was watching her intently. "I really shouldn't say it like it is a fact. I only think it to be true, but I do not know it to be so. I could be way off base."

With that, Penny dropped her eyes to her plate and took a few bites. Horatio, Penny noted, did the same. But only a few bites and he spoke again. "But you are pretty sure. From what you overheard."

"Yes," Penny said, looking directly into his questioning eyes. She saw the acceptance there. He believed her. That Kimmy was planning something.

Horatio began eating again, so Penny did as well. But she kept part of her attention on Horatio, ready to respond if he had more questions. When the silence stretched, Penny spoke again. "I guess you didn't notice the changes in that file."

With Horatio's one eyebrow up question look appeared, Penny added, "I sent the new information to the file on your laptop as soon as I had made the changes. And removed it from my computer."

"Um... No. I didn't notice it."

Penny was pleased that Horatio did not question her as to whether she had really removed the information from her system. He believed her. And then he surprised her when he stated, "You have it all in your head, though, anyway."

"Yes," Penny admitted. "But I would never use the information. I don't know how to get it out of my memory, but I do know how to keep from accessing it."

Horatio met her gaze again and saw Penny's need for him to believe her. He did believe her. "I know." His eyes still on hers, he suddenly asked, "Just how smart are you? Do you have a photographic memory? What's your IQ?"

Penny dropped her eyes back to her food and took a quick bite. Horatio continued to eat, Penny noticed, but had his attention on her.

"That's kind of personal," Penny finally said, meeting his eyes for a moment and then looking away. And then look back. "Like asking a woman her age. Or her weight."

Horatio was studying her, and Penny knew it. After a few moments she saw him nod. "Yes. I guess it is. But you'll answer. You are not the... average woman. You'd even tell me your age and weight, if I asked."

Now it was Penny's turn to study Horatio for a few seconds. He was very perceptive. He had accepted the information about Kimmy much more readily than Penny had expected.

"I'm twenty-three. Weigh eighty-eight pounds." She had met his gaze when she answered. But when she continued, her eyes were down on her food again, though she was not eating. She sighed slightly, but said, "I'm in the top one-half percentile in intelligence.

"But I don't really have a classic photographic memory. I can call up many things, but not everything." Penny glanced at Horatio again, but cut her eyes back down as he continued to look at her with no real expression on his face. "I'm... I'm considered a polymath by many people that are into definitions."

Penny looked up again when Horatio calmly said, "I'm going to have to look up polymath."

Silently Penny took out her Smartphone, made a few swipes and typed for a moment, and then handed Horatio the phone.

Horatio read the article and then handed the phone back to Penny without saying a word. At least for a few seconds. Penny could not take her eyes off Horatio's face. "You've been given a hard time before about your... abilities. I'm sorry."

Penny had to blink back the sudden tears that formed in her eyes. Horatio really did have some special abilities of his own, Penny decided. She had sensed it even before she had met him, just from having heard what people had told her in passing, and he had shown it since they had met that morning.

"Yes. A few times, actually. Not to mention having been interviewed, and tested, and poked, and prodded for years, from the time I was three years old. Until I was eighteen and put a stop to it and decided to just be what I wanted to be, and not what other people thought I should be, due to my 'gift'. And being doubted and mocked for being fey and acting on those feelings, too."

Penny's voice had been even, and soft. Horatio heard all the anguish and pain that it expressed, though. And felt inordinately proud of the fact that she was definitely her own woman, despite everything.

Horatio nodded once and Penny managed to blink the tears away without any falling. She was right about him. He understood. And accepted. Without judgment. She felt a stirring she had never felt before. A passion that was not about a subject. But about a person. *"Uh-oh,"* she thought to herself, *"this is going to get complicated."*

Penny apparently had the same thought that Horatio had. They both concentrated on their food for a while. Horatio finished first, but Penny was not far behind.

Their server was on the ball and was clearing their plates shortly after they put down their utensil. "Some desert this evening?" asked the server.

Horatio did the one eyebrow thing again and Penny nearly giggled. That quirk of his absolutely fascinated her. "Do you mind?" she asked Horatio. "I'm not very big, but I do have a very fast metabolism. I eat a lot, for my size."

"Ah. Good to know," Horatio said. "I'll have whatever she is," Horatio told the server. They both looked at Penny.

Penny did not hesitate. She ordered the lava cookie with ice cream, and a cup of hot tea. "But it is a bit too much, even for me," she added, looking at Horatio. "I don't mind splitting it with you."

Horatio nodded and looked over at the server. "We'll do that. Just one and we'll share it. I'll have coffee, too."

The server grinned and left to put in the order.

The two were distracted for a few minutes by a birthday celebration at a booth across the way. Both were smiling when they looked back at each other after things settled down. The desert arrived right after that and there was no talk while they consumed it, Horatio amusedly watching Penny eat the lion's share, enjoying it immensely in the process, he noted.

Horatio held Penny's jacket for her when she stood up after he paid the check and she slipped into with a smile over her shoulder to him in thanks.

Again, his hand went to her lower back as they walked out of the restaurant into the cool evening. "Thank you for dinner," Penny said when they were in the Impala, headed back to Horatio's house.

Both were silent until Horatio pulled up to the garage door of the house and stopped. Penny turned to Horatio before he opened the driver's side door. "I'm sorry about what I had to tell you."

Her eyes were on his when he looked over. Horatio saw the compassion in them. She felt bad about what she had told him, but not what she had done.

"I know," Horatio said softly. "But thank you for telling me." Though his hand was on the door handle, Horatio did not open it. His eyes were still on Penny's. "There is one more thing... That you mentioned..."

Penny cut her eyes away, but quickly brought them back to Horatio. He had proven to her that he could and would deal with whatever the realities were that she had witnessed.

"The naked guy... and that Kimmy was naked..." Horatio said tentatively. Penny saw the hurt in his eyes, and the hesitation there in bringing it up.

Penny kept her eyes on his, again the sympathy in them obvious to Horatio as she replied to the implied question. "I'm sorry. I really am," Penny said. This time she did reach out. To put her hand on his upper arm.

"Tell me," Horatio said. "Please."

"He was an average size guy," Penny said quietly. "It was already pretty dark and I didn't get a good look. Plus, I had to get Kimmy out of the water... Had pretty long hair, I noticed. Very dark hair, I remember. But a skinny, very pale body. Like he never got any sun."

Her eyes still on Horatio's Penny continued, though she really hated to. "I... uh... I heard them. It was quiet there for a few minutes as I was unloading, just before the bass boat came barreling in.

"He was pretty loud... but I heard her, too... They were definitely... well... You really do not want me to say it, do you?" Penny asked.

Almost too low for Penny to hear, Horatio said, "No. I guess not." His eyes were a bit glazed, as if he was a thousand miles away, but they cleared and met Penny's again. "It was Beauford. Beauford Goodard. Her ex-boyfriend." Horatio sighed. "Or I guess, not ex. He's a VP in her father's bank. She left him after she met me. Or I thought she did. Now I'm not so sure.

"Her father has been after me to move everything over to his bank from where my family has banked for generations. Been pretty aggressive about it, actually. And Kimmy has been pressuring me, too."

Horatio sighed. "I'll deal with it later. Right now, I want to go in and get a shower and go to bed. It has been a long day." He opened the door before Penny could say anything else.

As she waited for him to open the house door after he'd escorted her from the Impala up to the house, Penny tried again, "I can go to the storage place and get the truck. It isn't a problem for me to sleep in it. I don't need to invade your space like this."

"No. You're staying here. I am not going to let you sleep in your truck. It isn't a problem for you to be here another night."

"Okay," Penny said, no longer willing to push the point. She stepped inside when he opened the door and then headed for the hall bathroom.

Horatio was waiting for her in the living room when she came out. "You... uh... need anything?" Horatio asked.

"No," replied Penny. "I'm fine. Um... I guess I'll see you in the morning."

"Yeah. I guess so."

Penny turned and went back down the hall and turned into the guest bedroom. She closed the door. Horatio stood where he was for a few moments, silent. He shook his head and then went back out to the Impala to get the suitcase he had not brought in earlier. He carried it to the master bedroom suite and got ready for bed.

Chapter Two

-

Horatio groaned and rolled over in the bed the next morning when his alarm went off. He had slept during the night, but it had not been restful. Dreams of Beauford and Kimmy had been disturbing. And then there had been the dreams of Penny. Also disturbing, but in a much more pleasant way.

A quick shower and a few minutes to get dressed and Horatio headed to the kitchen. Thinking about the well-stocked refrigerator, Horatio was anticipating a good breakfast for a change. As soon as he opened the bedroom door his nose alerted him to the fact that he probably would not be preparing breakfast himself.

"You didn't have to do that, you know," Horatio said when he entered the kitchen and saw Penny at work at the stove. He was careful to control the quick intake of breath when she leaned over to take a pan of biscuits out of the oven.

Penny was wearing another knee length sundress. And this one, like the one she had worn the day before, had a tendency to ride well up her thighs when she bent over.

"I know," Penny replied, totally unaware of what she was doing to Horatio's libido. She glanced over at him. "But it really is true that breakfast is important. Fuel for the start of the day. You have a busy one again today and need the sustenance. Besides, cooking is a hobby. I like doing it. Well. Every once in a while."

Penny glanced over at Horatio as she set things out on the kitchen counter for them. "I take it by spells. I am just on a cooking kick now for some reason. Other times I eat pretty simple. Sit down. It's ready."

Horatio did not argue. The ham and eggs looked delicious and the biscuits just as good. "Is that red eye gravy?" Horatio asked when he saw the gravy boat on the table, the contents of which smelled delightful.

Penny grinned. "I take it you are familiar with it."

"I haven't had it forever," Horatio said. "My grandmother used to make it when I was a kid. I didn't even know you could get ham anymore that you could make redeye gravy with. It is all ham and water product now, it seems like."

"Well," Penny said, taking a seat across the counter from Horatio, "salt cured, hickory smoked Virginia hams can be found if you know where to look on the internet." She looked over at Horatio. "I ordered a couple when I was stocking up the... Well... No big deal. Dig in."

Horatio intended to pursue this particular subject, but the lure of the ham, eggs, cottage fries, biscuits, and redeye gravy was too strong at the moment, so he simply enjoyed the breakfast.

Horatio noticed that Penny seemed quite pleased that he enjoyed it. She was as relaxed and open as he had seen her as they ate. She did tense up a bit when Horatio insisted on helping her do the cleanup.

And then even more when they headed for the door to leave for the office. "Why don't you just ride with me?" Horatio asked when Penny said she was going to the bedroom to put on her leathers.

"Unh-uh," she replied. "No telling what might happen. I want my own transportation available. And gear."

It was not until they were on the road, Penny on the Harley conversion, and he in the Impala that it registered that Penny had mentioned not only the bike, but her 'gear', as well. That was something else he needed to talk to her about.

It was not just the cleaning. He had already decided that Penny was something of a neatness and organizational type person, but the stocked refrigerator and pantry, and a couple of references to her gear was another matter.

It suddenly occurred to him that she had mentioned moving some of her things and bringing her truck to get the rest. *"How in the world was she going to move anything on that bike?"* he asked himself. *"And what is the deal with the research on the lake? And the diving?"*

Horatio found that those additional questions would have to wait, because Penny jumped right into work when they arrived at the office, and his first appointment was only a few minutes after nine. But due to Penny's work in the office, he was ready for it, and the one after it.

And then he was busy with other aspects of his practice. He wondered for a moment how Penny had managed to schedule a conference call with just the people he needed to talk to about one of his more difficult cases. He had been trying for a month to get everyone together. But he forgot about the how and simply took advantage of it to reconcile some difficult problems with those involved.

Again, a lunch showed up on his desk at noon, while he was engrossed on an analysis that Penny had written the week before concerning his next appointment. *"Criminey,"* Horatio muttered almost silently. *"She has a brilliant analytical mind, that is for sure."*

With the points she had made, Horatio was able to dissuade the woman and her attorney wanting to sue Horatio's client for everything he had from doing so, and get them to not only withdraw the case, but agree to pay Horatio's fees, and pay a nominal settlement to avoid Horatio's client from suing them for defamation and harassment.

Horatio was not entirely sure he could have managed it all without Penny's report. He was sure that Kimmy would never have come up with anything like it. And he would have been hard pressed himself to have gotten everything together on his own, in time to handle it now, rather than later, which would have made it even more difficult.

With everything caught up for the moment, well before five, Horatio, rather reluctantly, opened up his personal file on his laptop and took a look at what Penny had sent him.

After double checking his old records he confirmed that not one cent of the money in the various accounts had been touched. Only the accounts had been moved. Also reluctantly, Horatio called two of the account executives that had handled some of the accounts and casually questioned them about the activity on the accounts before and after the transfers.

He did some quick double speak explaining on why the accounts had been moved. But he did find out that there had been some attempted access to the old accounts only three days after they had been moved. And he knew he had not been trying to get into them.

After only a short hesitation, Horatio called his friend Andy. Despite his obvious feelings about Kimmy, Andy was a bit evasive, and then reluctant to discuss Kimmy with Horatio. But he finally spilled his guts of everything he knew. And it was quite a bit. Things he had held back after Horatio had essentially told him in no uncertain terms to mind his own business when it came to Kimmy.

Horatio put the telephone receiver down slowly after the last call. He was not sure why he had believed Penny from the beginning. But he had. And what he was finding out was confirming that her fey feelings had been correct. Someone had tried to access his accounts. There really was only one person that could have. Kimmy.

He was lost in thought when Penny knocked on his open office door some time later. "Horatio?" she asked quietly.

"Um... Yes?"

"Look," Penny said, firming up her voice. "It is still fairly early. I am going to go get my truck and..."

"I am not going to let you sleep in your truck!" Horatio said just as firmly.

"You know," Penny said, arms crossing in front of her chest. Which drew Horatio's eyes to the area. He had noted first thing that morning that she was not wearing a bra again. Just the shelf bra in the sundress. He had managed not to think about it all day until just now.

Quickly putting the thought out of his mind, he looked up at her face and concentrated on what she was saying. Which rather annoyed him and really took his mind off the other matter.

"You are not the boss of me... I mean, outside this office. And that is temporary. I am going to go get the truck." She saw his even more determined look and raised her right hand up in a *stop* motion. She sighed. "Look... Take a look at the truck. You will see why it isn't a problem for me to stay in it. And... Well... Until you find a replacement paralegal, I will keep working. I had planned on being in the area for a while, anyway. But I will find another place to live this weekend.

"It is going to make it even more awkward for you to deal with Kimmy if I am staying in your house. So, me being out of there is the only logical thing to do."

"I won't let Kimmy hurt you..." Horatio was saying. He saw the complete change come over Penny.

"Oh, you just do not worry about that woman hurting me," Penny said forcefully. "I can take very good care of myself. She only got the slaps in on me because I let her. She needed to vent, and I could understand how she was feeling at the time. But she will not lay another hand on me, ever. And the verbal stuff... Well, that just slides off me like water off a duck's back. So, do not start thinking you have to take care of me."

Horatio was rather taken aback at not only the fierceness of her attitude, but the absolute surety that what she was saying was true. "But you are so..."

Again, a hand went up. "And no comments about my size. It doesn't apply in this case, and very seldom does in any others, either. I can, and will hold my own with Kimmy, if she ever does try something."

Penny's voice softened slightly. "And to be honest, I do not think she will, anyway. Not with me. You, on the other hand... You are in for some rough times."

Horatio heard the sympathy in Penny's voice and it annoyed him more than her previous words had. "You can't possibly think Kimmy might try anything physical with me!"

"Uh... Well... Not in a fighting sense... No." Penny drew the *"no"* out rather dramatically, leaving the rest of what he suddenly realized she was thinking left unsaid.

Horatio knew he was turning bright red in the face when the thought came to him. Quickly he said, "I assure you I am not susceptible to that kind of persuasion. At all."

Penny's somewhat disbelieving, "Uh-huh," had him turning even more red. He opened his mouth to reiterate the point, but Penny spoke again before he could. "Doesn't matter. None of my business now, anyway. But I am going after my truck."

She turned to go, but slowly turned back. "Uh... But after you see it... and if you don't want me to leave it parked at your house, I will move it. You know. So no one gets the wrong idea."

"What? What are you talking about?" Horatio asked, lost again, as he was finding he often was with Penny.

"Well, you might not want people to get the wrong idea..."

"Oh," Horatio said, realizing what she meant, finally. "You mean Kimmy."

"Or anyone else," Penny said. "For any other reason, either."

Again, Horatio was not sure what she meant, but he let it pass. "Okay. I guess I can't stop you..." At her firm look, he added, "or have any right to, for that matter, I will see you at home, then?" He rather hated the fact that he was asking more than making a statement.

"Yes. Won't be long. And think about what you might want for dinner. I have plenty of options that only need heating up."

Penny saw the stubborn look. "And if you insist we are going out again, it will be my treat this time, make no mistake about that. I'll leave you to finish up and lock up." With that she was gone, before Horatio could think of anything remotely likely to change her mind.

Horatio, more curious than he wanted to admit, hurried to finish up and shut down the office, fully intending to be at the house before she arrived.

"What in the blazes?" Horatio asked himself when he turned down his street and saw what was now parked in his driveway. Fortunately, it was a long driveway, with the way the house was set back from the street. For a driveway much shorter would not have allowed the vehicle to be parked there.

Penny was perched on the front bumper of the vehicle, waiting for him. Which was rather easy for her, considering the construction of the bumper. Horatio knew his mouth was hanging open when he got out of the Impala and stood looking at the rig.

For rig was the only term he could come up with. Because it sure was not the compact pickup truck he had for some reason expected her to show up in. Why he had thought that, after having seen the Harley conversion, he was not sure.

"What is that thing?" he finally asked, cutting his eyes away from the rig, finally, to meet hers. He frowned slightly at the amusement in her eyes and on her face at his expression of wonderment.

"Just my truck. Well, and trailer, of course. For the Harley and its trailer."

"The Harley has a trailer, too?" asked Horatio in a rather squeaky voice.

"Yeah. It's in the garage. I was going to have it loaded up, but I forgot I had given you the key back."

"Oh," Horatio replied, taking another look at the trailer that Penny had backed up to one of the garage doors. He caught himself just in time, before asking Penny if she had backed the trailer up herself with the *truck*.

"Now," Penny asked, "see what I mean about being able to stay in the truck without a problem? The sleeper is plenty big enough. And comfortable."

Horatio looked back and forth at the length of the rig. He scratched his head. He had never seen anything like it. "Well..."

"Oh, for crying out loud," Penny said. "Come on. Take a look inside the sleeper." Penny had dropped down off the bumper of the truck. She took Horatio's arm and led him over to the driver's side rear passenger door of the crew cab custom Chevy 5500 Kodiak truck. She opened the door, saying, "Follow me."

Horatio quickly closed his eyes as the hem of Penny's sundress flipped and swirled as she reached up, stepped up, and lifted herself into the cab of the truck. Sliding past the left side Captain's seat Penny looked back at Horatio as he groaned, catching him just opening his eyes.

Without any sign of embarrassment, she muttered a *"sorry"*, and stepped rearward between the seats. She turned and waited as Horatio clambered into the cab and moved to join her, having to duck his head inside the crew cab, but able to stand upright, just barely, inside the sleeper section of the truck.

Penny did a slight arm wave, and Horatio took a good look around. He realized that what he was seeing was essentially a complete living area, albeit quite compact. There was a tiny L-shaped kitchen along one side and against the rear of the crew cab, with sink, two burner range with oven and hood, and a nice size refrigerator, with some counter space left over. When

Penny slid open a pocket door he saw the wet bathroom, complete with shower.

On the other side of the space was a set of bunks with storage below the bottom one and above the top one. The top bunk looked like it would fold down to give sitting headroom on the bottom one. There was a fold up table that would act as dinette or work table.

A narrow door gave access to the rest of the long truck, which Horatio soon learned was a nine-foot long pickup type bed with a custom topper on it. He looked through the glass of the rear door and saw the bed was filled side to side, top to bottom.

Penny made a motion and Horatio went forward and then out of the cab of the truck. Without even thinking about it, he turned around and took Penny by the waist and set her down onto the ground when she started to follow him out.

"Oh!" Penny said rather breathlessly when her feet touched the ground, amazed with the ease with which Horatio had accomplished the feat, and not having expected the assistance, anyway.

Horatio had already taken a step back to look over the outside of the truck in more detail, and Penny took a quick moment to compose herself, not having felt quite like she had just felt ever before. It was a very nice feeling, and she was not quite sure why she was feeling it.

As Horatio continued to stare at the truck, Penny began to explain, as she had so many times before. At least when she felt like it. Usually she just ignored everyone that looked at the rig with shock and awe.

"As you can see, there is a custom bumper up front. The overhead rack just over the top of the cab is the same height of the sleeper. It extends from the front of the sleeper out over the hood, supported by the stanchions on the corners of the bumpers.

"The extended height sleeper section, of course, and then behind it, another rack on the topper from just above its roof to the height of the sleeper, the length of the topper. And the custom rear bumper.

"The trailer is custom, too. Uses the same size tires as the truck. Room for the Harley conversion and its trailer, plus lots of tankage and storage space.

Penny walked to the rear of the truck and worked a remote control in her hand. The topper hatch lifted, and the rear barn doors of the pickup bed swung open sideways. Horatio saw Penny touch another control on the remote and a drawer assembly began to slide backwards, over the tongue of the trailer. "Everything is on slides so I can access it easily," Penny explained.

She pointed to the dark glass panels on the side of the topper. "Those open, too, so I can access things on the upper level in the topper from outside if I want. There are fold out steps so I can reach them. And the space under the bed, along the side of the frame that isn't taken up with tankage is storage space. You can see a couple of the access doors."

Horatio turned to look at Penny, amazement on his face. He was not sure how to describe the sudden feeling in his chest when Penny scrunched up that pixie face of hers, which was surrounded by that deep copper colored hair, and said, "You are not going to ask me if I really drive this thing, are you?" Her hands went to her hips. There was a twinkle in her eyes when she added, "Or comment on compensation issues?"

He knew he colored again, at least slightly, when he realized he actually had been about to ask that very thing. And make the comment. Either. Or both of them. "Of course not!" he managed to say with a straight face.

"That is good," Penny said, working the remote again to close everything back up. "Because I have been known to maim people for those kinds of questions and statements." She cut him a sideways glance, a grin curving her lips.

"I have absolutely no doubts," Horatio said.

He gave the rig another look. "Interesting color scheme." He could not quite figure it out. It was not a conventional camouflage pattern, with splotches of different colors.

There were multiple colors, and some of the colors were actually brighter than he would have thought, but every single color blended into every single other color, wherever they were next to each other. It was actually rather difficult to make out any shapes, for the blended colors just trailed off around all the edges.

And the tarpaulins that covered the bumpers and both roof racks continued the color scheme, and with the irregular shape they had, it made it even more difficult to make out the shape as he walked away from it, even no further than they were from it when they got up to the front door of the house.

Horatio, with one last look over his shoulder, opened the front door of the house and stepped aside, to let Penny precede him inside. She put her purse on the table by the door and headed for the kitchen. "You decide on what you wanted for supper?"

"I still think..." Horatio shut up quickly when Penny turned and glared at him from the end of the kitchen dividing counter. "Uh... You have some kind of beef dish?"

Penny grinned. "Yep. Sure do. Steaks, meatloaf, stuffed bell peppers, lasagna…"

Since it looked like she was going to continue for a while, Horatio quickly interrupted and said, "Meatloaf sounds fine."

"Okay. Escalloped potatoes and corn on the cob okay with it?" Penny asked, going the rest of the way into the kitchen.

"You actually have… Uh… Yes. That is fine," Horatio said after first starting the question.

"Hot or cold dessert?" Penny asked next, after she had taken some things from his large refrigerator.

"Uh… Surprise me?" Horatio asked after hesitating, having no idea what to ask for.

"Sure. I can do that." And just loud enough for him to hear, though ostensibly under her breath, she added, "As if I'm not already."

Horatio grinned. She sure had that right. He went to his bedroom to take off his suit jacket and tie, returning just a couple of minutes later. Penny was nowhere in sight. But she came out of the hall bathroom moments later and Horatio relaxed. He had not felt himself tense up at her not being right there, but he realized he had. And that bothered him a little.

"Dinner won't take long," Penny said. "You mind if I watch the Weather Channel while you check your mail and stuff?"

"Sure, go ahead," Horatio said, suddenly distracted by a couple of the envelopes that had been delivered that day. He did not realize that he had dropped onto the sofa near Penny, as he concentrated on the mail in his hands, until she got up to go to the kitchen.

He went right back to the mail until Penny called him to the dinner table. Horatio looked up in surprise. The table was set, the serving dishes were on the table, including a salad she had not asked him about, as was a bottle of wine and two wine glasses, along with the filled water glasses.

Horatio glanced down at his watch and then cut a look over at Penny. She had seen him check the time before he looked over. "Told you it was quick and easy," she said with a grin.

"Uh… Yeah. You sure seem to make it so." Horatio joined her at the table, but suddenly realized she had not taken her chair. With dawning realization, he quickly moved behind her, pulled out the chair she was standing beside for her, and scooted it back in when she sat down, with a quiet, "Thank you."

"She sure seemed to expect that," Horatio thought to himself as he took his own seat, at the head of the table, which put Penny at his right hand,

near the kitchen. He remembered suddenly that the hostess at the restaurant had seated Penny the night before.

And then it dawned on him that he had seen a firm pillow on the chair when he had pulled it out. No wonder she was sitting much closer eye to eye with him. He resisted the urge to look under the table to see if her feet were dangling, despite the high heels she was wearing.

When they had finished up the meal, and it was time for desert, Penny said, "Don't get up," swung around in the chair, and stood up. She was back in just a couple of minutes, carrying two dishes, with brownies and ice cream on them.

She set down the plates and turned her legs around under the table. Horatio was rather proud of himself that he had managed, though barely, not to be looking at her chest when she did.

Horatio sighed mightily after finishing his dessert, which brought a rather shy smile to Penny's face. "So, it was okay? Not everyone likes my meatloaf."

"Best I have ever had," Horatio admitted. "Not sure what the difference is. My mother always made a good one. But yours is better."

"Why, thank you, Horatio!" Penny said. "That is very kind of you to say."

"Just the truth." Horatio put his napkin beside his plate, and as Penny made a move to get up and clear the table, Horatio quickly added. "Can we talk a bit more?" looking over at her.

Penny could see the hesitation in his face and she hesitated herself. But then she was saying, "Of course. But let's do it in the living room. I don't like talking serious stuff at the dinner table. Even afterwards. Just let me clear the table and get things into the dishwasher."

Horatio nodded, but then he got up he began to help her. Working together silently they moved everything to the kitchen, and as Horatio put the few leftovers into containers to go into the refrigerator, Penny loaded the dishwasher. She started it and then headed for the living room as Horatio closed the refrigerator door.

Penny sat down on the sofa, where she had been before, and turned slightly to face Horatio as he sat down at the other end, after picking up some of the mail he had been reading earlier.

Horatio looked over at Penny, then down at the papers in his hands. "Actually, this can wait." He turned and put the papers on the coffee table.

After looking at her again Horatio spoke. "I'd like to know more about you. And that amazing truck. And..." He stopped suddenly and shook his head.

Penny gave him a quizzical look.

"Actually," Horatio said, "That can wait, too. For right now..." Horatio sighed, looked away, and then back at Penny. She kept her eyes focused on his.

"Look. You have made it quite clear that you really can stay in that truck just fine. For some time, I suspect. You do not actually need to stay here."

Horatio fell silent again, studying Penny's face. She stayed quiet, letting him think.

"But I would like you to stay here, in the house, until I find another paralegal." Quickly he added, "And as good as dinner was, and believe me when I say I enjoyed it immensely, you do not have to cook. And you certainly do not have to clean.

"I would just feel better if you continued to stay here, rather than move out into the truck and go someplace else, even if you continue to work for me."

Penny had to think a few moments herself before she spoke, not quite sure what to say. She thought she had been prepared for this and was simply going to say she would rather stay in the truck. But those words did not come as easily as she expected them to come.

"You know Kimmy is going to be livid. It will not help your situation with her when she discovers I am still here in your house."

"To be honest with you, Penny, I really don't care. While I need to make it very clear to her, which will probably take some doing and probably some time, I am done with her.

"I confirmed all your suspicions... Your fey sense is apparently very accurate... And your hearing ability and powers of observation are also very good." Horatio sighed. "My main worry is that you will wind up in the middle of this... ending... with Kimmy. And that really isn't fair, but..."

"Don't worry about that, Horatio. I may be small, but I am surprisingly resilient, and very tough." She suddenly grinned at him. "Might even make it easier to resist her persuasions, hunh, with me in the house?"

Horatio flushed and Penny laughed aloud. "That thought actually crossed your mind, didn't it?"

He really wanted to deny it, but would not, since it would be a lie. What he did say was, "Really not going to be a problem, either way."

And then Penny surprised Horatio, and herself even more, when she firmly said, "Okay, Horatio. You have a deal. With conditions. I will cook and clean whenever I want to; I will pay you rent, a practical amount, deducted from my salary; which you will pay me, retroactive to the day I started at the office."

And then, even as Horatio started to protest what she had already said, Penny quietly added, "And you will let me help you with the Kimmy situation, if there is any way in which I can."

Penny then warned him, "Don't even try to argue it, Horatio. Those are the terms. Only under them will I stay here any longer than this one more night."

Oh, Horatio wanted to argue. Every single condition. But there was determination in Penny's eyes. And he had learned what she could do, and deal with. And would do. Finally, after long moments he nodded and said, "We have a deal."

"Good," Penny said brightly, rising gracefully from the sofa. "So, if you will excuse me, I think I will go to bed. Tomorrow is going to be a busy day at the office, I suspect."

Horatio suddenly wondered how much of that statement was just normal conversation, and how much of it might be Penny's fey at work.

Since she was going to be staying, Penny rode with Horatio in the Impala to work the next day.

Horatio was about to decide that Penny had missed the mark the evening before about how busy they would be. There were a couple of appointments that morning, early, but they had gone quickly and well. Plus, he was catching up on some reading he had been needing to do. So, he was feeling relaxed and easy when he left his office and went to get a cup of coffee.

All that relaxed feeling disappeared in a hurry just as he came back into the reception area, and Kimmy came through the front door of the office building.

Horatio winced at the screech Kimmy let out upon seeing Penny. "That home wrecker is still here? Is that her monstrosity in your driveway?" Kimmy glared at Penny for a moment longer and then turned toward Horatio. "I told you to get rid of her! I am back to work now, and…"

"Hold it Kimmy," Horatio said. He noted peripherally that Penny had left her chair and come around the side of the desk. The thought flashed through his mind, *"She should have kept the desk between her and Kimmy. But she doesn't seem concerned at all."*

But it was only tiny fraction of a second, and he continued addressing Kimmy. "You no longer work here, Kimmy. Not that you actually worked that much when you were here. But when you decided to not open the office when I was gone, you also decided you no longer worked here at all, whether you intended to or not."

Kimmy screamed. There were no real words, just sound. Horatio flinched. A glance at Penny had him wondering how she could hear that and not react.

"Where have you been, anyway?" Horatio asked, proud that he was not matching tone for tone. "Since you left the house the other night I have left a dozen voicemails, even more e-mails, and I don't know how many texts, to try and set up a time and place where we could discuss this… situation."

"We will discuss it here and now!" Kimmy declared, taking a step toward Horatio's office. "Just as soon as that she-devil leaves this place!" Kimmy was glaring at Penny. And becoming more infuriated by the second as Penny stood still and just looked at her calmly.

Kimmy turned furious eyes on Horatio and stamped her foot. "I demand you tell her to leave and never come back! Right this instant!"

"Kimmy," Horatio said, still keeping his voice calm, "We are not going to do this here. This is a place of business, and not the place to conduct personal… whatever. I have a client coming in shortly, no thanks to you…"

Horatio made the mistake at glancing at Penny, who had managed to get the appointment set up with someone he had been trying to get to talk to him about taking over as her legal counsel for some time.

Kimmy let out another wordless scream and took a step toward Penny. Penny still refused to budge, Horatio saw out of the corner of his eye even as he stepped forward toward Kimmy. "We are not going to have a scene here, Kimmy. I will not allow it. Do not make me call the authorities to have you removed."

With an incredulous look on her face, which turned white, Kimmy exclaimed, "You would not dare!"

Horatio closed his eyes for a moment when Penny calmly said, "I would," and Kimmy screamed again.

When Horatio turned his head just enough to see Penny, and still keep the fuming Kimmy in view, Penny was picking up the phone receiver and punching in a number. Three digits. *"Oh, Criminey!"* thought Horatio. The phone beeps were loud in the suddenly silent room.

"I will be at the house at five this evening, Horatio," Kimmy yelled. "And she had better not be there. Or else!"

"No, Kimmy," Horatio said. "I will text you a location and time where we can talk. Check your phone, for crying out loud, sometime this evening."

Horatio could see Kimmy getting ready to lunge past him toward Penny and prepared to intervene. But a siren sounded in the distance. "You will pay for this, you... you... you... Shrimp!" Kimmy was red in the face again as she turned and stormed out the front door of the building.

Horatio took just long enough to let out the breath he was holding and then spun around and said, "Call the police! Quick! Cancel that 911 call! Tell them... Oh, shucks! I don't know... you think quicker than I will ever hope to be able to. You tell them something!"

Penny just smiled and hung up the phone. "I didn't call 911. I punched 411. I didn't think Kimmy would know the difference in the tones."

"You didn't call 911?" Horatio asked, feeling himself relax significantly. "But the sirens..."

Penny shook her head. "Those were fire department, not police. Convenient, but unrelated. I guess Kimmy does not know the difference in those, either.

"And I wouldn't call 911 on a whim," Penny continued. "Not for a tantrum like that," Penny assured Horatio. She shrugged her shoulders and turned to go around the desk again, not seeing Horatio's agonized expression at having seen what that shrug had done to the bodice of her dress.

Horatio gathered his thoughts for a moment and started past the desk, where Penny was now sitting calmly, working on the computer. He stopped for a moment, debated, and then asked, "You would have known the difference in the phone tones, wouldn't you?"

Penny did not even look his way. "Oh, sure. They're easy."

Horatio shook his head and went into his office, to do the final preparations for Mrs. Benito's appointment.

Happier that he probably should be, all things considered, Horatio turned to Penny after escorting Mrs. Benito to the front door and said, "That just made my day! She isn't going to turn everything over to me immediately, but she is going to give me some work to check out my abilities. And if she is happy, she may switch everything over to me.

"Thank you for arranging for her to come in, however you managed to do it. I don't know how to thank you."

Penny smiled. "It wasn't a big deal. You keep pretty good notes. When I read some of the things you had written about Mrs. Benito that you would use to try to persuade her to use you, they sounded very professional and like good advice.

"So it was easy to convince her to come in when I talked to her at the club. Uh..." Penny quickly cut her words off and dropped her eyes.

"You were at her club? Wait. Which one? She is in several." Horatio was trying to think of any possible connection that Penny and Mrs. Bonito might have.

"Well..." Penny said, hesitating, and then, as she often did, as Horatio had noted before, she rushed through an explanation. "It was at the Country Club. After the Historical Society meeting Sunday before last. I called an acquaintance I have here and told him I would be willing to do a short presentation if the Society was interested.

"I was a bit surprised, but he called me back and said they would be... I think the words he used were *'They would be delighted.'* Anyway, I gave the presentation and then brought up your practice when I was talking to Mrs. Benito afterwards. Anyway, it was no big deal."

Penny lifted her eyes after another moment and found Horatio watching her. "You gave a presentation to the Historical Society? They are so... persnickety. And you know someone here that has influence with them?"

She could tell he was not doubting her, just that she confused him. It was obvious he had never met anyone like her. "I have many interests. And contacts. This one happens to be one of my internet friends that is also big into paleoclimatology and its effects on physical anthropology.

"He also has an interest in the Civil War history of the area. Had family fighting on both sides. So, he is a member of the Historical Society."

"Uh... anthropology I know... I know what that is. Paleoclimatology?"

"Ancient climate," Penny replied.

"And the Historical Society was interested in this?" Horatio was having a hard time making the connection.

Penny nodded. "Yes. Of course... well... the early humans in Tennessee part, primarily. I didn't really get into the palaeoclimatological aspects of it. That is of more interest to Jimmy and me. But the Society does have an interest in pre-Columbian life here. They were quite receptive to the presentation."

"Okay... I guess. Anyway, it seemed to have worked. Thank you." Horatio went past her desk and was almost to the door to his office when he turned and quietly added, "And thank you for... well... dealing with the Kimmy thing so... calmly."

Horatio saw her shoulders lift and drop in a shrug, though she did not turn around. "No big deal," she said, also quietly. "Personal relationships can be difficult at the best of times. I don't really want to make it more difficult than it already would be."

She still did not turn to look at Horatio, but he could see her back stiffen slightly as she added, "But I will only accept so much..."

"I understand," Horatio replied and went into the office. He needed to come up with a place where he and Kimmy could get together and he could give her the official word that he was ending things with her. Officially. *"Thank the Lord I didn't propose before I left on that trip like I was planning,"* he thought. *"If she hadn't insisted on going to that party instead of coming over that night before I left..."*

Horatio actually shuddered slightly at the thoughts and quickly put them out of his mind. "Where is the best place?" he mused aloud, as he sat down in the desk chair and leaned back, to stare at the ceiling.

After having thought of, and then discarding two dozen places where he could talk to Kimmy, he was still at a loss when Penny knocked on his open door an hour later.

"Yes?" Horatio had not heard the phone ring, and there were no more appointments on the calendar for today.

"Horatio," Penny said, and then paused. "Look, Horatio. Obviously, Kimmy has been by the house and seen my truck. It won't take me ten minutes to get the Bunkhouse trailer out of the garage where I have been keeping it and onto the truck's trailer. I can disappear for a few hours if you want to talk to Kimmy at the house."

"I thought we agreed..." Horatio was protesting, but Penny stopped him.

"We did, Horatio. And I stick to my agreements. But just not being there for a few hours doesn't mean I won't be back. I will. I promise. But dealing with Kimmy in a public place might not be the best way to handle things..."

Horatio sighed. "I know, I know." He ran a hand through his hair, mussing it significantly. Penny felt the sudden urge to run her fingers through it to smooth it back into place but managed to resist it and stood still.

"But I feel like I'm putting you out. You've done so much for me. And... Well... I just don't like the idea of Kimmy making you do anything." Horatio's eyes met Penny's. He was surprised at the humor he suddenly found in them.

"Horatio, you've known me only a short time, I know, but in that time, has there been anything at all to give you the idea that I would let Kimmy make me do anything at all that I didn't really want to do?"

It took Horatio only a moment to think about it and come to the conclusion that Penny was right. Kimmy did not have it in her power to make Penny do anything. Penny did what Penny wanted to do. Period.

"Good point," he admitted. "Okay. I guess if I keep her out of the kitchen and the guest bedroom, she might not think about you being there, if you aren't there."

Horatio snorted. "It isn't likely she'll go into the kitchen. She has an aversion to them. And the only bedroom she wants into is mine." Realizing what he had said, Horatio turned pink and dropped that line of thought.

After studying Penny's watching eyes, Horatio added, "Okay. But you have to let me make it up to you."

Horatio saw Penny start to protest, but she relaxed almost instantly and nodded. "Okay. Fair enough. I will leave now and be gone well before five. I will call you from your house to let you know when I am ready to leave. I will be working on my computer, so you can e-mail me when I can come back."

Penny turned to leave but Horatio leaped up from the chair and said, "Wait a minute! How are you getting there? You rode in with me. I can take you home and come back…"

"That is silly, Horatio. You need to be here in case something comes up. This is no problem," Penny said. "I will call Jimmy. He can be here in just a few minutes. He won't mind chauffeuring me around."

For some reason that did not sit well with Horatio, though he studiously avoided thinking about why that was. But he had no real valid reason to object. He did need to stay at the office until the usual closing time. There was some work he needed to do for a case that would be going to court early the next week.

"Okay," Horatio reluctantly said. "But I will make this up to you. Thank you."

"Better call Kimmy," Penny said, walking over to her desk.

Horatio was a little disappointed when Penny squatted down to get her purse out of the bottom desk drawer. Usually she bent over.

Horatio quickly went back to his office, thinking, *"Get you mind off those legs, Horatio!"*

Halfway hoping Kimmy would not answer, so he could tell Penny she did not have to leave the house that evening, Horatio dialed Kimmy's number.

Rather to his surprise, Kimmy answered immediately. He was not at all surprised at her words when she answered. "I hope that harlot is gone."

Horatio glanced through the office door. Penny was already going through the front door of the building. Feeling like a traitor for some reason when he replied, Horatio said, "She is gone. But Kimmy…"

Kimmy cut him off. "I do not want to hear any further nonsense about her or anything else. I will be at your house, waiting, when you get home. Where is that key you said you hid? I don't understand why you never gave me one, anyway. I am your girlfriend, after all. We will get all of this this straightened out this evening."

Thankful that Kimmy was not screaming, despite not at all liking what she was saying, Horatio agreed with a simple, "Okay. I will see you shortly after five." With that he ended the call, sighed, and pulled up the file for the case he needed to work on.

He had not been working all that long when he got a call from Penny. "I'm gone," was all she said before she ended the call after he answered. Horatio set up the contact immediately, so he would have her cell number.

Later, when Horatio noticed the time in the lower right corner of the computer screen he muttered and quickly closed the file he was working on. *"No need to set Kimmy off any more than she already is by being late,"* Horatio thought.

Still, almost as an act of defiance, Horatio carefully went through the office shutdown procedure Penny had instituted before he went out to the Impala. He saw the envelope on the driver's seat when he opened the door.

Horatio picked up the envelope and sat down in the seat. He opened it and took out the three pictures it contained, and the single sheet of paper. He read the few lines of information and studied the pictures for a moment. Then Horatio headed home.

Kimmy was in her Mercedes, windows closed, engine running, doing something on her phone when Horatio parked beside her. He could hear the radio in her car blaring, despite the closed windows when he got out of the Impala.

She lifted a finger when she saw him and continued talking on her phone. Horatio went up to the house and unlocked the door, setting his computer case on the stand next to the door and turned to wait for Kimmy.

It was at least five minutes before Kimmy finally got out of the Mercedes. Horatio realized just how much gall Kimmy actually had when the first thing she said was, "What took you so long? I have been waiting for hours! Do not, and I repeat, do not forget to give me a key before I leave in the morning."

Horatio let it pass, even knowing full well Kimmy had not been waiting for hours. Probably less than ten minutes, five of which he had been there. And the key was not going to be a factor, as Kimmy was not going to be spending the night. Not now, not ever. And Horatio was going to make sure she knew that. Very shortly.

Kimmy brushed past him, taking a quick look around, obviously looking for Penny, despite Penny's rig not being in the driveway. It suddenly struck Horatio that Kimmy must have driven by at some point after Penny had brought the truck over. *"Hm,"* he thought, but was quickly distracted.

Kimmy turned to him, a seductive smile suddenly on her face. One that Horatio knew, and had at one time eagerly anticipated. Not this time, however.

"I think we have a few minutes before we go get dinner, Sweetheart. It has been a while. I was so lonely while you were gone."

Kimmy moved to put her arms around Horatio's neck, but Horatio caught her wrists and put them down at her sides. "No, Kimmy. None of that. No sex, no going out for dinner. You are here for one reason, and one reason only. To explain what happened while I was gone, and for us to have a chance to put a close to this relationship."

Horatio guided her over to the sofa and seated her at one end and then he sat down at the other.

Horatio saw the expressions flit over Kimmy's face, one after the other. Shock. Disbelief. Fear. Anger. Unsureness. And then they repeated, in various orders, several times. Not surprisingly, the one that settled, was anger.

"Now you listen here, Horatio! I do not care what that little tramp has told you, but..."

"Leave Penny out of this, Kimmy. This is me and you. And only me and you. I am willing to hear you out, about why you didn't bother to open the office. And why you and Beauford were naked on the houseboat when it sank. And why, when I checked on some of my financial accounts after I got back, you had tried to gain access to them."

Kimmy blanched at Horatio's last words, having turned red at first. But she was soon red again, anger shining through, as she began to talk. Horatio managed not to wince as her voice became a screech.

"How could you expect me to go into work after that terrible woman sank my houseboat on purpose? I was distraught. I nearly drowned. I couldn't possibly think about work. I had to go shopping for new clothes. And Daddy insisted I stay at the house to recover from the ordeal."

Kimmy glared at Horatio for a moment when he did not say anything immediately. She tried to put on a hurt look, failing miserably. "You wouldn't expect me to be thinking about that silly job at a time like that, would you?"

"I see," Horatio said, his voice noncommittal. "And the other?"

Kimmy stiffened. "That other is just outright lies. I don't know who told you I was with Beauford... If it was that miniscule slut... well, she simply is lying about it. And of course, I never tried to get into your accounts.

It had to be her. You will be bringing charges against her for that. I certainly am for sinking my houseboat. I have already filed the complaint. I don't know why she hasn't been arrested already."

"I told you that this is not about Penny. She did not sink your houseboat. And she didn't try to access my accounts." Horatio knew he was kind of stretching when he said the last. Penny had not tried to access them. She had accessed them. But that was not what he had referred to, anyway.

"But if she didn't than who…" Kimmy knew she had made a mistake when she saw the look change on Horatio's face.

More emotions flashed across her face, and then she was quickly saying, "Well… Okay. I suppose I should 'fess up about that. You see, Daddy asked me to see if I could talk you into bringing over an account or two to our bank. I was just checking to see what might be the most appropriate ones to…"

Horatio was shaking his head. "Won't fly, Kimmy. They told me that whoever tried to access them was trying to empty the account. They already knew what accounts and how much money was in them. Information that I made the mistake of discussing with you one time."

"How dare you accuse me!" Kimmy screamed. Then she slapped him. And started to slap him again, but Horatio caught her wrist, amazed when he remembered that Penny had said she let Kimmy slap her. More than once. Because she understood Kimmy's anger and need to vent. *"Geez! She slaps hard! And Penny let her do it more than once? Geez!"*

"It was Beauford!" Kimmy was desperate, and Horatio could tell. "It was Beauford! He made me, Horatio! He said he would tell you I'd got back with him and slept with him if I didn't do it! That is where that rumor got started. It has to be. You have to believe me, Horatio!"

Again, she got the seductive look and reached for him. But Horatio was having none of it. He moved back out of her reach, getting up and going around to stand behind the sofa. "No, Kimmy," Horatio said. "You were seen. Beauford was on the houseboat that night. And the two of you were naked, having sex on the top deck when the houseboat went down.

"You shouldn't have tied up that close to the club house. "People actually heard the two of you. And Beauford was seen running down the docks naked after the boat went down."

"Well, I wasn't naked!" Kimmy hissed. "Ask anyone there! When people saw what happened and came running down I was fully clothed. You can ask them!"

"I know you were," Horatio said. "And I know where you got the clothes. Several sizes too small for you, but just big enough to cover up everything."

Kimmy screamed. "That witch! I am going to kill her!"

"No, you are not, Kimmy. You are going to walk out of this house, and out of my life. You will not ever do anything to Penny, or cause anything to be done to Penny. If you do, I will drag your name so far through the mud that Beauford Goodard won't come within ten feet of you, and not even your own precious Daddy will have anything to do with you."

Kimmy turned white again and her voice was hushed in fear when she replied, "You wouldn't dare! And you couldn't, even if you did dare!"

Horatio moved over to the computer case and extracted the envelope he had put in it after having looked at the contents in the car. He walked back over to the sofa and handed the envelope to Kimmy.

Her hand began to shake when she slid the contents out. Suddenly she threw everything at him, screaming, "You'll never prove this! It is all fake! All of it! You can't prove it!" but her voice had lowered in acceptance.

Kimmy stood up, walked around the sofa and out of the door, slamming it behind her forcefully.

Horatio, more ashamed at the relief he felt than shame at having used the information, walked over to the entry and looked through the sidelight.

"Oh, give me a break!" he muttered. Kimmy had just walked between her Mercedes and the Impala, her keys in her hand. She left a long scratch down the side of the Impala before walking behind the Mercedes and back up to get into the driver's seat. She squalled the Mercedes' tires when she hit the accelerator after backing out onto the street.

Slowly Horatio went back to the living room and gathered up the pictures. One of a newborn baby, one of front and back of an endorsed check for one hundred thousand dollars, and one of a birth certificate and adoption papers. And the paper with the names and details of Kimmy's birth to an illegitimate daughter, her giving the baby up for adoption for money, the details of who the father was, and where he now was.

Horatio put the papers back in the envelope and the envelope back into the computer case. He sat down for a few minutes, and then he used his phone to e-mail Penny.

All he said was, "It's over."

Horatio heard the ping of a notice for a new e-mail just moments later. It was Penny. "I'm sorry. I will be there in a few minutes."

His mind essentially went blank after that. He was a bit startled when the doorbell sounded. Horatio climbed to his feet and walked over to the door to let Penny in.

When he closed the door and turned back around Penny's eyes were searching his face, staring into his eyes. "Had to use the information, didn't you?"

When she saw his lower lip tremble, she put one arm around his chest, and used the other to bring his head down to rest his cheek on the top of her head, the closest she could get to him. "I am so sorry. I really was hoping you would not have to."

Horatio took a deep, shuddering breath, and then straightened up. "I am sorry, too," he said. "But thank you. I am not sure what else it would have taken to get her to accept the way things have to be."

With her looking up at him, Horatio looked her right in the eyes and saw the determination in them. "There is more to it, isn't there?"

"Yes. But it is something Kimmy will have to deal with. Hopefully with her family's help. I won't say more, Horatio. Please don't ask me."

"Okay. I have a feeling I already know. I won't ask you for confirmation." Horatio took another deep breath. "Okay. You are back. I said I would make it up to you. Please tell me how I can do that. And dinner out on me tonight is just the start."

Penny did not argue. "Okay. But the other stuff later. Dinner is good enough for now. Maybe we can stop somewhere and see how much fixing the key scratch will set you back."

"You noticed, huh?"

"Oh, yeah. Pretty noticeable." Penny turned back toward the door. "You know a really good steakhouse?"

"I do for a fact," Horatio said, already feeling much better. "And remember. This is just the start. I will still owe you."

"I know. I'm not arguing. A deal is a deal. And I do have some ideas. I just want to ease you into them."

Horatio did not think too much about her last statement until much later. For the moment he just enjoyed the relaxed feeling he was having. Something he had not experienced in quite some time he realized with a start as he seated Penny at their table in the steakhouse.

The two had talked about the various cases that Horatio had pending on the way over, but Horatio decided that as much as he was enjoying it, he did not want to talk business at dinner. Not with Penny.

"Enough business," he said when Penny brought up another case after they settled in at the table. "My mother never let us discuss business at the table."

"Tell me about her," Penny immediately said, more than willing to change the subject. What had started out as a project brought on by a feeling of responsibility had begun morphing into something much more personal. Penny had quickly acquired the knowledge she needed to help at the office, and about the situation with Kimmy. But now she was interested in Horatio as a person, not someone that needed help.

"You would have liked her," Horatio said, with a distant look on his face. "She was very personable, outgoing, but could be quite focused when she needed to be. Very strict in some ways, like my father, but so open about so many other things.

"When my father basically insisted I follow him into medicine, and I decided to go into law, Mother made sure I was able to follow my dream."

Horatio's eyes focused on Penny again. "Not that my father was domineering or anything like that. But he was the fourth generation of doctors in the family and had always assumed I would also become one.

"Since I had always shown such an interest in medicine as I was growing up, when I discovered law in my junior year in high school and quit following his career so closely, he couldn't quite understand. Mother got him to understand by the time I left for college. Somehow."

"You said 'was'. Are your parents still living?"

"Sadly, no. I lost Mother five years ago. Cancer. I think my father's inability to prevent her death from it weighed on him heavily. He died just eleven months later. A heart attack, despite being in very good health, and taking care of himself to prevent just such a thing. But the stress... Even in good health, the stress did him in."

"I'm sorry," Penny said, reaching over to cover his hand on the table with hers. Quickly she changed the subject again. "What do you do for fun? What are your hobbies?" Penny grinned. "Besides bowling. I saw the bag in the closet."

"I would not call bowling a hobby," Horatio said with a smile. "It used to be a real passion with me." He shook his head. "I haven't been in quite a while. Just sort of drifted away from it. Andy has been after me to join them for a night out."

"So," Penny said, "when are you going?"

Horatio looked at her closely. "Well... I don't know... I just haven't had the time for a while. So many things going on..."

"Some of which will no longer be going on," Penny said gently. "You will have time now."

Horatio shrugged. "I guess. Maybe."

"Would you teach me?" Penny asked.

Horatio looked over at her in surprise. "You don't know how to bowl?"

"Not really," Penny said. "I've been a few times with a couple of friends. More as cheerleader than participant."

"Well sure!" Horatio said eagerly. "I would love to teach you!" He hesitated, but Penny gave him an encouraging look. "There is open lane time before the league games start tomorrow night... Is that too soon?"

"Of course not. They have food there?"

"Yes. Pizza and things like that. Why?" Horatio asked.

"I'll spring for something there, so we can go direct from the office to the facility."

Horatio was nodding. But suddenly flashed on Penny's proclivity of wearing sundresses. He really did not want any of the guys seeing her in one of those while bowling. "Uh... You might want to bring a change of clothes tomorrow... Well... If you plan on wearing..." Horatio knew he was turning red. "I mean, when a person bowls they are leaning really far forward, and..."

"Ah," Penny said, "I get it. No problem."

Horatio was amazed that she seemed not the least bit embarrassed about the implication he had been making. And he was red as a beet. Penny did not seem to notice.

Rather, she was glancing around the restaurant. "This is a nice place. Jimmy mentioned that we should come here. He wants to discuss some additional aspects to the presentation I gave at the Historical Society."

Penny turned back to Horatio. "What's the matter?" she asked, seeing the look on Horatio's face.

"Nothing. Nothing," Horatio quickly said. His sudden annoyance toward Jimmy was uncalled for and he knew it. Who Penny saw while she was here was no concern of his. Or should not be.

Penny's head tilted slightly as she watched him look away from her and fiddle with his napkin and flatware. "Do you know Jimmy Hendricks, by chance? He's pretty reclusive. Does get out for the Historical Society meetings, though."

"He seemed to be available to give you a ride today." Horatio was not sure what prompted him to bring it up. Or the flat tone of voice when he said it. Again, he felt bad about his attitude, but again Penny did not seem to notice.

"He's a nice guy. We meshed pretty good when we met at the meeting."

Horatio felt another pang. Especially when Penny laughed. But he suddenly felt better when she continued. "He's a big old bear of a guy. Looks like a mountain man. I don't have any idea how old he is, but he is still quite active. I think he has decided I am his long-lost niece or something."

"Niece?" Horatio asked.

Penny laughed again, the sound sending a pleasant tremor down Horatio's back. "More like grand-daughter, I guess. He said I remind him of his oldest daughter's little girl. Who is ten. Said I was her spitting image. Kind of takes it out of a grown woman to be compared to a ten-year-old."

"You definitely are not ten years old," Horatio said before he realized it, feeling much better suddenly.

"Nope," Penny said, looking him in the eyes for a moment. "I definitely am not ten. Twenty-three. Remember?"

Horatio cut his eyes away first, but he did manage to say, "Oh, yes. I remember," before he did.

Their server's assistant arrived with water, bread, and butter. Horatio and Penny picked up the menus to decide what to order. When the server came over only a few minutes later, they were both ready. After the server left, Horatio looked at Penny again and finally asked something he had been wanting to for some time.

"I've been wondering. You never said why you were out on the lake, diving. Or why you are here in Tennessee at all. I'm curious, I must say."

"Oh. That. A project I have been working on for some time. It is the main reason I am here in Tennessee, but only one them. There are a few more."

Penny watched, fascinated as always, when Horatio lifted one eyebrow in question. "I guess you would like to know some details, too?"

Horatio nodded. He could see some reluctance in Penny's face. But after only a slight hesitation, she began to explain. "Well, you see, one of my interests is treasure hunting..."

He could not help it. Horatio knew his eyes bugged out a bit and his mouth dropped open. This woman never ceased to amaze him. "Treasure hunting?"

Penny sighed. "Yep. I am afraid so." She cut her eyes to him. "But only in a fairly limited way. Has to be gold involved, fairly well documented, and in very hard to get to locations."

"But if the treasure is fairly well documented, wouldn't it have been found already?" Horatio asked.

"Much has," Penny admitted with a shrug.

Horatio quickly lifted his eyes back up to Penny's. He was not sure, but he had a feeling that this time he might have been caught looking at her chest. He turned pink, but since she did not say anything, he did not either. But he did see a bit of a glint in her eyes. Perhaps even some amusement. He just was not sure.

Penny continued. "However, only in the last two or three decades have some of the documentation come to light, as more and more old records, especially personal letters and such, are being posted up on the internet.

"Some people put up such things simply as historical documents to give a sense of what was going on in those times; and some simply want to preserve the history of their family, or community, with no real thought or interest in any information that might bear on known or unknown lost treasures.

"There are some people into treasure hunting that keep a close eye on new releases of information that might shed some light on the location of these treasures. Or indicate that there might be a new one that has not been revealed before.

"I have a data analysis program that I developed that scans the internet for possible treasure information. I got a hit a couple of months ago on a possible location of both a known treasure in the area, plus one that is entirely new, as far as I could determine from my subsequent research. Both in this area.

"So, since I had some plans in this area anyway, I decided to come down early and take a look around to see if I could find anything. Now, in Tennessee, anything over one hundred years old, that does not come under Federal Laws concerning treasure troves, belongs to the State. If I had found the lost Civil War treasure, I would have turned the location over to the proper authorities.

"However, the other possible find in the lake is less than one hundred years old and has provenance. I contacted the heirs of the original owners and cut a deal to recover it, if I could, for one-third of it."

When Penny stopped talking, Horatio waited a few seconds, and then asked, "And?"

Penny grinned. "It can get tricky taking things off public property. TVA in this case. The local authorities have it and are in the process of contacting the owners for verification of my right of recovery." Penny leaned forward and whispered conspiratorially, "One thousand each 1924 Saint Gaudens gold double eagles, and 1924 Peace silver dollars.

"All in Atlas EZ-Seal half gallon glass canning jars. All still sealed and unbroken. Right where I expected them to be from the description the family sent me after I contacted them. Just had to move a bit of debris, some silt, and there were the oak boxes, still intact. A bit of a pain to get into the boat, but I managed."

Horatio was staring at Penny. Her eyes were wide with excitement. "You did all that on that one boat trip?"

"Oh, no!" Penny said quickly. "I just located the boxes, rigged lifts on them, activated a locator beacon, and set a remote release that first evening. I logged the GPS when I got back in the boat and then went back a couple of nights later to do the actual recovery."

"You did all that alone? Penny! That could have been dangerous! Aren't you supposed to always dive with someone? Buddy system or something?"

"Uh..." Penny said, her eyes downcast for a moment, but then she looked up and her eyes were sparkling, her mouth curved in a huge smile. "Yes, of course. And I usually do. But I just didn't have anyone here I could trust. And with that information out there...

"Well, the family was getting more inquiries, most of which wanted the information and were not giving much of a guarantee of sharing the find with them. I couldn't let that stash go to just anyone."

After Horatio's, "Hm," they both stayed silent as their appetizers were delivered. But as soon as the server was out of earshot, Horatio looked over at Penny again and asked, "What kind of guarantee could there be, anyway? I mean, I sure trust you, from the first, but..."

It was Horatio that shrugged his shoulders this time, and Penny had to admit to herself that those broad shoulders were something to see when he moved like that.

"Well..." she said slowly, after a long hesitation.

And Horatio thought to himself, *"Here it comes again."*

Penny started talking at a fairly normal pace but was soon talking rapidly. "I really wanted to find that treasure and get it to the family. They can really use it. And I wanted the finder's fee. You will find that I am very mercenary at times. Anyway, to make as sure as I could that they wouldn't give out any other information, until I had a chance to come down here to look, I put a million in escrow for them. If the treasure wasn't delivered to them within six months, they got the million."

Penny's eyes were carefully on the shrimp cocktail she was slowly eating when she finished.

"Let me get this straight," Horatio said, trying to make sure he understood what he thought she said. Because he was pretty sure he was misunderstanding her.

"You put a million in escrow... Dollars?" He saw Penny nod. Horatio took a deep breath. "Just how much is that stuff worth?"

Penny looked at him in surprise then. "A thousand Saint Gaudens 1924 almost uncirculated double eagles and a thousand almost uncirculated 1924 Peace silver dollars? Horatio, that is worth over a million two right now. And gold and silver prices are down a bit.

"And there could have been a lot more. The family just knew their great grandfather sold his business and retired in 1924. He converted to gold and silver coins, the sly old dog, and socked it away for a rainy day. He dipped into it from time to time, of course, to live on, up through the depression and then died about the time they started the dam.

"His kids had moved away when he retired and were doing okay. They did not know just how much he got for the business. They didn't realize he still had much left, from what the letters that were found said. But when his great grandchildren found some of his documents and a couple of letters, they figured it out. They just thought the money would be gone. Ruined by the water."

Penny shook her head. "They didn't even think about it being in gold until I contacted them. They just assumed it had been in currency."

"That is amazing!" Horatio said, and then finally took a bite of one of his stuffed mushroom caps. "What happens now?"

"When the paperwork clears and the family gets the physical metal, I get the escrow money back. Then they will sell coins to a reputable dealer and give me my four hundred thousand and keep the other eight hundred thousand. I'll convert mine to US Mint Gold and Silver Eagles."

Horatio stopped eating again. "Wait. You had a million dollars you could put in escrow?"

Penny winced. "I'm... uh... pretty well off, actually. It wasn't a problem." She concentrated on her shrimp cocktail for several long moments of silence. When Horatio still had not said anything she looked up to see him watching her.

She dropped her eyes again. "It's not a big deal, Horatio. I've uh... well, I've invented a couple of things, come up with some processes... made a discovery or two... and made some investments the last few years..." Penny looked up again.

"And you want me to teach you to bowl?" Horatio asked, astonished.

Penny had almost a pleading look in her eyes. "I do, Horatio. Honestly. I don't really socialize much, even now, when I can. I just… don't have that much experience with it. I want to learn some new things. Things other people enjoy. That I can enjoy with them.

"I love my work and my hobbies and my research… But I do most of it alone. My parents are happy on their homestead they were finally able to get and… well… I don't want to bother them."

Horatio studied Penny's face for a moment, and then nodded. "Of course, Penny. I promised you I would make things up to you for helping me out. How about I help you out a little in return? I'm no social animal, much to Kimmy's formerly constant dismay, but I know how to have some fun. Really I do."

Penny grinned. "Never doubted it for a minute. And you might just find some of the things I may get you to do entertaining, as well as educational."

"Just what things did you have in mind for me?" Horatio asked as the bus person cleared their appetizers and replaced them with salads.

Penny shook her head. "Still trying to decide the particulars. For the moment, tell me more about yourself. What do you do besides bowling in your spare time? I know you must have other hobbies."

Horatio could tell Penny wanted to get the subject away from her. And that was okay. It was just fun talking with her about anything. And everything.

"Well, though I do not have the time for it anymore, and will not likely have any in the future, but I like to work on cars. Well, not just cars. I helped my grandfather rebuild a tractor once when I was a kid. That was as much fun as working on my first car. An old rust bucket of a 1977 Chevrolet Impala I bought with my own money."

Horatio shook his head. "My mother and father insisted I work for spending money from the time I was old enough. And that meant I had to pay for my own car, when I wanted one. I tried so hard to wheedle Mother into talking my father into loaning me the money. But she told me flat out that if I wanted something like a car, I would have to earn it myself."

When Horatio glanced over at Penny she was smiling. "Poor baby," she said, laughing.

"Yeah. Right. Anyway, I rebuilt that car from the ground up. My parents would not let me put it on the street until it was in tip top condition. But they didn't prevent me from turning it into a very classy, and fast, ride." Now Horatio was grinning.

"I take it you have been a fan ever since," Penny said. "Still driving one."

"Yeah," Horatio said. "I do like the Chevy Impala line. The only cars I have ever owned." His face took on a wry look. "Never had one keyed before, though."

Penny grunted something he could not understand but did not ask her about it as the server was there with their entrees, and the bus person was clearing the salad plates.

"This looks really good," Penny said. "I can certainly cook steaks to my own satisfaction, but they are one of my weakest skills. I love a perfectly grilled filet." Penny picked up her fork and steak knife and cut into the steak. When she took a bite, her eyes closed and she moaned slightly. "Perfect!"

Horatio had to clear his throat twice before he could speak again. That moan of pleasure had him ready to groan, thinking about making her recreate that sound for other reasons.

He quickly cut into his own steak and took a bite when Penny looked over at him. After he had chewed and swallowed, he did manage to say, "This is the best place in town for steaks. Though I must say, I can hold my own on a grill.

"One of the things my father taught me. He always said it was a man's duty to be able to cook fresh meat properly in the out of doors. Every once in a while, there was a bit of cave man in my father that he let show."

Horatio grinned. "And from what my mother implied a few times, she kind of liked that side of him."

He almost groaned again when Penny gave him a calculating look and said, "Yes, I think I would have liked your mother. We seem to have some things in common."

They ate in silence for a while, and then Penny cut her eyes up to Horatio. "What are you thinking?" she suddenly asked.

Horatio looked startled. His eyes had been on her when she looked up. "I..."

"It's okay, Horatio. I know I can put people off..."

When she dropped her eyes again Horatio felt a pang at having caused her distress, even if it was unintentional. "Penny. Penny look at me."

When she met his eyes again he saw the sheen of unshed tears. "Penny, it is nothing bad. Honestly. You just fascinate me. I don't know what to expect at any time, with you. That isn't a bad thing, Penny. I've just never been... surprised... by a woman before. They've always been... I don't know..."

Horatio shrugged. "Just there. Nothing special. All mostly just a variation on a theme. You, on the other hand... You don't fit the mold that the women I have had fairly close personal dealings with all came from."

Penny continued to look at him but sighed. "Yeah. I'm different, all right. I'm all the things guys don't really care for in a woman. I'm short and not very curvy, I'm smarter than most, I have my own money, I speak my mind, I have oddball interests... guys have never been into me very much. Not that I have had much time to find out."

Putting her eyes down on her plate, Penny cut another bite of the steak, not really expecting Horatio to say much about what she considered something of a self-pitying tirade.

"None of that matters to me, Penny," Horatio said after another long pause. "If you must know... well, that not being very curvy is a crock."

Penny looked up, eyes flashing, mostly, at first, in annoyance at Horatio contradicting something she had said, the flash turned to something else when Horatio continued, especially when he turned slightly pink.

"Your curves are fine. Maybe not glamor girl curves, but what you have, you... Aw, heck, Penny. You're beautiful. And sexy. Don't ever doubt yourself about that. If other guys haven't noticed, that is their absolute loss. Take my word for it."

It was Horatio's turn to stare at anything except the person across the table. But when Penny just made a, "hm," sound, Horatio looked over at her again.

"And the other things?" she asked.

"They fascinate me," Horatio said. "Like I said. They aren't turn offs, not to me. I'm amazed, and curious. I feel bad every time something you do surprises me. I mean it is the twenty-first century. Women can do almost everything men can do. I don't really know why it catches me by surprise. It shouldn't."

"Just the total package, I think," Penny replied, all signs of the tears and sadness gone now. "Some things don't seem to go together, where individually, there is no second thought about them."

Horatio nodded. "I do admit the package, as you said, is what is the amazing thing. But it is a very nicely wrapped package. Don't ever doubt that."

"That is sweet," Penny said. "Thank you."

Horatio cleared his throat. "You mentioned something about not having had much time to... figure out boys... men."

"Another self-pity story," Penny said. "You sure you want to hear it?"

Horatio found himself grinning. "I have a feeling there is a lot less self-pity than there is interesting background and self-determination."

"Well. I don't know about that. But here goes," Penny said. "When it was discovered I had an exceptional ability to learn, when I was three, my parents sort of didn't know what to do about it. They wanted me to have every opportunity to take advantage of it. To be whatever I could be. To have a better life than they had, growing up and then as a couple.

"So, they more or less signed my care over to the scientists. Oh, they were there, whenever the team allowed it. But my life was not my own for a long time. The team was careful to have my psychological needs met. So, they thought. It was more of an experiment though, to check my reactions to various stimuli and see how I reacted psychologically.

"I knew the intricacies of the human body by age eight and the mechanics of sex and reproduction by the time I was ten. But I never had a chance to figure out the girl-boy thing, not really. From age eleven on, I was in pure learning mode. Every day was another specialist teaching me their specialty. All the sciences. Math. History. Languages. Literature. Economics. Law. Political systems. Engineering. Medicine. Geology. And on and on and on.

"Then I was enrolled in advanced college classes when I turned thirteen and got several Bachelor's degrees, and then a few Master's degrees in various subjects over the next few years.

"Not until I was eighteen and could legally make my own decisions was I able to disassociate myself from the think tank that had controlled my life for so long.

"I don't think they counted on me rebelling before then, because I had always been eager to participate in everything. And I was. Really. I loved the learning. But despite learning everything I was, I just felt like I was missing something. Something important.

"Not long after I was seventeen a new guy was assigned to the team working with me. He was just out of college... and such a dreamboat. I immediately developed a huge crush on him. I knew what it was intellectually, of course. But I didn't understand the feelings, not really.

"So, when he fell in love with another of the researchers, and they got married, all within a year, I decided that I wanted to find out more about real life. Not the sheltered, controlled life I was living. The day I turned eighteen, I went to the facility administrator, basically signed myself out, and left.

"One thing I will give them, everything I came up with during those years was duly attributed to me, patented, copyrighted, or trademarked where needed, and any money that came from the ideas socked away in trust funds. So, I had money. But I could not access it until I was twenty-one.

"But I was given an allowance all those years for personal expenses. It wasn't like I was locked away. I did visit my parents fairly often, for a weekend or holidays. And we did do field trips quite often, so I did have some money for things like that.

"But even then, I was pretty frugal, and without much experience at life, didn't really know what was available to be purchased. So, I had enough money to get by for a while if I was careful.

"I headed home, of course. I was so homesick suddenly I don't think I could have done anything else. And my parents were very understanding. They only wanted the best for me. Always had. And understood that doing what I wanted was what was best for me. So, I moved back into a home I'd never really lived in before.

"After a week of vegging out, I was so bored I wanted to scream. So, I went looking for a job, just for something to do, until I decided what I did want to do."

Penny paused, for the first time, and grinned. "I am proud to say that I was hired on the spot at a restaurant as a bus person. For minimum wage. And I was very good at it, too."

Horatio laughed. "I bet you were."

"Yeah. But, it did bother me that I was actually just rebelling, and only doing it just to prove that I could do anything I wanted. I do have a gift, and I knew it then, too. It was foolish to waste it on working in a minimum wage job, where I couldn't use my education to really help people, which I had decided was something I wanted to do, early on.

"So, I enrolled in some practical work classes. Paralegal was one of them, since law seemed to be important. But I got my general contractor's license, too. And a bunch of other things. I went ahead and finished up the last elements of three doctorial programs I had been well into before I left the think tank.

"I think I just avoided personal relationships during those three years, because I really had no clue what to do. And I stayed so busy I had an excuse not to date or anything else.

"I managed to come up with a few more things to increase my personal wealth in my spare time. I gained access to my trust funds on my twenty-first birthday, and that turned me loose to really pursue my interests.

"I set my parents up on their dream homestead, as part of the property I had been watching for some time and was finally able to purchase. It is my home base, as well."

Penny paused then, her eyes going to her plate. She took the last few bites. Horatio continued to watch her, finishing up what was left on his plate, as well.

"The last two years," Penny said, having finished, "I've dated a few times... Nice guys, for the most part. Guys I met in more or less normal societal activities. I would get asked out... but never got a second date."

Penny looked at Horatio, a rather forlorn look in her eyes. "I just don't know what I'm doing when it comes to guys. I have certain moral standards... and those get in the way, too. And I am afraid I am running out of time."

Her last words did not really register on Horatio, because of the idea that had just popped into his head because of what she had said shortly before.

Despite being just a little uncomfortable about what he was going to say, because there were some underlying aspects of it he did not really want to admit to, Horatio said it anyway. "Look, Penny. Perhaps I can help."

Penny looked over at him as she leaned back so the bus person could clear the table. Horatio waited until the woman was out of earshot before he resumed. "It's not like I'm an expert, or anything... but maybe I could help you out with that. I do owe, you, you know. Give you a few tips and pointers when it comes to dating..."

"You'd do that for me?" Penny asked, holding her sudden eagerness in check. This was verging on being too good to be true.

"Sure," Horatio replied, rather calmly, considering the way his heart was suddenly beating in anticipation. "I mean, look at tonight. It isn't really a date, but this is the kind of thing people do on dates. Just talk. Get to know each other. It doesn't have to be anything special.

"And tomorrow could be the first step. Make it a date training event. Like a real date, not just helping out a friend, like we talked about before. How does that sound?"

"You'd be honest with me, wouldn't you? Tell me true if I do something that puts you... would put off a guy I was out with?"

"Of course," Horatio said.

"Well, then, I guess it is a date," Penny said. "Now. That's settled. Do I get dessert?"

Horatio laughed. "Of course, you get dessert." He lifted his arm slightly and the server was there within moments with the dessert cart.

They made their choices, and then enjoyed them in companionable silence. There was no hesitation, nor a second thought given by either when

Horatio again put his hand on the small of Penny's back as they left, or when Penny took his arm as they walked to the Impala out in the parking lot.

Neither had much to say, other than "Good night" when they reached Horatio's house and entered.

Again, Horatio awoke to the smell of breakfast being prepared. He decided to just enjoy it. *"No need to make Penny uncomfortable,"* he told himself.

They discussed the upcoming work day over the breakfast and clean up. Penny detoured to her bedroom to get a small bag before they went out to get into the Impala to head for the office.

When Penny asked Horatio if she could listen to the news on the way he had no objection. He realized that he had not seen Penny watch any television, except for the Weather Channel. And now she was intent on the news.

"You like to keep informed," Horatio commented as they waited at a traffic signal.

Penny nodded and said, "There are so many things going on now. I like to keep up. Never know… well… things can happen."

Horatio cut a quick look over at her but had to get his eyes back on the road. Traffic was fairly heavy through this area in the mornings, and it seemed people were more and more aggressive in their driving habits.

There was no time for Horatio to pursue the train of thought. They were soon at the office and deep into work. It appeared that Penny was quite a task maker. She had Horatio's schedule full, though it left plenty of time for him to prepare for each appointment or activity.

Before, he had been at a loss of what to do at times. He had been doing fine, business wise, but had more free time on his hands during the day than he felt like he should. If he had that much time, he should be filling it with productive work.

And Penny had done that. Mrs. Benito was not the only new client she had managed to bring in. His file of potential clients was rapidly shrinking as his client base expanded.

It was with a great deal of relief that he met Jimmy Hendricks that day. His unease with Penny mentioning him several times, even though she had explained that he was more of a grandfather figure than anything else, was allayed when she introduced him as a potential new client.

"Hey there ol' son," said Jimmy as he nearly crushed Horatio's hand in his when they shook hands. "Hearing good things about you from Penny here. Figure if she's willing to help out here for a while you must be worth knowing. Needing a good lawyer. Got some planning to do, you know. Won't live forever. Gotta make sure the youngsters have a good stable base to continue with life after I'm gone."

"Well, I am sure I can set up things any way you want," Horatio said.

"Yeah. Gotta be extra careful with the way this country is going. Government trying to take over every aspect of people's lives. Not going to let them take what I've got that has been meant for my family from day one. I worked hard for what I have. And the g'vment is not going to get more than what it is truly entitled to. Don't mind paying for what the Founding Fathers set things up to be but be danged if I'll give a penny more."

Horatio contained his amazement at Jimmy's words but gave Penny a questioning look as he let Jimmy precede him into the office. Penny just gave him a reassuring look.

By the time the first consultation was over, Horatio realized he had some research he needed to do to handle Jimmy's requests. He also realized he was intrigued with the subject. But Jimmy seemed quite happy with what Horatio had said he would do to get started.

Penny was wrapped up in a bear hug before Jimmy left, almost disappearing in the man's arms.

"Interesting man," Horatio said.

"Oh, yes." Penny's eyes sparkled. "Not at all what one might think just seeing him on the street."

Horatio nodded. "I suppose you are right. I have to admit I would not have given it a thought that someone that looks like that would be so involved in finance and politics."

Penny grinned. "Bear wrestling and banjo picking, perhaps?"

Horatio had a sheepish grin on his face when he admitted she was right. "You know some interesting people."

"You don't know the half of it," Penny muttered without looking at Horatio. Before he could reply, she added, "I'm going out to get us some lunch. Chinese okay?"

"Sure," Horatio said. He watched her tiny, trim figure as she left the building, sundress skirt swirling around her legs. She was buttoning up the sweater she had put on, since, though the day had started out sunny and nice, it was already cooling down as clouds rolled in.

Horatio was busy the rest of the afternoon after lunch, right up until Penny knocked on his door just before five to tell him she was ready to lock up.

Almost apprehensively she asked, "We still going bowling?"

Horatio looked up, surprised. "Yes. Of course. I am looking forward to it." He then remembered their new agreement. "Oh. And don't forget that this is a date."

Penny nodded. "Believe me, I won't." She hesitated a moment. "And you'll let me know if I do something wrong?"

"I doubt you will do anything wrong. But, sure. If you do, I will let you know," Horatio reassured her.

She started to turn away but looked back at Horatio. "Uh… Jeans are okay for bowling, aren't they?"

"Sure. As long as they aren't so tight you can't move in them." Horatio shook his head. "Why women wear jeans so tight they can't even bend over is beyond me."

"Uh. No problems there. I will change and be ready in a few minutes."

"Okay," Horatio said. "I'll shut down and get the car started."

Horatio looked over Penny appreciatively when she came out of the building. He was leaning against the Impala on the passenger side, waiting to open the car door for her.

The jeans she was wearing were well worn, and fit her trim body well, but were not skin tight. She was moving easily in them. The green blouse she wore set off her hair and eyes. Her copper hair was back in a long ponytail.

This was the first time Horatio had seen her when she was not wearing heels. She had on athletic shoes, instead. She looked tiny. But she sure as heck did not look like a little girl, Horatio realized immediately.

"Is this… okay?" Penny asked, lifting her arms to indicate what she was wearing. A leather jacket was hanging on one finger and her bag was in her other hand.

"Perfect," Horatio said. He opened the door and watched as Penny shrugged into the jacket. It was much different from the motorcycle jacket she wore when riding the bike. This one was sleek, feminine. Horatio liked it. A lot. She tossed the bag onto the back seat of the car.

He seated her in the Impala and ran around to get in the driver's side just as a light rain began. "Where is your jacket?" Penny asked after he started the car.

"Didn't think to bring one," Horatio admitted.

Penny gave him a look he could not quite decipher. "Need to be ready for things, Horatio. Never know when something might come up."

"You're probably right. I'll be sure and bring one tomorrow. It is supposed to be like this for a couple of days."

"Three, actually," Penny said as she buckled her seat belt.

"You said you've been bowling before…" Horatio prompted.

"Yes. A few of times. A girl… a friend… or so I thought at the time… anyway, yes. I have been. But never bowled. I was just along to cheer on my friend. I do know what to do, and how to score a game."

Horatio could tell it was not a pleasant memory. And not because of the bowling aspect. "Well good. The scoring is the hard part. At least for me. I have no doubts you will pick up the physical aspects quickly."

"I am fairly athletic," Penny said. "Just no real experience with bowling."

During the short ride to the bowling center, Horatio went over the basics with Penny. She listened eagerly, asking him to clarify a couple of points in proper technique. "Okay. If you run me through it a few times I think I can probably do okay. Well enough not to embarrass myself too much."

Horatio laughed. "Do not worry about embarrassing yourself, Penny. Some people take bowling very seriously. But like almost every other participation sport, there are people that do it just for the exercise and for the fun. Gutter balls abound. But people have a great time and enjoy both themselves, and the people they are with."

Penny smiled over at Horatio, expressing her appreciation of his comments. Horatio felt a tug at his heart.

The center was still lightly occupied. Not many people came out on league nights, except those involved in league play. They had the lanes almost to themselves.

They got Penny shoes, and a ball, and Horatio opened his bowling bag and took out his ball and shoes. A few minutes later they were at a pair of lanes, ready to go. "Now remember Penny," Horatio said, "You are just a bit handicapped because of the lighter weight ball you have to use. There just will not be as much momentum in it as there are in heavier balls, even given good speed on it."

"I understand," Penny said. "That means I have to make it up in technique and ball placement. Can I watch you bowl a couple of frames? Observe how you do it?"

Horatio nodded, hoping he had not set her up for disappointment. Then Penny said, "Give me a couple of minutes to loosen up." Horatio was distracted more than a little as Penny went through a quick stretching routine. He could not keep his eyes off her rear end every time she bent over.

The jeans were not the super tight ones some women wore, but they were form fitting. And fit Penny's form very well. But she could still move effectively. And that seemed to make it even worse. Every little movement she made emphasized what was under those jeans. And blouse when she happened to be facing him.

His breathing was just a bit uneven when she stretched one last time and said, "Okay. I am as ready as I am going to be." She looked at him expectantly.

"Oh... Yeah... I'll bowl a couple of frames..." Gathering his wits about him, Horatio picked up his bowling ball and lined up. Suddenly he was more nervous than he had ever been at a bowling alley. At least since the first time he bowled in front of a girl. And that had been several years previously.

Penny said not a word when his first ball took down only four pins. She just continued to watch as his ball returned and he picked it up. After taking several calming breaths, Horatio lined up again and made his throw. It was with more than a little relief that he saw all six pins go down.

"Well done, Horatio!" Penny said.

Horatio felt her eyes studying his every move as he continued, moving to the other lane. After he had bowled each lane three times Penny said, "I want to try now."

Penny looked over her shoulder at him when she picked up her ball and started to line up. Horatio quickly moved forward and adjusted her foot placement and stance. Then he stepped over to one side and nodded.

After studying the lane for what seemed a long time to Horatio, Penny began to move. His eyes locked on her body, he noted her graceful form as she went forward, her execution of her swing, slide, and release, and his breath caught in his throat as she followed through. *"Lord she is poetry in motion!"* was the thought in his mind until he looked down the lane.

And he saw the ball curve toward the gutter. His heart dropped. Her first attempt was going to be a gutter ball. But the ball was spinning, with an amazing amount of English, he realized, and though the ball was within an inch of going into the gutter, it curved back and took the pins right on the three pin. The one and two pins stood rock steady, but the others tumbled.

"I did it!" Penny shouted as she turned and jumped up and down three times, her shining eyes on Horatio. "I did it!"

"You sure did!" Horatio said. "And did it very well, I might add."

"You are a great teacher," Penny said, moving to the ball return to wait for the ball as the pins were reset.

"Oh, I think there is some natural talent there, too," Horatio said.

Again, Penny looked over her shoulder at him when she lined up. "Now, how do I get the other two?"

Horatio placed her for the follow up throw and stood to the side again. It was a good throw, but she hit the one pin slightly off center and it skipped past the two pin by a hair, leaving it standing.

Cutting his eyes to Penny he waited for the disappointment to show there, but there was none. She was not expecting perfection. Nine in her first frame satisfied her.

She was lining up and throwing completely on her own by the third frame. Penny had yet to make a strike, but she was not leaving more than three pins on any frame.

"Can we bowl a game now?" Penny asked after that last throw on the third practice frame.

"You sure you don't want some more practice first?" Horatio asked.

"Naw. I want you to have fun, too. We're here to bowl, both of us. I have no hopes of competing with you. I just want to bowl with you."

"Oh," Horatio said, feeling touched by her sentiment. "Then sure."

Horatio was loosening up and got three straight strikes in his second, third, and fourth frames. Penny was just as excited for his as she was for the one she made in her fourth frame.

Penny had obviously had a good time when they finally had to give up the lanes as the league players showed up and needed to get in some practice throws. Horatio reviewed the scores in his mind and was amazed that Penny had done as well as she had on her first outing.

But thinking on it as they changed back into street shoes, Horatio realized that he was right. She was a natural athlete. And that would probably translate into more than acceptable performance in just about any sport.

And her understanding of angles and the use of English was outstanding. That definitely helped her in bowling. Horatio was holding one of the spectator tables behind the lanes while Penny was getting them something to eat when he saw Andy and his girlfriend approach.

They were just shaking hands when Penny returned with a tray loaded with pizza slices and soft drinks. When Penny put the tray down Horatio introduced her to Andy and Vicky.

"Hi," Penny said, shaking Vicky's hand and then Andy's. She was aware of the scrutiny she was receiving but watched Horatio for his reaction.

"Penny is working for me for a few days until I find a replacement paralegal.

Vicky was looking at Penny, though she addressed her words to Horatio. "Andy told me Kimmy was out of the picture now. Lucky break Penny was available on such short notice."

"It was for a fact," Horatio replied evenly.

Vicky rolled her eyes and leaned closer to Penny. "Guys, huh? Never admit to just how luck plays a part. Always their perfect planning."

Penny grinned. "When it is usually us that do the real planning."

"I like you," Vicky said. "You are my kind of woman. You know the real score. Where are you from? And how did you meet Mr. Attorney?"

"Kind of strange, that," Penny said, taking her seat. Vicky sat down beside her. Andy had motioned Horatio to join him several steps away.

"I met him through Kimmy, believe it or not."

"What a witch. I am so glad Horatio is out of her clutches. She got between Horatio and Andy. Almost ruined their friendship. How did you get involved with her? I just can't see you being friends. No insult intended."

"None taken, believe me," Penny said. "It was a random encounter. She mentioned in passing that Horatio would need a paralegal and I decided I might as well look into it. I am in the area for a while and a woman needs to keep busy, you know."

Vicky nodded. "Well, I guess luck did play a part. And good luck in this case. Horatio needed someone besides Kimmy working for him. The stories Andy has told me…" Vicky's words faded away when Andy and Horatio returned to the table.

"You ready to get in some frames?" Andy asked Vicky.

"Yep," Vicky replied. She stood, but leaned over and faux whispered to Penny, "We'll talk later."

"Sorry about that," Horatio said. "Vicky doesn't like Kimmy."

Penny smiled. "No problem, Horatio. It was fun. Almost like real girl talk. Another first for me."

They were interrupted again as more of Horatio's former bowling team showed up and Horatio introduced Penny to them. There were many speculative looks at Penny from the men and the two women that were with two of the men.

Horatio did not invite the others to join them, but Penny did not mind. She was pleased with the way things were going and was having a good time. They did agree to leave fairly early, while league play was still going on. Horatio and she said good-bye to everyone and then headed for home.

Penny frowned when Horatio became soaked getting to the Impala since the rain had started coming down much harder while they were inside the bowling alley. And it was a cold rain, too.

When they arrived at the house and went inside, Penny insisted that Horatio take a hot shower. He did not argue much, since he had taken a bit of a chill on the way home despite having the heater going full blast.

When he came out of his bedroom wrapped in his robe, he expected Penny to already be in her bedroom. But she was in the living room watching the Weather Channel. When he came in, she popped up and went to the kitchen.

Horatio followed her and she sat him down at the counter, placing a cup of something hot in front of him. "Drink this," she said.

"What is it?" Horatio asked, watching the steam rise from the nearly clear liquid.

"A version of a hot toddy. Hot lemonade, with honey, and a little bit of PGA. A drop of a couple of different essential oils."

"PGA?" Horatio asked, lifting the cup to take a tiny sip.

"Pure grain alcohol," Penny replied. "Everclear, one ninety proof. Just for the alcohol content. No need to waste the good stuff in a hot toddy."

Horatio made a face and set the cup back down with a grimace.

"It is not that bad, Horatio. Drink it. It is good for you. It will help you sleep and might just keep you from getting something with your immune system lowered due to getting a chill. I know getting cold will not give you a cold but getting cold can stress the immune system and make you susceptible."

"I'd rather have some dessert. We didn't get anything at the bowling alley."

"Drink the hot toddy and I'll make us some dessert. How about coconut cream pie? I have one made. Just need to defrost it."

Horatio's eyes lit up and he picked up the cup and took another sip. "Okay. Deal," Horatio said. "I love coconut cream pie."

Penny smiled and turned to the refrigerator. "I'll even make some of my special hot cocoa." When she turned back to face him, pie in hand, she added, "And we can have a shot of Irish Mist in it. That is pretty good stuff."

Horatio smiled back. This was turning into an even better evening than he had been anticipating and hoping for. And it continued as Penny put the pie in the microwave to defrost very slowly and they went into the living room to wait.

Again, with the Weather Channel on in the background, Penny talked about the bowling, and how to improve her game, asking Horatio's opinion from time to time as she essentially worked things out in her own mind.

The hot toddy was long gone when the microwave dinged and Penny took the empty cup into the kitchen. Horatio followed, despite Penny having told him it would only take her a few minutes to prepare the hot cocoa and slice the pie.

But she did not object when he sat down at the counter again to watch her. "One of my fondest memories of the times with my parents," Penny said as she took out the things she needed to make the cocoa, "was making hot cocoa with my mother.

"She never bought the mixes. She always made it with Hershey's cocoa, whole milk, and real vanilla." Penny grinned over at Horatio. "Of course, only she and Pappa got to add Irish Mist to theirs, way back then. I just got an extra dollop of whipped cream. And it was always fresh whipped cream. No artificial whipped topping or anything. Never marshmallows in cocoa. Just real whipped cream."

Penny paused and smiled again fondly. "But we did use our share of marshmallows making Rice Krispy Treats. That was a favorite, too. I never got things like that at the think tank. Only healthy foods."

"I don't think I've had them," Horatio said. "I've seen the snack packages in the store, though, I think."

"You don't know what you are missing," Penny said. "Momma always made them with extra marshmallows so they were extra gooey." Penny looked over at Horatio. "I'll make you some one of these days. If that is okay?"

Horatio nodded. "Of course, it is."

Penny turned back to the stove to stir the hot cocoa as she added the milk. "I take it I have whole milk now," Horatio said.

Looking over her shoulder, Penny grinned at him. "You sure do. Whole milk or no milk, is my motto. I can't stand low fat milk."

Horatio laughed. He had not felt this relaxed and had this much fun, doing essentially nothing, in a very long time.

Time seemed to pass to quickly for Horatio, for Penny was soon placing plates of pie on the counter, filling cups with hot cocoa and adding shots of Irish Mist and large dollops of whipped cream to them.

It was a fleeting thought, but Horatio wondered what else Penny had stocked his pantry with. He had not had any Irish Mist in the house before her arrival.

"Oh, this is so good!" Horatio said after the first bite of the coconut cream pie. He took a sip of the hot cocoa and gasped. "I've never had hot chocolate this good, ever!"

It was all he could do, suddenly, not to wipe the whipped cream off Penny's pert little nose after she had taken a sip of her hot cocoa and left a bit of the whipped cream on it. But she was already wiping it away, fortunately, before Horatio could act on the impulse, saving him from what was sure to be an embarrassing moment.

Horatio stretched things out for as long as he could, taking a second piece of pie and another cup of the hot cocoa before Penny gently chided him about getting to bed, since they had to get to work the next morning and it was getting late.

He helped her clean up and walked side by side with her to the hallway. She stopped at her bedroom door and turned to Horatio. "I had a fun time, tonight, Teach. And learned a lot. Can I have another lesson soon?"

Oh, how Horatio wanted to give her one right that very instant. A lesson in good night kisses. But he managed to control himself. Barely. "Of course. You are not just an excellent student," he said, "But a very nice date. Thank you."

Penny's heart stilled. She gulped slightly and stared up at Horatio's eyes, trying to read just how much of what she was seeing was friendship that was developing, and how much might be something more.

"Thank you, Horatio. I found it to be a very nice first date, too. Does that mean I might have another?"

Her voice was so low that Horatio was not sure if he had heard her correctly. But assuming he had, he quickly said, "If you would so honor me with accepting the invitation."

Penny managed to nod her head yes, but then fled through the bedroom door, not quite sure what to do next, knowing she did not dare do what she wanted to do.

Chapter Three

-

The rest of the week was busy with work, since Horatio would be in court at least two days the following week. Penny was a help with that case, but also took over working with the investigator that Horatio used for some types of cases.

The investigator, Olivia Ferguson, was somewhat standoffish when she came into the office the first time after Horatio had returned. Penny picked up on the fact that Olivia, quite good looking, and very personable, had not been on good terms with Kimmy. Enough so that Olivia had been avoiding contacting Horatio for over a month.

But it did not take Penny long to set Olivia at ease after Horatio made quick introductions and asked Olivia to work with Penny on two pending cases.

During a break, as Penny and Olivia got something to eat and drink in the break room, Olivia told Penny, "I had heard through the grapevine that Kimmy was out of the picture. But I had a hard time picturing it. That woman was something else. Clingy to beat it. I thought she had her hooks into Horatio tight."

"Horatio managed to de-claw her, from what I understand," Penny said easily. And kept her voice unconcerned when she added, "He's a free agent now, companion-wise."

"Hm…" Olivia said thoughtfully. "He deserves a good woman. Especially after that she-cat. I may let my cousin know he is available again."

Penny was actually fairly skilled at keeping her emotions under wraps, having learned the skill working with the scientists that had been her daily companions for so many years. Though she did make sure that Olivia was not looking at her when she spoke again.

"Oh. I would have thought you would give it a shot. You are nothing like Kimmy in terms of personality, but you have the same beautiful model looks that Kimmy has. He obviously likes that look."

Penny turned and took a sip of her tea, watching Olivia over the rim of the cup. "Not me," Olivia said with a quick shake of her head. "He's a nice guy, quite a catch, but my heart is with someone else. I expect him to propose any day now.

"Horatio has never been on my want-to-date list. Too... tame. I am not sure exactly how he wound up with Kimmy. I figure it was all her doing and he didn't really have a chance."

"You could be right," Penny said. She was pleased that Olivia did not have any designs on Horatio. And she would deal with Olivia's cousin, if that situation ever came up. Though Penny was not sure why she was thinking that way. Horatio was only helping her out with her lack of experience with dating, not actually dating her.

Horatio tried to talk Penny out of going into the office with him Saturday morning, but she pretty much refused to agree and went in with him. He knew he had not tried as hard as he should have. Things just went better at the office when she was there. And he just liked to be around her, even at work.

But they knocked off shortly after one in the afternoon, having skipped taking a lunch. When Horatio offered to take them to a late lunch at the marina, Penny did not even hesitate to say yes.

It was only when they were nearly there that Penny looked over at Horatio and asked, "You sure you'll be okay taking me there? It is one of Kimmy's hangouts, after all."

"Kimmy is not going to interfere in my life," Horatio said calmly. "I was going to the marina long before I met Kimmy. Actually, that is where I met her. Her father, actually, first. He introduced Kimmy to me a couple of weeks after I met him for the first time. She accompanied him to lunch and I also happened to be there."

Horatio seemed at ease talking about the situation, so Penny asked him, "Are you into the Lake scene? You really haven't mentioned it."

"Not really," Horatio said with a shrug. "Andy is a fisherman, so I come out to support him when he is competing. I like the lake, and all, and even fishing. But I'm not much into the bigger doings on the lake. I spent more time on Kimmy's houseboat tied up to the dock than I ever did on it out on the lake.

"We went to some of the important functions at the Club, but... well... that was all Kimmy."

Penny nodded. "I love the water," she said. "Being out on boats and ships. Swimming and snorkeling and diving. I didn't have much chance growing up, and really got into it after I got away from the think tank. Just for the experience at first, but found I liked it."

Horatio smiled over at Penny. "Is there anything you don't like doing?"

Penny grinned back at him. "Oh, yeah. Lots," she said. "But just as an eclectic mix as the things that I do like. For instance, I love to dance. But never really took to ballet. I learned all about it in my education and took lessons as exercise at the think tank because the staff thought it would be good for me. But I just could not get into the rigidity of it. Or the pain. Lord, ballet can be painful!"

Horatio laughed. "So what kind of dancing do you like?"

Penny gave him a sideways look, which he had already learned was a sign that she was a bit unsure of how he would take something. "Actually, I don't know how to 'officially' dance. I learned ballet, of course, like I said.

"And Mother and Father taught me the waltz once when I was home on a holiday. But other than that, I never learned any other steps. I just dance in private. I just move to the music I like. I'm not even sure it can be called dancing, actually."

"Hm," Horatio said, giving her a speculative look as he parked the Impala. As he escorted her into the marina Clubhouse, he asked, "What kind of music do you like to 'move' to?"

Penny was letting the greeter take her jacket to hang up when Horatio asked. She turned to him and looked up at his face. "You are going to laugh," she said.

"Try me," Horatio said.

"I like the Oldies," Penny said, dropping her eyes. She cut him a glance. "Oldies rock and roll. And some big band music, too. I have always been envious of the dancers I've seen in old fifties movies. And I love the dance movies from the thirties and forties, too.

"One of my instructors used to bring me some of those movies, after I commented on how I liked the music when it was on in the background when we were working on something where the music would not be a distraction."

"Hm..." Horatio said again, bringing Penny's eyes around to him as they were taken to a table overlooking the lake.

"What?" Penny asked after he had seated her.

"I was just thinking," Horatio said, putting his napkin on his lap, "that going dancing would be a good practice date. I'm actually a fairly good dancer... Or so I have been told." Horatio met Penny's eyes.

"I'm not sure I could learn to dance that quickly. Not like bowling. That's all just geometry and calculating angles and English. Dancing is... knowing what you are doing. I did pick up ballet quickly, because it was all rote. The same with the waltz. But dancing dancing... I don't know."

"You said you just move to the music," Horatio said. "That's all we would have to do. It is more the social interaction... the dating aspect... Not the actual dancing. Lots of people can't dance very well and enjoy going, just to be going out."

"Oh," Penny said thoughtfully. She hoped the hopefulness in her voice was not audible when she asked, "You'd be willing to put up with my feeble attempts at dancing, in public?"

Horatio grinned. "Of course. Dancing is fun, no matter what skill level a person is. Just being out on a dance floor together…" Horatio's words faded and he cleared his throat. "Yeah. I would be more than willing to take you dancing on another date."

"Well… Let me think about it," Penny said.

Both picked up the menus and began to check them, to avoid any further conversation about a date to go dancing.

They stated their choices when the server came by, and there was silence for a moment. Penny saw Horatio's eyes widen suddenly. "It just occurred to me…" Horatio said, lowering his voice, "When you mentioned the treasure… You said, they would sell the gold and silver and give you the money. But you also said you would buy… What was it? Some other gold coins? Why sell those you found, just to buy more?"

"Those that I found are numismatic coins," Penny explained. "Worth much more as collector pieces than the worth of the gold they contain in the case of the Double Eagles, and the worth of the silver in the Silver Dollars.

"Plus, there is an odd value of gold and silver, respectively, in the coins. I can take the money from the sale of my share of the coins and buy the new US Mint Gold Eagles and US Mint Silver Eagles, get much more actual gold and silver, and the content of the coins is exactly one ounce of silver in the Silver Eagles and I can get one-tenth, one-quarter, one-half, or one full ounce Gold Eagles. So, everything is easy to track and calculate based on spot prices, rather than collector value."

Horatio was nodding. "Okay. That makes sense. But it just occurred to me… Why gold and silver, anyway? Wouldn't the old coins be more fun?"

"Oh, Horatio, gold and silver are not 'fun' for me. They are much more involved for me than that," Penny replied. She tilted her head slightly. "Are you sure you are ready for this? It really is something I would like to discuss with you, but it might be outside your comfort zone."

Horatio frowned slightly. "My comfort zone? How so?"

Penny sighed. "Perhaps I better explain a little more about myself first." She fell silent for a moment, her eyes on her hands in her lap. But she looked over at him again. "It might change your opinion of me quite a bit."

"I doubt that," Horatio said.

Penny smiled wryly. "It has happened before," she said softly.

"Come on, Penny," Horatio said. "I think I have taken things in stride pretty well, so far."

Penny had to grin. "I have to admit, you have bounced back pretty good from some of the things I have thrown at you since that first day."

Horatio grinned back. "Exactly."

"Okay. Here goes." Penny took a deep breath, released it, and began another explanation she was not sure of what the result would be. "You know what a prepper is?"

"You mean like on TV? That *Doomsday Prepper* thing?"

Penny saw that he did look a bit unsure but was trying to control it so he would not be what she was afraid he would be.

"Well, the name is the same, but no, it is not like the *Doomsday Prepper* show on TV. That is a very… distorted… view of prepping. What I do, and what I am involved in, is much more subtle, and complex, than what they imply prepping is on that show, and some of the other things shown on TV and in the movies.

"It is a lifestyle for me, as it is for many others. We simply try to be prepared for a wide variety of possibilities that we can see could happen in the future. Things that have happened in the past and will undoubtedly happen again in the future."

Penny studied him for a moment. "Actually, it might be good that this came up. I was intending to do some shopping after we left here. There is some bad weather coming, and I wanted to top off the supplies at the house. And pick up a couple of additional things. For just in case."

Horatio nodded in acceptance, if not complete understanding.

"So, anyway," Penny continued, "the gold and silver coins are just part of my preps. They are a store of wealth for when dollars are not worth anything."

Horatio looked rather alarmed at the idea.

Penny smiled slightly. "Edging out of the comfort zone a little?"

"Uh… I keep an open mind," Horatio said firmly.

"I know," Penny said. "But let's leave it at that for the moment. Might be better to ease you into this a little at a time." She smiled over at him.

Horatio looked sheepish. "Yeah. Perhaps that is a good idea. But I do want to know more about it. It seems to be a large part of your life, from what you just said, and some of the things I've noticed about you are staring to add up now."

"Does that mean I'm losing my air of intrigue?" Penny asked, astounded at her boldness.

There was a moment of silence, and then Horatio laughed loudly. "I would not say that, exactly. More that I am just adjusting. I'm learning, so what you do doesn't surprise me so much."

Penny saw the look on his face change slightly just before he added, "You are still definitely intriguing. In more ways than one."

She had to clear her throat before she could speak again. "Um... Okay." Their appetizer arrived, so Penny was spared having to think of something else to say. At least for a while.

Then the 'visits', as Penny began to think of them, began. She began to wonder if Horatio was getting tired from all the getting up and sitting back down he was doing as people came up to say hello to him. And look Penny over.

After the seventh or eighth time, right after their entrees were served, Horatio leaned forward and, with his voice lowered, said, "I'm sorry, Penny. I didn't mean for you to be put on display like this. I had decided that I would not let breaking up with Kimmy affect my actions, but I didn't think about what it would mean for you."

"It is all right, Horatio," Penny replied. "People are curious. Can't blame them for that. And so far, the people that have stopped to say hello have been quite friendly. You are well known in the area, and obviously well liked. For you. I have not seen one person whose sole interest was in Kimmy, rather than you."

Horatio leaned back. "You are something else, Penny. Thank you."

Penny blushed slightly. "No big deal... Uh-oh..."

Horatio saw Penny's demeanor change, but only slightly. She was still relaxed but seemed much more aware suddenly. Horatio turned to look in the direction that Penny's eyes had gone.

He frowned. It was Kimmy and her father. And Beauford Goodard was with them. Horatio could tell the moment that Kimmy saw him and Penny. Her eyes flashed, but for only a moment. She took Beauford's arm and turned to speak to her father, ignoring Horatio and Penny.

"Well, well, well," Horatio said softly, turning back to Penny. "Seems that she might already have me out of her system."

"Don't you believe it, Horatio," Penny said. "She learned a lesson, yes. But she will seek her revenge at some point. But do not worry about it right now. Just be aware. For now, deal with your life any way you want, without worrying about her. When it does happen, you will know what to do."

Horatio frowned. "You seem so sure."

"I am sure," Penny said. "I have dealt with people like her before. And studied them as a matter of fact. Just as I have many other things. I do not let people like that worry me. They are not worth it. I just deal with them as needed."

Penny looked at Horatio hopefully. "I hope you can do the same. I do not want you to let her ruin things for you now."

"It's not for me that…"

"I know that, Horatio," Penny said, interrupting him. "You are worried about me. But don't. As you have seen already, I can take care of myself. As long as you don't let her get to you, she can't get to me."

Horatio slowly nodded. "Okay. I get your point. No problem then. So. How's your catfish?"

Penny laughed, low in her throat, sending a shiver up Horatio's spine. "It is quite good," she said. "Good to see you getting on with your life. How is your pasta?"

Horatio had to laugh in return. "Fine. Just fine. As always here. I like your spirit."

Penny grinned. "Good. Now. Tell me something else about yourself. Winter is coming up. What do you like to do in the winter months? You an outdoors person?"

It caught Horatio a bit by surprise, but he was learning that nothing should surprise him about Penny, or anything she did. So, he let himself just enjoy the experience of being with her.

"Kind of fifty-fifty, I guess. I do like being outdoors during the winter. Sometimes. Other times, I prefer to hole up inside with the heat up and a good law book to study."

"Oh, you poor thing!" Penny chuckled. "Law books. Of course, they are fine when working. But it is hard to beat challenging oneself against the elements sometimes."

"I bet you do that often," Horatio said.

"Well, perhaps not often. But yes, I do love to go winter camping sometimes. Especially when there is going to be a good snow accumulation." She smiled over at Horatio. "Comfort zone challenge again. I have an igloo building tool that I use to build an igloo, even when there are only a few inches of snow on the ground. Instead of using a tent for shelter."

Horatio knew his eyes widened. He could see it in Penny's amused look. "You would."

"Might just get a chance here in the not too distant future," Penny said, watching Horatio with more intensity that she realized.

"You mentioned that there was some bad weather coming. You really think we will get snow this early?"

"Possible," Penny replied. "With this first system that is coming through, I doubt it. But there are two more systems coming after this first one that could turn more severe."

"You really are a weather bug, aren't you?"

Penny nodded. "I am for a fact. It is a fascinating subject." Penny decided to change the subject. "Since this isn't really the dinner table, perhaps we could discuss the trial case scheduled for next week."

Curious about Penny's additional thoughts on the case, Horatio eagerly took her up on discussing the subject. He was finding that she was an excellent sounding board for his ideas. Just as eager to point out problems as she was to encourage him on other ideas.

It was actually edging over into dinner time by the time they wrapped things up on the late lunch and left the marina club house. Horatio felt the chill in the air as they walked over to the Impala. "I think you are right about the weather."

Horatio glanced over at Penny as she buckled her seatbelt after they were in the car. "You don't think the weather will interfere with the court date, do you?"

Penny was shaking her head before Horatio finished his question.

"I don't think so, Horatio. It will be nasty out, but I don't think there will be any problems with the infrastructure in that timeframe. But that could change by next weekend."

Penny looked over at Horatio. "Do you mind if we do some shopping before we head for the house?"

"Of course not," Horatio said. "You mentioned it before. I figured we could stop on the way."

"Hm..." Penny hesitated, but when Horatio looked at her with a question in his gaze, she continued. "I was thinking more we could go by a couple of other places, besides the grocery store. Not too far out of the way."

Horatio shrugged. "Okay. Sure. Just tell me where."

Penny gave him the address of the first place she wanted to stop. Horatio gave her a quick look but headed toward the place.

Penny, Horatio noted, was an intense shopper, when they got to the store. She pulled a cart from the line, but immediately shoved it toward Horatio, expecting him to follow her with it. So, he did.

"Have you been here before," he asked her at one point. "You seem to know where everything is."

"Not this one. But most of them are laid out the same. Come on. I want to get some additional tarps."

When Horatio tried to pay for the cartload, Penny gave him one look, took out a store card and handed it to the clerk. "My choices, I pay," she said quietly to Horatio as the clerk began to scan the items Horatio was putting on the belt for Penny, since it was a bit difficult for her to handle some of them.

It was much the same at the second store. The trunk of the Impala was full when they reached the last store, the grocery store where Horatio usually shopped for food.

And this time, though Penny made the actual selections, she stood back and let Horatio pay for it when they reached the checkout counter. Everything fit on the back seat, and on the floorboards when they took the cart out to the car. Just.

"I may never have to shop again," Horatio said as they headed for the house as twilight changed to darkness.

Penny chuckled. "You never know. Better to have and not need, than need and not have."

Horatio looked over at her. "That motto seems to come naturally to you."

"It is one of several by which I live my life. Now start thinking about what you want for supper. I'm thinking something pretty light, since it was a late lunch, and a good one, at that."

"How about tuna fish sandwiches?" Horatio asked. "I haven't done those in a long time. And I noticed you got canned tuna."

"A staple for me," Penny said, without elaborating. "Sounds good. I… we… um… you have everything we need." She grinned over at him. "I even splurged for you and added a bag of chips. I don't usually buy chips. One of the worst things you can put in your body. Just like colas."

Horatio laughed. "I noticed no cola but did see some root beer and orange soda."

"Just a twelve pack each," Penny said. "Should last for a while." She was grinning over at him. "Gotta have a root beer or orange float once in a while, just for fun."

Horatio laughed. Being with Penny was fun, he found, despite her often very serious manner at times.

"I'd go ahead and park in the garage," Penny suggested when they got to the house. "I noticed you don't always."

"Yeah. Usually have to clean it before…" Horatio realized he had not been in the garage since he had come back from the trip. He touched the garage door opener control when he pulled up the driveway.

Sure enough, there was plenty of room for the Impala. And from what he could see, nothing had been removed, just reorganized. He cut his eyes over to Penny, but she was studiously avoiding his gaze. He realized he should have made the connection when Penny had mentioned that her motorcycle trailer was in the garage.

When they got out of the car and Horatio closed the garage door, and then opened the door into the kitchen, Penny finally said, "You don't mind, do you? I just needed something to keep me busy one Sunday afternoon."

Horatio smiled. "No. No, I don't mind. I feel bad that you have done all this work around the house, and I haven't done anything in return…"

"You are letting me live here, Horatio. That is enough. Now, let's get these things inside."

Horatio decided that Penny really did not want to discuss it, so he kept silent and helped her move things, following her guidance. Some things went onto the newly organized shelving units along one wall of the garage, and the rest into the house.

Some of the things that went into the house were put in the entry closet, some in the pantry, and most of the rest in the kitchen. Penny took a few things into the bedroom she was using, and she gave Horatio a box with some things for him to take to his bedroom, with instructions to put them in his walk-in closet, close to the door.

With everything put away, Penny ushered Horatio out of the kitchen, to look for something interesting on television to watch, and she began the preparations for their tuna fish sandwiches.

It did not take Penny long, and when she carried the tray of sandwiches, chips, and drinks into the living room, Horatio was still looking at the cablevision guide channel.

"I don't know," Horatio said. "Not much of interest on. At least to me. You pick something."

Penny chuckled, put the tray on the coffee table, and took the remote. Horatio just kept his mouth shut as Penny scanned through the channels as fast as the system would let her. "How about an old movie," she said, stopping the scrolling suddenly.

"Sure," Horatio said. But Penny heard the hesitation in his voice.

She laughed suddenly. "Not a chick flick." Horatio relaxed and Penny chuckled again. "How about *Jurassic Park*? I have not seen that in a very long time. It is just about to start."

Horatio perked up. "Okay. That sounds good. Uh… You aren't a screamer, are you?"

Penny cut him a look, debating just how risqué she could pull off. "Well… for movies, not too much. Other than that… I really don't know."

It took Horatio a moment to figure out her second meaning. Penny saw him glance at her, flush, and look away. "Um... Yeah. Well, good. Used to have a girlfriend that screamed at all the scary parts. Right in my ear. Not the best date I ever had."

"No worries then," Penny said. She sat down on the sofa at the other end from where Horatio was sitting. She started the movie, picked up one of the plates from the tray, and sat back.

Horatio got his plate and drink and did the same. Penny paused the movie halfway through, after they had finished their sandwiches, so she could clean things up, and both could use the bathroom.

"You want some popcorn?" Horatio asked Penny as they met in the living room again.

"Sure. Can I make caramel sauce for it?" Penny asked.

"Hm... If we do the trilogy..."

Penny grinned. "Glutton for punishment. I like that. Okay. But I am sleeping in Sunday."

"Works for me," Horatio said. It did not take long for the two to have the popcorn popped, and the caramel sauce ready for it. With fresh drinks, and the big bowl of caramel popcorn, the two went back to the living room and started the movie back up.

Since both had seemed to never give it a thought to get two bowls out for the caramel popcorn, Horatio and Penny sat side by side on the sofa this time, to share the single large bowl.

The first couple of times their fingers met in the popcorn bowl each would freeze, but after the third time, neither hesitated to grab another handful.

They did watch the first three *Jurassic Park* movies, but they were both yawning broadly by the end of the third one. After quick good nights they moved to their respective bedrooms, though each gave the other a long look when the other was not watching, before they did.

True to her word, Penny slept in on Sunday morning. It was five after nine when she rolled out of bed and belted her robe. With her clothes for the day in her hands, she stuck her head out of the bedroom door and listened for a moment. When she did not hear anything, she went to the bathroom and did her morning routine.

When she entered the kitchen a few minutes later she was smiling. Apparently, Horatio was even more tired than she had been. It might just give her time to do a special breakfast. With the weather outside miserable, being wet and cold, this breakfast would be perfect.

Humming softly to herself, Penny got to work. When she heard the TV come on, she smiled again. Horatio had tuned to the Weather Channel. Penny looked over her shoulder when Horatio cleared his throat to announce his presence.

"Something smells good." Horatio chuckled. "Not that it always doesn't."

"Thank you," Penny said. "I thought with the nasty weather something especially warming would be nice. How does biscuits and sausage gravy sound, followed with some chocolate gravy to top it off?"

"Chocolate gravy? Never heard of that," Horatio said. Penny turned and grinned. "You will either love it or hate it. Personally, I love the stuff so much, I only make it every once in a while because I would eat too much of it otherwise."

Horatio looked over Penny's trim figure. She was in jeans and a shirt again, with the same athletic shoes on she had worn bowling. "You're sure doing something right," he said without thinking, bringing a blush to Penny's face.

She turned back to the stove, smiling, as Horatio tried to come up with something to say to get past what had slipped out. But with Penny ignoring it, he decided to do the same. "I'll set the table," he said and moved back into the dining area.

It was only a few minutes later that Penny was placing everything on the table. Horatio was ready and seated her when she stepped up to her chair.

"You were right about this weather," Horatio said shortly after they started eating. "Nasty out. Listen to that wind and rain."

"What did the Weather Channel have to say earlier?" Penny asked.

"Just what you told me. We should be fine for the next few days, but there are a couple of systems headed this way that could dump quite a bit of snow on us."

"When we get to the office tomorrow, I will check the schedule and make sure there won't be any problems with appointments while the weather is bad."

"Oh, my Lord!" Horatio said a few minutes later after his first taste of Penny's chocolate gravy on her homemade biscuits. "This is wonderful!"

Penny smiled. "It is my mother's recipe. I will let her know she has another convert when I talk to her this afternoon."

"You're pretty close to your parents, aren't you?" Horatio asked as he leaned back in his chair, stuffed from the breakfast. He cradled a cup of coffee in his hands.

"Yes. Despite being away from them so much... Or perhaps because of it," Penny said, "I am very close to them, now. I talk to them at least a couple of times a week, and almost always each Sunday."

Horatio hesitated, but then plunged ahead with his question. "What do they think about this situation? With what has happened to you here?"

Penny smiled down at her cup of tea. "Well... They don't know all of it, of course..." She looked over and met Horatio's curious eyes. "They are... Mom especially, curious about you. And Daddy is a bit... disconcerted that I am living here. But they know me. Know nothing inappropriate is going on."

Horatio almost cut his eyes away, but Penny was looking at him so openly he could not. He did not want her to think that he thought anything other than what he was trying to project. Nothing inappropriate was going on between them. He could not voice the thought that inappropriate thoughts had occurred to him.

"That is good. Trust is a very elusive thing in this day and age."

"I know," Penny said. "It is something I value highly, also taught to me by my parents. They would like you, you know." Penny grinned. "Even if you are an attorney."

"Hey!" Horatio protested. "What's wrong with attorneys? Didn't you say you almost decided to become one?"

Penny laughed as she got up. Horatio quickly did the same and began to help her clear the table. "My father would have supported me, of course," Penny said, still smiling. "But he is not a big fan of the legal profession."

Her smile faded. "He was not too happy with the terms of the agreement that he and my mother signed when I was sent to the think tank to... When they agreed to turn over custody. Neither one really understood everything the lawyers put in the documents, until much later."

"I'm sorry," Horatio said, placing a hand on Penny's shoulder after they had placed the things on the counter in the kitchen.

"It's okay, Horatio. It all worked out okay. It is just that my parents do not trust easily. Never did, really, and especially not after that." She smiled up at him. "And you would not believe what they think about the media!" She laughed.

"Trust issues again?" Horatio asked, smiling.

"Oh, yeah," Penny said. "I have a few problems with the media, too. But a story for another time. Let's get these dishes done. I have a few things I need to do today."

They worked companionably in the kitchen until the breakfast things were put away, and Penny's initial preparations for their lunch and dinner were completed.

Horatio was a bit surprised when Penny sat down on the sofa with her cell phone when they were finished in the kitchen. He sat down on the other end of the sofa with the Sunday paper and began to read. But it was hard to completely tune out Penny, as she spoke to her parents.

She was making no effort to keep her voice especially low, so, though Horatio kept the paper up and his eyes on it, his concentration was on Penny.

It was essentially impossible to follow the conversation, hearing just Penny's side of it. But Horatio could tell it was a good one, with the humor and love in Penny's voice obvious. He could also tell when Penny began talking to her father, instead of her mother. There was a slight difference in tone, not to mention the 'Hello Daddy.'

Horatio did put the paper down when Penny suddenly said, "Daddy wants to talk to you."

Penny's eyes were on him when Horatio put the paper aside and took the phone from her. "Hello sir."

Horatio's eyes cut back to Penny's quickly when Allister Arcade said, "I understand you are an attorney, young man."

"Yes, sir. I am."

"You a good one?"

"I… I believe so, Sir. I try to do the best I possibly can for my clients."

"I see. Penny almost became a lawyer, you know. Decided against it, thankfully. As much as I worry about her getting into trouble at times, the way she does, I think I prefer her doing what she does than if she had become a lawyer. No insult intended, son. Attorneys are a must, but I have met a few that I had no use for. But Penny has told me you use the law to help people, not disadvantage them. So that is good.

"Penny would have been the same way, of course. But the law is too tame for her. She needs some excitement in her life to keep her interested. That is why she does what she does, sometimes. And she is certainly capable of taking care of herself. But I still worry about her. Since she still has some things to do in the area, I would appreciate if you could keep an eye on her for me. You know. Just to lend a male hand if needed. Not that she needs it, mind you. But still…"

"Yes, Sir. I understand. I would anyway, but since you have mentioned it, I certainly will do what I can. She has helped me out significantly, and I owe her a debt of gratitude."

"That is my girl, for sure. Here. Hang on. Momma wants to talk to you."

Horatio glanced over at Penny. Penny had not said anything, but she was watching him with interest. "Your mother wants to talk to me, too," he mouthed to her. She gave a tiny nod.

"Horatio? May I call you Horatio?" came the woman's voice.

"Yes, Ma'am. Of course. Mr. Arcade said you wished to talk to me, Mrs. Arcade?"

"Yes. Just to say hello. And ask you to watch out for Penny. She is so self-confident that sometimes she gets herself into things she probably shouldn't. She has always gotten herself out of any problems, but it would be nice to know she has someone out there she can lean on and depend on, if she needs to.

"My little girl PP, as smart and capable as she is, can be a handful. So, feel free to be quite forthright with her if you think she is getting into something that you would prefer not to be involved with. She can be very persuasive, you know, PP can."

Horatio glanced over at Penny. She was still smiling calmly, as Mrs. Arcade continued. "And feel free to call us if you need some advice on how to deal with her."

"I certainly will, Mrs. Arcade. You can count on me."

"Oh, and Horatio?"

"Yes, Mrs. Arcade?"

"Do not feel too bothered if PP doesn't act like most of the young women you know. It is nothing personal. She is a tomboy at heart and sometimes can be rather... intimidating when it comes to men. Especially ones that think that because she is small that she is not capable of doing not only what most women can, but often even more than most men."

"Oh, yes, Mrs. Arcade. I have discovered that about her. And it is no problem. I quite respect PP's capabilities."

"Oh, no!" said Mrs. Arcade. "Never refer to her as PP. That is my pet name for her, and as you can probably tell, it isn't suitable for public use. I am so sorry I slipped and used that reference." There was silence for a moment. "Perhaps I should talk to her again..."

"Yes, Ma'am. Here she is." Horatio tried very hard not to grin at Penny's red face, which was planted in her hands, until she lifted it to take the phone. She suddenly glared at him when he told her, "PP, your mother wants to talk to you again."

Horatio could not help it. He started to chuckle as he handed the phone over, but quickly clapped a hand over his mouth to hold the sounds in. But Penny could tell he was still laughing, because he was shaking so hard.

"Hello Momma. Yes, I know. It was just a little slip." Penny glared over at Horatio. "He is a very nice man. He will not tease me about it, I assure you. Tell Daddy I said 'bye and that I love him. Love you. Good-bye."

Penny ended the call and stared at Horatio until he managed to get himself under control. "It is not PP as in tinkle, Horatio. It is the first letters of my first name and middle name."

Horatio nodded, but still did not trust himself to speak for a moment. But seeing the firm look on Penny's face starting to change to one of chagrin, he did get out, "I understand, Penny. I'm sorry if I upset you. It just caught me by surprise. Things just popped up in my head... I'm sorry."

Penny sighed. "It's okay, Horatio. I do understand. It is a natural reaction. Not the first time mother has used the name. Fortunately, not very often."

Back under control, wanting to ease any tension or embarrassment Penny might be feeling, Horatio asked, "What is your middle name."

Penny sighed again and looked down at the floor. Horatio could barely hear her when she replied. "Pound."

"What? Did you say Pound?" Horatio made sure his voice was normal, despite the sudden urge to laugh again.

Penny looked over at him again, finally. "Yes. My middle name is Pound. I am Penny Pound Arcade. As in, 'In for a penny, in for a pound.' My parents have a somewhat warped sense of humor. And I was quite a surprise when I came along. They didn't think they could have children. They had been trying since they were first married. I didn't come along until several years later."

Horatio, back in full control nodded and said, "I understand, Penny. I promise I won't tease you about it. It is over and done now, and I will not bring it up again. It just caught me by surprise, is all."

Penny's smile lit up the room, Horatio decided, when she looked at him with grateful eyes and the ends of her lips turned up. "Thank you. I was teased unmercifully for a little while when I was about nine, I guess it was. There were a couple of other kids at the think tank, visiting their Aunt. She was one of the scientists studying me.

"She referred to me as P. P. Arcade once in front of them. She didn't mean anything by it, but her niece and nephew were quite the obnoxious pair. As soon as their aunt was out of hearing range the teasing started.

"I really did not know how to handle it and just... well... took it. And then cried myself to sleep for three nights in a row, until they were gone. Their aunt never knew."

"Oh, Penny. I am so sorry. I never should have even mentioned it when your mother used the name."

Penny smiled again. "It is all right. I trust you, Horatio. You are not the type to use it against me. Now, I guess I better get on with my plans for the morning."

"You didn't really say what you are doing today. It is just me and the paper and then some games on the TV in a little while."

Horatio saw her hesitation. "You don't need to tell me. It is your personal business."

"No. It is okay. Just… might be out of that comfort zone kind of thing for you."

"I really need to do something about that comfort zone. If you don't mind, I would really be interested."

Penny smiled. "Okay then. Just remember you asked. Let me get my laptop. I'll be right back."

Horatio gathered up the paper and set it on the coffee table as he waited. Penny was back in only moments and it took only moments more for the laptop to boot up and connect to the Wi-Fi that was part of Horatio's cable connection. He did not bother to ask how she had figured out how to get on.

"Okay," Penny said, "I need to update my financials, since that money came in from the family with the treasure. It was a lot faster than I expected."

"You said you were going to buy some more gold and silver?"

"Yes. I need to transfer the money to my PM guy. He will make the purchases over the next few days and take them over to my parents' place for me."

Horatio looked confused. "You aren't just going to buy them? Can't you get them on line?"

"Oh yes. And many people do it that way." Penny paused. "And now for the comfort zone stuff. Horatio, I do not trust the government very far. When it comes to precious metals, there is a historical precedence for the government requiring privately held gold to be turned in to the government. In the thirties, when FDR signed the Executive Order, gold was turned in and everyone that did was compensated, at the then official rate.

"Not long after that the government increased the official conversion rate. Now they never really went after very many people that didn't turn in their gold. But things are different now. There is a chance that if PMs are declared illegal for Americans to own, the government will take much more severe measures to ensure that the laws are enforced.

"So, anyone that has purchased gold or silver in normal commerce, with a paper record of it, will be at risk of having everything taken from them, with or without compensation. So, all of my precious metals holdings have been bought for cash, with no record, other than a cash ticket at times, but with no name on it."

Penny watched as Horatio thought about it. "You really think that could happen?" he asked, looking over at Penny curiously.

"It is not an absolute. Nothing is. But there is a precedent, as I said. And the government has already instituted some tracking legislation, and every time any government starts tracking something, they invariably wind up using that information to take whatever it is from the people they are able to track.

"Precious metals, guns, money that goes out of the country, large cash withdrawals from banks, purchases of certain other types of goods, even long-term storage foods... all sorts of things. Often, even usually, the reports are made without the person's knowledge that they are being reported."

Horatio looked surprised. He did not doubt her, as she had proven to be totally accurate with everything she had told him that he had checked out himself.

"That is disturbing." Horatio had a thoughtful look on his face, and Penny stayed silent. "But... But why would they?" Horatio finally asked, his eyes back on Penny.

"Horatio, you read the paper and watch the news. You are seeing the same things I am seeing, every day. Just think about what you are reading and seeing, but with your mind open to what might not be being said, and about what the ultimate results are going to be, given the fiscal and financial policies of the government and the Federal Reserve."

"Hm. Why did you separate the Government and the Federal Reserve. The Federal Reserve System is part of the government." Horatio saw Penny shake her head. "Isn't it?"

"No, it is not. It is a private corporation, given legal responsibility in 1913 to loan money to the government, when requested, which is then paid back, with significant interest, using taxes collected by the government. Private banking interests have direct control of many aspects of the US economy."

"Are you sure?" Horatio asked. "That just does not sound logical."

"I am sure, Horatio. And no, it isn't logical. It isn't even technically legal, according to the Constitution, but the legislature of the time made it into law, and the system has been operating since 1913. They are not going to be willing give up that power that they have. And with the Federal Reserve

System operating, Congress has the power to do many things it would not be able to do if there was true fiscal responsibility by the government, as intended by the creators of the original Constitution."

"Wow. This is a lot to take in." Horatio was thinking again, Penny could see, so again she kept silent, to let him work some things out in his mind.

"Okay. Given that. And I certainly have no reason to doubt you. What does this actually mean... I mean, in reference to me, personally? I have money in the bank in CDs and I have an IRA that is invested in the stock market, and shares in some independent mutual funds. The money in the bank is protected, right? By the FDIC?"

Penny smiled a sad smile that Horatio picked up on immediately. "Horatio, certain amounts in banking establishments are protected. But only some types of instruments, and only up to a limit. And in normal circumstances, a person will get their money from the FDIC, if the FDIC considers the situation to come under their rules, and after attempts are made to correct the situation, and if the FDIC still has enough funds left to make the payout.

"You see, if something really major happens, the FDIC will run out of funds quickly once they start paying out and would have to go to Congress to get more, which could take a long time, especially if things are in a turmoil. The FDIC, like many government entities, works only marginally well in normal times. In crisis situations, they often do not work at all.

"That FDIC protection, even in the best of times, may not put food on the table for a family when the family's bank accounts are frozen during the investigation and afterward. The family will, in normal times, eventually get the money. But it could be weeks at best, months or even years, at worst. Government guarantees are not something that can be counted on.

"They are just like all guarantees, only worse. Even good guarantees simply state that you will get the value of the item back at some point, except for the limitations in the fine print, of which there are usually many, not that the item will work as stated, or that the events will unfold as stated, or whatever it is the guarantee is about.

"A guarantee gives you compensation when something does not go as planned. It is not an absolute promise that things will go as planned or work as advertised."

Horatio actually paled slightly. "I... I guess I knew that... As an attorney... of course I did... But I never really thought about the practical matter of depending on a guarantee to ensure that the guarantee would not actually be needed." Horatio's eyes widened at the thought.

"Now you have it," Penny said. "Too many people have come to believe that the word guarantee is some kind of promise that things will be as stated, not simply that they will be paid if things are not as stated."

"Yeah... Yeah... I do understand that. Now." Horatio's eyes cut quickly to Penny again. "But about my finances... Wait. I do understand what you just said. I realize what guarantee means. But the economy... there really could not be a situation where any of it matters, could there?"

Again, that sad smile that Horatio was beginning to dread to see. "Horatio, you saw all the news about all the bailouts over the last several years, haven't you?"

"Yes. My point exactly. The government won't let anything too drastic happen. It can't." Seeing the look on Penny's face, he added, "Can it?"

"Did Argentina happen? Russia? Zimbabwe? Greece? The US is umpteen trillions in debt. Our financial rating has been downgraded. The dollar is about to lose its position of international reserve currency. The petro-dollar is about to become a non-entity as countries bypass it and deal directly country to country with commodities, gold, and their own or alternative currencies other than the dollar.

"There is no guarantee, of any kind, other than implied, that the US economy will not tank, to a degree even worse than it did during the Great Depression, despite all of the so-called safeguards that have been instituted. For every safeguard put into place, there has been a new way to create apparent value with nothing backing it at all.

"Now that more and more people are starting to realize that the money and other financial instruments they own not only might be devalued, but become totally worthless, almost overnight, those people are getting out of those instruments in larger and larger numbers, causing the financial system to go to greater and greater lengths to turn the tide, by making even more apparent value out of thin air to bolster the numbers so they look good."

Horatio slumped back against the sofa. "I am no Bill Gates or Warren Buffett, but I do have some assets. Some I inherited, that I have grown, I am proud to say. I do not want to be the Billing's family member that loses it all."

Turning worried, yet hopeful, eyes on Penny, Horatio asked, "What should I do?"

"Oh, Horatio! Don't ask me that! I do what I do, because I believe what I believe. It would just kill me if you did some of the things that I do and wind up unhappy with the results."

"But you do them for what I am beginning to see are sound reasons. But I... I couldn't just sell everything and buy gold with it. I couldn't handle that."

"Of course not, Horatio," Penny said, putting a hand on his arm. "One never puts all their eggs, financial or otherwise, in one basket. I don't, and I would never recommend that to anyone. And, believe it or not, despite some of what I have just explained, I do still have some more or less conventional investments.

"Because they make me money now, and because it could be quite some time before things get so bad that the alternative financial instruments are truly needed, and because it might just never happen the way I think it will, anyway."

"Well..." Horatio hesitated. "It isn't fair to ask you where your money is... but could you at least give me some ideas to look into?"

Penny looked at him for a moment, and then she nodded. "Yes. I can do that. But you have to promise me you won't jump into anything blindly. We don't have a whole lot of time, but we do still have enough to do this right." Suddenly her eyes dropped and Horatio saw it. It was a sure sign she had said something she wished she had not.

Horatio thought for a moment, and it hit him. His voice rose slightly when he said, "You think it is going to happen soon! Not the next few days, of course, but soon... Um... How soon?"

"I don't know, Horatio," Penny said, meeting his eyes again. "I really don't. But I think we are talking many months, to, at most, just a few years. Four or five on the outside."

"Less than five years?" Horatio slumped back again. "That is a lot to take in."

"I know, Horatio. I did mention it might get outside your comfort zone. Always remember, this is all just my opinion. It is based on facts, that you can check out yourself, but my conclusions are mine. Others certainly have come up with different ones. Just look at the stock markets, the bond markets, the currency markets, the commodities markets, among just a few. They all are operating with the absolute belief that what they are doing is the best way to use and protect their money."

Horatio sighed. But he straightened up again and squared his shoulders. "Okay. I understand. And I will study up on all this... starting with the Wall Street Journal on Monday after I get a subscription. But for now, could you lead me through some possibilities? Some things you would do, if you were in my position?"

"I can do that, Horatio. No problem. I already have a list that I have posted up on some of the prepper forums. I will e-mail it to you and you can look it over while I get the rest of our lunch ready."

Even as she spoke, Penny's hands were flying over the laptop keyboard. A few seconds later she closed the laptop and put it aside, saying, "Done. It won't take long to get our light lunch ready. Would you set the table?"

"Sure," Horatio said, though he really wanted to go get his laptop out and look at that e-mail. But it would have to wait until after lunch.

Since breakfast had been later than normal, lunch was light and quick. Sandwiches and Penny's recipe for tomato soup that had been in the smaller of Horatio's two crockpots since breakfast.

Horatio's "Aw, man! This soup is fantastic!" brought a smile to Penny's face.

"Thank you," Penny said. "One of the dishes my mother taught me. Better even than the one the culinary expert the think tank brought in when I said I wanted to learn to cook."

"Well, whoever taught you to cook sure knew what they were doing. I have not eaten this well for… well… forever."

They were silent for several minutes as they ate. The Weather Channel was on, the sound low, but loud enough for them to hear the updates for the weather in their area.

Now more than a little curious about Penny's activities, after the lunch things were washed and put away, Horatio asked Penny, "What is on your agenda for this afternoon. If you don't mind me asking, of course."

Horatio really liked the smile that Penny gave him when she said, "I don't mind you asking anything, Horatio. But do not take offense if I decline to answer any given question. Some things I just do not talk about."

Penny paused until Horatio nodded, and then she told him, "Well, next I am going to do a little more research on the area. I am looking for a piece of property."

Before Penny could continue, Horatio, trying to contain his excitement, asked, "Here? In town?"

Penny shook her head. "No. A large tract, on one of the rivers or streams that feed the lake. Preferably on the lake, too, but not absolutely necessary, as long as it is on one of the tributaries large enough to get a good-sized boat up to the property."

"Oh…" Horatio replied, let down more than a little. "I… Hm… I know a couple of real estate agents. Perhaps I could help?"

Penny smiled. "That would be great, Horatio. Thank you. I doubt if many, if any, of the main agents around here deal with raw land like I am looking for. Most likely homes and luxury lake properties."

Horatio nodded thoughtfully. "I think you may be right. The two I know are always talking about selling me a place right on the lake. A house and lot. But not what you are looking for, sounds like."

"Probably not. But I would appreciate you asking them about any such property, and whom I would need to contact about it."

"I will do that Monday, first thing we get to the office," Horatio said. "So, you are moving to the area, then?"

"Not necessarily," Penny said, looking at the laptop screen as she typed. "I need another place with good facilities. Something east of the Mississippi, but not too far from my parent's place in the Ozarks. I have my own place there, too, of course.

"And a place in Wyoming. But I would like at least one more place for safety's sake."

"Safety's sake?" Horatio asked.

Penny looked up. "Yep. That comfort zone thing again. I think that there are some things that could happen that would make having more than one place available that could sustain one a good idea. I do not like, and will not, put all my financial eggs, my livelihood, or a safe place to live all in one basket, so to speak."

Horatio was thinking, and Penny watched the emotions play over his face as he considered what she had said.

Finally, he looked over at her again. "You take this... prepping very seriously, don't you?"

"Very seriously," Penny said. She hesitated for a moment. Horatio gave her a questioning look. "I tell you what. Another reason I am in this area is that a Prepper Convention is being held near here, in two weeks. I am planning to go. Would you... would you consider going with me? To get a look at some of the things I have talked about? You don't have to, of course. I..."

Penny had started talking rapidly. Horatio lifted his hand slightly and she stopped talking. "Yes. I think I would like to go. Let me check my calendar. I don't think I have anything..."

Horatio checked his Smartphone. Penny had set it up so the calendar synced with the computer at the office, and with his laptop. Penny did not tell him that he did not have anything that weekend. She was well aware of his schedule for the next several weeks.

"Nope," Horatio said. "Nothing that weekend. Actually, there is nothing scheduled that Friday, work wise, either." Horatio looked over at Penny.

Penny was a bit surprised she did not blush. She had kept that Friday clear on his schedule, just in case she could talk him into going to the convention. "Actually, I was going to ask you for that Friday off. I want to go over the day before and get set up, so I have the full two days at the convention. I like to take in some of the demonstrations and training classes."

"Oh," Horatio said, looking interested. "They have classes, too?"

Penny smiled. "Yes. There is a great deal of sales talk from the vendors, of course, but even some of those can be very informative, with useful information that applies far beyond what their particular product might be."

"Okay then," Horatio said. "Let's just take Friday off, close the office, and go to the convention."

"I would like that, Horatio. Thank you." She dropped her eyes for a moment. "I need to take my rig... In case I buy some things... And I just do not like to travel without my gear, anyway. So, you could ride over with me. I'll be staying in the rig."

Horatio nodded. "Sounds good to me."

"Well... You could get a motel room, if you wanted. Would probably need to book it pretty quick."

When Horatio looked surprised and said, "Good point. I will do that right now." He started to get up to get his laptop.

"You know," Penny said quickly, "There is plenty of room in the truck sleeper for you, too. There are two bunks. You would not need to get a room, if you didn't want to."

Horatio sat back down. "Wouldn't that really crowd you? Not much privacy..."

Penny shrugged. "I trust you to stay in the cab for those times when I need extra privacy. And I would certainly do the same. It is not a problem for me. Really."

"Um... Your father might not think too highly of the idea," Horatio replied.

"Daddy trusts me to know who I can trust and whom I cannot. As long as he knows I trust you, he would not say a thing." Penny grinned. "Now, he might give you one of those guy-to-guy looks, but that would be the limit of it."

"Guy-to-guy look, huh?" Horatio said, smiling. "Yeah. I get that."

"Okay," Penny said. If you are okay with it, then we have a plan. I am not sure you could have found a room close, anyway."

"Really? The Prep Convention is that big?"

"This one is," Penny replied. "Plus, it is in a more rural venue, so they can set up some of the larger outdoor gear. And there is at least one other event going on in the area too, which takes many of the rooms available in the area."

Horatio nodded. "Okay. Then that is the plan. What else do you have to show me this afternoon?"

An idea shot through Penny's thoughts, but she quickly suppressed it. "Well," she did say, "I can lead you through the action plan in case this coming storm is worse than expected."

Horatio, finding he really was not that surprised, asked anyway, "You have an action plan for that possibility?"

"Of course," Penny said, her eyes on her laptop screen again, fingers flying over the keyboard.

"It is a basic plan, that I modified for this particular event."

"Okay. Good. Tell me what part I play in this plan."

With that, Penny motioned Horatio to sit a bit closer to her so he could see her laptop screen, and then began to go over the written plan. That really did not take long, but Horatio was more interested than he expected to be, and asked questions that led them to other situations and plans, and what Penny thought of the probabilities.

Horatio soon had his computer up, looking up some things online while Penny explained some of them to him. They were busy until the kitchen timer went off, signaling that the crock pot roast was ready for their evening meal.

While Horatio set the table, Penny finished up the preparations in the kitchen and then carried things out to the dining room table. Horatio seated her, as was now his custom. They continued to discuss prepping subjects over the meal, and afterwards, Penny linked her computer to Horatio's home entertainment system to play a movie she had on her laptop.

"This movie was one my Mother and Father insisted I watch when I was thirteen and home on one of the breaks I had from the think tank. Russia and China were both rattling swords to intimidate the US and my parents wanted to introduce me to some additional prepping concepts beyond self-sufficiency.

"It is *Panic in Year Zero*, one of the earliest, and more realistic, of the nuclear war movies that were coming out in that time frame. It made a real impact on me. Ray Milland, one of the stars, was also heavily involved in the production. He was big into Civil Defense. Even made some information and training films for the government.

"They gave me a copy of the book *Alas Babylon*, by Pat Frank, then, too. I took it back to the think tank and read it when I had a chance. Those two things made me realize that prepping for such things, along with simply being self-sufficient, were going to be a part of my life the rest of my life."

"Wow. That is amazing," Horatio said. "I have to admit, I have not given these things much thought. Just kind of thought... I don't know..."

"That it will never happen here. And if it does, FEMA and Red Cross will take care of it."

Horatio colored slightly, but nodded and said, "Yeah. I guess that is what I thought." He looked at Penny thoughtfully. "But you know that won't be the case, don't you?"

"No one can know for sure anything," Penny replied. "There are no guarantees either way. But I have learned that those that help themselves tend to live better lives than those that rely on someone else to take care of them."

Horatio nodded again and leaned back to watch the movie. He decided he would order a copy of *Alas Babylon* the next day.

Chapter Four

Things were busy, with the court case Horatio was involved with, the first four days of the next week. And the storm did blow in, both earlier than initially forecast, and more severe.

Horatio was glad to let Penny pick him up from the courthouse Wednesday afternoon, and then take him to and from the office and courthouse Thursday as the heavy wet snow covered the streets to a depth of five inches in the matter of a few hours early Thursday morning, bringing the total to seven inches.

Without adequate snow removal equipment, the city could not keep up with it, and as good a car as Horatio's Impala was, it was no match for that amount of wet and then frozen snow.

Horatio was more than a little impressed at how expertly Penny maneuvered her truck through the mess, stopping more than once to help people stuck in the drifts. She had insisted they leave early Thursday to allow for those delays.

He felt bad about not being much help, at least at first. But after some instruction from Penny, and the loan of some winter gear that he could use, Horatio was able to hook and unhook the front winch while Penny stayed in the truck and pulled out the vehicles, making it go much more quickly.

When things warmed back up on Friday, Penny took Horatio down to the courthouse to pick up his Impala. Even then, he was slipping and sliding around more than he was comfortable with on the way back home. He was rather glad that Penny was following him home in her truck.

Horatio worked his aching shoulders after they entered the house, tense from the drive. "Stiff?" Penny asked, setting aside her bag after seeing the look of stress on his face.

"Yeah. A little. It has been a long time since I have driven on roads that slick. Tensed up some."

"Here," Penny said, taking his arm and leading him to the sofa. "Sit down. I will work on your shoulders a bit before I start supper."

"Penny you don't have to…"

"Sit down, Horatio," Penny chided. "I know how it is when a person is stressed over something. There for a while, when I was unhappy at the think tank, just before I left, I was in knots."

Horatio reluctantly took a seat on the sofa, with his back to one arm, and his legs stretched out on the seat. "Oh, Lord," he moaned moments after Penny's deft fingers began to dig gently into the bunched muscles in his shoulders. "That feels good…"

Penny smiled and continued to work on him as he continued to moan slightly with almost every movement of her hands. "Where did you learn to do this?" he asked not long after she moved down a bit lower to work on his mid back.

"It was part of the holistic medical training I insisted on when the think tank staff decided I needed to learn some more advanced medical techniques. I knew I did not want to ever be a medical professional fairly early on, but I did like learning first-aid, and even taking the paramedic courses they wanted me to have.

"But I wanted more than just current medical technology and techniques. By that time my stubbornness was fairly well known, and they did not give me much argument when I insisted on the holistic training. Massage, essential oils and their uses, herbal and other alternative treatments and remedies."

"How much medical training do you have?" Horatio asked.

"Just EMT Paramedic, officially, plus a Master's of Science in Herbal Medicine, and a massage therapist license."

"Just?" Horatio said, with another moan of pleasure. "There is nothing 'just' about you, Penny."

Penny's hands stilled for a moment at Horatio's comment, but she quickly continued the massage, going back up to Horatio's neck for a few minutes. Then she let her hands drop to her sides. "That's about all I can do. Your neck, shoulders, and back seem to be more relaxed now."

"They are," Horatio replied, swinging his legs around off the sofa so he could stand. "Thanks to you. And I definitely owe you a massage. But it will be from a pro. I would probably break you if I tried."

Penny managed not to say she was willing to risk it, but it was close. Instead, she turned and headed for the kitchen. "Supper won't be long. I hope crockpot pork roast is okay for tonight."

"Everything you cook is all right with me," Horatio said. "I'll set the table." As the two worked, Horatio asked, "What do you want to do tonight? I kind of had another evening planned… you know… a practice date… but I know we shouldn't go out tonight in this weather."

There was silence for several moments, and then Horatio stepped around the corner and looked at Penny. She was standing still, looking down at the dish in her hands.

"Penny?"

"Oh!" she said, slightly startled. "I was thinking," she said, keeping her eyes down. "We could watch another movie, I suppose," she said after another moment of silence.

"We've done that," Horatio said, watching her. She moved toward him, and the dining room, still not meeting his eyes. "I know," Horatio suddenly said, picking up another serving dish to carry to the table.

Penny did look over at him then. "What?"

Horatio was smiling. "I think it is time we do some dancing."

"Dancing?" Penny nearly squeaked, cutting her eyes up to him.

"Yes, dancing. And since we probably shouldn't go out, we can get some practice in tonight, so when we do go out dancing, you will have a few steps under your belt."

"Oh," Penny said, "That... um... sounds... doable."

"Of course, it's doable," Horatio said, returning to the kitchen with her to carry out the rest of the food to the table. "I do not think there is anything you can't do, when you want to."

Penny smiled. "Well, since you put it that way... Okay. Dancing it is."

Neither actually hurried to finish the meal, but then neither lingered over it, either. Horatio even suggested they have their desert, since it would keep, after the dancing practice. But Penny did insist on getting the dishes done first.

Comfortable around Horatio now, Penny had been changing into sneakers or flats after getting home, but for the dancing, she went to her bedroom and put on a pair of heels while Horatio moved some of the living room furniture out of the way, and the two throw rugs that covered much of the hardwood floor.

When Penny returned to the living room, Horatio was programming his entertainment system. When the music started, Horatio lifted his arms and Penny stepped into them. Penny knew to keep her eyes on Horatio face rather than her feet, but after only a few moments of eye contact she lowered her eyes to his upper chest, right in front of her.

Horatio had to clear his throat before he could begin to explain the moves he was making. "I remember this," Penny said. "The Tennessee Waltz."

It took very little to bring Penny closer to him, Horatio found when he increased the light pressure on her back. Despite their height difference, Horatio and Penny seemed to be a natural fit for dancing together.

"You are a fast learner, Penny," Horatio said after only a half an hour had passed. "You already have the basic steps down for four dances. You want to try a few more advanced moves?"

Penny glanced up at his face, still in his arms, though the music had stopped. She nodded, and then said, Yes. I think I would. If you think I can."

"I am sure you can," Horatio said, releasing her to go to the entertainment center. Penny went to the kitchen to get them some water while Horatio selected songs. Both took a few moments to down a glass of water each before Horatio held his arms up again.

A minute of instruction, and then Penny was whirling in multiple fast turns. She began to laugh in delight as Horatio spun her one way and then the other, took her around his back, threw her away from him and then pulled her back against him, only to repeat the moves time after time.

Both were breathing hard when the third song ended and Horatio stopped moving. "You," he said, after taking several deep breaths, "are a natural. I've never danced with anyone that could follow as well as you on those fast moves."

Penny had to breathe a bit herself before she could reply. And it was not all from the exertion. Being in Horatio's arms in some of those moves had been breathtaking. "Thank you," she said. "You move pretty good for a stodgy lawyer."

Horatio threw back his head and laughed. "Stodgy, huh? I'll show you stodgy!" The next song was already several bars in when Horatio took her in his arms again and began to dance. It was a wild, fast dance, and at the end, Horatio dipped Penny until her head was almost touching the floor before he lifted her back up.

There for a second Penny thought Horatio might kiss her while she was deep in the dip. But he did not. She had no idea just how close he had come, though. It had been tough for him not to do so.

Horatio cleared his throat and released Penny. "Um… I think that better be it for this evening. Don't want to overwhelm you."

Penny saw his eyes dip to her heaving chest and then snap quickly back up to her face. "Yes," she said rather breathlessly. "I think you are right. Uh… I'll… I'll go get desert ready."

With that, Penny hurried off to the kitchen and Horatio simply went to get the remote and turn off the music and turn on the TV. He flipped to the

Weather Channel, knowing Penny would want to see what was expected during the night and next day before they retired for the night.

They were both silent for a while as they ate the desert Penny had prepared and watched the weather forecast. But Penny put down her spoon and told Horatio, "Thank you for the dancing lessons, Horatio. You are a good teacher. And I had fun."

"You are quite welcome," Horatio replied. "Mmm... Would you feel comfortable enough already to go dancing one night this coming week?"

Penny nodded quickly. "Yes. I think so. As long as things weren't too intimidating."

Horatio had to laugh. "I don't think anything will intimidate you."

Penny grinned back. "Yeah. Probably not. Just don't want to embarrass you in your home town."

"That would be impossible," Horatio said, rather softly, his eyes on Penny's.

Penny dropped her eyes first and took another quick bite of the desert.

Neither stayed up much longer, each for the same reason. Emotions were running high, and Horatio and Penny were both thinking that they might just do something that the other might not welcome. So better to have an early night than risk things.

Horatio had a couple of commitments he had to meet that weekend. He thought about asking Penny to go with him, but when she mentioned the need to get some things done before they went to the convention, he left her to her own devices and went to meet with several other attorneys on Saturday, and then go golfing with a college friend that was in town for the day on Sunday.

The four days of the work week that followed went quickly. Horatio helped Penny load her things into the truck Thursday evening. All of her things. He wanted to ask her if she would be coming back but decided there might be a better time to ask. He would not admit to himself he did not want to ask now and find out she would simply be dropping him off after the convention, and then be on her way.

He watched in amazement as Penny readied the bike, truck, and trailer for the trip. She serviced the bike, changing oil and checking the other fluids, and air and fuel filters. Then she did the same on the truck, using a built-in fluid changing system for the engine.

The manual transmission, transfer case, and both differentials were checked from underneath. Penny extended hydraulic jacks at the four corners of the bumpers, and then put jack stands under the truck to hold it securely.

There was enough clearance for Penny to easily get under it on a mechanic's crawler she had in the slide out trays in the back of the truck.

Horatio knelt down and watched her lubricate the universal joints in the drivelines. "What are those big knots in the drivelines?" he asked at one point.

"Remco driveline disconnects and Sonnax over-torque protection units. I can disconnect the drivelines remotely so I can tow the rig without all the driveline parts spinning all the time. And the protection units will pop a pin instead of twisting or breaking a driveline if something happens to over torque them.

"Like rolling backward with a heavy load and hitting the accelerator too hard. The engine has a blower and turbo both, so it has a lot of power. The running gear is more than tough enough to handle it, but in extreme situations, the drivelines are protected, anyway."

Penny next lubricated all the other grease points from the two remote lube panels inside the front and rear wheel wells on the passenger side. She topped off the coolant tank, and the window and headlight and tail light washer tanks.

The fresh water tank was topped off, using a hose from one of Horatio's water bibs on the house, running through a purification system. Then she did the same to the fresh water tank on the trailer.

Horatio helped her stock the food they had picked up on the way home Thursday night in the sleeper cabinets and refrigerator. He went with her to fill the fuel tanks after that. He stood and watched amazed as she put a total of one hundred fifty gallons into the tanks on the truck and trailer.

"Never got around to topping them off after I got here," Penny said when Horatio mentioned the amount of fuel.

He was even more shocked when she casually added, "I wasn't too worried. Still had three hundred gallons in reserve on board." Penny double checked the fuel caps and then climbed back up into the driver's seat of the truck and they headed home.

On the way, Horatio suddenly said, "Let's eat out tonight. I just remembered there is a live band at Rembrandt's. We could practice your dancing again."

"I'd rather not stay out too late tonight. I was planning to leave about six in the morning. I need to get there pretty early to check in with the organizers."

"Oh. Okay," Horatio said, his disappointment obvious.

Penny felt a tug at her heartstrings. She also really wanted to dance with him some more. "Tell you what," Penny said, "If we make it an early evening, I don't see why we shouldn't go. I probably need the practice."

"Well..." Horatio said, "You're already pretty good. But practice never hurt."

"Okay then. We dressed okay for it?"

They had not changed out of their office attire, so were fine to go to the club, according to Horatio.

Penny was very glad she had acquiesced. But no more than Horatio. Both enjoyed their dinner, and then both were reluctant to leave, as they were having a great time dancing. The band played an eclectic mix, and both Horatio and Penny asked for two songs apiece that the band agreed to play.

But promptly at ten, Penny gathered up her coat, and Horatio stood to help her on with it. His hand on the small of her back, the two went out to the truck.

"You want to drive it home?" Penny asked before they reached it. They were well away from the rest of the vehicles on the large parking lot. "Get a feel for it before we hit the road in the morning, just in case you have to drive for some reason."

"Really?" Horatio asked, looking at the truck with a mixture of awe, excitement, and a bit of trepidation.

Penny grinned. "Sure. You can drive a stick, though, right?" she asked.

"Yes. I have driven some other trucks. But nothing this big. I think I can do it. Might have to let you back it up the driveway." He had noticed that she always parked so she was facing out from the parking area she was using.

"You might surprise yourself," Penny replied. "The backup camera system is great." She grinned at him. "And I can activate the rear steering and it is just like pushing the trailer with the front."

"You're kidding! You can steer the rear wheels, too?"

Penny nodded and laughed. "Yes. There are a few other features I haven't thought about mentioning, since they haven't come up. This truck is very capable, if I do say so, myself. A truck in a prepper fiction book called *Rufus*, influenced me somewhat when I designed this."

"Rufus, huh?" Horatio asked, a bit distracted as he carefully adjusted the seat and mirrors to fit his much larger body. Penny coached him through the diesel startup process and pointed out the various controls for lights, wipers, and such. And then Horatio put the truck in gear and they were off.

Horatio was slightly pink in the face for a few moments, but he got the hang of the clutch and the shifter quickly, and only ground the gears the one time. Penny had not said a word.

And when they reached the house, Penny had him pull around, facing away from the driveway. She activated the rear wheel steering and showed Horatio how to use the joystick to guide the truck with the rear wheels while keeping the front wheels straight ahead.

It took him only moments to have the trailer back up to the garage door accurately. "Wow! That was easy," Horatio said, looking over at Penny and smiling.

"Yep. I can back it without using it, but it is so much easier with it, since the trailer is not all that long. Longer trailers are much easier to back up."

When they were inside the house, Penny stopped Horatio before they headed for the bedrooms and said, "Thank you for taking me dancing, Horatio. I had a really good time." She really wanted to give him at least a kiss on the cheek but could not get the words out.

Horatio felt much the same way, though her cheek was not what he wanted to kiss. Her luscious lips would be his preference. But he merely said, "You are quite welcome, Penny. I had a great time, too. Um…" It was almost a question when he said, "Good night."

"Good night," Penny said softly. Before she went into her bedroom she turned and said, "See you at five, don't forget."

"Five… right. We leave at six."

Penny nodded and went through the door, closing it behind her. She took a deep breath and sighed. She fell asleep wondering what kissing Horatio would be like.

Those thoughts were still in her head the next morning when the two met in the kitchen for breakfast. But she quickly put them out of her mind as they ate, and then locked up the house. They pulled out of town just after six and were on the interstate shortly after.

They talked some, but traffic was heavy, and Penny needed to concentrate on the road. She took a moment to show Horatio how to use the on-board satellite internet and WiFi so he could use his laptop to get a few things done for the next week.

He looked up when Penny reached for a hand mike after they had travelled quite some distance. He heard her give her Amateur radio call sign, and then ask for weather conditions ahead of them.

Horatio listened as Penny talked back and forth for several minutes, not only to the station that had given her the weather conditions, but a couple of others that wanted to talk to her since she was in a moving vehicle.

"That was cool," Horatio said, looking over at Penny after she hung the mike back on its hook.

Penny smiled over at him. "Been an Amateur Radio operator for a long time. I got my license when I was ten. Didn't use it much after I got it, until I went out on my own."

"Have you ever thought about ham radio?" Horatio asked.

Penny grinned over at him. "It is the same thing, Horatio. Amateur Radio is the official name. Ham is just a very common nickname."

"Oh," Horatio said, turning pink again. "I didn't know that. So, how far can you talk?"

"On HF, like I was, basically around the world depending on the HF band I am on, and the atmospheric conditions. On my two-meter radio, which is in the VHF spectrum, just a few miles, unless there is a repeater system I can access. And there often is, nowadays. Then sometimes for dozens of miles. Even hundreds on a linked system."

"I see," Horatio said musingly. "Is it hard to get a license?"

Penny shook her head, her eyes still on the road. "Not really. A Technician license is really easy, but it has a lot of restrictions. Pretty much VHF and above, with one small segment of the ten-meter HF band.

"I have a General license, which lets me use much more of the HF bands, where the long distance talking is done. And it is not all that hard. Extra class, on the other hand, is much more difficult. And it only adds a few frequency segments. I never really had much interest in it. General does me just fine."

"You... uh... You think you might help me get my license?"

"Sure," Penny said, cutting him a quick look. "You are more than capable of passing the tests with some studying and doing practice tests. When we get back, I will set you up a learning program."

"How hard is the Morse code to learn?"

"Not that hard," Penny replied. "But you don't have to know it to get even the General license. I learned, because I wanted to know how, but it isn't required. It is a lot of fun though. And in some emergency situations, Morse code will get through when various voice modes won't."

"I see," Horatio said thoughtfully. After a moment he looked over at Penny again and added, "I look forward to learning what I need to know."

Penny cut him a smile, but then was slowing the truck very quickly. "Uh-oh," she muttered. "That looks bad!"

They were stopped behind a big rig and Horatio could not see what Penny was seeing past the truck. "What is it?" he asked.

"Wreck. And I see smoke! Hurry! Call 911 and then pop the cover on the rear bumper and get the fire extinguisher there and I'll get the one on the front bumper!"

Penny was unbuckled and sliding out of the truck before Horatio could move. When he made it to the rear of the bumper and had the large fire extinguisher, which was on a cart for easy movement, Penny was already at the site of the crash, playing the nozzle of her fire extinguisher at the base of the flames running up the side of the upside-down SUV.

"Keep doing what I'm doing," Penny told Horatio. "Base of the fire. I need to get some tools and my medical kit." Penny took off running back to the truck, the hem of her dress swirling.

There were several people milling around. Only the truck driver was helping, and he only had a small five-pound extinguisher, compared to the twenty pounders that Penny had.

Horatio almost grabbed at Penny as she ran back up to the SUV. He had just put out the fire with the last of the chemical from the extinguisher when Penny seemed to slam her hand against the passenger side window of the SUV.

The window shattered and Penny was down on her knees, dragging the large AMP-3 Outfitter medical pack closer to her. "Open it up while I check vitals," Penny commanded. She already had on a pair of exam gloves. Horatio wondered for a moment where she had got them and when she had put them on.

But he quickly did as he was told, unrolling the well-organized medical kit. Penny said over her shoulder, "Someone keep everybody back. That fire might flare up any second."

Giving Penny a worried look, he watched as she carefully felt around the person hanging upside down from their seatbelt. "Get me a big pad bandage," Penny barked. "The pouches are marked."

Horatio found the bandage immediately and handed it to Penny. She ripped the package open with her teeth and half crawled into the SUV to put it in place.

"Bandage wrap! Hurry!"

Horatio dug into the pack and quickly handed her the wrap. Horatio could see her working, laying on her back now, wrapping the thick bandage on the woman's leg with the bandage wrap.

He thought he would have a heart attack when Penny scooted back out of the SUV and he saw the blood covering her hands, arms, and chest.

Before he could say anything, Penny was up, running around to the other side of the SUV, calling out, "Bring the Outfitter pack!"

Again, she was on her knees. This time Horatio saw the tool she had in her hand when she slammed it against the driver's side window, shattering it like the other one.

Horatio heard the sirens coming, but Penny did not stop working. She was on her side, reaching up past the steering wheel. She wiggled back out. "This one has a good pulse and I do not see or feel any blood."

Next, Penny ran around to the back of the SUV and took out the hatch glass. Horatio heard whimpering, and then a weak bark as Penny pulled out a small dog, covered in blood.

The dog was trying to lick Penny's face as she checked it over for injuries. "It's okay," she said after a moment. "Hang onto it and keep it out of the way," Penny told Horatio, thrusting the dog into his hands.

Then Penny disappeared into back of the SUV through the glassless hatch. "Penny!" Horatio protested, leaning forward, the dog still in his arms, to look inside. Then she saw her dragging something backward. He ignored the way her dress was riding up her legs, and held the dog with one hand, as he reached in and grabbed the object.

He felt sick when he realized what he had in his hand was the collar of a jacket on a youth. Penny spun around on her knees when Horatio began dragging the youth back. Scrambling to her feet, she helped guide what was now obviously a 'tween girl up and over the lip on the SUV hatch window surround.

Horatio saw the tears on Penny's face. "She wasn't buckled in. She must have been thrown over the rear seat." Penny checked for breath and pulse, and then was doing chest compressions on the girl. Horatio could only look on, not knowing how he could help.

Penny was still going strong when Horatio saw flames begin to flicker on his side of the SUV. "Penny!" he yelled. "More fire! You have to move!"

Horatio reached down to lift her up but she shrugged off his hand and kept pumping. "Penny! Please!"

"Another fire extinguisher on the roof rack at the back!" she managed to gasp out. Horatio ran, nearly throwing the dog to one of the bystanders as he passed the dozen people watching the tragedy. It seemed to take forever to get the third fire extinguisher off the roof rack, after unsnapping the flap he had not noticed before he went looking for the extinguisher.

He was again directing the fire suppressant on the fire beneath the SUV, which was leaking fuel, draining toward Penny's legs as she knelt on the shoulder of the road.

"Penny! You have to move! I'm almost out!" But she continued the compressions, ignoring his plea. When the extinguisher was empty, Horatio moved toward Penny, intending to bodily pick her up. But just as he got to her he was roughly shoved out of the way. A paramedic was kneeling beside Penny and took over the compressions as her partner knelt down on the other side of the girl and opened up an AED to defibrillate her heart.

Penny climbed to her feet and turned toward Horatio. When she saw two more paramedics running up she joined them and began to fill them in on the other two victims, explaining what she had found and what she had done.

Horatio and Penny were both caught in the spray as firefighters began to spray the SUV with foam as the flames caught again, suppressing them so the paramedics could continue to work. One of them motioned Penny and Horatio back. Grateful for the reprieve, Horatio guided Penny toward the truck, just as two State Troopers pulled up, lights flashing and sirens sounding.

They killed the sirens and both quickly moved up to the crowd and began to move them away from the scene. Horatio was standing at the front of the truck, Penny at his side, watching for a moment. But he turned when he heard Penny faintly say his name. "Horatio?"

He caught her before she collapsed to the pavement. He carried her over to the grass in the median and gently placed her on the ground. Calling to the closest firefighter, he asked for help, but Penny's hand touched his arm. "I'm okay. Just exhausted. That CPR did me in..."

Suddenly Penny was ensconced in Horatio's arms. He was hugging her almost to the point she could not breathe. "You scared me to death! Don't ever do that again!"

Penny's startled eyes met Horatio's concerned ones when he finally released her and eased her back onto the ground. "Wow..." she said softly.

Penny could tell that Horatio was about to apologize for his outburst, but she did not want him to do so. So, she quickly held up one hand. "Help me up. It is cold on the ground." It was all she could do to lift that arm, they were so rubbery from the CPR.

"But you need..." Horatio protested.

"I'm freezing now," Penny insisted, starting to rise on her own.

Horatio was not about to let her exert herself. He squatted and scooped her up into his arms and carried her toward the truck. Penny managed not to squeal, and the thought that she should insist he put her down crossed her mind in a flash, but she made the conscious decision to just stay in his arms. She even lifted her arms to put around his neck to help support herself.

With her still in his arms, Horatio got the rear passenger door open. He put Penny inside. Her eyes scanned his face, but then dropped to his chest. "Oh, no! You are covered in blood! Are you alright?"

Horatio saw the concern in her eyes. "No, Penny. This is from your clothes. You are soaked in it. No wonder you are cold."

Penny looked down at her dress. "Oh. Yeah. Maybe I better shower and change."

"Good idea. I will wait out here. I am sure the State Troopers are going to want your statement. I will keep them occupied until you are ready. Take all the time you need."

"But you need a..." Penny started to protest.

"I'm fine. You get your shower." His voice was firm.

Penny could tell it was rough from concern for her. "Okay," she said softly. Thanks."

Horatio nodded and closed the truck door and took a few steps away. Penny watched for a moment, seeing his head drop and his shoulder droop. "Wow," she muttered. "He really cares..."

With that thought in mind, Penny dragged herself into the sleeper compartment and stripped out of her clothing, careful not to get the blood all over anything.

She sighed in pleasure when the hot water began to beat down on her cold, tired body. Penny allowed herself to warm up but cut the shower shorter than she would have liked. She wanted to find out what was going on. How the victims in the SUV were faring.

Quickly pulling on underwear, jeans, and a polo shirt, Penny grabbed a jacket and climbed down out of the truck. She saw Horatio talking to one of the troopers and walked over. "You need to get a shower and change, too," she immediately told Horatio.

"I will when things are wrapped up," Horatio said. "Penny, this is Trooper McGee. She needs to ask you some questions."

"Alone," said Trooper McGee. "You have already given me your statement."

"I'm her attorney. I'm staying," Horatio insisted, without looking at Penny. "I do not want any implications made about liability."

"I'm sure..." Penny began to say.

Horatio gave her the look that told her his stubborn side was going to be showing, no matter what. Again, she looked into his eyes and saw concern there. "Okay," she said, turning to the trooper.

The trooper nodded in acceptance, and began to interview Penny, writing quickly as Penny spoke. Penny paused often so the trooper could keep up, since Penny was giving many details, including some medical terms.

It did not take as long as Penny expected. Trooper McGee seemed to be satisfied with everything. As the trooper headed over to the other one, who was now directing traffic around the scene, Penny saw the paramedics loading up the victims in three different ambulances.

"I need to find out how they are," Penny said. "You go get your shower and change," she added, without looking at Horatio. Her attention on the paramedics, she did not notice that Horatio simply followed behind her to the ambulances.

"How are they?" Penny asked immediately.

"You the one that worked on them?" asked the paramedic.

Penny nodded.

"You saved two lives, Miss. All three will eventually be fine. The girl... Lord, why won't people wear their seatbelts? She has a concussion for sure, at the least. But her heart is going strong now. The other two... The woman would have bled out if you had not put on the compression bandage. The driver is banged up, but not too bad. He will be fine."

Penny sighed in relief. "Good. Good. Oh. How is the dog?"

"What dog?" asked the paramedic.

"The Trooper took her," Horatio said, startling Penny.

She spun around. "You're supposed to be showering!"

"Soon. But not until you finish up and can rest while I do."

"But..." Horatio's stubborn look again shut her up. "Okay."

Penny took a card case from one hip pocket and handed it to the paramedic. "Call me if there are any questions about the treatments. And please let me know how everyone turns out."

The paramedic took the card and nodded. "I will. Okay. They are ready. We are heading in." He went over to one of the fire trucks and climbed in.

One after the other, the fire trucks, the recovery truck with the still upside-down SUV on it, and the two State Patrol vehicles pulled away. Penny and Horatio went back to the truck, taking the depleted fire extinguishers and medical pack with them.

After they were stowed, Penny turned to Horatio. "I'm not taking no for an answer this time, Horatio. In the shower you go, if I have to put you in there myself." Penny gave him a hard look.

She had to hide her smile when he looked at her incredulously. "You do not honestly think you could do that, do you?"

"Oh, I could," Penny said. "But it would not be pleasant for you."

Horatio turned away quickly when the thought of Penny and him in the shower together flashed through his mind. But Penny saw the red creeping up the back of his neck as he moved toward the sleeper and wondered if the same thing had occurred to him as it suddenly had to her.

Putting it out of her mind, Penny headed for the driver's seat of the truck while Horatio went through the rear door and into the sleeper. "I'm going to log this in my truck journal so I do not forget anything," Penny said over her shoulder, pulling a leather-bound book from a pocket beside the driver's seat. "Take all the time you need."

Horatio pretty much just grunted an acknowledgment, without saying anything, and Penny smiled as she opened up the log book and began to write. After she was done, and Horatio still in the sleeper, Penny left the truck. She was back inside, in the front passenger seat when Horatio joined her.

Horatio took the driver's seat. When Penny glanced over his hair was still damp, but he had on clean clothing.

"I heard some noises from the back of the truck. Is everything okay?" Horatio asked as he put the truck in gear and eased back onto the highway, during a long gap in traffic.

"Fine," Penny replied. I pulled items from storage to replenish the AMP-3 Outfitter medical kit and went ahead and swapped fresh extinguishers for the spent ones." At Horatio's look, Penny shrugged. "I just like being ready."

"Yeah. I have learned that," Horatio said. But he was smiling.

Penny had entered the destination in the truck's navigation system. So, when Penny fell asleep a few minutes later, he just followed the computer's instructions, staying silent, thinking.

Horatio had to be careful to keep his eyes on the road. They were constantly drawn to the sleeping Penny. She was so different than the women to which he was usually attracted. But there was something about her that was working its way into his psyche and soul.

And then his mind went to some of the things she had said. Horatio began to think about the world situation in light of the insights Penny had imparted. Things just were not the way he had always believed and accepted.

It was worrisome. He had pretty much thought he had a nearly ideal life, with a bright future.

But now... Horatio shook his head. He should probably think things were looking terrible now, with what Penny had clued him in on, but he actually thought things looked brighter over all. And then paused again. "With Penny in it, anyway," came the thought.

Then Penny began to stir and Horatio sucked in a sharp breath. She stretched mightily and groaned, causing shivers in Horatio's spine. That cat like purr did something to his insides.

"Where are we?" Penny asked, looking over at the navigation display. "Oh. Getting close. I slept a long time." She looked over at Horatio. "Thank you for driving. I would have had to stop and rest. I don't want to be late getting there."

Horatio turned surprised eyes to Penny before looking back to the road. "I did not realize you were in a hurry."

"Not really a hurry. But I want to get a good parking place, and I promised to help a friend set up his booth. He's in a wheelchair and has some trouble managing it. And really hates to ask for help."

"But he asked you?" Horatio asked.

Penny grinned over at him. "No. I simply made it clear that I would be there to help. Period."

Horatio chuckled, understanding exactly what she meant. His attention was diverted when a pickup truck shot by them, but suddenly slowed, and eased back even with Penny's rig. The two guys in the truck gave the rig a long perusal before the driver hit the accelerator again and took off up the interstate once more.

"That was strange," Horatio said, glancing over at Penny. He noticed the frown on her face. "What?"

"That was Lucas and Travis Pontain. Couple of lowlifes, if you ask me. They do not like me and I do not like them. They are some of the ones that the media love because they are everything counter to the real prepper movement, yet operate around the edges of it, tainting everything they touch."

"Whoa!" Horatio replied. "I've never seen you... not angry... annoyed like this. You really do not like those guys."

Penny shook her head. "I'm sorry. But, no, I don't. I have a feeling you will get a chance to see why before the weekend is over."

Suddenly Penny brightened. "I see Oliver and Tess. That GMC motorhome up ahead. I am glad they were able to make it. One of their children has been ill and they were not sure they could come. Just follow them the rest of the way. I like being set up near them."

Horatio nodded. He began to see what he was beginning to recognize as prepper vehicles of one type or another. Lots of big pickup trucks, several motorhomes, SUVs equipped much like Penny's truck. But there were plenty of other types of vehicles taking the same exit Horatio took, still behind the GMC motorhome.

They were some ways from the nearest large city, but there was a nice sized community they went through before turning onto a well maintained two lane highway out in the middle of a forested area.

A couple of minutes later they turned and went through a fancy set of gates. Horatio brought the rig to a stop behind the GMC motorhome when it, like the traffic in front of it, halted.

There were several people in identical outfits going along the row of vehicles. Penny pulled something from her purse and handed it to Horatio. "Tickets?" Horatio asked, his left eye brow lifting again.

"Parking voucher. Should get a packet of information now, or after we set up camp."

It was now. Horatio saw that the man that stepped over to the Chevy had a large messenger bag over one shoulder. He pulled a large manila envelope from it and handed it to Horatio when Horatio handed him the parking voucher. "Nice rig," was all the man said before moving on to the vehicle behind them.

A few minutes later Horatio pulled into what was, thankfully, a pull through parking slot in what appeared to be a relatively large commercial campground.

Penny was out of the truck in a flash and hugging the couple that exited the GMC motorhome.

"Penny," Oliver asked, his eyes on Horatio, who is this?"

Tess nudged him. "Hush, Ollie! I am sure Penny will introduce us."

Horatio was not sure who was more embarrassed, Penny or himself. It was Penny that said, "I'm sorry. This is Horatio Billings. Horatio, this is Tess and Oliver Twill."

The two continued to stare at Horatio, and Penny turned even more red. Horatio was becoming amused as Penny literally squirmed slightly.

"Tess!" Penny said with a hint of desperation in her voice.

"Oh dear. Oliver, stop staring at the boy. I am sure there is a good reason he is with little Penny."

Penny sighed slightly at the 'little', but quickly spoke up. "Of course, there is. He is a friend."

"But you don't have…" Oliver was saying when Tess elbowed her husband rather forcefully.

Horatio almost said something at the flash of hurt in Penny's eyes at Oliver's almost statement. But Oliver was looking quite contrite, and Penny ignored it.

Oliver cleared his throat. "How long have you known our girl, Horatio? And where will you be staying?"

At the look that Penny and Horatio shared, Tess quickly said, "You are welcome to stay in the GMC with us if you don't think you can get a room..."

"Tess, Oliver," Penny said, rather firmly, Horatio thought, "Horatio is staying in the sleeper. With me. We are not a couple, but we are good enough friends for it not to be a problem."

Horatio saw Oliver start to protest, but Penny gave him a stern look and he did not say anything. Tess, however, gave Penny another hug, and took advantage of it to take Penny's arm afterward and guide her around behind the GMC motorhome.

"I think I better go check on... Uh... some things," Oliver said, and made himself scarce in the other direction.

Horatio shook his head, and then, after looking over the hookups, figured how to position the Chevy truck so the utilities could be connected easily.

He had just straightened back up from making the last connection when Penny came around the GMC. Horatio noticed that her face was red as a beet. He bit back a smile and then asked, "Third degree?"

Penny nodded, and then cut her eyes up to Horatio's. "Did Oliver..."

Horatio shook his head quickly, hoping to keep Penny from being any more embarrassed than she already was. "Got the rig hooked up."

Penny noted the pride in his voice and smiled, the embarrassment fading. "Good. Let's go register."

Penny was concentrating on getting to the motorhome with the convention logo on it they had seen finding their parking spot. Horatio, on the other hand, was looking all around as he followed Penny. There were so many vehicles equipped so differently than he had ever seen, until meeting Penny, that he could not help but stare at some of them.

But Horatio's attention was drawn back to Penny quickly as person after person stopped and greeted her by name. Handshakes, but mostly hugs, from men and women both, with more than a few children of just about every age thrown in, seemed eager to meet with her.

Finally, they made it to the convention motorhome and had a moment of peace and quiet. "You are quite the popular lady in prepping circles," Horatio said quietly, bringing the expected blush to Penny's cheeks.

"I am just one of many," she quickly and quietly protested. "Oh, phooey! There is Antonio. Stand in front of me." Penny quickly made herself as small as possible and styed right behind Horatio. So close he could feel the heat from her body.

Horatio suddenly stood tall and made himself look as large as possible. The glint in Antonio's eyes simply grated on Horatio's nerves. "Seen a shrimp of a redhead around here? She should be checking in any time."

Even Antonio's voice grated on Horatio's nerves. "Sorry Ace. Haven't seen any shrimps of any kind around here. If one were to show up, with any color hair, I will warn... er... tell her you are looking for her."

Antonio bristled, and Horatio bristled right back, glaring at Antonio, but standing firmly in place.

"Yeah. Ace. You do that. Maybe we'll see one another when there ain't so many people around," Antonio said with a sneer.

When Horatio pointedly looked around, Antonio flushed, as there was no one even close to the motorhome except them.

"Looking forward to it," Horatio said then, looking back at Antonio. He had to suppress a slight grin when he felt Penny poke him in the back sharply.

Horatio started to whistle softly as he stood and watched Antonio angrily walk away. A few seconds later he felt Penny shift slightly, to poke her head around his side.

"It's okay," Horatio said. "He's gone."

"What was that all about?" Penny asked, moving in front of him, her arms akimbo, fists on her hips. "'Looking forward to it.'"

"Nothing," Horatio said, shrugging. But then added quietly, "Just whatever he might want to make of it."

Penny frowned but spun around when someone standing in the door of the motorhome called her name.

"Mattie!" said Penny and rushed forward to follow the woman into the motorhome. She paused and motioned for Horatio to follow her inside, which he did.

Suddenly the office, which the motorhome was converted into, was crowded. With "We'll catch up later, Mattie," Penny took the document package from the woman and headed for the exit.

The line was out the door, and another ten to twelve people were in line. Horatio looked at the campsite as they walked back toward the truck and noted that quite a few more rigs had pulled into some of the open slots. The park was nearly full now.

"Penny, what was that with that Antonio guy?" Horatio asked.

Penny appeared as if she would answer him, but she was called to again. Horatio decided that rather than forcing Penny to 'explain' him time after time, with his presence beside her, he would go back to the truck and get inside. He was needing to go to the bathroom, anyway.

Horatio did not catch the wistful smile on Penny's face when she saw him edge past the group of people now surrounding her. Fortunately, neither did any of the group.

He decided to fix them a bite to eat, since it was getting late afternoon, and they had not stopped for any lunch after the accident. Horatio had just finished the preparations and was debating on whether or not to call to Penny to come in to eat when she opened the door of the truck and then came into the sleeper.

"Sorry. I just now got away."

"You hungry?" Horatio asked.

Penny gave him a grateful smile. "Starving! Thank you." She took the plate with bowl of soup and sandwich and moved to the rear passenger seat of the truck to eat so she could see out and keep an eye on things.

She was obviously in a bit of a hurry, so Horatio quickly ate, too, so he was ready to go when Penny said, "I need to get to the center. Let's just leave the dishes until later."

"Okay," Horatio said. He grabbed a jacket when Penny did and followed her out of the truck.

There were more calls of greetings as they headed for the large building adjacent to the campground, but Penny just answered back and waved, keeping up the pace.

She stopped by the doors of the facility and gave her name. She was handed another packet and stepped aside. She opened it up and handed Horatio a Special Guest pass. One eyebrow lifted when he fastened it to his jacket lapel.

Penny colored slightly but did not say anything as she pinned on a like pass. "Come on. I need to find Bradley."

Horatio's head was again on a swivel as they moved through the large exhibit area. Penny more than once nudged him out of the way as vehicles pulled down the wide aisles to unload. He managed to follow her as she worked her way toward the right front quadrant of the area.

They turned around one row of the booths and Horatio saw the booth Penny was obviously heading toward. A large man, looking like he could be a lumberjack if he was not in the wheelchair. "Bradley!" Penny called.

The man spun the wheelchair around. A huge grin appeared and he opened his arms wide. Penny gave him a hard hug and then stood back. "Okay, Bradley. Where do we start?"

Horatio hid his smile when Bradley started to protest, drawing a frown from Penny as her fists went to her hips. "You really want to argue with me about this, Bradley?"

"Uh... No?" Bradley replied, obviously not willing to force the issue.

"That is what I thought," Penny said. She motioned to Horatio. "This is Horatio. He is going to help, too."

Horatio could tell Bradley wanted to protest but held his peace. He simply began to issue instructions, which Horatio jumped to follow, to prevent Penny from attempting to handle some of the heavier items, which drew an appreciative nod from Bradley.

It did not take long for them to get the booth ready, as Bradly did a great deal of the work himself, despite the wheelchair.

Only after the booth was complete and Horatio got a good look at it, rather than piecemeal, did he do a double take. He looked over at Bradley. "You made all of these?"

"Amazing, huh?" Bradley asked, but he was smiling.

Horatio flushed slightly. "Yeah. Sorry. I just never met anyone that made knives... and swords... themselves..."

"Much less in a wheel chair?" Bradley was grinning.

"That, too," Horatio said, managing to smile back. He cut a look toward Penny to see if she had heard the exchange. She and Bradley were obviously good friends and he did not want Penny thinking he did not appreciate Bradley's skills.

Unfortunately, Penny was looking right at him, her hands on her hips again.

"Give him a break Copper Top," Bradley said. "It is a shock for most people."

Penny frowned for a moment, but then shrugged. "True." She looked pointedly at Horatio when she added, "Many people have some type of limitation, yet do quite well at things one might not think would be possible. Don't you think, Horatio?"

"Of course, Penny. Of course. I have my own set of limitations." He added, under his breath, "Mostly mental."

The corners of Penny's mouth flickered slightly, but she did not smile, or give any other indication that she had heard his words. And Bradley was at one of the display cases, making a few minor adjustments to the placement of the sharps items.

Horatio's eyes were drawn to one of the knives that Bradley handled. He walked over and took a long look at it in the case when Bradley rearranged the literature on the table.

When Bradley looked over, Horatio was still studying the large knife. His eyes cut to Penny. He recognized her stance. She was pretending to be busy but was watching Horatio out of the corners of her eyes.

Bradley rolled back over to the case and asked Horatio, "Want to handle it?"

"Uh... Better not," Horatio said, obviously reluctantly.

"Just finished it for the convention," Bradley said conversationally. "It is a Mediterranean style Bowie knife. Damascus steel, brass accoutrements, and black walnut scales. Thirteen-inch blade, clip point, full tang. One of the pre-production knives of a group of knives I made for a series I am planning. Be several knives per set in the series.

"Mediterranean Bowie; eleven inch Batangas style butterfly knife with six inches of the blade exposed when folded; six-inch conventional butterfly knife; six-inch hunter sheath knife; five-inch skinner; four-inch caper; three-inch hook slitter; butchering axe; bone/meat saw; butchering scissors; and butcher knife set in a leather case; folding fillet knife; fishing Swiss Army Knife and fishing multi-tool in a belt pouch; small game and upland bird Swiss Army Knife and matching multi-tool in a belt case; three blade pocket knife; utility Swiss Army Knife and matching multi-tool in a belt case with additional pockets; and survival Swiss Army Knife and matching multi-tool in a belt case with additional pockets for fire starters and tinder, flashlight, wallet survival cards, and other survival gear.

"The prototypes are mostly high carbon and tool steel. Made several versions until I got exactly what I wanted. I have all the pre-production knives made, in Damascus, brass, and black walnut, with premium leather sheathes and pouches.

"The production models, which I will farm out to a shop I trust, will be stainless, high carbon, and tool steels, depending on function, and various options for fittings and pouches/sheaths. "Ten thousand for the production set in basic trim. Fifteen with premium options. Some items available separately for various prices."

Horatio lifted his eyes up to meet Bradley's. "You anticipate many sales?"

Bradley grinned. "Sounds pretty high, huh?"

Horatio tilted his head slightly but did not speak. He felt Penny move over to stand beside him. "He will sell them," Penny said. "His production knives sell even better than his fantasy and specialty work, and they sell as fast as he makes them. For his price. But he is reasonable."

Penny smiled at Bradley. "For what he does." Though Bradley saw it, Horatio did not, when Penny quickly cut her eyes to Horatio, and then away, just before she asked Bradley, casually, "Any offers on the Damascus pre-production set?"

"Yep. From a couple of my regular customers. Probably sell to one of my regulars, when I get the offer I want." Bradley smiled slightly at Penny's small frown.

"How could you part with them?" Horatio asked. "If the others are anything like as spectacular as this one, and I am sure they are, I would never give them up. They could be family heirlooms for generations."

"Very true," Bradley replied. "But I have some things for my kids that I will pass down. These are just tools to me. Fancy ones, but tools never the less. What I have to pass down is… well… they have special meaning."

Horatio and Penny were both nodding. Penny glanced at her watch. "Well, I want to see a couple of other people, see if they need any help. We'll see you tomorrow, Bradley. Good luck with sales."

Bradley nodded. "Thanks. And thanks for the help. Nice to meet you, Horatio." He held out his hand and Horatio shook it, realizing quickly that if Bradley wanted, he could probably break Horatio's hand, just in a handshake. When Penny turned to leave, Bradley's eyes cut to Penny and then back. With a look into Horatio's eyes that held much meaning, Bradley squeezed ever so slightly more and then released Horatio's hand.

Horatio nodded slightly, the message in Bradley's eyes and handshake clear. Treat Penny right or suffer the consequences.

A couple of strides and Horatio caught up with Penny. He continued to glance around as he accompanied Penny to several booths in various stages of set up. But the couple of offers to help that Penny made were politely declined, and Penny finally headed for the exit, dragging slightly, Horatio noted.

"Tired?" Horatio asked.

"Yeah. More than I realized, suddenly. I'm for a bite of supper and then sleep. I want to get an early start tomorrow. Lots to see and do here."

Horatio nodded. He could only agree. And he did not know the half of it yet.

Chapter Five

-

True to her word, Penny was up at five the next morning. Horatio gave her privacy to get ready for the day, moving to the cab of the truck to check his e-mail and do a little work on his computer, through the internet connection that was part of the truck's communication system.

When Penny came out of the sleeper to do the same, Horatio swapped places and got ready. Penny was engrossed in her laptop when Horatio was dressed, so he went ahead and made them breakfast.

"Oh. Thanks, Horatio. I was going to get something ready…"

"You looked entranced," Horatio replied, sitting down beside her to eat.

"Unfortunately, so. There are so many things going on right now… I am not sure what is going to happen, but it will not be long. I am trying to get ahold of someone I keep hearing about on-line but have not been able to make connections. He seems to have some insights into what is likely to happen the next few months to a year."

"Who is it?" Horatio asked, after taking a bite of the instant oatmeal he had prepared for them.

"Guy called TOM. For Tired Old Man. He writes post-apocalyptic fiction. Uses a great deal of technical detail and information in his stories. He has slowed down recently, due to his health. I hope he is still okay."

Horatio nodded and continued to eat. Penny, still working the computer with one hand as she ate with the other was silent. Horatio was able to watch her, without her noticing. "Lord, she is beautiful," he thought to himself, after she had glanced at him for a moment and smiled, before turning back to the computer.

Soon enough they were finished with breakfast, and Penny insisted on doing the dishes from the evening before and from breakfast. They were finished up by eight and headed over to the convention hall. With the passes they had, they were able to go in, ahead of the public, for whom the doors would open at nine.

Horatio could see a few people putting last minute touches on their booths, but most were as ready as they could be, and were visiting among themselves. There would be little time during the convention public hours to do any checking with other vendors, or even see any of the presentations and classes that were scheduled. Horatio did not expect that to be a problem for Penny or himself. Boy, was he wrong.

No sooner than the announcement that the doors were being opened to the public did Penny excuse herself. "Need to do something, Horatio. Just wander around and check out the booths. If you have any questions I can help you out in a little while."

Two minutes later, while Horatio was checking out the booth they were near when Penny excused herself, Horatio looked up, startled, as Penny's name was announced.

Horatio quickly went looking for the stage where Penny was apparently going to give a presentation. Penny was carrying a step stool out to the podium. She set it down, stepped up onto it and adjusted the microphone on the podium.

Grabbing the last available seat, with more people gathering to stand and listen, Horatio watched Penny on stage. She was poised and received a great deal of applause before she could speak one word.

"Hello everyone. Thank you very much! My name is Penny Arcade..." She waited for the polite laughter to die down before continuing. "Welcome to the convention! It's great, isn't it?"

Thunderous applause sounded. Penny, smiling, waited for it to die down again before she continued. For the next twenty-five minutes Penny talked about the need for preparing, and about how to get started. When the twenty-five-minute presentation was complete, Penny opened the floor to questions.

"How short are you?" came the first shouted question. More than one person frowned and made disapproving noises, as they looked over at the man.

Penny maintained her poise and simply ignored the man, motioning to someone that had their hand up. "Yes? You have a question?"

Horatio was totally amazed as Penny answered question after question, on a whole gamut of subjects. She never faulted or hesitated, and only once said she did not know, but would find out. She gave an e-mail address as her hour was up, promising to answer other questions people might think of after she left the stage.

Horatio joined the standing ovation as Penny stepped down off the step stool, picked it up and went off the stage. He hurried around to the back of the stage when Penny did not immediately come from behind it.

He found Penny taking deep breaths, still holding the step stool in her hand. "You okay?" Horatio asked, taking the step stool from her.

Penny sighed, look up at him and nodded. "I am. I just hate being up there in front of everyone."

"You sure did great," Horatio said as Penny began to walk along the back wall of the building. "I had no idea…"

Penny smiled up at him. "Thank you. I do okay, I guess. I am always afraid I will give someone bad information…"

"I do not think anyone there thought any of it was bad advice," Horatio said firmly.

"Except the 'short' guy." Penny huffed.

"Yeah. Idiot," muttered Horatio.

"It was Lucas Pontain. He is always trying to get my goat. If it is not my height, it is being female, and if not that, it is something else."

Penny shook her head. "Never mind. There are Tess and Oliver. I need to say hello. Oh. Would you take the step stool back? That is the convention's."

"Sure," Horatio said. He was not particularly looking for more questions about him and Penny from Tess or Oliver.

When he returned to where he had left Penny with the other two they were gone. "Probably for the best," Horatio muttered, seeing Antonio approaching.

"Where is that witch? I saw her head this way after her so-called presentation. I wasn't able to get there in time to catch her."

"Who would you be referring to? I have not seen any witches. A bastard or two. Now and again."

Antonio did not like it, and it showed. But after a quick look around, with the growing crowd, he did nothing but mutter a curse and move away, looking for Penny.

"Nuts," mutter Horatio. "I had better find her first…"

Paying little attention to any of the booths, Horatio took advantage of his long legs to cover a great deal of ground, going up one aisle and then down the next.

His blood pressure spiked when he found Penny. It was not Antonio that did it. It was Lucas and Travis Pointain. Penny was obviously trying to calm down the situation. Tess and Oliver were gathered close to Penny, in protective stances, as the two men glared at the three. Oliver's voice was beginning to rise as he told the two where they could go.

Penny tried to shush Oliver. "Oliver, let it go. You'll have security over here any minute and I do not want that."

"Well, they better just keep their mouths shut about you around me." Oliver growled.

"Goes for me, too," Horatio said, striding right up to stand between Penny and the men. He had not really meant to do that, but, like Oliver and Tess, he was in protective mode, especially after his run in with Antonio.

Obviously cowards, and with two of the convention security people approaching, Lucas grabbed Travis' arm and pulled him away, saying, "This isn't over, Red. You owe us for that truck."

Someone called over to Tess, who then looked at Penny and said, "Penny, we have to see what she wants. Will you be okay?" Tess looked at Horatio.

"I will see to it," Horatio said, preparing himself for the quick poke in the side he knew he would probably get from Penny. He was not wrong.

"I can take care of myself," Penny protested quietly.

"I know," Horatio said, beginning to walk, Penny at his side as the two security people listened to their earpieces and moved off in another direction. "But I still aim to be there if needed," he added stubbornly.

Penny was not averse to the idea, though she was not about to admit it. "Besides," Horatio said, "Antonio is on the prowl for you, too. I ran into him near the stage."

Horatio felt Penny grab his arm. "He didn't... Um... You okay?"

"I am fine. What is it with him? And the Pontains? I cannot feature you ever doing anything that would have anyone upset with you."

"You forgetting Kimmy?" Penny asked.

"Uh... Well... No. But still..."

Penny decided explaining was easier. "Lucas and Travis, as I said, are what gives survival, survivalists, and now preppers and prepping a bad name in the media. They were trying to start an illegal militia up near where I live. Now, I am all for state and even independent militias. They are important to the safety and security of a free state, but these two were looking to set up a private army to run roughshod over people if something ever happens.

"Well, they had this fancy military truck all tricked out with equipment. And illegal automatic weapons. Again, I do not think they should be illegal for private individuals to own in any jurisdiction, but they are not at the moment there, and those guys would not have been using them for anything peaceful. So, I talked to the Sheriff and let him know about them.

"The Pontains managed to get rid of the automatic weapons before the Sheriff found the truck, but the idiots were using it to transport stolen goods and the truck was confiscated. Their lawyer managed to get them off for the possession charges, since they were able to claim they did not know the things they were hauling were stolen. That they were duped."

"Dopes, sounds more like it," Horatio muttered.

Penny chuckled. "Yes. Definitely. But they do not like me and give me grief whenever they can."

Horatio nodded. "And Antonio?"

Penny sighed. "He believes I cheated him out of a big contract to produce some parts for the military."

Horatio stopped to stare at Penny. "You... uh... What?"

"I came up with a couple of things the military was interested in. Antonio found out and decided to try and beat me to getting a patent and going into production. I was able to get it done before he did and won the contract. I would have won in the end, anyway, because I have the proof of when and how I came up with the thing. Antonio would never have been able to hold the patent or the contract."

Penny tugged Horatio's arm. "Come on. We're blocking people. It's not a big deal."

"Yeah. Right," Horatio said. "I'd like to hear more." When Penny frowned at him, he added, "Later."

Horatio did not at all mind Penny continuing to hold his arm, hers now intertwined with his, letting him lead them through the heavy crowd. But Penny controlled where they went. She stopped at probably two thirds of the booths, to exchange a word, or look over one of the products. She asked a few questions but was questioned many more times than what she asked.

Horatio found he was getting quite the education in prepping, mostly from Penny, as the conversations went on, one after the other. Distracted for a moment at one of the booths, Horatio turned to find the vendor at the next booth over gushing over Penny.

"I tell you Miss Arcade; your design is the best thing going. I am selling them like hotcakes. Everyone that has bought one has been pleased. Not a single complaint or return."

Penny glanced at Horatio and blushed slightly when she saw his admiration. "So, you don't just talk a good prepping game. You make prepping stuff, too?"

"Not a big deal," Penny whispered, after thanking the man and tugging Horatio away from the booth. Her voice low she explained. "I mostly just make improvements on some existing items. Or buy the rights to some good ideas that are not being made well and produce quality versions. Just small stuff. Nothing major."

"I see," Horatio replied. Unwilling to press her for more information at the moment, he accepted what she said and let it go at that. But he was continually amazed as he continued to notice a product here and there that had what he discovered was her business logo on it.

Different booths had different items, depending on what their product line was. There was one booth, however, that carried Penny's logo. And Penny stopped there. "Horatio, would you mind? I need to talk to Alicia and Billy for a bit. It could take a few minutes, as busy as they are..." Penny looked at him hopefully.

"Sure," Horatio said, though he really wanted to stay and hear the conversations. "I will go get us something to drink and a snack."

Penny cast him a thankful look and turned back to the young man and woman manning the booth with the help of one other person, a bit older than the two.

Horatio took his time, perusing booth after booth as he worked his way toward the concession stand. His mind was reeling with the overwhelming amount of information he found available at the booths. Horatio was deep in thought when he returned to the booth where Penny was now helping a customer, since all three of the others were also occupied with people asking questions.

He stood and watched the animated conversation Penny was engaged in. "You continue to amaze me, Penny," Horatio murmured to himself.

Horatio started slightly when a voice whispered in his ear, "An amazing woman, young and slight as she is." Turning to see who was speaking, Horatio was surprised to see a rather nondescript looking man, about Horatio's height, slender, but with a wiry look about him.

"Yes. Yes, she is," Horatio said. "And you are?"

"An old acquaintance. No one important. Just tell her that property she inquired about a year ago is now available."

"Who should I say..." Horatio was saying, but the man gave a little wave and moved away, mingling with the crowd immediately.

"That was strange."

"What was strange?" asked Penny, having moved over to join Horatio when she saw him standing there, staring at the crowd.

Horatio turned to Penny and handed her the soft drink and bag of nuts he had picked up for her. "A guy... said he was an old acquaintance. Asked me to tell you the property that you were interested in a year ago is available now. I tried to get his name, but..."

Penny looked excited, her eyes flashing, and she was bouncing on her toes. "Joe! About your height, but real... leathery?"

Horatio nodded. "That could be him."

"Dang. I wish I'd seen him."

"I could go after..."

"You'd never find him. He hates crowds. I am sure he just checked a few things here, saw me, and then took off. He never hangs around more than just long enough to buy a few things, check a few things, and then he is long gone."

"Who is he?"

"He was one of my instructors, way back when. He was one of the people that taught me survival techniques when I insisted on learning things like that when I was at the institute. Even back then he was a bit distant, though he always gave me all the time I needed to learn what I wanted. And I think he threw in a few things that the institute would not have appreciated him teaching me." Penny grinned.

Horatio laughed. "Why am I not surprised. He did seem quite fond of you, from the look he gave you."

"He's a dear. Just a loner. I am glad he came. Good for him to get out and about. Now. Let's find a place to sit down and rest a bit. And I need to make a couple of calls, in light of what Joe told you to tell me."

Penny did not offer up any more, but Horatio stayed silent as they made their way back to the concession area and found a table and a couple of chairs.

Absently, Penny ate and drank, working on her phone the entire time. Finally, Penny looked up. "Got it!" she exclaimed, a look of pure joy on her face. But suddenly the joy faded and she looked startled. Her "Oh," was soft and rather sad.

"Are you okay? Everything alright?" Horatio asked, his concern obvious.

"Well... Yes... and no..." Penny sighed and Horatio had to look away as her chest heaved slightly with the sigh.

"It means I got the property I really wanted over near the lakes. But that also means I do not have to keep looking in that area. And there is no reason to stay there now when we go back. At least until I can come back and start developing the property the way I want."

It puzzled Horatio for a moment, but then he realized what Penny was saying. She would be leaving after they got back to his place.

Penny looked up at Horatio and met his eyes. "I don't think it will be too hard to find someone to work the office." She cut her eyes down. "I guess I haven't been looking all that hard recently."

"Penny..." Horatio said, but before he could continue, Penny's name was announced, stating that her class on medicinal plants would be next in one of the meeting rooms.

"Oh, my! My class starts in just a few minutes. I better get going."

"But Penny," Horatio said, feeling an emptiness that was painful.

"I'm sorry, Horatio. I have to go." Penny got up, leaving behind what was left of her drink and bag of nuts, and hurried off.

Horatio thought about going to the class, but decided he needed to do some thinking before he talked to Penny again.

By the time the doors were about to close, Horatio decided that Penny had been avoiding him. He had continued to browse the convention, even taking in a couple of classes when he could not find Penny anywhere. But she finally joined him as he waited at the exit, just as they were about to lock up the doors.

"Horatio! I thought you would have gone back to the truck."

"Of course not. Not without knowing you were okay."

"Of course, I am fine." Penny started walking quickly toward the campground.

Horatio had no problem keeping up with her. He walked beside her silently until they were almost to the truck. "We are going to discuss this, aren't we?" Horatio finally asked as Penny unlocked the truck.

She dipped her head and sighed, before opening the rear cab door and climbed up into the truck, going into the sleeper compartment. "Give me a minute?" she asked without looking at Horatio.

"Of course."

Horatio sat down, lost in his own thoughts. He was not sure how long he sat there, but suddenly he turned his head and there was Penny, in the opening to the sleeper, watching him with inquisitive eyes.

"Horatio? What are you thinking?" she asked softly.

"About you. Me. Us. Is there an us?"

"I don't know, Horatio," Penny replied, taking the other rear Captain's chair. She glanced at him and then away, staring forward. "Horatio, I am not any good at things like this. I have no experience. I do not know what to expect. I don't know what to do. How to proceed. I... I like you, Horatio. A lot. But we've only known each other a few days... I don't know if you..."

"I like you, too, Penny. But you are a special person... I'm not sure..." Horatio could tell when Penny started to cry. "Penny..."

"Let's fix something to eat and get to bed. Tomorrow is another long day."

Horatio was at a loss for words. He had no clue what to do. He had hurt her, he was sure, with what he had said, but was not sure what to do about it. "Okay," he said softly. "You must be exhausted."

Penny nodded. She did not look at him as she got up and went into the sleeper. Horatio followed her. It was the first awkwardness between them since the first few days they had known one another.

The only time either one became animated was when the conversation turned to the mechanics of prepping while they were eating.

But that faded when they finished up and prepared for bed. Things were silent between them until the next morning when their respective phone alarms sounded. The awkwardness was gone, but so was the spark they had felt before.

It was only when they were headed over to the convention building again that Penny spoke about anything but the mundane. "You know, if we leave a bit early, we can go by that property and look it over, before we go ho… before we get back to your place."

"That is okay with me, if that is what you want, Penny."

Penny nodded but did not say anything else. Nor did she meet his eyes. She excused herself as soon as they entered the convention, stating the need to get ready for her first presentation of the day.

Horatio found himself left to his own devices until shortly after noon. Penny called him on his cell and asked him to meet her at the main doors.

"Give me a few minutes to make my good-byes and I will meet you at the truck," Penny said without any preamble.

"Sure," Horatio said, feigning cheerfulness. "I'll get the truck ready for the road."

"You don… Okay. Thanks, Horatio."

Horatio nodded and headed back to the campground as Penny turned back inside. Horatio was waiting in the front passenger seat, working on his laptop when Penny joined him a half an hour later.

"Ready?" Penny asked, reaching for the start button on the dash.

"As I am going to get," Horatio said. He put away the laptop and turned to watch Penny as she drove out of the campground.

"Are you okay?" he asked after they had been on the road for ten minutes, the silence between them palpable.

"Of course," Penny replied.

Horatio could tell she was trying to be cheerful but was not succeeding very well. "Can we talk about this, Penny?"

"What?" Penny asked, keeping her eyes on the road.

"This… whatever it is between us."

Penny did steal a glance at Horatio, but seeing his eyes on hers, she looked back at the road. "I… I… I guess. I'm not sure what there is to talk about, Horatio. We're friends, you know. Even no longer than we've known each other, I consider you a friend. A good friend."

Horatio heard the strain in her voice. "I agree," he said softly. "Definitely friends. Do you... Do you think there might be more? Sometime?"

Horatio could have kicked himself when he heard the slight gasp from Penny when he had added the 'sometime'.

"I don't know, Horatio. Perhaps we should just leave things be. I am going to be tied up with this new property for a while. And I know your client calendar is full after we get back."

"Is that what you really want?" Horatio asked, more than a bit disappointed.

"I think it best," Penny said. She waited until Horatio was distracted with something on his side of the road before she quickly wiped the tears from her eyes. She did not think Horatio noticed. He did not say anything. But he noticed.

It was still light but getting late when Penny hit the turn signal lever again and pulled off the county road they had been on for an hour. They were well away from the interstate and had passed a few small towns on the state road, one just before Penny had taken the country road.

The gravel road was rough and got much rougher as they made a couple of turns through the heavy forest that was on both sides of the road.

Penny stopped at the steel pipe gate set between large steel pipe uprights, from which some split rail fence disappeared into the heavy woods on each side of what was now a rutted dirt track the gate gave access to. She started to climb down, but Horatio quickly opened his door and said, "I'll get it."

Penny nodded. "Unless they changed it from before, the combination starts one left, two right, one left, one right, and is one, five, three, zero."

It took Horatio only moments to have the well-maintained lock unsnapped and the gate rolled back. "Go ahead and lock it back up," Penny said, leaning out of the truck window when Horatio started for the truck. "We'll just stay here tonight. I'm too tired to go on."

Horatio thought about offering to drive the rest of the way through the night, but quickly decided against it. He waved and closed and locked the gate back up.

Once back in the truck, with Penny driving slowly, avoiding what pot holes and ruts she could on the winding track, Horatio began to wonder why Penny would want a place with such terrible access.

And then she went around another turn and drove onto a wide, hard surface road. Horatio could not tell exactly what the surface was, as it certainly was not asphalt, and did not really look like concrete, either.

"Whoa! That was unexpected," Horatio said, looking around the area they were entering. It was much more open woodland, rather than the dense forest they had passed through earlier. Just a bit further on, after another curve, Penny stopped at another gate.

This gate was totally different from the previous one, and even more formidable a barrier. Once Horatio figured out that it was, in fact, a gate in a wall, and not just a wall at a dead-end road, he studied it for several moments.

Instead of open pipework, this gate was like two large concrete planter boxes. Each had heavy vegetation growing in them. There was a tall, heavy duty chain link fence with three strands of out-facing barbed wire atop installed all the way around the rim of the planter boxes.

They were placed just behind tall walls of the same construction, except for the fact that the plants were planted in the ground, and there was a solid block wall behind the plants, and only the one chain link fence facing the direction from which they were coming.

Horatio was reaching for his door handle again, to get out and see if he could figure out how to open the gate, when Penny drove to the far left side of the driveway and stopped beside a slanted steel post with some type of metal box on the end.

Horatio quickly cut his eyes away from Penny's rear, when she had to raise up some, so she could reach out and down through her window, to manipulate the buttons on the gate control box.

When the gates began to part in the middle, sliding to each side, she plopped back down into the seat. Realizing the show she had probably given Horatio, she suddenly cut her eyes over to him. His eyes were studiously on the gates.

When he did look over at her, she made no indication that she had realized what she had done, instead, simply driving through the opening. Horatio felt the slight bump as they crossed the small metal tracks that carried the heavy gates.

The view changed again, the gently rolling ground now sporting large areas with spaced out trees, that Horatio suspected were probably fruit and nut trees. Then he saw grape vines. And another area had round, stepped tower like structures with some type of plant growing on them.

As he looked closer, he noticed that though everything was nicely laid out, everything had a bit of abandoned, uncared-for look. Then Horatio noticed that the large area was surrounded on three sides with a very dense hedge, with close spaced trees growing in it.

And there were more of the hedges here and there, Horatio saw, with stout gates closing off the openings that were in the hedges.

Horatio looked around some more after Penny stopped the truck on the large paving stone pad that was at the end of the driveway. He was sure he saw the glint of water through another stand of fairly open trees. It was only when he and Penny got out of the truck, and Horatio looked back toward the entrance that he noticed the solar panels on a concrete block structure that apparently held the mechanics of the gates in the wall.

The pad was near the center of a large, level area with lush grass growing, with the pond or whatever it was, down a gentle slope. North of the pad the ground rose slightly toward more of the hedges that continued where the wall came to an end quite some distance from the gates.

Looking over to the east, Horatio saw another hedge, with a gate in it, and heavy forest beyond. To the west, it was much the same, but Horatio noticed that the forest beyond the hedge on the west was heavy in some areas, but similar to the orchard in areas, though mostly much taller trees, more closely spaced.

"This is amazing," Horatio said, keeping his voice low for some reason of which he was not sure.

It seemed that Penny felt the same way, for her voice was also rather soft. "I know. I wanted it the minute I saw it two years ago. I had given up on it since the owner was adamant that he would never sell. It was to be his and his family's refuge in times of trouble at some point. As you can see, he had made many improvements, but had not been able to start the building program he wanted to do before he was in an accident several months ago."

Horatio saw the sadness on Penny's face when she continued. "It is sad that his family has no interest in his prepping and what he was trying to accomplish for them." She shook her head. "They could not wait to sell after he died. As soon as the will was settled, they put it on the market. And though they are getting a decent price from me, it is nothing like what it is worth, considering what their grandfather put into this place. I might have offered more than the asking price, but they were so rude and disrespectful of their grandfather's wishes."

Biting back a smile at the annoyance in Penny's voice, Horatio nodded. "I understand. This really does look like a great place. I had my doubts as we were getting here."

"That is deliberate, by the way," Penny said. "The road was actually in better shape all the way here when Rudolph acquired the property back in

1920s. He has let it deteriorate, and actively damaged parts of it to make it more difficult to get here, to discourage people from coming this far in to the property. Which, by the way, extends the other three directions about the same distance as what we came in, and has even worse access.

"This is a very rare piece of property in this area. Almost six thousand acres in one block, in the heart of the forest. Nine sections. About three miles on a side, but not nearly square. More a slight trapezoid shape."

"We only came three miles... Wait. Halfway would be a mile and a half. We only came a mile and a half in from the road?" Horatio was incredulous. "I thought it was miles."

Penny grinned. "Nope. About a mile and a quarter, actually. The main living barrier fencing encloses a little over seven hundred acres, a bit over a square mile, again not quite square, more pentagonal in this case."

"Barrier fencing? You mean that block wall goes around... uh... four miles around the place this area?"

Penny was shaking her head. "No. The sections with concrete block back fence and chain link facing are only sections where there are gates like the one we came through. The rest of that perimeter fence around the seven hundred acres is just living barrier fence.

"Thorny blackberry brambles, thorny rosa Ragusa rose brambles, with closely spaced honey locust trees inside the brambles. There is quite a bit of light welded wire fence in parts of it that were used to provide a psychological barrier in the early days. Most of that has rusted away over the decades, as the living fence was planted, but you can still see parts of it here and there. The living fencing has simply covered it over and corroded it.

"Some of the barrier is well over eighty years old. But all of it is at least twenty and fully mature. Same with much of the orchard, especially the nut trees. Black walnuts and pecans were planted early on and are fully mature. The full-size fruit trees were added later, as were the grapes, with some semi-dwarf and dwarf fruit trees added much later for variety. The berries, other than the blackberries, are fairly new, but are well established."

"Those stepped tower like structures?" Horatio asked.

"Yes," Penny explained. "Rudolph liked berry towers. I agree with him. But I plan to add some additional things, too." Penny fell silent as she looked around the property, turning slowly as she did.

"I cannot believe I got this piece of property," she whispered when she was almost turned to face Horatio again. "It is a true dream property. All the long lead things are done. I would be old and decrepit before I could have another place like this, starting off fresh." Penny's eyes cut up to Horatio's.

He looked a little surprised. "You already have a place like this?"

She nodded. "Well, not exactly. But close. Two, actually. My parents homestead, right next to which I set up my own place, which had many of the features on it when I bought the land for us. And the first one I bought elsewhere for myself is well on its way, but it will be a few years before the black walnuts are in full production, other than the ones already grown when I bought the place. And there is still quite a bit of metal fencing visible in the living barrier fence lines."

"You make really long-range plans, don't you?" Horatio asked.

There was a sudden catch in Penny's voice when she stammered out a soft 'yes'. She turned away. "It is almost dark. Can't really see much more of the property now. We can take some closer looks at parts of it if you want in the morning. I'm ready to eat and hit the hay now."

Horatio decided to just go along. For the moment. "Okay. Sounds good. You want the sleeper first to get ready for the evening?"

"If you don't mind. Thank you," Penny said as she headed for the truck again.

Horatio stood leaning against the truck as the darkness deepened, feeling small movements of the vehicle as Penny got ready. It was full dark when the outside light that illuminated the area around the truck doors came on and Penny told Horatio the sleeper was his.

They were both up early the next morning. Penny seemed fairly cheerful as she prepared a hearty breakfast for them. With it eaten and things cleaned and put away, Penny led Horatio on a foot tour of the immediate area, to show him things that were not obvious in the general look of the night before.

Horatio discovered that many of the living barrier fences enclosed different types of fields and pastures. Penny pointed out which were which and explained how they would be rotated from production use to lying fallow to recover with green manure crops grown on them.

The explanation for three of the smaller fields brought one of the single eye brow lifts that so fascinated Penny. They were the composting fields, where all sorts of organics from on site and off would be brought and spread out to be allowed to decompose to make rich humus to be added to the various fields as they lay fallow.

After walking around that area, the two got into the truck and Penny began to drive over the rest of the property, along what Horatio finally realized were actual paths for the purpose, though they were grown up in lush grass, and in a few places, brush and small saplings that Penny drove right over without hesitation.

"I'll cut those out, of course," Penny said matter-of-factly. "Rudolph hasn't done much on the property, except the parking pad and the finished section of the road, in several years."

Penny stopped at what turned out to be a small, spring fed lake. The lake was in a natural depression, with the far end dammed off. Pointing out the large diameter standpipe that kept the lake from getting too high, she said, "You can see the concrete spillway, just in case the standpipe is blocked, or the inflow is too great for it to handle.

"The dam was constructed long before the restrictions on private water rights issues, fortunately. I would not be allowed to create the lake now, if didn't exist."

Horatio saw her smile. "Just one more of Rudolph's foresights, or maybe they were just fortunate circumstances. Anyway, along with the lake, the property sports five other developed springs, two with heavy flow, and three smaller ones. They are out in the middle of the various forested areas, but with decent access, ready for use if needed."

When Penny went around the lake, and they could see the spillway of the dam, she pointed out the small concrete block structure, from the base of which the water exited the standpipe. She was grinning when she said, "Even back then, Rudolph anticipated micro-hydro. There is no power unit in the generator house, but the main standpipe is gated, and the water can be diverted into two valved penstocks for water turbines.

"It would not be a great deal of power, but more than enough to run most of the things I would want to run off that source of power when I get it installed."

"Wow," Horatio said softly.

Penny drove on, went through another of the heavy gates in the living barrier fence into rough forest, down to the edge of the small river that was the recipient of the lake's overflow. "Big enough for plenty of fish, but too small for boats of any size to get up to the property from downstream. Even kayakers and canoeists do not bother with it, until well past where the property ends. That is the line for this side of the property."

Continuing the tour, Penny went through several tight sections of path, just big enough for the truck and trailer. "This track is just inside the perimeter of the property," she said. "If you look close you can see the living barrier fence through the forest. Rudolph kept this wildland strip all around the edge of the property."

From this side of the barrier fence, there was not much to see, except the forest. "Along here, inside the fence, there is a group of large fields set up for commercial crop production. The groupings are scattered over the acreage in spots best suited for them. The largest ones are one hundred sixty acres, with many eighty-acre fields, and quite a few more of forty acres. Approximately, of course, depending on the lay of the land in each case.

"The rest of the property that will be used for annual planting consists of various smaller fields. And all the rest is either rough forest, orchards like we saw near the main building site, some different natural habitat areas inside the fences, coppicing firewood lots, pastures, some additional building sites, with, of course, the connecting equipment paths."

There was another gate right where Penny made a sweeping turn near another edge of the property. They went back inside the fence line and Penny finished up the tour. "I guess we'd better head on out," she said when they came back into the main estate site.

"This is a wonderful place, Penny," Horatio said.

Penny nodded, lost in thought for a moment. "I am fortunate to be able to own it," she said after a moment. "It is as about as ideal as one could want, for what I want it for."

Horatio nodded, and Penny put the truck back in gear, and headed for the main entrance. "What is this driveway?" Horatio suddenly asked, just as they were about to leave the hard surface section and return to the rutted dirt track.

Penny looked over at Horatio and grinned. "It is a Roman road," she said. An eyebrow lifted on Horatio's face and Penny giggled slightly. "I'm not kidding. Not from Roman glory days, of course, but Rudolph had something of a love affair with ancient Rome and planned to use several of their design and building principles to create this place.

"About the only one he got around to was the driveway and the pad. They use traditional Roman construction methods, except the road has a final topcoat of crushed concrete with fines over the stone blocks that would be exposed on a true Roman road.

"I do plan to keep this section just the way it is, but I have my own ideas, using some more modern methods that produce an equivalent permanent road surface. But I will still have a very rough section, at the first gates, for the same reasons Rudolph did."

"I understand." Penny seemed more like her old self, so Horatio kept things light as they travelled back home. He even got her to laugh a few times. Even when they arrived back at the house, things seemed to fall back into their easy routine of before the Prepper Convention.

Things were busy at the office from Monday, through Thursday, but they were caught up by Friday afternoon. That is when Horatio found out just how busy Penny had been the first four days of the week. Especially when he was away from the office several times.

When Horatio looked up after Penny knocked on his open office door, he was surprised to see three files in her hand. He already had the files he needed for the case he was working on. "Yes, Penny? I have the files…"

Penny cut him off. "Yes sir. I take it you did not check your calendar this morning. I had to make a couple of changes…"

She was not meeting Horatio's eyes and he began to have a bad feeling. "What changes?" he asked, watching her carefully.

"The candidates for paralegal I found for you are here for interviews." Penny had slowly entered the office and placed the files on Horatio's desk, still not meeting his eyes. "I will send in the first one."

Before Horatio could think of anything to say, she had spun on her heel and hurried out. A woman he did not know came into the office and the door closed behind her.

She was smiling and held out her hand. Horatio automatically took it. "I'm Melissa Anderson."

"Ms. Anderson…" Horatio picked up the three files, found the one labeled *Anderson, Melissa* and opened it. Rather numb, Horatio went through the motions of conducting a professional interview.

And then did the same thing twice more. With two more excellent candidates for the position of paralegal. Any of the three would be fine, he knew. But he did not want any of the three. Trying to decide what to do, Horatio waited for perhaps a minute and a half before he went out to the reception area of the offices.

He saw the note on Penny's desk. He walked over and picked it up. *'Horatio, I locked up after your last interviewee left. I have enjoyed my time here. But I must go. I would suggest Ms. Anderson as your new paralegal, but any of the three can start Monday, as noted in their files.*

'Good-bye Horatio.'

A sinking feeling in his stomach, Horatio hurried out to his car and broke a couple of traffic laws getting home. But just as he suspected, not only was Penny's truck and trailer gone, but so was everything of hers from inside the garage and the house.

Horatio flopped back onto the sofa. She was gone. Penny was gone. Horatio sat up suddenly, the thought coming to him that he would just go after her. But he flopped back again, realizing he had never found out where she had come from, much less where she might be going.

Not only did he not know where her parents lived, but he had no clue where the other properties she owned might be. He did rouse himself long enough to check his phone records for Penny's parent's phone number, but nothing showed up that he did not recognize. Penny had not used his land line for anything except local calls. She had used her cell when she talked to her parents.

Horatio sighed once again. For the next week, Horatio moped. But Penny had been right. Melissa Anderson was a good paralegal and kept things on an even keel. Horatio knew that was, in part, because of the way Penny had reorganized the office and the excellent notes on how Horatio wanted things to operate she had left behind for whomever he hired.

Deciding he was being foolish, Horatio hired a detective the next week to look for Penny. His own caseload was too heavy for him to do the detective work on his own, though he had realized that Penny probably was not trying to actively hide from him, he just did not know her address. And he was not comfortable asking Olivia Ferguson to do the job.

Still, not knowing just how long it would take for the detective to find her, Horatio decided that she had invested time in him, and he could not bear to waste it, so he began a crash program of prepping. And when a realtor called, asking for Penny, he took down the information on the piece of property that the realtor had found for Penny.

That weekend he went to check the place out. Looking around, trying to think the way he thought Penny would, Horatio suddenly got excited. While he realized it was way too small for what Penny had been wanting, other than that, it had most of the other requirements she had been seeking.

Horatio spent most of Saturday, and all of Sunday going over the heavily wooded property, part of which surrounded a small finger bay of the lake. The bay had a very narrow opening, and the heavy forest grew right up to the water on one side of it, with more dense forest on the point of land that narrowed the entrance of the bay.

Like the access to the property Penny had purchased, the access to this tract of land was rough. He had rented a Jeep to go look it over after the realtor had taken him to the dirt road that intersected the county road just before it dead ended at one of the lake's boat access ramps.

The only other access that he found after roaming over the property Sunday was a very deteriorated track that angled off a fire road where the land abutted the State Forest.

With the potential it had as prepper property, Horatio spent another week negotiating, through the realtor, to get the price down to what he could afford to pay off in less than a year. He was a bit smug that he was able to use all the prepper positive aspects of the property, to bring the price down. The lack of good land access and water access, the heavy forest, the remoteness, the lack of commercial utilities, the steep hill and bluff that faced almost due south, leaving only some of the property suitable for conventional house building.

Two days after he closed on the property, the detective called and gave him five addresses where Penny might be, including three PO Boxes and two street addresses. But there was a total of nine telephone numbers associated with her.

It was late when the detective dropped the information off at his home, but he could not stop thinking about her, barely getting any sleep that Friday night, and waking up groggy Saturday morning. Forcing himself to shower, dress, and get some breakfast in his belly before he made the first call, Horatio thought continuously about what he would say to her.

When he reached for his cell phone to call the first of the nine numbers two conversations with Penny suddenly leaped into his mind, clear as the time they were spoken.

"Horatio, I am not any good at things like this. I have no experience. I do not know what to expect. I don't know what to do. How to proceed. I... I like you, Horatio. A lot. But we've only known each other a few days... I don't know if you..."

"I like you, too, Penny. But you are a special person... I'm not sure..." And Penny had started to cry.

And then, later:

"Can we talk about this, Penny?"

"What?"

"This... whatever it is between us."

"I... I... I guess. I'm not sure what there is to talk about, Horatio. We're friends, you know. Even no longer than we've known each other, I consider you a friend. A good friend."

"I agree. Definitely friends. Do you... Do you think there might be more? Sometime?"

"Oh, my Lord!" Horatio whispered. "I gave her the idea... But I didn't mean special in any bad way... and '*Sometime?*' What was I thinking? She must think I have all kinds of doubts, and I don't have any! I love her! But even if... Maybe she does just want to be friends..."

The cell phone was lying in Horatio's hand, forgotten for the moment as he tried to come up with something, anything, that he could say to her to break the idea she must have about how he felt about her. He racked his brain for hours, finally falling asleep on the sofa again, neck cocked awkwardly to one side.

When Horatio woke up early the next morning, with a very stiff neck, he dragged himself to the master bath to begin his routine, still at a loss as to what he might say to Penny when he found her. He just did not think blurting out "I love you," would work. It would just embarrass her and cause her to close off, even more.

"She has trust issues, for one thing," Horatio muttered on the drive to his office. He had started talking to himself right after Penny left. It was a habit now. One he was going to have to break. He had already been cautioned about expressing his thoughts aloud in the court room at inopportune times.

But he was not breaking it right now. "And she really does not think she would be suitable for me, either, I think." Horatio sighed. "What am I going to do?"

He stewed for several more days, still not having called. But that next Saturday, he was reading the paper and wound up in the Classified ads section. When he saw the ad for a restored military Jeep he suddenly had a new resolve in him.

"I have the property now," he muttered as he headed out to the car. "Need a suitable prepper vehicle. Maybe Penny would think marrying a Prepper might not be so bad. Instead of a stogy nine-to-fiver like I am now."

With thoughts crowding his mind on what he needed to do now, Horatio finally found the address for the Jeep owner. He felt anxious when he saw three vehicles parked on the street, with five people standing around the old Jeep parked on the driveway of the suburban house.

He parked and walked up to the men just as two of them shook hands. The other three looked disappointed and headed for their vehicles.

"I'm too late, I take it," Horatio said to the man standing where he was as the other took the keys from him and went over to the Jeep.

"Yep. 'fraid so. Just sold 'ol Betsy. Sorry my friend."

"Oh, well. There are bound to be some more older rigs out there somewhere. I guess the Jeep was gas fueled, anyway," Horatio said as the new owner of the restored Jeep started it up, a huge grin on his face.

"Y'all looking for a smoker?"

Horatio turned back to the man. "Smoker?"

"Yeah, yeah. You know. A diesel?"

"Oh," Horatio said. "Uh… Yes. I would like to find a diesel truck. But an older model. Before all the electronics." Penny had explained to him what she had done to her truck to protect it from EMP and other electrical and electronic dangers.

"Well, boy, my cousin Jimmy-Joe has a rig he's working on. Not quite done, but gonna be one sweet crawler when he is done. It's got a diesel.

New crate engine. Cummins, you know. One of them 6BTs you read about in the truck magazines."

Horatio's left eyebrow raised. A Cummins 6BT was what Penny had in her Chevy. "6BT, huh? Why does he want to sell it? Or does he?"

"Yeah, yeah. Boy does he! His wife's got one in the oven and he needs the money for baby stuff."

"I see," Horatio said. "You said '*crawler*'. What kind of truck is that?"

"Not actually a truck, you see. Be an old Suburban. Big for a crawler, but Jimmy-Joe always liked to have the biggest and the best. And he might just get it with this rig. If he didn't have to sell it."

"I didn't see a listing in the Classifieds this morning," Horatio replied.

"Naw. Jimmy-Joe figures to sell to one of his buddies in the Crawling club." The man looked sad and shook his head. "Most of them good ol' boys ain't got the folding money to get what Jimmy-Joe has in it. And he needs at least that much to get what they need for Linda and the baby on the way."

"Do you know just how much that is?"

"Well, the engine was expensive, being brand new, and all, but he got most of the rest of the stuff pretty cheap. The Suburban parts was offen wrecked ones at Ollie's Junk Yard he saved from the crusher. The frame he got is actually from a one-ton crew cab dually.

"Longer than the Suburban, but since he had to do a bunch of sheet metal work anyway and had four bodies to work with, he just stretched the body to fit the frame. That boy is an Einstein when it comes to fixing sheet metal. Can't even tell it ain't factory." The man shook his head and smiled. "'bout all Jimmy-Joe is good for, fixing cars at Jimbo's Auto Repair, but he is really good at it."

"I see," Horatio said. He had not understood some of what the man was saying, but he was now intrigued. Even if he did not want to buy it, he did want to see it.

"Could you give me... uh... Jimmy-Joe's address? I might be interested in the... Suburban."

"Naa. Never find it. Iffen you'll bring me back, I'll take you out there after I drop the Jeep off for this fellow."

Horatio nodded. "Sure."

Glad the man, named Bogas, first name or last, Horatio was not sure, had suggested he guide him out to Jimmy-Joes. It was well out away from town, down a long winding gravel road. There were no street names, though there were numbers on the mail boxes at the ends of each of the driveways that teed off the gravel road.

"Here she be," Bogas said finally, pointing to the dirt track that headed into the forest by the big mailbox that looked like a small Jeep. Rather proudly, Bogas said, "Jimmy-Joe made that mail box. Pretty nifty, huh?"

"Very nice, yes," Horatio said, as he turned onto the driveway. It was dirt, but in surprisingly good condition, Horatio decided. A couple of minutes later they came to the modest bungalow house that looked to have been recently re-painted.

Horatio looked the place over when he stopped. Though there were several vehicles in the yard, they were neatly aligned, and the yard was in good shape.

"Give a honk. He's probably out back. Don't want to get out until Clyde is corralled."

"Clyde?" Horatio asked.

"Biggest dang Rottweiler you ever seen, and mean as the devil, 'cept with Jimmy-Joe and his wife and her two young-uns. Let's them kids crawl all over him, pull his ears, pound on him, and ever'ting." Bogas shook his head. "But any stranger gets close to them and he could be a mad dog with the lock jaw rabies the way he gets."

Though he was feeling like he needed to check the Suburban out to satisfy his curiosity and get Bogas dropped off, so he could start looking for another vehicle, Horatio decided to do as Bogas suggested. He tooted the horn twice, quickly.

"Yonder he is," Bogas said a moment later.

Horatio saw the tall, thin, but well-muscled young man walking toward the Chevy, Clyde walking beside him, looking rather like a pony by his size.

Bogas made no move to get out of the Impala when Jimmy-Joe got to the car.

"What'cha want'in, Bogas? And who's this guy? Nice car."

Pleased at the compliment about the car, Horatio leaned over and said, "I am Horatio Billings."

"Thinkin' 'bout buying the Suburban," Bogas added, looking up at his cousin.

"Mmm. Sure. Let me get Clyde inside. Drive around to the shop."

"All righty. Just between them two Ford pickups, and around the house. Careful about any stuff the kids might have left out. They love them big toys of theirs."

Horatio maneuvered the Impala, in relatively tight quarters, around the house and stopped before a large pole barn, with wings on each side. There were six more vehicles parked in two rows, three on each side of the large concrete pad in front of the double wide garage doors in the middle of the building.

Horatio almost gasped. There were four more vehicles inside the cavernous shop. Or parts of four. They were all neatly arranged, up on work stands.

When Bogas got out of the Impala, Horatio did the same, walking over into the open garage doors. He looked around with interest. It seemed to have everything a well-equipped commercial shop would have, with a whole wall of tool boxes and racks with more tools.

There was even a vehicle lift mechanism, which had what Horatio figured out was the Suburban Bogas had told him about. Though he was not all that familiar with various SUVs, he could tell that this one was special. When he looked at it from the side it looked long. Almost too long for the vehicle lift.

"What'cha think?" Bogas asked.

Before Horatio could answer, Jimmy-Joe walked inside the pole barn and came over to Horatio.

"Jimmy-Joe Jenkins," he said, putting out his hand for Horatio to shake. Horatio did so, feeling like Jimmy-Joe could probably crush his hand with his own if he wanted to.

"Nice to meet you." They released hands and Horatio turned back to the Suburban. "Bogas has been telling me about the Suburban. That you... well... basically built it from parts."

"Yep. True as the day is long."

Horatio heard the pride in Jimmy-Joe's voice. Then sadness as he continued. "Was gonna be sweet when I finished. But my wife is having a difficult pregnancy, and we need to sell off some things."

With a movement of his head, Jimmy-Joe indicated the other vehicles outside. "Won't have no trouble selling the others, when the time comes, but I would like to go ahead and get the Suburban sold so I don't have to see it sitting here, ever'day, so I can concentrate on other work. The thing keeps drawing me to it and I am wasting too much time on it."

"How much is left to do?" Horatio asked.

Jimmy-Joe walked over to the Suburban and opened the front and rear doors on the driver's side. He sighed and answered Horatio's question. "Not really all that much. I was gonna make a rock crawler out of it, but when

I found out my wife was pregnant I decided to just finish it out regular like, you know?"

When Jimmy-Joe looked at him, Horatio nodded. He was looking at the interior of the Suburban. What there was in it. Which was not much but the bare metal of the body. No seats even. Excepting the Homer bucket behind the steering wheel.

Horatio was more than a little disappointed. "I see. I don't think I could do all this work..." He had really wanted to see what the thing would look like. He had finally figured out what rock crawling was, after remembering seeing some ads for a major competition in the area coming up.

He backed out of the open door and looked at Jimmy-Joe. "I'm not going to be able to buy it, but I would like to see the engine. I've heard about them..."

His disappointment showing, Jimmy-Joe nodded. "Sure."

"Bogas said it was a crate engine. I didn't see one in here. Is it outside?" Horatio asked as Jimmy walked along the side of the Suburban. Horatio thought he was headed for the open door at the other end of the barn.

But Jimmy-Joe stopped at the front of the Suburban and fiddled with the hood latch, giving Horatio a surprised look. "I wouldn't leave an engine outside, even in a crate," he said, lifting the hood.

"Power train is the first thing I get ready, to make sure everything is hunky dory. Frame and running gear next, drive train, and then install the engine and tranny. Thing is ready to go, except for the interior."

Jimmy-Joe reached over to a panel on the driver's side of the engine compartment and pressed a button. The Cummins came to life. It sounded just like the one in Penny's Chevy. If anything, it was even quieter.

"Wow," Horatio muttered, thinking, "Definitely need to have something with one of those engines..."

He turned back to Jimmy-Joe. "Had it all over the property," Jimmy-Joe said. "Even snuck it out on the road and did some high-speed runs one night after I got the body on."

Again, Horatio's left eyebrow lifted. "Guess that explains the bucket," he thought to himself. Aloud, he said, "So it's ready to go, except for the interior?"

"Well... depends on what else you would want. I haven't done the bumpers yet. I was going to do a winch up front and a rack on the back for a spare and fuel cans. Air and power connectors in both. The lines are run, but not connected to anything obviously."

"So, if I put a seat in it, I could drive it home?" Horatio asked.

"Well sure," Jimmy-Joe said, looking rather hopeful now. "Wouldn't take no time to put the factory seat back in to get you home."

Jimmy-Joe hesitated before he asked, "Uh... What'cha going to do with it, iffen you get it?"

"Oh," Horatio said, looking intently at the rig, "I have some ideas." He looked over at Jimmy-Joe again. "Rig it as a Zombie Hunter, maybe."

"Zombie hunter, huh? Make a good one, that's for sure. Don't interest me, but I helped at the shop on one and it was pretty cool, I guess."

Surprised at the positive reaction, when he had mostly been just joking, rather than admit to planning on making a prepper vehicle for the future Post-Apocalyptic World.

"Gotta tell you, mister," Jimmy-Joe said, down to all business now, "Gotta have cash, up front. Can't do no financing like the last guy asked. And I gotta have my price. I won't take less than what I got in it, plus a little for my labor."

Sure he would not be able to afford the truck, even in its unfinished state, he asked, "How much would that be?"

Glad he had learned to control his facial expression for the courtroom, Horatio managed not to show his absolute surprise when Jimmy-Joe told him what he had to have for the Suburban.

Making a snap decision, Horatio said, "I can give you a check right now..."

"He said cash," Bogas said.

"Oh," Horatio said. "I thought... Well, I can do a cash check and bring he money back..."

"Works," said Jimmy-Joe. "You got yourself a Zombie Hunter." He looked a bit wistful. "Wish I could help you out with the finish work, but I'm working full hours at the shop and I gotta keep an eye on my wife and the kids when I am off."

"Who would you recommend?" Horatio asked.

"Well... Let's see. The shop can't do that kind of work anymore. There's the Lone Ranger... Jiggs..."

Jimmy-Joe snapped his fingers. "Willis could do it. He needs the money, bad, since he lost the job he thought he had. Just bought that fancy welding truck and all that fancy equipment he's gotta pay off. He's working at Walmart right now, but I bet he could do it in his off time. He ain't gettin' many hours."

"Let me give him a call..."

Two minutes later Jimmy-Joe handed his cell phone to Horatio.

"This is Horatio..." He could barely get a word in edgewise. Willis was a talker. And explained, in great detail, why he would be an excellent choice to finish out the Suburban since he already knew it inside and out. And would work for a very reasonable rate, too.

Horatio had to hold back the chuckle when he handed Jimmy-Joe back his phone. Willis, with no participation on Horatio's part, had talked himself down in labor price twice. Not sure exactly what professional welders and fabricators got, Horatio was pretty sure he was going to get a bargain on the finishing as well as on the initial purchase.

Jimmy-Joe took the phone and said, "I'll take it on down there, if you want to go get that money..."

"You can drive it to Willis'?"

"Sure," Jimmy-Joe said. "He's down at the end of the road, there on the lake."

"Oh... Well, sure." Horatio looked over at Bogas.

"I'm sittin' on dead ready," said Bogas, turning to go out to the Impala. "Need to get going if you're going to get that cash today outta the bank."

"Yes," Horatio said. He shook Jimmy-Joe's hand and hurried out to the Impala.

Two hours later and Horatio was consulting with Willis on what he would be doing on the Suburban. With some basic work decided, Horatio said, "I will have some plans drawn up and out here next weekend. Will that give you enough time to get this preliminary work done?"

"Sure 'ting, Boss. No sweat."

They shook hands and Horatio headed home, wondering what he had gotten himself into with his impulsive behavior. He sighed as he went into the house, thinking, "Well, Grandmother always said my trust fund was for my future, if I ever really needed it. Looks like prepping is my future."

Horatio did a great deal of research the rest of that evening. He was not able to do much more the first three days of the week, but Thursday and Friday he was able to devote much of his time to the various sets of plans he had going, including the additions to the Suburban.

He also, finally, joined a couple of the prepper forums that Penny had mentioned. And immediately recognized the user name she had told him she went by. He killed several hours reading threads with posts she had made during the last year. They both confirmed what he had already learned from her and other places and gave him new insights and ideas for his prepping. There was a deep longing in him when he shut off his computer that night.

When that next Saturday rolled around, he finalized the plans for the Suburban, and for the property. Horatio headed out to drop off the Suburban plans with Willis. They went over them for an hour, and then Horatio left town to go to the next city over that had several businesses that were not available in this town.

He spent the rest of the afternoon, and part of the evening, making arrangements with several of them to go to his property to do estimates on the work he wanted each to do, and work out a time frame for the work to be done.

That taken care of, Horatio next did some legal and financial things for himself. He worked late into the night, setting up things for the future he was beginning to believe was on its way at a very rapid pace.

Horatio was almost late getting to the office Monday morning, after his late night. But he made it, and was hard at work when the first of the calls from contractors came in. Fortunately, he had no appointments scheduled, and was able to talk to each one, on the phone, through e-mail, or Skype.

He was smiling when the last person called that he had sent out to the property. Everything he had asked about was doable, and well within the budget he had set for the project.

Horatio picked up the phone, ready to call Penny and fill her in on his plans. Before he could call Melissa knocked on the open door. "A Mrs. Amstead is out here. She said she knows you and needs some advice..." There was a questioning look on her face.

"Of course," Horatio said, hanging up the phone. "Send her in."

When Alice Amstead entered the office, Horatio jumped up and moved around the desk to move the chair out of the way. Alice was in a power wheelchair.

"What happened?" Horatio asked. He was back in his chair, and Alice was parked at the front of the desk.

Alice waved her hand. "Just old age, Horatio. These old bones are not what they used to be. I fell and broke a hip and did more damage to my back. Looks like I'm stuck in this cotton-picking thing for the rest of my days."

"Oh, Mrs. Amstead, I am sorry! There isn't anything they can do?"

"Henry had some specialists take a look and they said there wasn't much they could do, considering the deterioration of my bones and spine. Especially considering my age."

Alice saw Horatio getting upset. "Now, don't you fret, young man. I am not spending good money on the very slight possibility that they could get me on my feet again. It wouldn't be for long, anyway. Don't have that much time left, to take advantage of it."

"Mrs. Amstead! You have many years yet! You're looking great, despite the wheelchair."

"Not so. My lord. You don't know the half of what is wrong with me. This last episode is just the tip of the iceberg." She lifted a hand when Horatio started to protest. "I am not going to go into it, Horatio. My time is limited. Just take my word for it. I need you to take care of a few things for me while I still have all my mental faculties. The time is coming when I won't be able to make decisions. I want the things I plan locked in before then."

As sweet as Mrs. Amstead was, Horatio knew just how hard headed she was. Her late husband used to joke about it. Horatio had started out as their paperboy, then began to mow their lawn for them when Bernie no longer could. He had become friends with both as he grew up, and they called on him to take care of things when they needed a hand.

So, he nodded and said. "Yes, ma'am. Of course. Just what can I do for you?"

Horatio had Melissa rearrange his schedule to accommodate Alice's needs. He was going to have to go out to her place in order to complete some of the work. It would take at least three days of steady work to accomplish what she wanted. He winced a couple of times during the discussion of what she planned.

There were a few people in town that were not going to like what she was doing. Including some of her distant relatives, the only ones she had left. And even a few of the locals would be impacted negatively when her plan was in place.

But Horatio set everything up as she asked, making sure every I was dotted, and every T crossed. Fortunately, Alice had already been to the nearest mental health center and had herself tested for anything that would be cause for her being considered incompetent to make the decisions she was making, in case they were contested. Horatio did not have to bring up the subject. He had dreaded it from the moment she explained.

Alice had him and Melissa in stitches more than once as she regaled them with tales from her past, sometimes in explanation of why she was doing what she was doing. By the time the papers were completed and filed, Horatio was feeling good about the situation, but a bit sad at the thought that his friend would soon be gone. But her legacy would live on. He would make sure of it.

Horatio, with Melissa's help, got caught up by Sunday. The next week would be a light one, so he made plans to be out of the office on Wednesday and Thursday. He would be on call if something came up that Melissa thought he should handle.

He took the Impala out to Willis' first thing Wednesday, to check on the progress he was making on the Suburban.

Willis was as good as his word. Everything Horatio had asked for was completed or being done. And Willis even had some additional suggestions that could be incorporated as he continued the work. Horatio gave him the go ahead.

Next, he went out to the property to meet the contractors that were scheduled to show up that afternoon. Everyone showed, on time, ready to start working.

One of the people he had hired would act as general contractor, supervising the other contractors. Horatio had wracked his brain trying to figure out how he could keep a better eye on the progress, but his practice was keeping him too busy to come out every day.

Just as he got back into the Impala, after walking to where it was parked just inside the property line, since it would not make it all the way to the building site, he snapped his fingers. "Got it!" he exclaimed and pulled out his cell phone.

He checked his contact list, hoping that he still had the number he was looking for, and that it was still valid. When he activated the call and it began to ring on the other end, he breathed a sigh of relief.

But it was not who he was expecting that answered the call. "Hello. This is Georgie. Who is this?" It was a woman's voice.

"I'm sorry. I must have the wrong number. This is the last number I have for Frank Goodwind. Sorry to disturb you."

"No! Wait! This is his number," quickly said Georgie. "I'm his wife. Hang on. I will get him for you. Who should I say is calling?"

Horatio kept the surprise out of his voice when he replied. "Horatio Billings."

"Frank's married? Never thought I'd see the day…" Horatio thought to himself. Then his friend was on the line.

"Horehound, you old dog! Good to hear from you. What are you up to these days?"

Horatio smiled at Frank's use of the nickname he had given Horatio the first day they met at college. He had not seen him in several years, since he had enlisted in the Marines.

"Still lawyering, Frank. How about you? I heard you mustered out last year."

"Sort of. Medical discharge." Frank quickly reassured Horatio. "Nothing major, buddy. But can't cut the mustard anymore, so I opted out when they offered. You know me and desk work."

"Well... Glad it isn't too serious. What are you doing now? Any chance you could get away for a while?"

"Depends on what you need, Horehound. I do have a few restrictions on what I can do, physically. But I can get lose for a while, as long as the invite includes Georgie."

"Yes. Of course, it does. And congratulations on your marriage."

Horatio heard Georgie laugh in the background when Frank responded. "Thanks. Never thought you'd see the day, I bet, after what I used to say about getting married and settling down. But when you meet Georgie, you'll understand."

"I look forward to it." Horatio decided that even if Frank could not do what he had been planning on asking, it would be great to see him again. "When can you come out? I'll cover the expenses..."

"No need. We can handle it nicely. Be about three days, give or take. We'll be driving. Got ourselves a sweet little motorhome. Been doing some travelling lately. Caught us at home by chance. We were heading out in a couple of days, anyway. We'll just change directions. I'll fill you in when we get there."

"Okay, Frank. Thanks. I am really looking forward to seeing you and meeting Georgie. Call me when you hit town and I'll give you directions to my house. I moved a few years ago."

"Sure thing. See you in a few. 'bye."

Horatio put away the phone. "Wow. That was a surprise," he muttered. "Hm. Still need someone to watch the place for me. Have to think on it."

He still had not thought of anyone suitable to act as supervisor and watchman at the property when Frank called for directions. Horatio gave them directions to the office and went outside to wait.

It was only a few minutes, though Horatio did not recognize the vehicle until Frank stepped out of it. Horatio's eyes widened. Frank had a cane in his left hand and he looked like he was leaning on it heavily. Horatio hurried over to the bright silver Class C motorhome.

"Hey, buddy! Great to see you!" exclaimed Frank. He held out his right hand and Horatio shook it, noticing that it was still just as firm and strong as when he and Frank were in their twenties.

"Yeah. You, too, Frank."

"Come on around to the back of the Airstream. I'll introduce you to my wife."

Frank did not limp all that much, but Horatio could tell he was dependent on, what he now saw was a fancy walking stick, not a simple hook cane, as Frank walked down the length of the motorhome.

"Honey, this is my old college buddy, Horatio Billings. Horehound, meet my wife, helpmeet, good right arm, and nurse, Georgie."

She was not at all what Horatio was expecting. Frank had been into busty blondes and redheads, always much shorter than his six two height, when they were in college. Georgie was tall, with a trim figure, and jet-black hair.

"It is so nice to meet you, Horatio." She smiled. "Frank told me you were the guy that got him through college."

Horatio shook her hand, and then glanced over at Frank. "Frank did it all on his own. He just needed a little push here and there."

"Push is right," Frank said, suddenly stepping forward and taking Horatio into a tight bear hug. "If it was not for you watching out for me, I never would have got into the Marines. And you know what serving in the Marines meant to me."

Frank stepped back. Horatio knew his face was a bit red. "Well..."

"I am in your debt, man. I got to do what I had always dreamed of doing. And despite everything that happened, it all led to me meeting Georgie." Frank gave his wife an adoring look.

"She nursed me through the worst of the recovery. I do not think I would have made it, without her."

Georgie put her right hand on Frank's shoulder. "You would have made it, Frank. I just pushed you to fulfill your potential. And you did."

Frank grinned. "Yeah. But not without giving you a hard time." Frank looked back at Horatio. He grinned. "But she is tougher than me. She kept me in line and made sure I did the therapy and did not go off the deep end."

Georgie smiled at Frank. "You're just an old softy."

Horatio grinned. "Yeah. I always thought that about him."

Frank harrumphed. "Right. Come on. Let me get the wheelchair out."

Georgie touched a remote and the rear of the motorhome began to lift. Horatio's eyes widened when the ramp went down and exposed not one, but three wheelchairs. One looked to be a conventional powered wheelchair. Beside it was a folded manual wheelchair.

But what really caught his eye was the tracked wheelchair next to the other powered chair. Horatio looked over at Frank, one eyebrow lifting in question. Frank grinned. "My rough country unit. I'll get it out later and let you get a good look. For now, I'm starving and would like to get some lunch."

Frank walked up the ramp and sat down in the conventional powered wheelchair, and then drove it out of the motorhome.

"I can get around alright with the stick," Frank explained as Georgie closed the ramp and then the hatch. "But any real distance and I get to a point that I am not comfortable that I could handle something if it came up."

Again, Georgie touched Frank's shoulder. "He is very protective of me. I can take care of myself. Frank made sure of that. But he doesn't want me defending him. He's determined to take care of himself, himself."

"Sounds like him," Horatio said. "We can go to a place here in the mall. Let me let my paralegal know I'll be back in a while. Head to the blue and white awning. I'll catch up in a minute."

Horatio hurried inside the office and then back out. Frank and Georgie were already at the restaurant waiting for him. It was a great lunch. Horatio listened, entranced, as Frank filled him in on his career in the Marines, the attack that partially disabled him, and his subsequent recovery. And then marriage to Georgie when she decided to leave the military herself, to be with him.

Finally, Frank asked, "Now, buddy, what did you need me out here for?"

"Actually, I was needing sort of a contractor supervisor and night watchman out at a piece of property I bought recently and am having some major work done." Horatio shook his head. "I will look for…"

"Not a problem," Frank said, looking at Horatio steadily. "I can handle it."

There was only a very small hesitation before Horatio nodded. "Excellent, then. Do you feel like going out now to take a look?"

Frank grinned. "You betcha!"

Horatio took care of the bill and followed Frank and Georgie back out to the motorhome. Horatio was studying the motorhome. "I don't know, Frank. It is really rough out…"

Again, Frank grinned. "Oh, don't discount this rig, either. It isn't just another pretty face. It is an Airstream, so it is pretty and well made. But it is on a one-ton four-wheel drive Mercedes-Benz Sprinter long wheelbase extended van chassis with a six-cylinder diesel. Very off-road capable."

"Oh. Did not know Airstream had something like this." Horatio was looking over the rig with interest.

"Frank had a few 'improvements' made, besides the wheelchair accommodations." Georgie smiled.

"I'll show you some of them when we aren't so exposed," Frank said. Georgie opened up the rear of the Airstream and Frank backed the wheelchair up the ramp and secured it in place. With walking stick in hand, he came down the ramp and around to the passenger side of the motorhome.

"We'll follow you out," Frank said.

"Okay." Horatio started to turn around and head for his car but stopped. "Uh... When we get to the edge of the property, I will need a ride..."

Frank laughed. "You can't even get on your own property?"

"Not yet," Horatio admitted. "But I'm having something put together that will manage."

"Sure, buddy, sure. Still driving an Impala?"

"Oh, yeah."

Chapter Six
-

When they reached the point where Horatio could no longer get the Impala down the track, he stopped and transferred to the Airstream, getting his first good look inside. The thing was gorgeous inside. And, he suspected, not just from what Georgie had said, not quite stock.

Squatting between the two front seats, Horatio guided Georgie to the construction site. Frank had not been kidding. The Airstream had no difficulty with the rough track.

Frank whistled when they reached the point where they could see the extent of what Horatio was having done. He turned and looked at Horatio. "You have changed. What happened?"

When Horatio sighed, Frank looked over at Georgie and then back at Horatio. "Have something to do with a woman?" Frank asked.

"Yeah. Sort of."

"Don't want to talk about it?"

"Not really. I'll tell you… But not right now. I want to show you what is going on."

Horatio watched as Frank carefully maneuvered to the back of the Airstream and entered the wheelchair garage. This time he strapped himself into the tracked wheelchair. Expecting the quiet hum of electric motors, Horatio was surprised when he heard a small diesel engine fire up. It was obviously well muffled.

When Frank got the wheelchair out of the Airstream, Horatio could tell he was showing off a bit as he worked his way toward the action. It was obvious that not only was the wheelchair a highly capable machine, but Frank was a master at using it.

Horatio waved over Elmer Coontz, the heavy equipment contractor that was acting as general contractor for the current phase. "Elmer, this is Frank. He's going to be out here as my on-site substitute. He will relay instructions and keep me advised on progress when I can't be out here."

"This guy?" Elmer asked, looking at Frank and the wheelchair with skepticism. He made no move to shake hands.

"Yeah. Me. Got a problem with a cripple being your boss?"

Horatio started to say something but decided to let Frank handle it. He had a feeling Frank had run into situations like this one before.

"I kinda do. What do you know about heavy equipment?"

"Mind if I just show you?" Frank asked. He did not wait for an answer but drove over to a D8 Cat with blade.

"Hey!" Elmer yelled when Frank moved from the wheelchair to the Cat, using his walking stick. But he was up in the cab before Elmer could get to it.

The D8 rumbled to life, and before Elmer could do anything else, Frank had the blade up and was moving toward where a set of grading stakes were set out. Ten minutes later, Frank parked the D8 back where it had been and climbed down.

Elmer rubbed his chin. "Well, got to admit, you did a decent job on that grading. I guess maybe you do know what you are doing." Elmer turned to Horatio. "Okay. I can work with this guy. Just don't expect me to cater to him."

Frank just grinned over at Horatio and gave him a wink. "I'm not worried about Frank," Horatio replied to Elmer. "Now, I am going to show Frank the place, so he knows what is going on."

Elmer did not respond, other than a slight wave of his hand, before heading over to the D8.

As Frank and Georgie accompanied Horatio around the property, Horatio pointed out what the plans were.

When they got back to the Airstream, Frank stopped in a spot where he could watch the work being done at several points within view. "Never expected you to go the survivalist route, Horehound." Frank gave Horatio a questioning look.

"Prepper," Horatio said quietly. "I'm a prepper now. Met someone that clued me in to what is happening, why, and what I can do about it to protect myself, no matter what the future."

"That is good, buddy," Frank said. He looked over at Georgie, who nodded. When Frank turned back to Horatio he said, "We've been prepping since before we got married. The Airstream is set up for prepping. We've been traveling around, looking for a suitable spot to set up a small homestead.

"We have enough capital to get one going to support most of our needs, with some ideas about what to do when things go south."

Horatio's left eyebrow went up. "I see. Hm… You thinking maybe in this area?"

Frank grinned. "Could be."

Horatio smiled. "Let's talk some more, later, at the house. I need to get back to the office."

They got back into the Airstream and Georgie drove Horatio back to his car. Horatio gave her the address and a key to his house before he got into the Impala. "Make yourself at home. I should be there well before six."

That evening was another eye opener for Horatio. Frank and Georgie, while nowhere as advanced with their prepping as Penny, where equal to Horatio, except for a good homestead property. Everything that was not with them in the Airstream was stored in their current home town, at their home, and in self-store units, one of which was climate controlled.

Just before they were going to go to bed, Horatio said, "You know, I can't really handle that place on my own. I am going to need help. I've planned on it, in terms of facilities, but have not figured out anyone I would be willing to risk asking to help out when the time comes. I was wondering... If you guys are interested in a permanent spot..."

Georgie and Frank exchanged a quick glance. "Let us talk it over, Horatio. We'll let you know pretty quickly. And if it is alright, we'll set up a semi-permanent camp out there and manage things for you until you have the place the way you want it."

"Definitely yes," Horatio replied, smiling. With that, Horatio headed for his bedroom, and Georgie and Frank the guest room.

Able to relax a bit, knowing Frank and Georgie were on the job, Horatio did not bother going back out to the property until the weekend. When he did go out on Saturday, after checking in with Willis, Horatio was towing a light trailer behind the Impala.

On the trailer was the custom ROKON two-wheel drive motorcycle Horatio had ordered on line and had Willis convert to a Hatz 1B40 electric start diesel engine in some down time he had when working on the Suburban.

Horatio parked the Impala just out of sight of the entrance to the property and unloaded the ROKON. He unloaded the other items he had purchased for use with the ROKON, including both trailers. One was an in-line single wheel trailer. The other was a custom tandem wheel trailer, much wider and a bit longer than the in-line trailer.

With the tandem wheel trailer hitched up to the ROKON, he loaded it down with everything else he had brought out, and then hitched the in-line trailer to the rear of the tandem.

Horatio was grinning when he pulled into the work area and Georgie looked up and saw him. She poked Frank, who spun the tracked wheelchair around. The grin on his face matched Horatio's.

"I see you came up with a way to get out here," Frank said when Horatio stopped the ROKON beside him.

"Yep. Thought this would be good to tool around out here. Where should I park and drop the trailers?"

Frank pointed out a spot on the far side of where the outdoor camp they had set up was located. Horatio drove over and unhitched the lead trailer, driving the ROKON back over beside the Airstream.

"Got a lot to report, as you can see," Frank said, getting down to business. Georgie handed him a clip board and Frank began to go over everything that had been done since Horatio had been there last. And made a few suggestions.

Horatio could see immediately the benefits to what Frank was suggesting and told him to incorporate them. When they had finished the work discussion, Horatio looked at Frank expectantly. "Well?"

Frank chuckled. "We're in, Horatio. Lock, stock, and barrel. Once things reach the correct point, we'll go get our things and move them here, and close down the other place. That okay?"

"Absolutely!" Horatio replied, shaking his friend's hand, and then Georgie's.

And while Horatio had made plans for additional people, Frank had more suggestions and a couple of requests for changes to accommodate him and Georgie.

With things going so well, Horatio had more time to think about Penny. He could not count the times he wanted to respond to one of her posts on the forums. But he did not really have anything to add. He just wanted the contact.

He finally could not stand it anymore. The first phase of the property enhancement was done, Frank and Georgie were headed to get their things, the Suburban was done, equipped, and loaded. Horatio cleared his calendar for three days and left on a Thursday evening. He did not have to be back until the following Wednesday morning.

Horatio had not called any of the numbers or written to any of the addresses he had for Penny. He decided that he would first go to her new property, just to see if she was doing what he was. Getting it ready, for when it might be needed.

Though the signs were subtle, Horatio had learned enough to recognize the fact that some fairly large equipment had come and gone on the road leading up to the outer gate of the property. Just inside were more signs of the heavy equipment traffic on the first part of the road he could see.

Horatio had parked out of the way of the gates, and sat in the Suburban for a while, trying to decide what to do, after checking the lock on the gate. The combination had not been changed.

He could get onto the property, but was debating if he should, without Penny's prior permission. He was not one hundred percent sure he would be able to get through the second gate, that gave access to the main building site. So, he sat in the Suburban and brooded a bit more.

The decision was made for him, when Penny drove up and stopped well away from the gate. Horatio sighed and started to get out of the Suburban and go over to her, but she already was out of the truck had the gate unlocked and slid back. She waved him through, so he shrugged, started the Suburban and drove through.

Penny followed him through the opening, stopped the truck, and closed and locked the gate. Again, Horatio started to get out of the Suburban, but decided that since she was letting him in, that he would just wait until they got to the building site before he got out to meet her.

She pulled around him, keeping an eye on the road due to its roughness, even worse now with the additional damage from the heavy equipment, and headed up the track. She stopped again at the gate controls at the inner gate, got it open with the keypad, and drove through.

Horatio followed her quickly, before the gate could close. His eyes roamed over the area, as amazed at the transformation of the place as much as he was when he had seen the transformation of his own place after the last inspection trip out.

Looking around delayed him, and Penny was already coming around the back of the Suburban when Horatio opened the driver's door and stepped out, turning around to meet her.

His eyes widened in concern when Penny looked at him, one hand going to her chest, and the other going to the Suburban to support herself when her knees seemed to buckle. He barely heard the whispered, "Horatio?"

He stepped toward her quickly, seeing her sway, and grabbed her on the sides of her waist to keep her from falling. Her eyes never left his.

"Are you alright?" Horatio asked in a worried voice, staring at her even more pale than usual porcelain complexion. She cut her eyes toward the Suburban, and then back to Horatio's face. He felt her straighten up and reluctantly let his hands slide from her waist.

She was nodding, but still had not said anything else, her eyes boring into his. He recognized several emotions as her eyes and expression changed rapidly from one to another.

Finally, she dropped both hands down in front of her, and clasped them together. Her knuckles were white, Horatio noticed, his eyes drawn to the movement.

"Are you sure you are okay?" Horatio asked again.

"I'm fine, Horatio. I'm fine. What... What... What are you doing here?"

Horatio shook his head. "I came, hoping to see you. Didn't you recognize me when you stopped at the gate? You waved me through... I thought you knew it was me."

Suddenly her eyes dropped to her feet and Horatio felt his stomach drop. "Um... No... No, I didn't. I was... am... expecting one of the contractors... I... I... thought you were him... You're in a Suburban... The Impala?"

"I knew it wouldn't get here. I had this put together recently. I still have the Impala."

There was a flicker of a smile, but it was gone just as quickly as it had appeared. "At least," thought Horatio, "she isn't looking at her feet anymore." Instead, she was looking over his right shoulder, avoiding his eyes.

"What... what did you want to see me about?" She did flick her eyes to his, but they were back looking over his shoulder instantly.

Before he could say anything, he saw her sway again. But she immediately straightened back up, turned to look at the small structure by which she had parked, and said, "I... uh... need to sit down. Let's go over to the construction office." She turned and hurried away before Horatio could respond.

His long strides caught up to her, and then slightly past, as he reached for the door lever and opened the door for her. Her eyes met his again for a moment, as she went past him into the office.

Hurriedly, Horatio thought, Penny went around behind the largest of the two smallish desks near the rear wall of the room and sat down. Horatio could tell she used the desk regularly, as she had made the slight jump up to get on the pillow riser she used when at a desk.

"Um... You... can sit down..."

Horatio nodded. But instead of taking one of the straight back chairs that were against the side wall, he pulled it forward and sat down right across the desk from her, keeping his eyes on her face.

Yet again her eyes met his, and yet again dropped. This time to the top of the desk. She glanced at the computer screen on the desk, and her eyes widened for a moment before she looked back at Horatio, meeting his eyes once more, just a bit longer this time.

"What is it, Penny? What did you see on the computer?"

"It's…" She fell silent. Penny glanced at him again, back at the screen, and continued speaking. "Something I am monitoring. Just noticed it start a few days ago."

"Something I should be concerned about?" Horatio asked quietly.

She shook her, head, but her eyes stayed on the monitor, flicking back and forth as she read. "I don't know," she said then, still reading. "Maybe… I don't quite have this figured out. It's looking like…"

Penny glanced at him, and then back at the screen. "I don't want to say. I am just not sure yet. It is a pretty fantastical thought…. Most people do not even consider it. One guy… mentions it from time to time. Never heard anyone else give it any credence. But I am beginning to believe he might be on to something."

She quit reading, squeezed her eyes closed for a moment, and when she opened them again, she looked straight into Horatio's eyes once more. "Horatio…" But her words faded away, and Horatio saw the vulnerability and pain in her he had seen when he had said what he had before when they had talked about, sort of, their possible relationship.

"Penny, I am sorry. So sorry. About how I made you feel that time… It wasn't what I meant to do… I didn't say what I meant very well. But it wasn't the way it came out sounding. Honestly. It wasn't."

Horatio knew there were tears in his eyes, but did not try to wipe them away, as tears shimmered in Penny's eyes, still locked on his.

"I… I… I don't understand, Horatio… What do you mean? When you said… When you said what?"

"When I implied that there wasn't anything between us now… Perhaps later there might be." Horatio's head dropped for a moment, but he lifted it again. "But that isn't the way I meant it. I meant now. Now… er… when we got back home. Not later, later. Just later than right then. I thought you would want to think about it a little bit. But just a few days. I hoped…" His words faded away.

"Hoped what, Horatio?"

Horatio barely heard her. But he did hear the quiver in her voice. And, he hoped he heard what sounded like hope in her voice.

Now his eyes bored into hers, searching for the answer to the question in the statement he began to make. "That there was something between us that could… would grow… into even more. Penny… I know we haven't known each other for very long. But even in the short time… Being around you made me a better person, Penny.

"You opened my eyes. To so many things. Kimmy for one. The real world around me. And prepping. But mostly to my real loneliness. My want for something more... Someone... Someone I could really love, without worrying about whether or not that person wanted me or my money and position.

"That wanted me for just me. That loved me. For me. That wanted to have children with me. And be with me the rest of my life. Not someone that wanted designer clothes, and a Jaguar, and parties every weekend, and Las Vegas gambling trips, and... and..."

Penny gasped slightly. She sucked her lips between her teeth and bit slightly as she stared at Horatio. His words had faded away, and he waited for her response. He could see the want and hope in her eyes, but still the fear.

He would have to risk his heart, he suddenly knew. He could not put the pressure on her to say it first. "I love you, Penny." The words were soft, but he knew she heard him, for her eyes went wide, her hands came up to her mouth, and then, faster than he thought possible, she was around the desk and in his arms, with him still sitting in the chair.

"I love you, Horatio. From the moment I saw you come into your office. I'd learned so much about you while you were away on that trip, and then, when you came through the door when you came home... I was lost. I fell in love with you that very instant."

Though her head had tipped slightly back, and she had leaned into him, Horatio could still feel her slight hesitation. He did not hesitate. His head came down and forward until his lips met hers.

It was not until she moaned that Horatio broke the kiss. They both gasped for air and stared at one another. An instant later, Penny's arms were around Horatio's neck and she was pulling his head down and herself up, to kiss him this time. Just as passionately as he had kissed her.

Finally, neither knew just how much later, they broke apart, lips plump and tingling. Horatio stood, but leaned forward, wrapped his arms around Penny and swung her around in circles as she laughed. "I love you! I love you! I love you!" she cried.

Horatio set her down, gave her another long kiss, and then stepped back. "I have a lot to tell you..."

Penny nodded. "The Suburban?"

Horatio shook his head but was saying. "Yes. The Suburban. But a lot more, too."

"I have some things to tell you, too, Horatio." But she whirled around without continuing when her computer on the desk dinged what was clearly an alarm annunciator.

"What is that?" Horatio asked when Penny hurried back around the desk.

"I am monitoring the news for specific types of stories." She glanced up at him, and then back down at the monitor as she sat down.

Horatio followed her around the desk and, braced with one hand on the desk top, leaned down to look at the computer screen with her. Penny was reading and scrolling faster than Horatio could keep up. He caught only snippets of the news story.

"I don't believe this," Penny muttered when she got to the end of the news story.

"What is it, Penny? I couldn't keep up." He moved back around the desk and sat down again.

Penny got up and began to pace the few steps available each way behind the desks. She shook her head. "This... This theory I have. That the guy I told you about triggered. She paused and looked at Horatio. When he nodded, she continued.

"It is something, at least the two of us, call addictive entertainment." At Horatio's questioning look, she added, "It is a whole class of activities." She finally quit pacing and sat down to face him again. She put her hands on the desk and kept explaining.

"It is when people get so caught up in their methods of entertainment that they make bad decisions based on their need to continue the form of entertainment. They quit spending time with loved ones, spend money they can't afford to on the entertainment, even begin to have trouble at work... even miss work... because of their addiction."

"I'm not sure I follow, Penny," Horatio said when she paused. He shook his head. "What kind of entertainment do you mean? Like movies and TV shows?"

Penny nodded. "Yes. But just in part. But there are many other things, too. Even things like golf, believe it or not. There are people that spend enormous amounts of money to play golf. Oh."

Her eyes widened when Horatio looked at her with a strange expression on his face.

"Not you, Horatio. Not people that play golf as a real sport, to challenge themselves, and have a little friendly competition. I mean people that invest thousands in clubs, lessons, green fees, trips to courses and competitions. With money that should be going to their family's needs. Even their own. Sometimes they neglect their health. And golf isn't the best example.

"The major professional sports, especially those with leagues that go all the way down even to toddlers. Football, basketball, baseball, hockey, tennis, gymnastics... all the major sports. People spend hundreds and even thousands of dollars on game tickets, game equipment for themselves and families, trips to playoff and championship games, memorabilia and souvenirs, decorations for their homes and vehicles, clothing. You know what I mean."

Horatio was nodding now. "I know a couple of guys that go overboard. Sure. But a danger? I'm not really sure..."

Penny nodded. "I know. Again, not the best examples of the dangers, but real ones, never the less, in my opinion. It affects the fabric of families, for one thing. And that drive, that addiction, can be, and I think is, used by the powers that be to control the population to one degree or another. I am sure you have heard the term 'Bread and Circuses' as it applied to ancient Roman times..."

Horatio nodded again. "Of course. The government used those programs to keep people occupied and their minds off... their... troubles... and what the government was doing." His voice slowed as his eyes had widened in understanding.

"Exactly, Horatio. But that is only one part of it, and the tip of the iceberg, as I see it. Those physical sports are one thing. Yes, they divert people, and the stress on families, when a member has one or more of the addictions, due to time away, or financial considerations, is definitely not good.

"But there are some other things that have started to get much worse in the last few years that started back in the 1970s."

Horatio's eyebrow lifted on the left side. "Let me guess. Computer games?"

Penny smiled and nodded. "Yes. Part of it. The main part. But let me mention what you did at the very first. Movies and television. Money can be a factor with them but is much less so. It is more the time that they keep family members isolated from each other. There are some programs that do bring families together to watch, but those shows are often shows that actually divide them and have them on very different sides of an issue. The best team. The best technique. The best dancer. The best singer. Many of the competitive shows really come between people.

"And that is, again, the tip of the iceberg. Movies and TV shows have a tremendous influence on what society thinks and does. There are people in the visual entertainment and musical industries that get their messages, the 'rightness' of their special agendas, to the public in ways that get people to accept them as normal, acceptable behavior and actions. Even though subliminal advertising has been basically outlawed in commercial productions, it does still exist in many forms.

"And propagandists have perfected many methods over the years that do not need traditional subliminal messages in TV and movies. There are even more subtle ways, that do not have a smoking gun left behind that can be found more or less by simply playing back the videos and music at slower speeds.

"No. Much more devious than that. Constant bombardment with ideas, using popular shows and actors to convey the messages is very effective in getting people to accept those ideas as normal. As good and right.

"And those behaviors and the attitudes that are bombarding people constantly, with most having no defenses against it, is polarizing the country as these people react vocally, and sometimes violently, against those that do see what is happening, or simply do not buy into the ideas being expounded."

Horatio sighed. "Yes. I am beginning to get the picture."

"Oh, I am just getting started," Penny said with a smile. "I wish I knew where my soap box is."

Horatio laughed.

"Speaking of soap…" she continued, "It isn't just prime time TV and big screen movies that are doing this. The soaps do their share, especially the cable and satellite broadcast ones. Pretty much the same as the primary network shows, but with harder edged propaganda, with appeal to adults, using sex and violence to push the agenda.

"Oh. And the shopping networks. They do their part, too. Less the propaganda about social issues and politics, but more of that than you might imagine. They build the must have, keep up with the Jones, got to have the latest thing competition between people. Not to mention, bring real distress to peoples' budgets when it gets out of hand in some people.

"The talk shows are some of the most direct and open deliverers of agendas. The news is much more subtle, using adjectives to color hard news stories toward the agenda they want, and giving what are really opinions and op-ed opinions as speculative interpretations of important events.

"Now, finally. The most dangerous aspect. The one you mentioned. Computer games and independent gaming systems. Early on they were essentially harmless. Times were different. Children, and adults, were limited in the time they could spend on the expensive devices. But as costs came down, programming became better, and society changed to one where the systems were used as babysitters and alternatives to TV and movies with the tamer early games, more and more adults, and especially children, were exposed to the messages being given in those games, for much longer periods of time. And the messages were presented using high intensity situations that the users could identify with in some way in their own lives."

"Before you go on, how did you discover this, Penny?" Horatio asked. "I've never really heard about any of these ideas. Media bias, I guess, but that is about all."

"Part of it goes back to when I was thirteen. Still at the institute," Penny said, now clasping her hands on the desk again. "The scientists brought in some of the games, already very sophisticated at that time, simply to be used to test my reflexes and thought processes.

"Some I liked, some I didn't, but I did develop some pretty good gaming expertise pretty quickly. But that interest faded just as quickly as I mastered the games. My attention turned to the programming that produced the games. And since I was studying programming anyway, the instructors never thought twice about me asking about the gaming software. So, they said nothing when I began to reverse engineer some of it to see how they got things to happen the way it did. Some of the theories, logic, and algorithms were very sophisticated and very advanced even then. It was fascinating.

"So, I did a little experimenting with gaming theory and programming. Even wrote a few sub-routines that have found their way into some major games. Mostly rendering, and some subtle logic loops.

"But that experience showed me how people can get caught up in the games as the graphics and outcomes of the games become closer and closer to reality. It is even more so, now, as all computer programming has advanced, gaming right along with it.

"Then, some time ago, it hit me. That these games were a perfect place to expose younger and younger children to the agendas that the world elite want pushed. In even apparently innocuous teaching games.

"After interactive internet gaming started getting big, I had another epiphany. Now, games did not have to be pre-programed with the messages, with little way to guide and direct the people once they were in their homes. And schools in many cases. Now, real time changes could be made on the game databases and operating programs. What could start as an essentially benign game, could be slowly rewritten over time, after players became acquainted with it, and, as usual, demanded bigger and better versions, to include what the elite wanted the population to assimilate and accept, without question.

"With the intense action, the powerful music, and realistic graphics, young minds, and less well-educated minds, were and are susceptible to having their minds programed with whatever the elite want."

Horatio thought he was going to fall forward off the chair when Penny stopped speaking. She had drawn him in and he had been leaning further and further forward, taking in every word she said.

"My Lord!" he said, half under his breath. The "How can we stop this?" came out a bit stronger.

"I am not sure we can, Horatio. More people do seem to be more aware of the possibility, and I and a handful of others are trying to get some evidence that it is not just speculation, but actually happening, and being directed by... well... government. Or persons unknown.

"We have hacked some of the online systems, and found some curious sub-routines and other programming, but nothing in any way a smoking gun or proof of intent. Certainly, no indication of who might be directing it. We do know who is writing many of the games, and it does not seem to be the major players in the off-line markets.

"But some of the smaller developers are beginning to look suspicious. And the interactive internet stuff is just a huge system, waiting to be messed with. And much of that is being done by anonymous programmers that are almost impossible to trace. It could be being controlled and directed by anyone."

"Oh," Horatio said, obviously disappointed.

"What I do know," Penny said, standing up again, "is that we need to be ready to deal with the outcome if their plans do come to fruition, before something else they might have in the works does first. Or a natural disaster of apocalyptic proportions occurs."

Penny came around the desk, her eyes on Horatio. She took his right hand in her left and tugged slightly. "Come on. I want to show you what I have accomplished on the property." She grinned up at him then and added, "And then I want to hear all about your Suburban."

Horatio followed her lead, as they walked side-by-side, Penny's hand firmly in his. There was still much work being done, in some areas of the property, with workers and equipment visible through the trees in several places.

He did a double take when he really saw the house that had been built. Horatio had, of course, noticed that a house had been built, but his attention was on Penny when they had parked. Now, his wide eyes took in the substantial structure.

"That is huge!" Horatio gasped, trying to take in the whole thing at once. It was well back from where the original paved area was, which should have put it down the slight slope. But, Horatio realized, there had been some dirt work done, actually putting the house on a slight rise in relation to the road and paved area.

"Not as quite as big inside, as it looks outside, Horatio," Penny replied. "Come see." Penny led him over to the entryway of the house. There was a ramp incorporated, as well as the steps. up to the enclosed entry porch.

"That is split face CMU, isn't it?" Horatio asked as he looked closely at the exterior of the home.

"Yes," Penny said with a smile. "Commonly known as concrete block, with a rough surface."

Horatio's eyes tried to take in everything, but Penny tugged his hand slightly, to get him to go through the double front doors. He suddenly looked more closely at the door frame.

"Wait," he said, studying the construction. "And the ICFs, too?" Horatio asked, turning to look at Penny.

Penny smiled. "Yes, it is. The CMU wall is twelve inches thick, filled with concrete, with basalt rebar all through it. But inside of that is a seventeen-inch thick insulating concrete forms wall, again with the concrete fill with basalt rebar throughout.

"The actual finish wall, inside," Penny continued, leading Horatio into the entry, "is a six-inch insulated framed wall with three-quarter inch plywood over three-quarter inch sheetrock, finished with the various materials you see."

"Wow! That is amazing. Just like you explained it to me before. And the whole house is like that?"

Penny grinned. "Yep. And you haven't seen anything yet!"

Up went Horatio's left eyebrow, and Penny laughed. "Come on. The upstairs is pretty standard, other than construction. The real important things are down below."

"Basement, I take it?" Horatio asked.

"Well, yes. But more."

"More?" Horatio asked.

Again, Penny grinned. "More. The basement, again, is pretty much standard open area, with columns here and there. But it does have a protection factor of well over one hundred thousand. The actual shelter is below the basement.

"All the infrastructure is in place, of course, but, like the rest of the place, it still needs the finishing touches."

As they went down to the basement, using the elevator that was behind the main staircase, Horatio tugged Penny closer to his side. "I've missed you, Penny."

"I have you, too, Horatio." She squeezed his hand.

Then they were in the basement. As Penny had said, the basement was structurally complete, but was not yet finished out, Horatio saw when the elevator stopped and the door opened. But Penny stayed where she was. She opened the control panel and pushed a button hidden behind it. The door closed and they were going down again.

When the elevator door opened this time, Horatio's mouth dropped open. "Holy Cow!" He turned wide eyes to Penny. "This is huge!"

Penny nodded. "Yes. The shelter is an independent structure, with supporting columns to support its roof, which has five feet of earth cover. Extra concrete columns and beams are in appropriate places to support the foundation of the house.

"The shelter has a PF of over ten million. Besides the elevator, there are three other independent entrances, and three hidden escape tunnels with camouflaged access points."

"You have really done it up right. Just like you talked about," Horatio said, more than a little impressed. "And the other things?"

"All on track. Almost completed. Will be in less than a month."

"Amazing," Horatio said, his eyes going from one thing to another as they wandered through the open area. Horatio saw the arrangements for enclosing various areas. And then he realized that the edges of the open area were not the outer walls, but internal walls, behind which were completed rooms.

Suddenly Penny stopped. "Wait," She said. "I just remembered. You said there was more than the Suburban?"

Horatio nodded. "Yes. I... uh... Well... You inspired me. I've been working on my preps non-stop since... Well, quite a while now. Um... I may have stepped on your toes a little," he said, putting his hands on her shoulders and looking down into her eyes.

"There was a piece of property you were checking out... On the lake. The realtor contacted the office, looking for you. I... uh... went out and looked at it... and bought it."

"Oh, Horatio! That's okay. I have this place. I thought I contacted everyone I had looking for places to cancel the search. I guess I missed one."

"You don't mind?"

"Of course not." She dropped her eyes, then looked up at his again. "I... You have a place here, Horatio. You know that, don't you?"

Horatio nodded. "Yes. I know. And the other place... It's a back-up now. You know. Just in case?"

Penny smiled. "Of course. Definitely my way of thinking. Come on. I want to show you the rest of what I've done."

Again, with Penny in the lead, they took one of the alternate entrances to leave the shelter and went up to look over the rest of the property.

It was almost dark when the two reentered the construction office. Two men were waiting for Penny, to discuss the next day's work schedule.

Horatio watched as Penny went over everything with the two men. It was obvious that they had learned to respect her, for they listened intently, and when they had their instructions, the two nodded and left the office, obviously more than willing to do as instructed.

Penny looked over and saw the look on Horatio's face. "Horatio?" she asked.

"You are amazing."

Penny's smile was shy. "Thank you. But..."

"No buts, Penny. You are. And have made me a better person for being so."

"What now?" Penny asked.

"Now... Well... I was thinking a short courtship... and then marriage?"

"I like that plan!" Penny said going around the desk and into his arms for another kiss.

"Come on. I will fix us some supper," Penny said, finally slipping from Horatio's arms. She led him to her truck.

"You aren't staying in the house?" Horatio asked.

Penny shook her head. "Not yet. It... I don't know. Until it's completely ready... I just kind of want to wait until it is complete, you know?"

Horatio nodded. "Yeah. I can see that. Actually, I kind of feel the same way. I had no intention in moving things into my place until it was completely ready."

Penny grinned. "I don't know if you are beginning to think like me, or vice versa."

With a chuckle, Horatio said, "Whichever, I sure am glad we are thinking it together. What can I do to help with supper?"

For the next few days, Horatio and Penny discussed anything and everything that came to mind. Including their plans for the future. It was left unsaid that there would come the time that Horatio would officially propose to Penny. For now, it was getting to know one another.

Despite the desire he saw in Penny's eyes, Horatio was careful to keep their romance limited to passionate kisses. He already knew enough about Penny to know that she was a woman that would not give herself to anyone without being committed completely through marriage. He would not put any kind of pressure on her, despite the longings he had.

Penny appreciated Horatio's understanding and showed him in many ways. She was affectionate, but very careful not to give him any false signs that she would consider anything but waiting until after they were married to take things any further than their kisses.

Tuesday rolled around, and Horatio delayed as long as he could before he kissed Penny one last time and climbed into the Suburban to head for home. Penny stood and watched the Suburban until the gates closed behind him. She sighed and turned back to begin the final phases of getting the place ready for whatever the future held.

Horatio did basically the same thing, including, like Penny, finishing up the work on his property. He was also reading the forums several times a day, and watching the news even more closely than before, looking for anything and everything relating to unusual happenings.

And he was not liking what he was seeing. With what Penny had told him about Addictive Entertainment, little things were beginning to add up. He was not discounting the other things that were happening, the political unrest, the economy, the social situations, and the many natural disasters that were seeming to hover, just waiting to bust loose.

But he kept coming back to one event that had happened the first day back to the office after his trip to see Penny. Melissa, usually punctual to a fault, came in almost ten minutes late.

"Are you okay, Melissa?" Horatio had asked.

She looked flustered as she answered. "I'm sorry, Horatio. Yes, yes, I'm okay." Melissa quickly put away her purse and sat down at the reception desk.

"My cousin's ornery son, Zach, had some kind of emotional breakdown. I had to get Shelia home this morning from the hospital."

"Hospital?" Horatio asked as Melissa booted up her computer.

Melissa shook her head. "Yes. They had to take Zach to the hospital. He was… well… violent, Sheila said. Then he just went catatonic all of a sudden. They called an ambulance and everything."

"I am so sorry, Melissa. Is there anything I can do?"

Melissa shook her head. "No, Horatio. The psychologist told Sheila that it would just take some time to get to the root of his problem."

"Do you know what caused the breakdown?"

"It is so silly. He was punished for not turning in his homework several times lately. Sheila put her foot down and pulled his gaming system and internet access, except for education sites. He's big into gaming, including the internet interactive games. Sheila said he has won some big-time competitions. I guess he just couldn't handle the punishment."

"I see," Horatio said thoughtfully. He turned to go back to his office but turned back to Melissa. "Melissa, do you know if there have been any other incidents like this in Zack's school and circle of friends?"

"Not that I know of," Melissa replied. But then she said, "Well, except for Audrey Paul. She didn't have a breakdown or anything, but Sheila told me that she has been causing problems at school. Violating some of the computer use restrictions in the computer club systems. Apparently. she managed to hack the system and get internet access to gaming sites for the other members of the club.

"Audrey can only use the school computers with direct supervision now. Sheila was surprised Audrey wasn't kicked out of the computer club and her access cut off completely to the school computers. But the computer lab teacher talked the school administration out of it. Promised that he would deactivate the access and keep a closer eye on her, and everyone else using the system. It is crazy. All this fuss over computer access." Melissa started typing.

"Yeah. Yeah," muttered Horatio as he went back to his office. He had plenty of work to get done after his short vacation and filed the information about the school computer situation in the back of his head.

When he called Penny that night, on the schedule they had set up, Horatio told Penny about Zack and Audrey.

"Has anyone checked the computers to see if access has actually been limited again?" Penny asked.

"I don't know, Penny. Surely that teacher would…"

"Horatio, anyone that is a gamer could be getting brought into that web. Things seem to be going faster than we anticipated."

"I will see what I can find out," Horatio said. Then the discussion turned to more personal matters.

A month later, when Penny came to visit Horatio and get a look at his new place, the first thing Horatio said, after he greeted Penny with a hug and a kiss was, "Glen Hastings, that computer lab teacher? He is a gamer. Apparently really big into it."

"Oh, no!" Penny said softly. "That is not good. Have there been any more incidents at the school?"

Horatio shook his head. "No. But when I made inquiries about whether or not the computer system had been inspected, I got the runaround from the school administration."

"Hm." Penny looked thoughtful, and as they went into Horatio's house she asked him, "Have you seen some of the other things going on? The attacks on parents by their children? Attacks on teachers by their students? And all the violent flash mob incidents?"

"Some of them, at least," Horatio said as they took seats on the sofa and Horatio pulled Penny next to him and put his arm around her. "Are you saying they are related?"

"I think so, Horatio. It is hard to get information about children's actions, since their privacy is protected by law. But from what I, and a couple of others have found out, that each one of the attacks was done by a gamer, or a fanatical listener to a dozen or so specific music groups.

"The flash mobs, in the few that we were able to get inside information about, were all set up by a small group of gamers in each area, though most of the actual participants were not actually gamers. They seemed to just get caught up in the violence when it started."

"Do you think..." Horatio shook his head. "Do you think that attack on the police headquarters in that medium sized town in Iowa was a part of that? Those weren't all teens."

"Horatio, there are a lot of young, and not so young, adults into gaming and some of that type of music." Penny frowned. "And I am worried about that movie of the week coming out next weekend. It is being touted as a family friendly movie, especially done so children could watch it with their parents."

"That's an animated movie," Horatio said. "What could there be..."

"It is one of the old fables. A fairytale. And Horatio, some of those old stories were meant to scare children into doing, or not doing, certain things. They were much more violent than their current sanitized versions.

"I do not know what this one is, but if they have taken one of those, and incorporated their propaganda into it, in the guise of a G-rated children's movie, there could be some unanticipated repercussions. Unanticipated, at least, buy many of the people involved. But if they... whomsoever 'they' are, have gotten their hooks into another media company, anything could happen. They are good at covering their tracks."

They left it at that, had supper, and then settled in for an enjoyable evening, which ended with Penny taking up residence in Horatio's guest room again.

The next day, a Saturday, Horatio took Penny out to his property, proudly explaining everything that had been done to the Suburban for him.

When they reached the site and pulled up to the main area of the property, Frank and Georgie were waiting for them. Horatio had explained that his old friend and his wife were going to be living on site.

Much to Horatio's amazement, Penny was out of the Suburban almost before it stopped and was running toward Georgie. Who, after an obvious moment of shock, began to move toward Penny.

Frank and Horatio shared a 'What in the world?' look and joined the two women who were now in a fierce hug.

"I can't believe it!" Georgie said, finally stepping back and looking at Penny.

"I know," Penny said. She looked at Horatio. "You didn't tell me it was Georgie Peterson!"

"Uh..." Horatio stammered.

"nee Peterson now," Georgie said. She put her arm around Frank's waist. "It's Georgie Goodwind now. This is my husband, Frank."

Penny shook Frank's outstretched hand. He looked over at Georgie and asked, "This is the Penny you are always talking about?"

Georgie nodded. Frank looked back at Penny, who turned bright red when Frank said, "Wow! You are quite a legend."

"Don't embarrass her, Frank. I told you she is rather shy." Georgie grinned at Penny. "So... You and Horatio, huh? He never mentioned you."

Looking at Horatio, Georgie added, "Shame on you, Horatio. This is one of the nicest people on the planet and you didn't tell us she was your girlfriend."

"Well... Uh..." Horatio stammered again.

"Oh, Georgie! Behave!" Penny said, taking Horatio's hand in hers. "We've just gotten together. Well, after meeting and then going our separate ways for a while." She looked at Horatio, and then back at Georgie. "But we are definitely together now."

Georgie nodded. "Well good. You deserve a good guy. And Frank has told me several times how good a man Horatio is. Congratulations. Both of you."

"How do the two of you know each other?" Horatio asked.

"We met online, on one of the prepper forums." Penny glanced over at Georgie before she continued. "As we got to know one another as our forum personas, sharing ideas on prepping, sometimes very different ones on a subject..."

Georgie laughed, but did not say anything, so Penny continued. "Finally, after each of us was comfortable with one another, we exchanged Private Messages on the forum, and discovered we were near each other. We finally decided to meet and greet and have been fast friends ever since. We just did not get to see one another as much after Georgie was transferred to another assignment."

"Those were some good times, girl," Georgie said, giving Penny another hug.

"Yes, they were," Penny replied. Her hand slipped back into Horatio's.

"You want the grand tour?" Frank asked Penny.

Penny looked up at Horatio. "Frank can give a better tour than I can," Horatio admitted. "He has been here far more than I have and supervised and been involved in the construction even more than I have."

Penny merely lifted her eyebrows when Frank went around to the other side of the Mercedes-Benz motorhome and returned on the tracked wheelchair. A few moments later the other three were following Frank as he went through the property, describing all the details.

Penny was suitably impressed, and said so to not only Horatio, but to Frank and Georgie for their part in getting the place put together. After the tour, Horatio and Penny headed back to town. First, for a few games of bowling, and then a nice dinner out before they went back to Horatio's house.

The next day, Sunday, both got on their respective computers and began to order additional stocks of many different items to add to those already on order for each, for delivery within another week. Neither had wanted to put in such a large single order that it would cause problems for the suppliers, and for other customers they might have. Better, both had decided, to space orders out.

It was especially important for Horatio since he did not have nearly as much storage space early on as Penny did at her place. They had discussed such things during the last month, among many others, and decided that each would put in monthly orders over the next several months, until they had what they wanted, or something happened that would prevent them from getting any more.

It was not just long-term storage food. The various orders included many other types of consumables, as well as third and fourth tier backups of much of the hardware and equipment, especially critical items.

Both computers sounded annunciators at the same time. Penny had helped Horatio set up most of the same online monitors on his computers that

Penny used on hers to keep informed about dozens of different types of potential problems.

Unfortunately, for several reasons, the monitors were sounding alarms almost every day for one thing or another. The search algorithm Penny had written to find news about anything that could be linked to her theory about Addictive Entertainment was finding far more incidents than even she expected this soon.

Many were very subtle connections, that most people would never even think to connect to any type of organized effort through gaming and the other venues that Penny was sure were being used to try and influence and control people.

But Horatio was as sure it was happening as Penny was. After her explanations in more detail, Horatio had no problem seeing the connections, tenuous as some of them were.

It was the Monday after that next weekend, the day Penny went back to her place, that it hit home for Horatio. The two had watched the Movie of the Week that Penny had mentioned the previous weekend.

It was just as he had feared. That 'sweet fairytale' story was loaded with messages that were part and parcel of the elite's agenda. There was something that Penny had not been aware of, as it apparently had been a closely guarded secret, right up to the beginning of the movie. An interactive online game started fifteen minutes after the movie started, based on what was happening in the movie while it was being aired.

The game not only continued through and just after the movie, it was going to be online permanently. Nothing seemed to occur until early the next morning. And at that, what did occur, only those looking for a connection would have any chance of seeing one.

But things were happing. Horatio could attest to that shortly after he got to work. Fortunately, Melissa had arrived early at the office, to get ready for a client meeting Horatio had scheduled for later that morning.

He had walked into the office just before the time Melissa usually arrived. A few seconds after the front door closed there was a strong explosion that rattled the doors and the glass in the windows.

Melissa screamed and dropped down beneath her desk. Horatio dropped down to his hands and knees, crowded up against the outer side of Melissa's desk. When nothing else happened, other than the shouts and screaming that barely filtered into the building, Horatio got back onto his feet cautiously.

He moved to the door, again, very carefully, ready to lurch back if something else happened. Carefully easing the door open, Horatio took a quick look outside. What he saw had him closing and locking the door quickly, and then activating the security shutters that he had added recently, based on Penny's recommendations.

Though he did not own the building, Horatio had been able, after considerable persuasion and agreeing to pay half the cost, to get the landlord to have them installed. Horatio paid the full cost of the enhanced security system he wanted, since the landlord deemed the existing one adequate.

It was a near thing, as quick as Horatio was. Something hit both the window and door, down low, before the shutters fully closed. But no damage was done, and the shutters locked into place.

Horatio hurried to his office and turned on his computer, saying to Melissa as he passed her, "I think you are safe to get up now, but go into the break room and let yourself calm down. I do not want you to have to listen to that banging."

The shutters were being pounded on with who knew what, and while there was no danger, it was a very annoying sound, and obviously frightening to Melissa.

With the computer up and running, Horatio looked at the separate large monitor that was the multi-image display from the outside cameras that were part of the new system.

"Geez!" Horatio muttered as he took in one image after another, from all directions around the building. There were hundreds of people, from older children, to middle aged adults milling around in groups of mobs, each one targeting one of the businesses in the mall.

He could see his own building with remote wireless cameras that had been installed on two of the light poles in the parking lot. Without permission, but so far, the mall management had not complained. They showed a much smaller mob banging on the shutters on the windows and doors, as well as what were obviously futile attacks on the brick walls of the building.

Horatio listened to the individual directional microphones one after the other. What little he could understand, with all the noise, was more or less gibberish. The occasional word shouted a bit more clearly than the rest varied but were of a common theme.

"Hate!"; "Unfair!"; "Kill!"; "Fault!"; "Oppressors!"; "Not Right!"; "Our Right!"; and several more words in the same vein.

When police sirens began to approach, many people started to move away from the mall, though very slowly it seemed to Horatio. But at least now he was able to hear a few more words. And got an extreme chill down his back when he recognized many of the words, phrases, and names of characters from the animated fairytale Movie of the Week aired the night before.

The police arrived while at least half of all those in the various mobs were still there. And the police were quickly outnumbered, by people that seemed more than willing to take some fairly extreme punishment. They attacked the police with anything and everything at hand that had been pulled from the attacked and looted stores. And, Horatio saw, some things that had to have been brought to the mall from outside as there were no stores in the mall that carried anything like them.

The most terrifying one was what appeared to be a homemade flame thrower. Fortunately, it did not work well, or for long, but well enough and long enough to set all five police cars on fire. And nearly caught several officers in its flames. The additional units, including fire and ambulance vehicles, got stopped and reversed out of range of the flamethrower just as the stream dribbled out and died.

The wielder, despite the several shots that had been fired at him by various police officers, managed to flee. Horatio saw him stumble once and was sure one of the rounds had hit the guy, but he straightened up and kept running. "Body armor," Horatio muttered to himself. "Penny knows her stuff, for sure," he added.

Penny had directed Horatio to a few specialty shops, along with many other prepper related businesses. One of them was a source of high quality, effective body armor. Another one, that Horatio had doubted very vocally was legal, but it turned out to be, was a flamethrower company catering to civilians. Producing much better, and more effective versions of the flamethrower that Horatio had just seen.

Things began to calm down as more and more people left the area on a run after the flamethrower use and the shooting, though, Horatio noted, the police and other public service personnel seemed to be every bit as agitated as those in the mob had been. Many were cursing loudly; kicking at things on the parking lot pavement; pounding vehicle hoods, trunks, and sides with their fists or night sticks.

Horatio sat up very straight when he saw a shop owner easing his way out of the shop he owned, looking around with care. When one of the police officers saw him, the officer shouted and several more ran over with him to the man. For a moment Horatio thought the police were going to beat the guy down, but a couple of other officers that seemed much more in control of themselves put a stop to it and the shop owner ran off while he had a chance.

"Not just... ordinary people..." Horatio whispered to himself. "Even those in authority..." Horatio's eyes widened. "Except the elite, of course, and those of us that have not been exposed to the steady, building influence of the Addictive Entertainment phenomenon."

Things seemed to be calming down outside now, and Horatio leaned back in his chair for a moment, still watching the monitor, but thinking, as well.

When his phone buzzed he picked up the receiver. It was Melissa. "Horatio?" she asked, her voice low and quivering.

"I will be right there, Melissa. Things are okay now." Horatio did not add the thought that continued in his head, "For the moment."

Horatio hurried into the break room to find Melissa huddled in a chair, half inside a storage closet. She was shaking, and had obviously been crying, although her tears had been wiped away.

"Come on. Get your things, Melissa. I will follow you home, so I know you got there safely."

"Oh, thank you, Horatio!" she said, getting up and running to him for quick, hard hug. "I was terrified I would have to go out there alone."

"Nope," Horatio said firmly. "I will be right with you until you are locked in your car, and then behind you all the way home."

Melissa nodded and hurried to gather up her coat and purse. She started to do the routine shut down as an afterthought, but Horatio told her not to bother. He would take care of it later, as well as deal with his clients.

Thankful for his words, Melissa went over to the door and stood aside while Horatio checked his smartphone and logged into his security site. The security system fed into the internet and he was able to access the cameras from his cellular phone as long as he had cell service. The police were well away from the office, though still present in the mall.

Horatio triggered the door shutter and was ready as soon as it was high enough to open the door. He did not bother locking the door again, just triggering the shutter down with the remote as he pulled Melissa close to him. "Where are you parked today? I don't see your car." he said.

Melissa softly said, "Over by... Oh Lord!" It was a half scream. One hand went to her mouth, and the other pointed to where several cars had been parked. Now most were on their side or roof, all with broken out windows and front and rear glass.

Melissa's car was one of those that was upside down. "I will get you home," Horatio reassured Melissa. "Try not to worry."

Horatio had taken to parking right next to the building, after getting the Suburban, to establish a bit of a pattern so people would be less likely to park in that spot, though it was not actually a reserved spot. He wanted to be able to plug the Suburban in to a set of connectors that he had managed to run out through a vent in the eaves of the roof, through some steel conduit, to a security box on the side of the building.

He could hook up an electrical connection to power the various winter heating systems in the Suburban, as well as a computer network cable so he could access the computers installed in the Suburban. The computers were not part of the vehicle system, but laptops that contained a myriad of prepping information as well as working programs.

He could interconnect through Bluetooth but did not want a signal that could be intercepted. Not only were the lines protected with flexible metallic conduit grounded through the building system, but the lines had EMP protective devices in-line so even if an EMP occurred, the pulse would be blocked before it could get into the Suburban, which had its own EMP protection.

But that had nothing to do with the current crises, Horatio decided, when the thoughts went through his head. So, he guided Melissa to the Suburban. It was untouched, in part, Horatio thought, because not only was it well away from any other vehicles, the subtle camouflage paint job made it relatively difficult to notice.

Primarily a tan color, with very carefully blended in other earth colors that created the very subtle pattern. Though it used different colors, the blending was reminiscent of that used in the camouflaged covers used by the Rebels in the *Star Wars* movie, *Revenge of the Jedi*.

Rather than sharp-edge color patterns, each color was blended into the adjoining one, so there were no lines to draw the eye. Other than the windshield, the camouflage pattern covered the other glass on the Suburban, using a tinting material with the pattern incorporated into it.

A click of his remote and Horatio had the front passenger door open and helped Melissa inside. He ran around to the driver's side and climbed in. He hit the door locks and activated the security system components that were used while the vehicle was occupied.

Driving carefully, but as quickly as was prudent with the many people still wandering the streets, Horatio made his way to Melissa's apartment building.

As soon as Horatio turned onto Melissa's street, Melissa let out another gasp, amounting to a soft scream. She stared at a building about halfway down the street, on their left. There were three police vehicles parked, lights flashing, and a dozen or more people milling around. There did not seem to be any violence, at least not at the moment.

Horatio stopped. "Melissa?" he asked gently, turning toward her in his seat.

Melissa was hugging herself, huddled in the passenger seat, crying mostly silent tears. "My parents... Could you take me to my parents' house?"

Her words were quiet, but Horatio saw the begging in her eyes and nodded curtly. "Of course, Melissa. Whatever you want."

Melissa managed to stutter out the address, and Horatio backed up into a driveway, turned around, and headed across town, taking a very roundabout route to avoid anything happening down town.

And there was much happening Horatio learned, at least in the few minutes he had the broadcast radio on. After a couple of reports of similar violence, Melissa whimpered, and after one quick look at her, Horatio turned the radio off. He would find out more after he dropped her off.

Though it took a while, Horatio got Melissa to her parents, settled in, with instructions not to worry about work until he got in touch with her. He reassured her that she still had a job, and they would figure something out about her transportation.

Horatio made better time back to his house, with the radio on now. He had also turned on some of the other communications systems, as well. The Public Service Band scanner was stopping again only moments after each transmission it picked up ended. Fire, police, ambulance, county sheriff, state patrol, city services, and even quite a few commercial service outfits such as tow trucks, power company, and more were handling incident after incident. Almost all of them were related to the same thing, though not everyone in positions of authority believed that.

There was quite a bit of local amateur radio traffic on the UHF and VHF bands, as well as the occasional conversation on the frequency he monitored on the HF band during that time of day.

He was hearing similar reports from all over the country, and there were reports of similar things happening in Canada, Mexico, most of Europe and Central and South America. Even in parts of the Russian and Chinese spheres of influence. Not much from Africa, other than South Africa and a few of the northern areas of that continent. But most were only the sketchiest of reports that indicated things were happening, but not in very much detail, when any.

Once home, Horatio was glad that Penny had got him into the habit of locking down the house every time he left. Just as at the office, Horatio had installed sophisticated security systems, including the door and window shutters.

As he drove into the garage, he could see a few rocks, several bottles, and one red brick lying on the ground at the garage door, front door and one of the front windows. There was no damage, of course, but the same could not be said for a couple of his neighbors.

He saw them walking over as he pulled into the garage, so stepped back outside as the doors went back down. His next-door neighbor, Alfonso Paine, was obviously agitated. "Can you believe those punks! Man, when I find out who they are they are, they are going to pay, I can tell you that much! Sue them and their parents for every dime they got!"

The neighbor on the other side of Alfonso, Juliette Manners, was trying to calm Alfonso down, without much success. Alfonso took a deep breath, ready to continue his tirade, but Juliette hurriedly spoke, cutting him off.

"It was terrible, Horatio. Terrible." She cut a side glance at Alfonso, hesitating just enough for Horatio to ask a question.

"What happened, exactly, or as close as you can come to it?"

Again, Juliette spoke first, and Alfonso was too much the old-school gentleman to interrupt her. "There were at least twenty-five or thirty of them, Horatio. All ages. Mostly younger people, but I saw one guy that must have in his late fifties or early sixties.

"They were all screaming some nonsense that I never did understand clearly. They just walked down the street, picking up anything and everything loose, and threw it at the houses. Sometimes one or more would come up onto a yard and throw something. Those are the ones that broke that beautiful picture window in Alonso's house.

"It scared poor Judith half to death, and Cuddles even more. They are lying down for now, while we watch for the carpenters to come out and board up our windows. Neither of us could get ahold of any of the glass companies."

Another quick eye cut to Alfonso, and Juliette could see he was still red in the face. Wanting to give him time to calm down, she spoke again before he could.

"Almost everyone on the block has some kind of damage. I only had the glass in my front storm door broken, and one window in my front bedroom. Some got it even worse than Alfonso. I think the Hendricks even had a fire start from something that was thrown inside through a window that had already been broken.

"I think your place is the only one unscathed. You were lucky you got those shutters installed."

Horatio did not mention that it was not luck. It was planning. Inspired by Penny, yes, but Horatio had seen the need early on in his process of learning about prepping.

Thankfully, Alfonso had calmed down somewhat. Like Juliette, Horatio had worried a bit about the event causing him enough stress to have yet another heart attack. He was prone to stress heart attacks, having already had three in the last eight years. Alfonso had gone to anger and stress counseling, but this event had been too much for the veteran to take.

He spoke relatively calmly when he addressed Horatio. "Horatio, would you take the case, if we find out who they were, and we sue them?"

Horatio was careful not to just dismiss the idea, not wanting to add to Alfonso's stress. "We will have to wait a bit before I can answer, Alfonso. Assuming they can be identified, the cases will have to go through criminal court before I could file any kind of suit."

Knowing there was no way a suit like that would ever be adjudicated, Horatio still told Alfonso and Juliette, "It would be a good idea to document the damage and get good clear receipts for any work done relating to the repairs. If it goes to civil court, you definitely want all your ducks in a row, and have all the information to present a clear and complete case."

Juliette and Alfonso were both nodding thoughtfully. "Good idea, Horatio. Thanks," Alfonso said. "Hey!" he suddenly added, "Why are you here at this time of day? I was sure you had told me you were going to be up to your eyeballs today and tomorrow, when we were talking about the weather a few days ago."

Horatio nodded. "Yeah. We got it at the mall, too. The office and the Suburban were fine, but Melissa's car was trashed and burned with a bunch of others, including some police cars. There were a large number of business invaded and looted, fires set, and even some shots were fired."

"Oh, my! We didn't know!" Juliette said, a hand going to her throat in shock.

"No. Power is on, but cablevision is off, and nobody is saying much on the radio," Alfonso told Horatio.

"I see," Horatio said thoughtfully, his eyes focusing off in the distance for a moment as he started tweaking his plan on how to handle such situations.

He brought his focus back onto Juliette and Alfonso. "You guys need me to wait with you? There are some things I should probably be doing for my clients, since there is no way they will let people in and out of that mall the way it is."

"No, no," Juliette quickly replied, glancing at Alfonso. "We'll be just fine. The carpenter said he should be here within another hour. We are first on the list on this street."

Alfonso nodded in agreement, back to his much calmer self.

"Okay, then. I am going inside and start making some calls." With that, Horatio triggered the remote in his pocket to open the front door shutters and went inside. Though he took a couple of steps away from the door, headed for the kitchen, he stepped back and triggered the door shutter to close.

The way Penny had set up the syncing system on the computers, Horatio's laptop had the same current information as the office system had. So, after cleaning up a bit, and getting something to drink, Horatio went to his study, fired up the laptop and got busy.

His first call was to the client with whom he was supposed to meet that morning. Just a few minutes from the time of the call, actually. Fortunately, although the man had headed toward Horatio's office, he had been turned around and sent home, despite being rather aggressive with the police that had cordoned off the area.

"Yes, Mr. Smotherman. Just as soon as I find out when I can get back to the office, I will call you and we will continue pursuing the case."

Horatio felt a chill when Tony Smotherman threatened Horatio. "You'd better, dude. You lawyers and judges and the cops and... all those others... they are destroying this country. And I will not stand for it. Not anymore. You mess me around and you'll be the first one we take out."

Smotherman had slammed the phone down. Horatio set his receiver down into the cradle a bit more slowly, more than a bit concerned. "Penny!" he suddenly said out loud.

He dialed the cellular number that was the number for the Chevy Kodiak's built in communications system.

Penny picked up immediately. They spoke at almost exactly the same time, the very same words. "Are you alright?"

After assurances from each to the other, and after Penny explained she was still on the road, on the interstate, with traffic being relatively normal, Horatio filled her in on what had happened with him. Including the threat Smotherman had made.

Horatio heard Penny gasp slightly, and then fall silent. "Penny?" Horatio asked, suddenly worried at her silence.

"I am here, Horatio. Sorry. I was... am... thinking. You are safe right now, correct? At home, locked down?"

Hearing some concern in her voice, Horatio reassured her that he was. Then heard a slight hesitation in her voice when she spoke again. "Horatio... Look, I know it is not my place... And I know how much drive you have to help people... But... Please, stay home for a while? Until I can figure out the best plan of action? The rest of today and tomorrow? I will not ask for more."

Horatio considered her plea for only a fraction of a second. "I will, Penny. I promise. Unless... Unless..."

"I know, Horatio," Penny said softly. "I will not ask you to make a promise that you cannot be sure you can keep. Just be extra careful, if you do have to go out."

"I will, Penny. I will. I love you, you know."

"I know Horatio. And I love you back with all my heart."

Horatio hung up slowly, still worried somewhat about Penny, but he was well aware of just how capable she was, and how intelligent. She would be fine. He sighed, picked up the receiver, and dialed another number.

It took another full hour to contact all his clients, check in with the courthouse, and make the arrangements needed to continue with his business, and meet the requirements the judges had laid down to keep the judicial system running during the next few days of the event.

And that was what everyone seemed to consider it. Just a group of isolated, coincidental, events, that would be taken care of and cleaned up in just a few days, to a week or so.

Horatio was not so sure. But, the last time he and Penny had discussed the possibilities that might occur after the airing of the movie, Penny was fairly confident that, although something would happen, that the activity would die down for a while. The movie was just a first major trial of what those that were doing this, had planned long term.

After Horatio had caught up the computer work about the changes, he finally realized he had not checked in with Frank, and that Frank had not called him, either.

Horatio hurriedly dialed Frank's cell phone number. He was relieved when Frank immediately answered. "You guys alright there in town? Been watching the news until it went off, and from what Georgie and I are hearing from the other sources, this rioting is pretty widespread.

"I thought about calling to see if you were alright but figured if you needed help you would contact us, and if not, a call might just get in the way of what you were doing."

"I am fine. So is the office and my house. Melissa's car was turned over, trashed, and burned. Penny is okay. I have talked to her..." Horatio paused when he heard Frank telling Georgie that Penny was alright.

"'K. Back." Frank said a moment later.

"Okay. I take it everything is okay out there?"

"Yep. If we had not been watching the news, we probably would not have known anything was going on. It is quiet out here. Though we did start hearing some boats whizzing around out on the lake through the security mikes and cameras monitoring the lake. Nothing even close to us, though."

"Good. Good." Horatio thought for a moment, and then asked Frank, "You guys comfortable about being out there on your own for the next few days? You can come…"

Frank cut him off with a bark of a laugh. "Horehound! Of course, we are comfortable out here. You forget who you are talking to? But is there anything in particular you want us to be doing the next few days?"

There was silence again for a few seconds as Horatio thought. "No. I guess not. Just be careful. Especially when you are out and about on the property."

"Sure thing, Horehound. We are already monitoring the 2-meter repeaters. So, if we lose cell contact, try that first, and if the repeaters go down, go to simplex."

"Yes. That sounds good, Frank. I will talk to you later. And if I come out there I will try to give you notice."

"Yeah," Frank said with a chuckle. "Very good idea."

With that Horatio hung up the desk telephone and leaned back in the desk chair. He was back on-line now, after the cablevision internet connection went down, and with it, his cable modem internet access.

Though not strictly legal, when Horatio had ordered the communications equipment for the facility, which included three satellite TV and internet small dish systems, he had included another in the order and he and Frank had installed it themselves at the house.

One was not supposed to have a dish if they were serviced by cablevision, and if a person had a dish, they were not supposed to be connected to cablevision. But Horatio wanted the redundancy and was now glad he had made the installation. Not only was he getting internet again, at least parts of it, he was also getting a couple of TV stations, though none of the major MSM stations.

Horatio continued to monitor the radios, TV, and internet until late that evening. He learned essentially nothing new and had lost both the TV stations and more of the internet by the time he went to get a late supper and get ready for bed.

He made sure his NOAA Weather Alert All Hazards radio was on, his cell phone plugged in to charge by his bed and kept a multi-band handheld Amateur radio on the nightstand in case he needed it during the night.

Horatio took a while getting to sleep, but slept soundly, with nothing occurring to wake him. He did hurry through his morning routine. After checking the Weather Channel, which was back up, Horatio checked a few other channels, and since Fox News was available again, too, he left it on, the sound up slightly, as he made and ate breakfast.

But he learned nothing to speak of, at least about what had happened the day before. After checking several other news sources, Horatio shook his head. Nothing relating to the violence, or where it was unavoidable, the violence was laid off to various other situations. Absolutely no mention of the movie of the week, or anything about gaming, computers, or anything related.

Breakfast done, Horatio went to his study, fired up his communications gear, and his laptop. More of the internet was available again, and Horatio checked several sites he was now very familiar with and found quite a few discussions were active about what had happened.

But other sites were not available. The more controversial ones. Still listening to the communications gear, turned low, Horatio made several business-related calls, confirming with his clients when and where he could meet with them until he could get back into his office.

With nothing else he could do business wise, Horatio took the Suburban out of the garage, re-closed the security shutters, and headed to his property, after letting Frank know he was coming out.

He talked to Penny as he drove out. She had made it just fine to her parents' homestead. Just as Horatio was planning to do at his place, Penny was helping her parents double-check everything on their homestead, getting a few things done that they had planned for a while, but had not been considered priorities.

With what was happening, all three decided it would be a very good idea to get them done now.

Doing much the same, Horatio talked things over with Frank and Georgie, discussing what they might have missed in the planning, creation, and supplying the facility. All three wound up shaking their heads.

Between them, and Penny, they felt like they had covered everything it was possible to think of ahead of time, with enough flexibility in the plans, and additional equipment and supplies, to deal with whatever might come up they had not anticipated.

They were in Frank and Georgie's house, which was inside their own small compound in the facility. As Horatio had done the night before and that morning, Frank had his monitoring gear turned on. Suddenly all three sets of eyes turned to the communications consol.

Frank stepped over and sat down in the chair before the console, and Horatio and Georgie moved over and stood flanking Frank. Frank upped the volume on the HF radio. There was a rather heated discussion on-going between an amateur in Tacoma, Washington and one in Dyersburg, Tennessee.

The man in Tacoma was raging about how terrible things were all over the country and was blaming various people and institutions. All directly in line with the message of the movie, and what Penny had explained as her best analysis of what the Elite and The Powers That Be, and possibly, the programmers behind the computer games, and even some of the entertainment industry, with full support of the Main Stream Media, wanted.

The woman in Dyersburg was trying to give a reasonable alternative opinion, but the man kept cutting her off, as his signal was much stronger than hers.

Suddenly there was silence on the frequency. But it was not the silence of a no carrier signal. It was a very powerful, very quiet, dead air carrier, that simply blanked out anyone that did not have a stronger signal.

When all three of them looked at each other first, in surprise, and then at the radio's signal strength meter, they were fairly sure that there would not be anyone with a stronger signal coming in, unless they were parked right outside, as the signal was a full 30dB over S9 in strength.

"Somebody has a very powerful jammer," Frank said, beginning to check many different frequencies on the Amateur Radio HF bands, using another receiver.

"Most likely several of them," Georgie said. "All over the country, unless I miss my guess." She reached over, past Frank, and checked several other radios.

She tuned in several broadcast radio stations. All of them were on the air and broadcasting their normal genre. But none of them, including the all-news stations, were mentioning anything at all about the events occurring in the US and all over the world. Including the jamming being done on the Amateur Radio frequencies, except for those above the 2-meter band.

"Hm..." Frank muttered, and tuned the all-mode, all-band general coverage receiver to several different Land Mobile Radio Service frequencies, usually just called Business Band. And although most business users obtained licenses for the VHF and UHF frequencies, there were HF frequencies allocated to the service. They, too, were being jammed.

It was the same on the International Shortwave frequencies in the Low Frequency, Medium Frequency, and High Frequency bands.

Only some of the Marine and Aircraft HF band frequencies were not jammed, although there was some interference on several of them from the jamming on frequencies close to them.

Frank sat back in the console chair, and Georgie and Horatio pulled chairs over and sat down near him. Suddenly the jamming stopped. After a few seconds, the woman in Dyersburg called for another station that she apparently talked with often on that frequency.

The jamming immediately started again. After several more minutes it stopped. Someone else tried to make a call on the frequency and once again the jamming overrode their signal. This happened a dozen times before there was continuing silence on the frequency, and most of the others, as it became apparent that it was pointless to try to talk. The jamming would simply start again.

Frank left the radios on that he usually monitored, including a Public Service Band scanner, which had not been jammed. More or less routine police, fire, and medical services continued to communicate, as did city and county services.

"That really puts a kink in things," Frank said shortly. "I had no idea that... well, whoever is doing it, could jam that many frequencies at once, and apparently over such a wide area. Takes away one of the best long-range communications methods preppers have."

Georgie moved to the kitchen to get them coffee.

"That is right," Horatio said thoughtfully.

Both men seemed to have the same thought at the same time. Both pulled out their cell phones and tried to make a long-distance call. Neither would go through. Long distance was down. Frank tried the land line. As with the cell phones, local calls would go through, but there was a recording that said that long distance was unavailable due to technical difficulties.

Frank looked over at Horatio. "I don't suppose you have any homing pigeons ordered?"

Horatio managed a smile just as small as the one on Frank's face as he shook his head. "Nope. Afraid not."

Something suddenly occurred to Horatio. "Frank! Do you have your copy of the plan book handy?"

"Sure," Frank replied.

Georgie was setting the tray with the coffee down and said, "I'll get it."

She came back a minute or so later with a tablet computer inside a Faraday cage bag. It was one of several on the property. Each contained not only the plan book, but hundreds of other useful documents, either on the tablet, or loaded on the handful of thumb drives also inside the Faraday cage bag.

There were, of course, also several hard copies of the plan book, and many of the other documents, but using the tablet was much easier than going through the paper copy.

"What are you thinking?" asked Frank.

"I think I remember something…" Horatio muttered, concentrating on scanning the plan book document table of contents.

"Maybe…" he muttered. Frank and Georgie shared an amused glance.

"Yes!" Horatio exclaimed. "Here it is. It is way down in the list of communications options." He began to read. *"In the event that the above methods of communications are unavailable for whatever reason…"* Horatio looked up. "That is pretty much all the other things we have checked, radio wise."

Then he began to read again, *"If a wideband HF transceiver is available, and both Amateur and Business Band frequencies are being monitored or controlled, an attempt may be made using Maritime and Aeronautical HF frequencies. However, this may bring unwanted attention, but should definitely be considered, using appropriate communications protocols to avoid risk."*

Horatio looked up at Frank and Georgie. "It goes on to list some frequencies. And a reference to the cypher section, and to the clandestine radio operating section."

Frank nodded. "Okay. So at least Penny, and probably her parents, would go to those frequencies if needed. I will get them into one of the scanning HF receivers."

"Good," Horatio said. "And, I suspect that there are some others in Penny's network of prepper friends, the close ones, probably have the same plan. But for the moment, I don't think it is something we need to consider."

"True," Frank replied, leaning back in the chair. "I know this is serious. But I simply do not believe it is a long-term event. A couple of more days. Tops."

Georgie poked Frank in the shoulder. "Don't be too sure, Sweetie. It might not be really long-term, but I have a feeling it may be more than a couple days."

Horatio nodded. "I am afraid so, too." Now he shook his head. "I sure hope it doesn't last very long. Not just because of the actual problems, but… I don't know. I just do not feel ready. For anything, really…"

Frank and Georgie both smiled. "You will get over that, Horatio," said Georgie. "New preppers almost never think they are as prepared as they often are."

"Then again," Frank interjected, "some new preppers think they are way more prepared than they are."

Horatio grimaced, and Frank laughed. "Not you, Horatio," he said then. "You really are well prepared. And no one is, or can be, prepared for everything. Mainly because no one can anticipate everything."

Horatio smiled. "Yeah. I know," he said. "Penny has told me the same thing. And we all have developed plans that are highly flexible, along with equipment and supplies that can cover so many things other than what we have planned for specifically."

Frank and Georgie both nodded. It had been pretty much what the three had agreed to earlier. But Frank and Georgie did understand Horatio's short spell of doubt. It was natural.

A few minutes later, with nothing having changed, Horatio said good-bye, and headed back to town. Knowing Penny was more than capable of taking care of herself. More so than even than he could himself. But still, he worried.

Back home, Horatio saw Juliette and Alfonso talking in front of Alfonso's house as he pulled up to his own house. He took a few minutes to talk to Alfonso and Juliette when they saw him and motioned him over.

They quizzed him about his security shutters. And then morphed into a discussion about what else might be done if such a thing happened again.

Horatio was careful of what he said. He had no problem with giving them all the information about the shutters. But he was very cautious about giving away anything about his preps, and his prepping.

He did give them some tips about what foods would keep on the shelf, and how much water a person used during a week. Finally, the two indicated that they understood, and each headed to their own house.

Horatio went to his house, and locked himself back in. After preparing something to eat, he went back to his study and turned on the monitoring gear again.

Since at least part of the internet was up, and his service was also working, Horatio got on, to see what he might be able to find out about the situation.

It turned out that was pretty much nothing. And when he went to check some of the prepper forums, Horatio found that all the ones he frequented, plus many others, were blocked. As were all of the prepper supply places, that advertised those types of supplies, plus a few other on-line stores that were not specifically prepper oriented, but carried goods that preppers found very useful, such as *Lehman's*.

In addition, when Horatio went looking, no gun; hunting; gun and hunting accessories; military type gear; or military surplus on-line store was available. That included even archery only stores, and camping supply stores and other stores that carried anything that might be remotely useful for preppers, militias, or anyone that might want to oppose the authorities in any way.

Horatio shook his head. "Man, they are really clamping down," he muttered, though he was not entirely sure who 'they' were. He no longer assumed it was always the government that was doing things, after his education from Penny.

So, Horatio continued to monitor his communications gear, and worked on the computer updating some of his prepping plans, making a few more, and making notes about many other things that he wanted to research more thoroughly.

He spent the rest of the afternoon and evening at the computer, and only stopped when he felt hungry, since he had not stopped to eat anything after the light snack he had made earlier.

After eating, Horatio tried to call Penny again, on both his cell and the land line. No luck. Skype was still down, as were all the e-mail services. With a sigh, Horatio turned in for the night.

The next morning, he was up and ready to leave the house at his usual time. Horatio had made arrangements to meet with a client at a Starbucks near the courthouse. Considering the state of things, Horatio decided to use the Impala, rather than the Suburban. He did not want to draw too much attention to himself.

While the Suburban would get him out of trouble, if needed, it drew quite a bit of attention in and around town, especially at the courthouse for some reason. Whereas his Impala was a more or less normal and accepted sight at the courthouse.

Horatio was surprised, at first anyway, when he got to the courthouse and found it in something of an uproar. There were people all over the place, many of them handcuffed, in the presence of officers from the various law enforcement agencies in the area.

Attorneys, family, courthouse employees, and the occasional just hangers-on made up the rest of the group. Seeing one of the court clerks he knew fairly well, Horatio went over. The woman looked frazzled and was talking to three people at once.

Horatio caught her eye and she made a small head movement, holding up one finger to indicate, "Just a minute."

Stepping over out of the way, but close to the small table she was using as a desk, Horatio waited. Fairly patiently. Lucinda had to wave away two more people, asking them to wait. She turned to Horatio.

"Horatio. Can you believe this? Things are crazy. We just got power back on this morning and everyone has been called in. Every office is in use, and everyone is filling in for those that did not come in. I am taking appointments! Can you believe it? For the Mayor, the prosecuting attorney, four judges, and Jim."

"Jim?" asked Horatio. "What does he have to do with all of this? He's the maintenance man, for crying out loud!"

"Yeah," Lucinda said. She sniffed and wiped away a tear. "I don't know what is going on, Horatio! All these people I am making appointments for… None of them are here, and can't seemed to be found, according to what I am hearing."

Wiping away another tear, Lucinda straightened in her chair, and composed herself. "What can I help you with, Horatio?"

Rather sheepishly, Horatio replied. "I just wanted to try to find out what is going on. I think I just did. I will leave you to what you are doing."

Lucinda nodded, and Horatio started to turn away and leave, but stopped and asked Lucinda, "Is there anything I can get you? How are you going to get lunch?"

Another tear appeared. "I don't know, Horatio. Judge Harrison was pretty adamant that we be here for as long as needed." Lucinda frowned. "That was before he disappeared. Have not heard anything since."

"Okay, Lucinda. I do not want you to worry. I will make sure you have something before noon. I will bring it back here, and make sure you have a chance to eat, and take at least a short rest."

"Oh, thank you, Horatio! I didn't know what I was going to do." Another sniff, and wipe of her eyes, and Lucinda turned back to the line that had formed, determined to do her best under the extreme circumstances.

Horatio headed for the Starbucks, leaving the Impala where it was in the courthouse parking lot. From the looks of it now, he had been lucky to get a spot when he arrived. The lot was completely full now, and people were circling around, looking for someone to pull out. On the street there was a steady flow of traffic looking for street parking.

The Starbucks was packed, as Horatio had expected. As he had walked over he checked his cell phone. Local service was available so, anticipating the crowd, he called in an order, hoping it would be ready when he arrived. Or shortly thereafter. Fortunately, he knew what Jennings like to drink, so he ordered that for him, as well.

It was well he had. The line was out the door. He worked his way inside to the pickup order spot. There were several things there, but none were his order. As he waited, every once in a while someone would come in and pick up one.

Horatio was keeping an eye out for Jennings and saw him enter the far entrance. Horatio lifted a hand and Jennings, looking for him, saw and waved back. Jennings pointed outside, and Horatio nodded. Jennings would wait for him out there. There was not a table or chair available inside.

It was a few more minutes before Horatio's order came up, but it did, and he grabbed the cups and headed outside to join Jennings. He found him at one of the two-person tables. He was guarding the other empty chair, as person after person came up, wanting to move it to another of the tables.

Horatio handed Jennings his coffee, and then shook his hand before sitting down. Jennings took a cautious sip of the coffee and set it down on the table when it proved too hot to drink at the moment.

"Man, have you ever seen anything like this?" Jennings asked, looking around, and over at the courthouse. "You said your office was attacked?"

Horatio shook his head. Jennings had a bit of a hearing problem and Horatio was not surprised that he had misunderstood what Horatio had tried to tell him over the phone.

"No. My office wasn't. But many of the other stores in the mall were. The police have it blocked off to keep looters and such out and let the repair people come in and fix the broken windows and doors. And get rid of the damaged and burned cars."

"Ah," Jennings replied. Then, the niceties concluded as far as he was concerned, Jennings began to question Horatio about the status of the case Horatio was handling for him. Horatio filled him in, clarifying several times when the talking around them got loud and Jennings had trouble hearing.

While Jennings did not look particularly happy, he did seem satisfied with the progress Horatio was making. "What is this mess going to do to the case?" he finally asked, making a sweeping gesture around them.

"I do not honestly know, Mr. Jennings."

Before he could continue, Jennings cut in. "It should get cleared up soon, I am sure. It shouldn't have much impact, should it? Nothing to do with my case."

"I hope not, Mr. Jennings. If it does 'clear up' quickly there really should not be much impact on the case. It might have some impact on the hearing date, but that would probably be all."

"Good enough, Billings. Let me know if something does come up." With that, Jennings rose, shook hands with Horatio, and walked away, his coffee in hand. As soon as Horatio moved, too, the table was grabbed by two more people, a fight almost breaking out between those two and several other people waiting for it.

Horatio rolled his eyes and headed back to the Impala slowly, sipping his coffee thoughtfully. He decided he had made the correct choice in not going into the possibilities of significant delays, and even worse, if the situation was not resolved, the way Penny, he, and many other preppers thought possible.

It would have not done any good, and Jennings would just have worried needlessly. Better for him to rest easy until it became clear just what was happening.

When Horatio reached his car and backed out of the parking slot someone pulled right into it, another driver honking angrily. Horatio decided he was not going to come back in the Impala, or the Suburban. Parking was just too problematic.

When he arrived home, he made himself something to eat, and as he ate, he prepared several things that would keep without refrigeration. When everything was ready, he opened the garage doors again and rolled out his newest vehicle. A Montague Paratrooper Pro folding military bicycle.

He thought about attaching the trailer he had for it but decided that the cargo containers on the bike would be sufficient. Horatio loaded the food and drinks onto the bike and headed back toward the courthouse.

Horatio got more than a few strange looks as he rode toward downtown on the bike, dressed in his suit. And even more when he arrived, carefully locked up the bike, and took the two canvas bags of food into the building.

Lucinda gave him a grateful look when he moved past the line in front of her table, amidst several protestations, to put the bags down beside her chair. When he did not try to cut in line, the protests died away. But, more were voiced when Lucinda announced she was taking a break for lunch as soon as she finished with the person she was dealing with at the moment.

Horatio gave her a wink at her resolve to take care of herself before he headed outside. Two other of the workers located near her gathered around when she pulled out the food. When Lucinda looked at him in question just before he got out of her sight he gave a slight nod. Lucinda handed her friends sandwiches and bottles of water.

As he rode back home, taking a roundabout way to look around, Horatio thought about what Penny had said about having humanitarian aid supplies as part of his preps. He had done it, as a matter of course, since Penny had recommended it. But with the experience today, he understood much better exactly what Penny had meant about the need.

When Horatio arrived home, he had a much better understanding of the realities of a disaster that did not include much physical damage. Setting up again in his study on the computer, he took quite a few notes to help clarify the thoughts that had come to him on the ride.

He spent most of the rest of the day working on his prepping plans, refining them based on the insights, that despite Penny's best efforts to educate him, he had not really taken to heart.

It was not until he turned on the television on his way to the kitchen that evening, out of habit, that he realized that both dish and cable were back on. Switching through the channels, on first one system and then the other, everything seemed to be on.

He watched for a few minutes on several different channels to see if anything was being said about the event. There was not, but everything else seemed to be being discussed.

As he continued toward the kitchen, Horatio realized suddenly that what he had seen had been orchestrated. There was no way that what had been happening would not be being discussed, in great detail, by a sensation seeking media, unless extreme pressure had been brought to bear. And it had to be from a source that was powerful enough to make hundreds, if not thousands, of people in the media fearful enough to follow the orders.

Horatio suddenly paused, his hand on the handle of the refrigerator, as something else struck him. "Not all of it would have been the fear factor," he muttered. "I'll bet that many in the media went along with it willingly, once encouraged to do so by those that had orchestrated the event, because they were made to realize that in so doing, it aided their own agenda.

"Crap," Horatio muttered a bit more loudly. He shook his head, rather disgusted with the whole world, the media in particular, and the powers that be that seemed to be controlling it.

He went about his evening routine and made his regular call to Penny as per their normal schedule. This time he got through alright.

Both laughed after both had said exactly the same thing to each other when Penny picked up. "Are you okay?"

After Penny told Horatio that she had not been much affected by the goings on, since she had been at home and had stayed there the last few days.

Horatio filled her in on what he had been doing, and then told her what he had been thinking earlier.

"I think you are correct, Horatio," Penny replied. "And as quickly as they have suppressed this, I am beginning to think this was perhaps just a test run.

"Oh, they accomplished a few real things, mainly sowing some seeds of discontent. But I do think that the main purpose was to see just how effective the efforts they have been putting in are going to be.

"I have a feeling that things will calm down for a while, as they analyze the results of the test, if that is what it was, and then make further plans. I am convinced, however, that they do plan to use these techniques to achieve their goals."

Horatio had been nodding in agreement as Penny voiced her ideas. "I am beginning to see that and agree that it is far from over. What do you think we should do now?"

Hearing Penny sigh, Horatio felt a pang of longing. He wished he could be there with her, to comfort her somehow. "About all we can do is carry on with getting ready for whatever does happen. There is no real way to know when they might put their full plan into operation.

"There could be some more test runs… they might even use them to reinforce the ideas they planted this time, and just keep building up the rage until they believe the time is right to do whatever the primary event is to be.

"Not to mention that there are still many other things that could happen that are not related to this. There are always natural events that happen, and the world political situation is tense. And with several people in positions of power that are very unstable, anything could happen before this group puts the final steps of their plan into action."

This time it was Horatio that sighed. "I know. I agree, now that you have clarified a few things in my mind. It is just a waiting game, I suppose, and keeping up with improving our prepping status."

"I agree," Penny replied.

There was silence for a few moments, and then Penny spoke again, nearly in a whisper. "I miss you. I love you, Horatio."

Horatio closed his eyes and groaned softly. "Oh, Penny. I miss you too, honey. And I love you, too. Desperately. You are the best thing that has ever happened to me. I am so glad you came into my life."

There was a catch in Penny's voice when she was finally able to reply. Horatio heard her clear her throat, and then could hear the emotion in her voice when she said, "I am, too, Horatio. I did not realize just how lonely I was, and how much I wanted what it is we are developing. I love you."

"I love you," Horatio replied, choked up now himself. After soft "Good-bye's", both hung up, and both sighed in longing.

Horatio sat quietly for a few minutes, not really thinking, just missing Penny. But with yet another sigh, Horatio got up, and went to the study to check online for anything important in the news, and when there was nothing of import, he got ready for bed.

Chapter Seven

Things did slowly return to normal. More or less. Horatio, now with a much keener eye for the news and what was going on around him, was not so sure it was even very close to the old normal.

Though appearing much the same, Horatio noticed that people seemed a bit more on edge. A bit more willing to speak up or speak out when certain subjects came up. Several of his clients, much like Tony Smotherman, had given some less than gentle hints that Horatio was considered part of the problems that the country was going through.

He had always had a few clients that were less than enamored with the legal profession. But this was a bit more than the client disgruntled with the basic premise that lawyers were needed, and they had to pay for them to get certain things done. It was now that the whole system, and everyone in it, was corrupt, and out to 'get' the common person. Namely, them.

Other than the threat from Smotherman, everything had been cross or distrusting looks, and snide comments. Still, Horatio was feeling the discontent aimed at him, personally, and the system in general.

He stayed in close contact with Penny, who was seeing much the same, though not directly against her. "You know, Horatio," she told him after he mentioned some of his clients, "that same attitude is being directed at many other parts of society. Law enforcement, who is pushing back just as hard.

"And survivalists and preppers, when people find out someone is one, they come under scrutiny, are accused of hoarding and the other standard things, but are being told as often as not that they will be targeted if the balloon goes up."

"Yes," Horatio agreed. "I am so glad you impressed upon me to keep my preps very close to my vest. So far, I do not think anyone knows about them that I do not want to know."

Horatio heard the smile Penny obviously had on her face when she said, "Yes. You did learn your lessons well."

"Um..." Horatio slightly stuttered, "When do you think we can get together again. I miss you so much."

"I know," Penny sighed. But her voice picked up suddenly. "I was thinking, though, that perhaps you might come up for Thanksgiving…" There was just a bit of hesitation in her voice.

"At your parent's place?" Horatio asked, his amusement obvious in his voice.

"Yes. We usually do it there."

Horatio actually laughed, bringing a loud huff from Penny. "Yes, Penny. I would love to. I really want to meet your parents in person. Make sure they approve of me and the way you have trained me."

"Horatio!" Penny exclaimed.

"I'm kidding, Penny. Just kidding. I really do want to meet the people that produced you. They must be amazing, just like you."

"Aw, Horatio…"

"Just how early can I come up, before?"

Penny laughed. "At least a couple of days. Even the whole week, if you can arrange it."

"Really? Alright! I will definitely see what I can arrange. I really want to see you and be with you for more than a couple of days at a time."

"Please do what you can, Horatio. I feel the same. Oh. And invite Frank and Georgie to come up, too."

"I will ask," Horatio replied. "I am not sure they will want to be away from the place very long. Frank is having a few more problems." Before Penny could react, Horatio spoke up again. "Nothing too serious. But something where he just does not want to be around people too much."

"Oh. Okay. Give him and Georgie my best. I really need to go. I have a project wrapping up and I need to be there."

"Okay, Penny. I love you."

"I love you, too, Horatio. 'bye."

"Bye…" Horatio slowly hung up. With a sigh, Horatio turned back to his computer and began working. He was now being even more careful about how he dealt with not only clients, but people in general.

It had started with Alfonso and Juliette when they asked him for advice on getting security shutters similar to his. He quickly put a stop to Alfonso's hinting around about getting a key to Horatio's place, so he and his wife could come over and be safe there, if something happened in the future.

Horatio quickly found out that Alfonso was not willing to pay what Horatio had paid for his installation. But he talked Alfonso through a selection process that would give them at least some protection, making very sure Alfonso understood that it would not be the same level as his.

Juliette, on the other hand, was more than willing to pay for a system very similar to Horatio's, including a security system and outdoor lighting.

While a long way from indicating she might become a prepper, she did ask questions about how to be more ready for things that might happen in the future. So, Horatio gave her the hand-outs that Penny had helped him develop, so he could give advice, without it really indicating he was doing more than what she might do, based on the documents.

Most of it was from on-line FEMA and Red Cross sources, with just a bit included that went a little further than the government and NGO suggestions. Things he simply was not comfortable not letting people know that he cared about in some way, since they were showing some interest, and that they really needed to be aware of and think about.

He and Penny had made sure that none of the material appeared to be from him, having used on-line sources with links that gave similar information, even though Penny had actually written most of the additional material, incorporating her own ideas.

One of the things that had changed, was some people's approach to gun control, or as Penny had taught him, the more accurate term, Civilian Disarmament.

Many people that had long called for Civilian Disarmament were changing their tune slightly. And so were quite a few people that had fought hard against Civilian Disarmament.

Those that had wanted widespread general Civilian Disarmament were joining forces with those that had not wanted any Civilian Disarmament, even a relaxing of the rules. They wanted selective disarmament.

Many that had been against civilian ownership of weapons wanted them for themselves, but not for selected groups. And those that had wanted relaxed rules now wanted to keep their guns as always but did want particular other groups disarmed.

People on both sides of the old argument, were agreeing that some elements of society should not have free access to effective weapons and ammunition. While there was still much mistrust between the two formally rival groups, they now stood united in wanting those people they both now feared to become unable to defend themselves effectively, under the guise of fearing attacks from them.

Much of what was not said though, became obvious to those that were the targets of the new legislation being proposed. That the groups doing the targeting, though they were somewhat afraid of the groups being targeted, were much more interested in being able to acquire what the targeted groups had, when the time came.

Also, to make it easier to be able to do whatever they wanted to those in the targeted groups, without much risk.

Survivalists; preppers; those living or advocating living off grid; homesteaders; herbalists, alternative, and homeopathic medicine practitioners; constitutionalists; hunters; and many other additional groups of people that had the capability of taking care of themselves and providing for themselves without reliance on "the system" were to be disarmed as soon as possible.

Additional legislation was being drafted to allow for the seizing of any type of equipment and supplies, to be designated at the appropriate time, from those individuals and groups.

In some cases, the entire holdings of some of the people in those targeted groups, and whole organized groups, would be subject to forfeiture, without compensation, if "the situation demanded it", again with both the decision to do so, and from whom, decided in the future, at "the appropriate time" and "for the good of all", as was being stated time after time.

Although it was rather counter intuitive to many, no one, whether they currently were included in one of those group definitions, or not, would be allowed to accumulate more than one week's worth of food and fuel, with many other consumables also listed individually on the restricted list.

Including toilet paper. It was the toilet paper that caused the most trouble with getting the legislation on the docket initially. Even non-preppers liked to have plenty of toilet paper on hand.

As well as a new drive to shut down as many gun stores and ammunition suppliers as possible, many of the businesses that specialized in other preparedness supplies, were to be closed down, or put under intense monitoring. Those that were not shut down would be allowed to sell products only to a group of approved civilian organizations.

The members of these organizations were those individuals that supported the new agenda and were considered useful enough by those in control to be exempt from the new rules coming into effect. These groups, government agencies, and select NGOs were the only ones that would be allowed to purchase prepper related items.

The duties of monitoring and policing the new policies were to be assumed by a new sub-unit of DHS, called "The Equability Enforcement Division."

Even with the new, somewhat more conservative administration in office, the extreme liberal components of The Powers That Be, the Elitists, Main Stream Media, the Entertainment Industry, most of those controlling Higher Education, almost all of the United Nations officials, and many other elements of the US, European Union, and much of the rest of the world, and given individuals and smaller groups with a liberal agenda, were able to block attempts to stop their activities.

They used every historic propaganda tool. Misinformation, false news, emotional blackmail, and several newer techniques that had been developed and honed by those with liberal agendas since World War II.

Despite many of the lower level groups now having this same agenda, they were being played against each other by those with the real power, just to keep the tension up and heighten the mistrust of one person or group against many others.

Of course, the MSM downplayed the machinations taking place. Either simply not reporting the activities or putting the kind of spin on them that convinced many people not actively supporting the agenda to accept the proposals as necessary, if even sometimes a necessary evil.

Horatio found himself under more and more scrutiny, not about his prepping, fortunately, but about his attorney work. Even though he did quite a bit of pro bono work, and the overwhelming majority of what he did benefited "the little guy" so to speak, he was still doubted.

He was often questioned heavily by some of his existing clients, as well as prospective new clients, and in a few cases, just people that knew he was an attorney would lecture him about how lawyers in general were evil people and the fact that he sometimes helped people did not make him one of "the good guys", like they, themselves were.

And much to Horatio's dismay, Penny finally admitted to him that she was under some pressure now, due to her involvement and support of the prepper movement.

"Penny, honey, have you thought about lowering your prepping public profile? Reducing the number of posts on the forums? Things like that?" Horatio asked her the week before he was to go up to her parent's place for Thanksgiving.

"Horatio," Penny said firmly, catching Horatio's attention immediately. He had seen Penny upset a few times, even somewhat angry a couple of times, but nothing really negative ever actually directed at him. This was different.

"I will not be intimidated by these people. Rest assured I have taken measures to protect all of us, as necessary, but I intend to fight what is going on, even if my efforts do not produce much effect. But I will not lay down and hide. What these people are doing is not only wrong, most of it is highly illegal. Some of it bordering on treasonous.

"I feel an obligation to speak out. I believe in what I do. And silence in the face of tyranny only allows that tyranny to succeed and makes it harder in the future to battle it when it happens again. And it always happens again."

Horatio had heard the heat and sincerity in her voice. The tone of it, and the firmness, as well as the words themselves. "Sweetie, I am sorry. I didn't... don't..."

"Oh, Horatio!" Penny said softly. "I am the one that should apologize. Obviously, this is bothering me even more than I realized."

Horatio heard the sigh just before she continued. "One of the people I began helping prepare a few years ago has been taken in by the rhetoric. We had become fairly decent friends. I thought. She called yesterday and told me, in no uncertain terms, that she blames me for getting her involved in... *This evil that is prepping*, is the term she used.

"She told me she is reporting me to the proper authorities, as soon as the new legislation is enacted." Horatio heard Penny's voice crack slightly and could barely hear her next words. "She hoped I went to jail for a long time, because I was always only thinking about myself, and had tried to get her to do such evil things as prepping."

"Penny, I'm sorry. You know that isn't true. Your only goal has been to help people."

Penny sniffled a bit. "I know, Horatio. I miss you, and her tirade just hit me hard. I will be so glad when you get here. Are Georgie and Frank going to be able to come, too?"

"I miss you, too, baby. And I am afraid not with Georgie and Frank. He is working on a solution to his new problem, and Georgie wouldn't even think about going without him."

"That is too bad," Penny replied. Horatio was thankful to hear her sounding more like herself. "Give them my best, and I will see you soon. I need to get back on a new project, myself. I love you."

"I love you, too, Penny. 'bye."

Horatio slowly lowered the receiver into the cradle. He leaned back in his desk chair, lost in thought. Suddenly he straightened up and rose from the chair. He opened the door of his office leading to the reception area and spoke to Melissa.

"Melissa, call Mrs. Amstead, and see if she would have time later today for me to come out and talk to her."

Melissa nodded, and picked up the phone. "What should I say it is in reference to, Horatio?" Melissa asked before she started to dial.

Horatio hesitated a moment, but then smiled. "Tell her it pertains to Bernie's 1962 adventure."

Melissa looked at Horatio, expecting him to elaborate, but he shook his head, a smile still on his face. "Can't explain, Melissa. But Mrs. Amstead will know what I mean."

"Okay, Horatio."

Horatio grabbed his jacket and added, on his way out, "I will be back shortly. As soon as you finish the call, lock up and go home. You will still be on full salary, but I do not want you here alone anymore."

Melissa looked uncertain but said nothing as Horatio went out the front door of the office. She made the call, scheduled the appointment, and called Horatio to let him know the time. Then, as Horatio had reminded her, she locked up the office, including lowering the security shutters, which was now standard procedure, and went to her new-to-her car. It was the replacement for the one totaled out during the riot.

"Should work out fine," Horatio said out loud when he ended the call from Melissa. "Enough time to find Eddie Mercer and set up something before I go to Mrs. Amstead's."

There was more than a little surprise on Eddie's face when Horatio walked into the small tattoo shop he owned and operated. Eddie quickly set aside the newspaper he was reading and rose from the client chair in which he had been sitting.

Horatio took in the massive amount of ink Eddie now sported. When they had met in college, Eddie had several tattoos, almost all hidden when he wore his standard jeans and T-shirt to the various classes the two shared.

In a muscle shirt and cut off jean shorts, all of the previous tattoos, and many more were visible. Horatio grinned. "Advertising the talent, I see," he said.

"You old son of a gun!" Eddie said, the big man enveloping Horatio in a tight bear hug. "What brings you by? Haven't seen you in ages!"

"Who is it, Sweetie?" came a voice from the hallway leading to the back rooms of the shop.

The blonde-haired woman came around the corner and squealed when she saw Horatio. Eddie had stepped back by then and when the woman launched herself at Horatio, he was prepared, and caught her when she jumped up into his arms and wrapped her legs around his waist, giving him a sloppy kiss on his cheek before dropping back to her feet.

She saw Horatio looking at her new ink, and did a pirouette, to show it all off. She, too, was wearing a pair of cut-offs, rather shorter than Eddies, and instead of the muscle shirt, she wore a short tank top over a sports bra. "What do you think, Horatio? Pretty cool, huh?" she asked, facing him again.

Horatio nodded, glanced over at the beaming Eddie for a moment, before saying, "The big guy is talented, for sure. And you do wear those with great panache, Misty."

Misty moved over to Eddie, who put his arm around here in a side hug, which she returned. "Thanks," they said, almost simultaneously.

"How is business?" Horatio asked, as they moved over to the waiting area and all sat down in the comfortable leather chairs and sofa.

Eddie shrugged. "Eh… Not doing much right now. Haven't been for a while. All the recent troubles up the street have not helped business. But you know we aren't in it for the money."

Giving Horatio a penetrating look, Eddie asked him, "And since I know you are not here for some ink, and we did not contact you needing help, what is up, and how can we help you?"

"Straight to the nitty gritty, as always," Horatio replied with a smile.

Misty patted Eddie's broad chest. "Yep. My guy is a straight forward, upstanding citizen, always ready to lend a hand. Never beats around the bush."

Horatio and Eddie both chuckled. Eddie looked serious then. "Man, you pulled us out of a disaster, Horatio. We owe you. So, whatever you need, it's yours. You know that, right?"

Misty nodded her agreement, looking at Horatio. Horatio took a quick look toward the door before he responded.

"You guys do not owe me anything. But, I do have a favor to ask. But I do not want to interfere with your business. I was hoping you could refer me to someone that can do a job for me."

"Job?" Eddie asked, his head tilted quizzically. "What kind of job would you need done that you need a referral from me?"

"I need some security work done, Eddie. I am worried about my paralegal. It is pretty tense at the mall, and… well… there are some… people… that seem to have taken a dislike to all things pertaining to attorneys, lawyers, judges, and the whole legal systems.

"Melissa's car was flipped over and burned during that riot, I have sort of been threatened…"

Both Eddie's and Misty's eyes went hard as Horatio continued. "I just do not want her to be at the office alone, even with the security measures I had already taken before the riot. I am even a bit worried about her getting to and from the office, if… if something else triggers another riot or something when I am not in the office."

Eddie and Misty exchanged a short look. Horatio realized they had the same kind of spousal visual eye-to-eye, non-verbal shorthand that Frank and Georgie did. Apparently, they came to a mutual decision.

"You got it, buddy," Eddie said. "Misty and I will take care of it."

"No," Horatio protested. "You guys can't do that. It will interfere with your shop here. I was just asking if a couple of your friends might be interested in the job."

"Man, you know I do not need to keep this shop open. It is just something to do when there isn't something else Misty and I want to do. Thanks to you, not only are we married, but we were able to get that inheritance straightened out. We don't need the money. And, speaking of which, do not even think about offering to pay us for doing this for you."

"But…" Horatio started saying, but Eddie and Misty were looking at him firmly, a glint in their eyes. After a moment, he nodded. "Okay. Thank you. Thank you both. I will make it up to you."

Horatio could tell that the two wanted to protest that, but he quickly turned and added, "I have to be somewhere shortly, but if you guys don't mind stopping at the office around five or so, we can go get some supper and work out the details."

They followed him to the door of the shop. "We will be there, Horatio. See you in a while."

Horatio looked back again. "Thanks guys. This means a lot to me."

"You got it, buddy," Eddie added rather softly.

Horatio drove out to Mrs. Amstead's home. The work she had told him she would be having done there, which pertained to the legal work he had done for her, was well underway. There were at least five contractor's trucks that Horatio could see, parked in the front area. He suspected there would be at least a couple more in back.

When he rang the doorbell, and the door opened shortly after, he was surprised to see Mrs. Amstead herself had opened it.

"Where is your nurse?" Horatio asked when she backed the wheelchair out of the way so he could enter. He closed the door behind him and followed Mrs. Amstead toward the study.

"I sent her out on some errands." She stopped the wheelchair and spun it around expertly in the hallway so she could see him. "Anything to do with Bernie's activities in 1962 are not matters for public consumption. You know that."

Properly chastised for having taken the situation a bit too lightly, Horatio humbly gave her his apology.

"Okay," she replied, a very slight smile on her face when she spun the chair around again behind the desk after they entered the study. "That is better. So. Since you did mention it, I take it your visit does have something to do with the Cuban Missile Crisis in some way? Just what would that be?"

She motioned to one of the chairs in front of the desk and he sat down, facing her across the expanse of the large, beautiful custom desk she had commissioned for Bernie while he was still in the Air Force.

Her eyes went to the framed portrait of Bernie in his Air Force flight suit, standing before a B-47 bomber. Then she looked at Horatio again, expectantly.

Suddenly at a loss how to begin, Horatio paused with his mouth barely open. "Get on with it, Horatio," Mrs. Amstead said gently.

"I'm... uh... worried... about some of the things that have been happening here, locally, across the state... The whole country, really. And internationally. I am not sure if you keep up on..."

"Of course, I keep up on things, Horatio. I am old, and not in great health, but I have already told you my mind is as sharp as ever." She suddenly grinned. "And I have the paperwork to prove it, if you remember."

Horatio smiled back. "Yes, you do. So, you do obviously keep up with what is going on. That is what I came out here to talk to you about. I know you said you did not have all that much time left, and I am not really sure just how much you meant. But I am afraid something very bad might happen relatively soon. Soon enough that you very well may still be around when it does."

"Um-huh. Go on," she said.

"And, well, I am worried about you. If something like I think might happen, you could be in some significant danger. You have always been one to speak your mind about things, just the way Bernie did. And while you are greatly loved by many people, there are some that... well..."

"Pretty much hate my guts and everything I stand for. Is that what you are trying to say without hurting my feelings, Horatio?"

Horatio nodded.

"Well, you haven't, and will not, hurt my feelings bringing that up. While I know it did not come through you, a few people have found out about some of the things I have set up in my will, and some of what I am doing now, to get ready for that time.

"Including a couple of my relatives, as well as three members of the city council, and a handful of other people. They are not happy campers, to coin a phrase. And that is on top of those that have not liked me or my beliefs for a long time, anyway. So, what has brought you out here, specifically. I am capable of defending myself, here at home. Not sure if you know that, or not. Or, I guess I should say, believe it now, since you know just how well I can shoot, when called upon."

Horatio nodded. There was no doubt in his mind that Mrs. Amstead would make a good accounting of herself if there was to be a one-on-one confrontation. But that was not so much what he was worried about. And he told her so.

"I am more worried about harassment and being in danger when you are out and about. Which, I am one hundred percent certain you will be, especially if what I think could happen, does."

"Really?" she said, watching Horatio carefully.

Horatio nodded again. "What I want you to know is that I... uh... have a place where you would be safe, pretty much no matter what might happen. I know you are moving out of here as soon as the work is done, and have a nice place to go... But it will not be all that secure..."

"I know. I have thought about that. In general terms," Mrs. Amstead replied, rather surprising Horatio. Suddenly she grinned. "You never figured it out, did you?" she asked.

"Figured what out?" Horatio asked, puzzled.

"The shelter Bernie and I had built in 1947. Under the barn, when we built it. Did most of the shelter construction ourselves. Had it all covered up when Franklin came out to put up the barn for us."

"You have a shelter? A storm shelter?"

Mrs. Amstead shook her head. "No, Horatio. Not a storm shelter. Though, of course, it is more than adequate for that. It is a bomb shelter. Actually, a combination fallout and blast shelter. Rather crudely equipped when we built it, but we have updated it as better equipment and supplies became available.

"That is what bothers me the most about leaving this place. Not having access to it if we ever do need it. Though, when I turn the place over to the Foundation, they will be informed of its existence and that makes me feel good, knowing that those that will be using this place will have it available to them.

"Because, like you, I am worried about the future. Have been for a long time. I am pleased to see that you have come around to the same way of thinking. That pretty little redhead have anything to do with the transformation?"

"Oh!" Horatio said, his eyes widening. "Um... Well, yes, actually. And because of her, I have a place. A safe place to go... I am offering you a place there. Now. Not just when something might happen. A place you would be safe, no matter what."

"I see," Mrs. Amstead said, again studying Horatio's face, making him squirm just a bit in the chair.

"That place you bought, out on the lake?"

Horatio shook his head. "I should have known you would know about it. I have tried to keep it as low key as possible."

"And you were quite successful. If it wasn't for Bunny fishing out there by your inlet, I never would have known. She kept me informed, like she does many other things when she is out and about."

"Oh. We thought no one…"

Mrs. Amstead grinned. "Bunny has a way about her. Never too noticeable, unless she wants to be. Been spying for me for years."

Horatio had to laugh at the grin on Mrs. Amstead's face.

"So, what do you say? Will you move out there when the time comes to leave here?"

"As long as Bunny has a place, too. And one other person, whom I trust implicitly."

She saw Horatio's hesitation over the second person, though he had not batted an eye about including Bunny.

Mrs. Amstead lowered her voice slightly, and even leaned forward a bit in the powered chair. "It is young Suzette Spannings."

"Suzette? I had no idea you even knew her."

"Oh, yes. She is the grand-daughter of Bernie's best friend. You remember us talking about Hiram? Hiram Berkenhiser?"

"Oh. Yes. I do, as a matter-of-fact. He and Bernie served together much of their careers in the Air Force."

"Well, Suzette followed in her grandfather's and father's footsteps and was in the Air Force for quite a while. Came back from Afghanistan several months ago, not doing at all well. Pulled some special operations types out of a tight spot, flying close air support, and wound up being shot down in the process.

"She has healed up, for the most part, but is having a hard time adjusting to civilian life. She intended to make it a career, and now is at loose ends. She lends me a hand from time to time, when I need it. And I do the same for her. She is more like family to me than any of my own that are left."

"Well, then of course. I do need to let you know my friend Frank and his wife are out there, sort of as caretakers, and are permanent residents, too."

"Frank Goodwind? The man you went to college with? Came home with you a few times on holidays. Went into the Marines, if I recall."

Surprised, though he was not sure why, as Mrs. Amstead had already proved her memory was a good as it had ever been, Horatio nodded. "That is him. He married the nurse that helped him through his recovery and rehabilitation when he was wounded. Her name is Georgie."

Mrs. Amstead nodded. "Good. Sounds like a plan to me. One I like very much, since I do not plan to let very many people know where I will be living. Partly so those that have a bone to pick with me will not be showing up on my doorstep any time they want to argue what I have done."

"Well, I guess that is it, Mrs. Amstead. Just let me know when you want to go out and see the place. You and Bunny and Suzette. Just to make sure it is suitable for your needs."

"You wouldn't have offered, if it wasn't. But, yes, of course. We will show up out there soon. I will let you see yourself out. I want to call Suzette right now. She has been looking for a place close to the home I had tentatively decided on moving to. I do not want her spending anything she does not have to. I tried to get her to move in here, but she refuses."

Horatio said a quick good-bye, and headed back to his office, satisfied, and pleased, that Mrs. Amstead had agreed to his sudden plan.

Eddie and Misty drove up to the office just as Horatio arrived. When Horatio got out of the Suburban, he did exactly the same thing Eddie and Misty did, when they exited their vehicle. Stared at the other's vehicle.

As Eddie and Misty took in the Suburban, Horatio was doing the same detailed look at the old Ford F-350 crew cab, long bed, four-wheel-drive pickup truck the two were standing beside.

The Ford had single wheels on the rear axle, and large tires all around. An obviously custom cargo rack went from stanchions on the front bumper to stanchions on the rear bumper. A set of tarps covered the load on the cargo rack. And just like Penny's Chevy and Horatio's Suburban, canvas covered the large front and rear bumper assemblies.

Horatio took in the cargo rack over the Ford's bed, which was part of a flat bed-cover protecting whatever was inside the pickup bed.

And then Horatio met Eddie's eyes. Though they were only on one another's a moment, because Misty touched Eddie's massive arm and then pointed to the office building.

Several more seconds elapsed before Eddie looked at Horatio again. "You've got some 'splaining to do, Lucy," Eddie said to Horatio when they gathered at the door to the office and Horatio activated the remote in his pocket to open the security shutters.

Twice more before Horatio had the doors open, Misty pointed out several things to Eddie. The various cameras, on the building and the light poles in the parking lot. And Eddie spotted the connection box on the side of the building.

They entered the office and Eddie and Misty looked around expectantly, but there was nothing out of the ordinary in the reception area.

"Horatio, I have a feeling we may have more in common that either of us thought possible," Eddie said, following him into his office.

"Uh… Yeah… I'm thinking the same thing. Oh. You guys want some coffee or something? The break room has…"

"I'll find it," Misty quickly said. "What'll you guys have?"

"Iced tea," both said, in tandem.

Misty turned and left. Eddie took a seat on the leather sofa, and Horatio took one of the leather chairs across the small table from Eddie. "You know she is on a mission, right? Scope out the place? Could be a bit before we get our tea." Eddie said.

Horatio grinned. "Of course. It is fine."

Both fell silent, neither knowing quite how to broach the subject they wanted to, without giving too much away, in case they were wrong.

Finally, Horatio cleared his throat and spoke. "About the job…"

"First, how about us exchanging a piece of information about ourselves, until we both understand just what is going on?" Eddie asked, leaning back against the sofa's firm button tufted leather surface.

Horatio smiled slightly. "Um. Probably a good idea. Where to start?" he wondered aloud. "Okay. You familiar with the term 'prepper'?"

"Very," Eddie replied immediately. "You know many… any… around here?" was his question.

"I didn't… or actually, didn't know I did until very recently. Found out one of my other friends and his wife are. And another individual that I had absolutely no idea was anywhere near being a prepper, actually was. Has been for a very long time."

Eddie nodded. "How do you feel about them now? How do you feel about the idea of prepping?"

"I am all for it," Horatio replied. "Might even be interested in learning more about it, if I knew someone that might be willing to help."

"I see," said Eddie, looking away from Horatio for a moment before turning his eyes back to him. "I might just be able to help with that, too. Along with the other job. If you'd take advice from an old, dedicated friend."

"More than happy to," said Horatio. "Of course, I wouldn't want anyone else to know…"

"'Course not. Ah, here's Misty with the tea."

Misty put the tray down on the coffee table and the two men reached for their glasses of the sweet tea. Misty took one as well, and sat down beside Eddie, their hips touching.

Eddie and Horatio were taking their first sips of the tea when Misty asked, as she looked around the office some more, you guys figured out each other are preppers yet?"

She looked at Horatio and then Eddie, who had managed to swallow a bit of the tea down the wrong pipe and began to cough. Misty pounded his back a couple of times until he caught his breath. "Geez, Misty. You don't just say it out like that! You've never done that before," Eddie managed to say when he had caught his breath.

"Aw, come on, Eddie! It is so obvious! You saw his rig. And the office. And he just bought that place out on the lake. The one there near that hot fishing spot Bunny told me about. I caught some nice small mouth bass out there the other day. I'd put a dollar to a donut that's his bug out location." She looked at Horatio expectantly.

"Ah… Well… I guess you could call it that. I just wanted something away from town, on the water, you know…"

Eddie laughed. "Oh, give it up, Horatio. It is pretty obvious now that I think about it. And just so you do not feel too exposed, I guess we can tell you we are looking to get a place, too. Somewhere we can do a nice off-grid prepper home. If you know what I mean?"

"Yeah. Yeah. I think I do." Horatio paused for a moment. "I am thinking you might not have all that much time to get a place ready. You know all the things that have been happening lately?"

Eddie and Misty exchanged a quick glance, before Eddie turned back to Horatio. "We know. There is something going on beyond the usual stuff. You know. Yellowstone, asteroids, nuclear stuff, the economy…

"We haven't been able to figure it out. But there have been a couple of incidents at the shop." Misty gripped Eddies arm and he put it around her protectively.

"Half a dozen of my customers… Preppy types. You know. Gen X or something. Been in to get a tattoo or two each. Minor stuff. Just a lark kind of thing. Usually with the girlfriends, who usually got an ankle tat or something else simple."

Eddie shook his head. Misty spoke up before he could continue. "It was awful, Horatio. They threatened Eddie."

Horatio's eyes widened at her words. That young professionals, even several of them, would have the nerve to threaten Eddie was almost beyond belief. But then Eddie explained.

"Not me, Horatio. Not really. But they very plainly implied that something could happen to Misty if I ever…" Eddie closed his eyes and tilted his head back for a moment. He then looked at Misty a moment, and then over at Horatio again. "If I didn't go along with what was 'right and proper' when they asked me for something. Either I would help them out when they needed 'muscle' to take care of some 'undesirables' 'when the time comes', or else…

"Oh. And Misty and I should start covering up our ink when we were in public. And even halfway suggested I shut down the shop sometime in the near future."

Still gripping Eddie tightly, Misty said, tears shimmering in her eyes, "I thought Eddie was going to take them on right then. When they mentioned me…" Her eyes went to Eddie's, and then back to Horatio. "He got this look in his eyes. Like that time… Well, you know. But somehow, he held back. Just looked at them silently until they left."

"Yeah," Horatio said softly. "I do know." His eyes studied Eddie for a moment.

Eddie met Horatio's gaze calmly as he spoke. "Too big a risk for Misty at the moment. I just will not risk her. Not after I almost lost her. But those guys… They just better stay away from her, no matter what happens."

Horatio understood the threat that Eddie was making. It would not matter what happened to him. What he might have to do. No one was going to hurt Misty, in any way.

It took only a couple of seconds of seeing the two look at each other again, worry in the eyes of both of them, to make the decision. "If you wouldn't mind coming out to my place on the lake, to take a look around tomorrow, perhaps we can help each other out. In more ways than one."

Eddie stared at Horatio for a long minute, as Misty studied Eddie's face. Giving a slight nod, Eddie agreed. He relaxed then, as did Misty. The talk then turned to them keeping an eye on the office, and Melissa getting to work, at work, and getting home when Horatio was not handy.

Plans made, the three decided to skip the meal for the moment. Misty gave Horatio a hug, and then Eddie enveloped him in another tight bear hug before the two headed for home. Horatio shook his head, watching them drive away in the big Ford F-350, and then he locked up the building and headed for home himself.

As soon as he got home, he called Frank to let him know that there would be some additional people at the facility in the near future and asked him and Georgie to get several of the guest quarters ready for occupancy.

Horatio could hear the humor in Frank's voice when he agreed, and then said, "I knew it wouldn't be long." Before Horatio could ask him what he meant, Frank hung up.

The next call Horatio made was to Penny, for their nightly talk. Penny seemed to understand immediately why Horatio had done what he had for his friends. She even told him his caring nature was one of the things she loved about him.

Finally, after they finalized their plans for Thanksgiving, the two ended the call. Horatio fixed a light supper, ate it in front of the computer, and then went to bed.

The weekend was a busy one for Horatio. It seemed everyone involved wanted to see Horatio's place. After receiving calls from all of them within a matter of half an hour Saturday morning, Horatio gave them all directions on where to meet so he could take them out there and guide them through the minor maze and security steps to get to the home site.

Bunny was driving Mrs. Amstead's converted van, which was now equipped to handle her power wheelchair. It was set up so Mrs. Amstead could drive it herself after locking the wheelchair into place, or a regular driver's seat could be slid forward into place so someone else could drive, with Mrs. Amstead's wheelchair locked into place in the passenger's seating space.

Suzette was right behind the van, in an old beat up ex-military jeep, from the looks of it. Horatio took note of the winch in the front bumper and the rack on the rear with fuel and water cans, a spare tire, and some pioneer tools. The jeep sported a roll cage, with a cargo rack on top. It was loaded, though whatever was in it was not very tall, as the tarp covering it was not very high above the rack rails.

Eddie and Misty, rather than the Ford, were both on Harley choppers, fully suited up in winter leathers for the ride out. There was no precipitation in the forecast, but the temperature was in the mid-forties.

Having made the decision that he could trust each of them, Horatio led them through the security procedures, including the diversions and non-lethal traps that were now set up and active. Each had their own password, code, or combination to get through various locks, both electronic and mechanical

Each also received a laminated card with emergency words and procedures in case any were ever compromised and needed to let those at the facility know as much about the situation as possible, without giving away what they were doing.

It did not take long for everyone to become acquainted with one another, especially with Mrs. Amstead breaking the ice, mostly by telling stories about knowing Horatio as he was growing up.

Suzette did hang back a bit, though Misty and Georgie both brought her into the fold without hesitation, making her quite comfortable with the group. She was laughing with the others and lending a hand as the other two younger women put together a lunch for them all.

Though, when by her actions it was clear to Georgie that she needed some time alone, both gave her the privacy she needed, with Georgie giving her a few suggestions on where some quiet, comfortable spots were on the property that she might want to check out.

Suzette gave her a grateful smile and made herself scarce for most of the afternoon, exploring on her own as Horatio took the others around on a tour of the entire place.

Frank and Mrs. Amstead used their powered chairs for the tour. By the time they all returned to the main house, before Horatio and the others went back to town, Mrs. Amstead had the information from Frank on where to get one of the tracked chairs like the one he used, since it would go anywhere on the property, and her conventional powered wheelchair was significantly more limited.

With Mrs. Amstead entering the van, Bunny took Horatio aside for a moment. "Horatio, I swear, you and that Frank, the dear man, have given Alice a new lease on life.

"She has been doing well, yes, but she has also been putting on a good front at times, too. I think being part of this is going to be so good for her. And seeing Frank in his tracked wheelchair has her interest peaked and looking forward to doing so many things now she did not think she would ever be able to do again. So, thank you, Horatio. You have made an elderly woman very happy. Two of us, actually."

Horatio did not quite know what to say but was saved the need when Bunny hurried over to the van when she saw that Mrs. Amstead was behind the wheel and ready to go.

Suzette was in her jeep and gave a slight nod to Horatio as he walked over to the Suburban. She led the way, opening the gates as she went, with Mrs. Amstead and Bunny in the van next, Eddie and Misty behind the van, and Horatio last to secure everything on the way out.

Horatio's Sunday was spent reviewing and ordering additional equipment and supplies, considering the new circumstances. There was not really that much he needed to do, as he had, with Penny's guidance, prepared for additional people.

But he did want to fine tune things for the specific people, and get the orders in while he could, before the new legislation was passed and took effect, and he would be unable to get some of the things he wanted.

Before bed on Sunday, when Penny called, Horatio filled her in on how everyone had reacted, and what he had done to up his preps. She made a few suggestions, and then told him she would be adding just a few things herself, just in case they all wound up at her place.

Horatio found himself tearing up slightly at her words, Penny's trust in him and willingness to support his actions and take in those that he had chosen to bring into his circle.

After a heartfelt "I love you," to each other, and good-byes, both went to bed, falling asleep thinking about the other.

Despite his fears, things had seemed to settle down significantly by the time Horatio loaded up the Suburban and hitched his trailer to it to head for Penny's parents' home for Thanksgiving. Nothing new had occurred, the rhetoric had lessened, and several issues had fallen completely out of the news, such as it was now. There even seemed to be some progress on the international political front.

It made Horatio feel better about things, although he took heed of what Penny continued to stress, that it was only a lull as TPTB analyzed the results of their previous efforts and fine-tuned whatever they had planned for the future.

Horatio had expected the Arcade's homestead to be very nice, with prepper elements, but he was not prepared for the full extent of it and Penny's adjoining property when he made the turn onto the driveway from the county road up to the house near the center of the property.

He slowed to barely moving as his head swiveled back and forth, taking in everything he could see along the long driveway. Besides quite a few fruit and nut trees, which he was expecting, and some crop fields, there were many more trees than he was expecting, both for fruit and nut production, and what he recognized as yellowhorn trees that produced seed pods that produced very good quantities of an oil that converted to good biodiesel.

There were several other forested areas that looked very uniform, in blocks. Horatio realized they were coppicing wood lots for firewood. Seeing the willow lots, he remembered that willow made good charcoal and also had medicinal qualities. And could be used to make fencing and such.

The crop fields, those that were not already harvested, looked ready. And were much larger than he was expecting, as well as there being more of them that he thought there would be.

He passed the same type of living barrier fences he was growing the way Penny had taught him, with going through each gap revealing something else.

Then he saw the group of buildings. Horatio knew his mouth dropped open. Penny had told him there were three barns, and a handful of other outbuildings, and a very nice prepper friendly house.

He was not sure why he had thought everything would be on so much smaller scale than what it was. Not only were the barns larger, as were the out buildings, but the nice two- or three-bedroom single level house he was expecting was actually a two-story brick house verging on being a mansion.

Thankfully, Horatio had his mouth closed, and his astonishment under control when he pulled to a stop on the large parking area of Penny's parents' house, at right angle to the two-double-wide-door-garage.

Penny ran to the Suburban and was standing ready to leap into Horatio's arms as soon as he stepped out. It was another thing that surprised him. Her open expression of her feelings for him in front her parents.

She was a bit pink cheeked when she turned around and led Horatio to where her parents were standing at the foot of the steps of the porch of the house, her hand in Horatio's.

"Mrs. Arcade, Mr. Arcade," Horatio said, stretching out his hand toward Penny's father.

"Boy," Mr. Arcade replied, "good to finally meet my girl's paramour." His eyes searched Horatio's face, and especially his eyes. A small smile curved his lips when he seemed to be satisfied and gave Horatio's hand one final firm pump.

Horatio felt like he had successfully passed some test that Mr. Arcade had just put him through. Mrs. Arcade, on the other hand, having seen how happy her daughter was now, and seeing the look on her face, and Horatio's when he looked at Penny, was already convinced. She pulled Horatio into a tight hug when he would have shaken her hand.

Despite her diminutive size, like Penny, Mrs. Arcade was more than strong enough to give Horatio a hard squeeze around his chest. "Welcome, Horatio. It is so good to meet the man that has captured my daughter's heart."

Apparently, the introductions were done, for Mr. Arcade said, "Come on, boy. We have some chores to finish. Gave the hands the holiday off, plus a bit. Been a decent year." He started to walk away, without a backward look.

Penny gave Horatio a rather sheepish look but did not say a word when Horatio looked at her. So, Horatio hurried after Mr. Arcade, thankful he had decided to wear jeans, a long-sleeved shirt, boots, leather jacket, and a wide brim hat for the trip.

Mr. Arcade lost no time in putting Horatio to work in the barn, working on a small combine. Horatio was thankful that Mr. Arcade was willing to explain what he wanted Horatio to do, and then led him through the work when there was something that Horatio had not a clue how to accomplish, which was often. And Mr. Arcade was never negative in any way when he did so.

He did expect Horatio to do the work, once it was explained to him, but seemed to have no expectations that Horatio would know how to do any specific thing but did not seem to mind that at all.

Horatio could tell that Mr. Arcade was fully expecting Horatio to learn what he needed, in order to accomplish the work, without hesitation or complaint. So, Horatio made sure he did just that.

Penny looked up toward the hallway that opened to the back porch, with the laundry room off one side of it, and the mudroom off the other. She noted immediately that her father had a hand on Horatio's shoulder, as the two men talked quietly back and forth.

She could hear enough words to know they were discussing something about one of the combines. Penny's next realization was that while Horatio's and her father's hands and faces were scrubbed clean, there were still a few dirt and light grease marks on their clothing, though obviously both had brushed themselves as clean as possible before washing up in the mud room.

Horatio's eyes suddenly turned to Penny. She thought she might just swoon when his lips curled up into a most amazing smile. Just a bit different from any she had seen him form before.

"Good worker, this one, Penny child," her father said gruffly, before he gave Mrs. Arcade a peck on the lips and then headed for the stairs to go change his clothing.

Horatio stepped toward Penny but looked down at himself and stopped just short of reaching her. "I don't want to get you..." he was saying when Penny took the remaining step needed to bring them together and stood on tip toes to give him a kiss much like the one her father had given her mother.

"I am used to getting clothing dirty, Horatio," she told him, stepping back, her eyes glowing with pride in him. "I took the bags up. Your room is third on the left from..."

"Penny," Horatio exclaimed. "Those bags are heavy! You shouldn't have carried them up the stairs!"

Penny grinned at him, just as her mother was doing, Mrs. Arcade having glanced over her shoulder from where she was doing something at the cook stove.

"Oh, Horatio! I used the elevator. I use the stairs most of the time, for health reasons, but it would have been silly to drag those lead weight cases up them. The elevator is much easier."

"They have an el..." Horatio looked chagrinned and took a quick look over at Mrs. Arcade to judge her reaction to what he had been saying, which could have been something of an insult, if taken wrong.

"Just like the ones in our places," Penny replied, still grinning at him. We aren't total hicks, you know."

Horatio winced, even though he knew Penny was just ribbing him. "Uh..."

"Leave the poor boy alone, PP. Let him go get a shower and changed. Supper will be ready soon."

Horatio managed not to laugh, nor use the nickname her mother used for Penny, when he said. "I'll go change. Something smells fabulous." He had seen Penny's slight wince at the endearment. He leaned forward, and gave Penny another peck on the lips, and then grinned at her and winked, before following the path that Mr. Arcade had taken.

Several minutes later, when Horatio came back down, showered and dressed in fresh clothing, he found Mr. Arcade sitting at the head of the table, talking quietly to Mrs. Arcade, who sat on his left, as Penny set the table.

"What can I do to help?" he asked, looking first at Mrs. Arcade, and then to Penny when her mother did not reply but looked over at Penny, too.

"Finish setting the table and then come get a serving dish. Things will be ready in just a couple of minutes," Penny told Horatio.

"You help out much in the kitchen, do you?" asked Mr. Arcade.

Horatio could not decipher Mr. Arcade's expression. So, he shrugged slightly and said, "Yes, Sir. Of course. My mother taught me to cook, as well as do everything else in a kitchen, as well.

"And my father taught me to grill. They thought a couple should be able to take care of all the different duties required around a household, in case one or the other was ill, or taking care of children, or for whatever reason. I've always felt it was just the right thing to do."

Mr. Arcade made a "Hm," sound, but turned back to his wife and continued their conversation. Horatio finished up setting the table, and then went into the kitchen.

Softly he whispered to Penny, "Does your father not approve of men helping in the kitchen?"

"Of course, he approves. He helps Momma all the time. If he said something about it he was just razzing you. He has a very subtle sense of humor sometimes."

Horatio straightened back up and shook his head. "Oh. Okay," he said. When Penny pointed at a large casserole dish on a metal trivet with her chin, Horatio picked it up and followed her out to the dining room.

"Here in front of me," Mr. Arcade said, making a gesture for Horatio to set the dish down in the clear area just in front of him. Horatio did so, and Penny placed the dish she was carrying down beside it.

"Tea is in the fridge, Horatio. And a water pitcher. I'll get the salad and we'll be set."

Horatio dutifully followed her back into the kitchen, retrieved the two large glass pitchers, and took them to the dining room after Penny carried the salad bowl.

A few minutes later, with Penny on her father's right, and Horatio beside her, Mr. Arcade said a short Grace. He then began to serve from the hot dishes as plates were passed to him, and then back, as Mrs. Arcade did the same with the salad and the covered basket of rolls.

Mr. Arcade guided most of the talk at first. He filled in Horatio what the homestead was producing in the way of crops and stock animals.

The questions Horatio asked seemed to please and satisfy Mr. Arcade, as he continued to talk, answering the questions succinctly. Halfway through the meal, Mr. Arcade said, "That's about the size of it, boy."

Mr. Arcade cut his eyes up to Horatio again, but this time they stayed on him as he asked, "How goes it with you? Business good?"

When Horatio began to speak, between bites, Mr. Arcade listened as he continued to eat, looking up from time to time.

"In some ways, yes, Sir, very good. In others… Well, not so much."

Mr. Arcade's eyes studied him for a moment. "How so?" he asked and then he looked down to cut another piece of the casserole on his plate.

"The work is there, but so many people are expressing great distrust about the laws, and lawyers, and judges. They seem to be angry about having to do certain things, legally, to do or have what they want. And are very disgruntled at the cost.

"And some of the things they are asking me to do, simply aren't legal. As well as some of it just simply not being right, morally or ethically. At least for me." Horatio had stopped eating and was looking at Mr. Arcade when he lifted his eyes again.

"I see." He glanced over at Penny for a moment, and then back to Horatio. He was still holding his fork halfway up off the plate. "Penny has run into a bit of that, herself. This country is falling apart, and there isn't a danged thing I can do to stop it."

He looked from Horatio to Penny, and back again. "It is good that my daughter has seen this and prepared. And it is good that she has someone strong and caring to stand beside her as this all plays out."

With that, Mr. Arcade turned to his wife and said, "Excellent meal tonight, sweetie. As always."

"Oh, Michael! You flatter you," Mrs. Arcade replied. "You know good and well PP made this dinner." Suddenly she looked over at Horatio first, and then turned her eyes to Penny. "I am so sorry, Penny. I will try harder not to slip."

"It is okay, Momma. Horatio makes nothing of it. Do not worry about slipping."

The talk, now led by Mrs. Arcade, turned to local events, with more than a bit of gossip. Penny obviously did not encourage it, and even tried to side track her mother a few times. But Janet Arcade was an inveterate gossiper. Penny finally quit trying, when Horatio winked at her after one of Mrs. Arcades more hilarious recountings of a local spinster.

After the meal, Mr. Arcade surprised Horatio. Horatio had risen and started to gather dishes to take to the kitchen, intending to help do the cleanup and wash the dishes. But Mr. Arcade said, "Leave it, boy. The missus and I will take care of this. You spend some time with your girl. I know she has been missing you."

"Well… Thank you Mr. Arcade. I have missed her terribly, as well."

A few kisses into the evening, Horatio heard a throat being cleared at the door to the living room, and he hurriedly straightened up, but continued to hold Penny's hand.

Mr. and Mrs. Arcade entered the living room. Horatio noted that they, too, were holding hands. They only slipped apart when Mr. Arcade settled into the leather recliner at one side of the sofa, and Mrs. Arcade took the one beside him. They were separated by a table with a lamp.

There was a short discussion, and it was decided on which movie to watch. After things were ready, Penny and Mrs. Arcade went to make popcorn and get some soft drinks ready. Mr. Arcade and Horatio discussed various movies they particularly liked. When the ladies returned, the movie was started, and the four spend a pleasant evening together.

None too surprised when Mr. Arcade and Mrs. Arcade rose after the movie and stated they were off to bed. What did surprise him just slightly was that Penny did the same. He was expecting Penny to spend a bit more time with him.

Penny must have noticed his disappointment. "Oh, Horatio. I'm sorry. I know you wanted to spend more time together this evening. But we do have plenty of time while you are here. I have a lot planned for you." Penny smiled mischievously. For tonight, I want you to get some rest. I know the trip was a long one."

Horatio smiled ruefully. "Okay, Penny. I understand."

She took his hand and led him to the stairs, flipping off the lights as they went. Mr. Arcade had already done the evening lockdown before he had turned in. Horatio walked Penny to her bedroom door, where he took both of her hands in his, leaned forward and kissed her. She kissed him back with fervor.

After the long kiss, Penny on her tip toes, and Horatio leaning forward, their foreheads touching, Penny said, "I love you, Horatio."

"I love you, Penny. More than I ever thought I could love anyone."

"Oh, Horatio... I better go in."

"Yes. Yes," Horatio whispered. "Probably a good idea." He gave her one more quick kiss, and stepped back. She slipped through the door, closing it softly behind her. Horatio walked back down the hallway and entered his bedroom with a smile on his face.

The next two days were both filled with activity. Horatio could not remember a time when he had so much fun. He discovered quickly that Penny had come by her mischievous and sometimes playful nature honestly. Her parents were the same, though perhaps not quite as often.

Part of the time was spent with Horatio helping Mr. Arcade. More was Horatio getting a full tour of both Mr. and Mrs. Arcade's homestead, and Penny's adjoining property.

Horatio was amazed again and again by how organized and well prepared the family was, at both places. All of the long lead aspects were complete. The living barrier fences, various orchards, and other permanent plantings were either producing extremely well, or were fully grown, doing the job for which they were planted.

Despite the amount of activity at the homestead, Penny's place, and the holiday activities in the nearby town, Horatio and Penny were able to spend quite a bit of time together.

Everyone was up early on Thanksgiving Day. A quick breakfast of pastries, juice, and coffee or tea, just to stave off hunger, and all four returned to the kitchen to begin the Thanksgiving dinner initial preparations.

After those preps were complete, Penny and Mrs. Arcade left Horatio and Mr. Arcade in the kitchen, after Penny smilingly informed Horatio that it was a family tradition for Mr. Arcade to prepare the second breakfast on Thanksgiving Day. And today, it would be with Horatio's help.

"Come on, boy," Mr. Arcade said, with a clap on his shoulder, "start chopping onions, tomatoes, and mushrooms." Mr. Arcade gave the occasional instruction to Horatio, and a short while later the rest of the two-part breakfast was ready.

Horatio rolled the serving cart into the living room as Mr. Arcade set up the folding tables in front of the sofa and chairs. Mrs. Arcade and Penny were watching the Thanksgiving Day Parades. After serving them, Horatio and Mr. Arcade took their own seats, and joined them.

Though the television was left on during the Thanksgiving dinner, only scant attention was paid to it, as everyone enjoyed the meal. But Horatio did notice that it was Penny, rather than Mr. Arcade, that did pay the most attention to the games, and the follow up shows.

Mrs. Arcade distracted him with some tales of Penny when she was growing up, when they were fortunate enough to have at home for one of her visits. The next time he thought to look, and ask her about her interest, the games were over, and other things were going on.

It was the best Thanksgiving Horatio had experienced since he was a child, and it equaled some of those, he decided. Despite more than a bit of reluctance from Mr. Arcade and Horatio, the four headed for the city, to do some Christmas shopping during the Black Friday sales.

With no intention of trying to make the openings of the various super sales, they took their time getting ready, and hit the city shortly after 10:00 AM.

Horatio was riding with Penny in her truck, while Mr. And Mrs. Arcade traveled in their beautifully restored 1974 Cadillac Fleetwood Talisman. Plenty of room for any amount of Christmas shopping the two might do.

Penny had wanted to come more to check out the situation in the city, rather than do much actual shopping. She quietly explained that to Horatio on the way in.

"Horatio, I am not sure if you picked up on any of the things going on during the parades, pre- and post-game shows, or the game itself, with the national commercials..."

Penny had looked over at him as her words trailed off. He shook his head. "What did you see?" he asked her.

"Very hard to pin down, or explain, Horatio," she explained as her eyes went back to the road and stayed there as she continued to speak. "It was all very subtle. I am not sure I would have picked up on any of it if I had not been watching for such things.

"And while I did pick up on some of the techniques, I have a feeling others, new ones, might have slipped by me. But, it was all basically the same as what we have seen before, just before the recent event."

Penny shot him a glance. "I believe they are priming the pump, so to speak. They might trigger something this weekend, if I missed something major…"

"Hm…" Horatio said thoughtfully. "I do not see it, Penny. The weekend is a letdown, not big emotion days the way Thanksgiving is, and Black Friday is, in a way. People will be buying Christmas presents, mostly, and obviously taking advantage of other sales, as well. I am just not sure what the objective would be right now.

"There are huge crowds, yes, but still…"

Again, she met his eyes when he stopped talking, quickly putting them back on the road when someone ahead of them hammered on his horn. They were getting closer to the city.

"Horatio, I think you are probably right. Which makes me think… We need to check out some of the games for the stand-alone systems, as well as computer games."

Penny shrugged her shoulders. "Well… Anything and everything, I suppose. And not just gifts for children through teens. Pretty much everything. Especially heavily discounted, new-to-the-market products."

"Yes," Horatio said, looking thoughtful.

The old Radio Shack MURS mobile radio that Penny had in the truck, matching the one in the Cadillac, broke squelch. "Honey, we are going to try to find a spot near the Macy's outside entrance facing west.

"If you can't find one close to us, just park anywhere and we will meet you in Macy's near the enclosed mall entry to the store."

"Yes, ma'am," Horatio said, picking up and keying the microphone. "Will do. See you in a few."

Satisfied with the situation, Mrs. Arcade felt no need to respond again.

It did so happen that Mr. Arcade lucked into a spot right near where they wanted to be. But there was not another parking slot anywhere close. So, Penny drove around until she found one with both slots facing each other open. She pulled in, but the truck was just too long to fit in one slot. It took both of them.

After locking up, they headed for an entrance, hand-in-hand. Immediately upon entering, they were bombarded with the sights and sounds of what would probably turn out to be a very electronic and technical Christmas present Christmas.

They hurried to meet up with Mr. and Mrs. Arcade. Setting a time and location where they would meet to get lunch, the two couples split up again.

Horatio had to use his long legs to full advantage, as Penny seemed to be moving faster than she should be able to with her shorter legs and high heels.

Penny's first stop was at the largest of the electronic gaming stores. Horatio watched Penny as she perused the advertising materials spread around the store. "You notice anything, Horatio?" she asked softly, though not quite a whisper.

"Lots of new games, and versions of old games?" Horatio replied, more a question than a statement.

"Yes," Penny responded. "But notice that there are no demonstrator versions of them on any of the try-out consoles. They have been hyping these games for a month now.

"But there have not been more than a couple of instances of showing anything from the games, other than a very quick look at a few of the characters, and just a few backgrounds. Nothing to really indicate just what they are about, other than the genre. First person shooter, strategy, empire building, and so on."

Penny glanced at him, and then indicated one of the posters. "And this one is entirely new. There is usually a huge introduction to new game series. Note the subject..."

Horatio took a good look at the poster. There was nothing overt about the images, he decided. There was a city street scene, with vehicles and people all about, with the tall buildings. Nothing really outstanding that he could see.

But then one sentence seemed to jump out at him. *Now it's **your** turn to see justice done.* Horatio took a closer look at the images. Suddenly he noticed the style of some of the buildings, and when he looked closer at them, he could read the engravings in the facades.

He spotted *City Hall, Court House, Police Station,* several international corporation logos, *Welfare Office, Social Security Office, Federal Building.*

When he looked even closer, though they were not really clear, assuming they were following the same pattern, Horatio was sure he could decipher business signs on some of the windows of a stretch of the street. Attorney at Law, Abortion Clinic, Medical Marijuana, Pharmacy, Wicca

Shop. There were more, but he just could not make out for sure what they were.

His eyes met Penny's. "This does not look good." And his words were a whisper.

Penny nodded, and then motioned him over toward a display of games. "Common theme," she simply said.

Horatio looked them over. Mostly the newest editions of some established games, but he did note a few new ones, according to the packaging. Again, nothing really stood out, but knowing what he did now, he could see the potential for some more than subtle opinion guiding possibilities in every one of them.

They left the gaming store and went into the nearby bookstore. Penny did not randomly walk the aisles between the bookshelves. She headed first toward the areas that had books supporting a prepper lifestyle, including off-the-grid books, homesteading books, gardening books, hunting, fishing, camping, and the like.

Horatio's eyes scanned the shelves the way hers were. "Not nearly as many titles," she muttered. Then Horatio followed her to one section after another. It was easy to see what she was looking for, as the books were all over the place.

Your Due was one title that popped out for Horatio. *What's Wrong with America* was another. Every title that Penny's eyes lingered on had something to do with making huge changes in American society.

And when Horatio thumbed through half a dozen of them, all but one had a section in the Table of Contents about how a person could bring about the changes. Reading a bit here and there in those sections and Horatio discovered that along with the standard, legal ways to change things, there were more than hints about making it happen, legal or not.

And the sixth book, while it did not have a chapter on effecting change, did have a chapter on forming and implementing 'Action Committees' to come up with plans 'to ensure that justice was brought to every person and organization that had created the problems the nation faces', with strong implication that they need not be peaceful plans.

The two exchanged worried looks. Next stop was a trendy clothing store catering to both men and women. Horatio did a double take as they approached the entrance. "Is that... Is that leather body armor?" He whispered the question to Penny.

"I am afraid so," she replied, also whispering. "And not just a few design elements relating to armor, but full on working leather armor, with fashion statements added to it."

"If people…"

"When people, Horatio. When people…" she interrupted him. "Look at the advertising, and then look at the customers. The stuff is flying off the shelves."

Horatio turned his attention from the products, to the ad displays. Violent street scenes in the background, and people sporting the leather wear prominent in the foreground.

They moved on without going inside. It was Horatio that shifted their path slightly toward one of the walkway kiosks. A sunglass business. A quick chin motion had Penny looking at what amounted to high fashion goggles. And not ski goggles, either. Goggles suitable for use in risky environments. *Industrial Chic* was the product line name.

"I wonder…" Penny mused, and Horatio followed her quick footsteps to one of the several hat shops in the mall. There were several. Some fancy hats for women, some sports team hats, some other logo hats, and some highly practical outdoor hats.

Penny found what she suspected she might. The two stood before a display of another *Industrial Chic* brand line of products. These were mostly fancy looking hard hats, identical to those workmen were required to wear in many industrial jobs.

And both noticed at the same time, the small ad across the bottom of the set of hat display stands, touting the special-order accessories. Including Steampunk style goggles, half- and full-face respirators.

Finally, going into a toy shop, they began to look around. They found, along with many of the classic toys, and types of toys, a couple of new types. One was blatantly labeled *Social Justice in Our Time*. Not only was there a board game, but several books, action figures, and a RPG version of the game, with included game master manual, dice, character development sheets, and character options lists.

Everywhere they went in the mall they found similar goods, all being touted for Christmas. None were more blatant than what they had already seen, and there more that were much more subtle.

The majority of products, of course, were benign. But the percentage of those that were not was very worrisome to Penny and Horatio.

The two did make several purchases, Penny guiding Horatio in his selection of presents for her parents.

Penny did not bring up the subject of addictive entertainment when they met her parents on time and had lunch. Horatio managed to join in the discussions that Penny kept light and upbeat, without letting his worries show.

After lunch, they split up again, this time with Mr. Arcade strolling through the mall with Horatio. Penny went with her mother. They would meet again at 5:00 PM, and head back home, with a stop to get something to eat.

Horatio found himself entranced as Mr. Arcade talked about life on the homestead, occasionally interjecting a comment about something he would see in one of the mall shops.

They went into a few of them, mostly technology and sporting goods types. But, much to Horatio's surprise, Mr. Arcade turned and calmly walked into Victoria's Secret. "Need a little privacy here, son," Mr. Arcade told Horatio. "No need for you to know what my wife likes to wear under her outer clothing."

Mr. Arcade winked at Horatio, and Horatio was again amazed when one of the store clerks greeted Mr. Arcade warmly, and headed off with him further back into the store, discussing something that Horatio was glad he could not hear.

Horatio considered, for a very short fraction of a second about getting something for Penny from Victoria's Secret. But decided just as quickly that it was not a good idea. At the moment, anyway.

He strolled around the other shops nearby, until Mr. Arcade came out of the lingerie shop, a well filled bag in his hand. "One more stop for me, for sure, and I will take these out to the car and get them secured away." Horatio just nodded.

Something caught Mr. Arcade's eyes in a Brookstone's, and he went in, with Horatio trailing behind, browsing as Mr. Arcade made a purchase.

Leaving Brookstone's, Mr. Arcade made a beeline to the See's candy shop. Watching Mr. Arcade make selections for custom boxes, Horatio decided that it was a pretty good idea.

Not for Christmas, so much, as he had already ordered chocolates from Godiva for Penny, Melissa, and several others, for Christmas. But for now. He wanted to give something to Penny right now, and would get Mrs. Arcade a few pieces, as well.

He had heard enough of Mr. Arcade's conversation with the clerk, who seemed to know Mrs. Arcade's preferences as well as Mr. Arcade did, to pick out enough of a selection for a small box for her.

Before Mr. Arcade headed for the parking lot to stow his purchases, he gave Horatio a bit of advice on what Mrs. Arcade might like to receive, after Horatio asked.

He had already picked up a few things for her, with Penny, but wanted something more. And Mr. Arcade gave him the perfect idea. There was something he had already seen, when shopping with Penny, but she had not mentioned it, and Horatio had not recognized as a good gift for Penny's mother.

Hurrying through the mall, he saw Penny and her mother discussing something in one of the shops and managed to slip past without the very situationally aware Penny spotting him.

He paid for the item, waited for it to be wrapped, and dropped the package in the store bag. But then immediately went into another store to pick up a couple of things, primarily just to get another bag. He could use the items, but it was the large bag that he wanted the most. He dropped the wrapped gift into that bag, discarding the original store bag.

Hurrying again to meet up with Mr. Arcade, he came to a sudden stop when he saw Penny and Mrs. Arcade in a jewelry shop. The display case they were looking in was the engagement ring and wedding ring case, according to the prominent sign on the top glass.

Horatio slipped past again, without being noticed, his mind suddenly very active as various thoughts came to him.

Despite the things that Horatio and Penny had seen, everyone was in a good mood when they left the mall and headed for the family's favorite restaurant in the area.

Horatio insisted on paying, despite Mr. Arcade's quick objection. But Mrs. Arcade's hand gently placed on his arm silenced Mr. Arcade and he acquiesced gracefully.

Knowing the plan for Sunday, Horatio made a few plans himself, without any of the Arcades knowing. Since he was heading back on Monday, it was suddenly imperative to do what he was planning that Sunday.

Saturday was spent processing the garden products that were now ready for harvest. Horatio was pleased that he was able to fit right into the activities, doing the tasks he was assigned quickly and well.

After finishing up late in the evening, Mr. Arcade slapped Horatio on the back as they headed in from the harvest prep kitchen to the house. "You did just fine, son! Took to it like a duck to water. We'll have you trained and integrated into this family in nothing flat."

Penny turned red, and exclaimed, "Daddy!" She turned to her mother and added, "Momma!", in a plea for her to stop her father from embarrassing her.

But Mr. and Mrs. Arcade just laughed, and when Horatio said, "It's okay, Penny. No big deal," and pulled Penny into a firm side hug, her blush faded and she hugged him back.

With it being so late, all four worked together in the kitchen, after cleaning up, to prepare a hearty, but quick, supper they enjoyed sitting together and watching another movie.

All turned in right after the movie, as the family usually went to the early services of the church they attended.

The next morning, Penny noticed that Horatio seemed a bit nervous, and tugged him in tight against her side as they waited outside the church before they needed to enter.

Suddenly, Horatio looked at Penny. "Penny, I am really worried about what is going on. Do you have any real feel for when The Powers That Be might make a move?"

"I don't know, Horatio," Penny said, now standing in front of him, both his hands in hers, as she looked up at his face. "I thought perhaps at Christmas, with what we saw at the mall... But that just does not seem like the best time for it."

Her gaze went distant, as she thought. Horatio could almost swear he could hear her brain processing information in her head, and see things swirling in her eyes. When her focus snapped back to Horatio, she continued as if she had not even paused for a moment.

She shook her head. "New Year's Eve? Day?" she asked herself tentatively, her eyes back on Horatio's. "I do not know, Horatio," she said again. I just do not get the sense that those days would be most effective for what they seem to be trying to do. We will just have to wait and see."

Horatio nodded. When Penny added, "I am in a near frenzy adding to my consumable stocks and repair components. It is not a good sign for me... but still... we will not know until it happens."

Again, she paused. "Well, possibly until just before it happens. I am sure there will be some signs of it that we will be able to recognize."

Mr. and Mrs. Arcade joined them, and they all joined the rest of the congregation entering the church. Horatio made his decision final, after what Penny had said. She glanced over at him when he squeezed her hand rather tightly, without realizing it. But he had immediately relaxed his, and she thought nothing more about it.

At least, not until the service was over, and she had introduced Horatio to the minister. Mr. and Mrs. Arcade were talking to some friends near the entrance of the church, just inside.

Penny took a step toward them, but a gentle tug on her hand had her turning toward Horatio. His eyes were on her as he walked, turned slightly backward, taking her several feet away from the rest of the church members.

When Horatio let go of her hand, his hand going to his suit jacket pocket as he went to one knee before her, Penny's eyes widened and she found she was holding her breath. Both her hands went to her mouth when Horatio snapped open the ring case he had taken from his pocket.

"Penny," he said, looking up into her eyes, totally unaware of those now staring at the two of them. "I love you. I have for a long time now. And we are facing some serious events in the future. I would very much like to face them together with you, not as just friends, but as husband and wife. Will you marry me?"

"Oh, Horatio!" Penny sighed, her hands now going to his to tug him up. "Of course, I will marry you!" Horatio slipped the ring onto her finger and put the box back into his pocket.

Reaching up, Penny tugged his head down to hers, and kissed him firmly. Until the applause and yelling registered with her. And then Horatio.

They both spun around to see most of the congregation looking at them, with her parents in the forefront, happy grins on their faces. Mrs. Arcade started forward, and Penny ran to her joyfully, to show her the ring.

Mr. Arcade joined Horatio, to stand with him, and they watched the two women hug, and then disappear into a group of women, all talking at once.

When the minister came up to Mr. Arcade and Horatio, Mr. Arcade immediately said, "Have you met my future son-in-law, Jack? This fine man is Horatio Billings. I can't tell you how happy I am to be welcoming him to the family."

"Penny did introduce me," said Jack, shaking Horatio's hand again. "She did not say, nor did he, that he was planning to propose to her in my church. Very auspicious start, Horatio. You have a very lovely and loving young woman in Penny. I congratulate you."

Jack put his hand on Mr. Arcade's shoulder but looked at Horatio. "Be sure you do not let Michael scare you away. His bite may be worse than his bark, but he very seldom actually bites."

Mr. Arcade chuckled, as did the minister. Horatio smiled. Mr. Arcade and Horatio drifted over to see if they could extract mother and daughter from the well-wishers so they could head home.

Penny and her mother spent most of the rest of the afternoon making plans for the wedding. Neither they, nor Mr. Arcade seemed to mind at all the short timeframe before the wedding, nor how simple it was to be.

Horatio was not sure if Penny had mentioned the whys and wherefores that prompted Horatio to ask Penny at this particular time, and the seeming urgency for them to marry quickly. It really did not matter much, since they accepted and supported the marriage.

With the preliminary plans made, Penny and Horatio were able to spend some private time later in the afternoon and into the evening. Monday morning came, and they said goodbye, reluctantly, with marriage plans in place.

They were to be married at Penny's family's church, a week before Christmas. They had discussed holding it at Penny's new place but decided that it would be better to keep that property as quiet as possible. It was the same for her parent's place and Penny's adjacent property.

So those that would attend would stay in town, in local motels, and then head back to their respective homes.

A four-day honeymoon, and they would celebrate Christmas at Horatio's house in town with their friends and Penny's parents. After that, they were not sure what they would do. Worried about what might happen on New Year's Eve or New Year's Day, they planned to simply see what happened, and act accordingly.

Chapter Eight

-

Things went pretty much as planned. And, if anything, everything calmed down even more around the world. Still, Penny and Horatio thought the risks were still high.

Even during their honeymoon, just the two of them at Penny's new place, they monitored what was happening in the world.

At Christmas, Penny noted that all those that were now living at Horatio's property never let on to any of the other guests in Horatio's house in town exactly where they lived, nor why, even though the majority were preppers themselves. But not all were, so the subject was not brought up.

It helped that things were calmer, so discussions tended to stay on much less worrisome topics.

Penny had been welcomed into the fold by Horatio's friends that she had not met before. Especially Mrs. Amstead. And a bit surprisingly, for Horatio, though he was not sure why it surprised him, Suzette and Penny had immediately formed a strong bond. Suzette was Penny's shadow whenever they in the same place.

It was not until the day after Christmas that the signs Penny was expecting to see began to appear. It was announced that Congress had passed, in a late-night session two days before their adjournment for the holidays, the legislation that had been written and introduced after the earlier events.

Unlike the original bills, the final laws that were passed were set to become effective January 1st of the new year.

Besides that quiet announcement, that very few people not involved with it were aware, other effects of the plan that Penny suspected was in place and now in action, began to show up.

The games, books, and other entertainment gifts received that Christmas were having an influence on people, just as the combination of the earlier movie and gaming had created.

"I don't know, Horatio," Penny said two days after Christmas. They were in the house in town, with Horatio ready to head in to his office, while Penny was adding her things to the household that she had brought down with her. "These are isolated events, again, though seemingly all over. But they do not seem to be coordinated in any way, like they were the time before. I can't quite get a handle on it.

"I was sure New Year's Eve or New Year's Day would be the time the major attack started, but this does not really point in that direction." She shook her head.

"All we can do is wait and see, Penny," Horatio said. He gave her a long kiss before heading out the door. Just before he left he turned and said, "Be sure to lock down. And if you come to the office, be extra careful."

"I will, Horatio. You be careful, too."

Worried, Penny continued to monitor everything she could. The aggression was not increasing, but there were constant incidents, over most of the world. Still no cohesion in them, and the MSM was not reporting much of the activity. Only local news reported on local events, and not all of the time.

Penny learned this from Amateur Radio operators she kept in contact with, and from a few foreign shortwave news broadcasts, also usually local in nature from their area.

The second day that Horatio was back at work, he had his first encounter with the new events. Pamela Jones, a longtime client, in her early fifties, came into the office for an appointment she had made before Christmas.

Horatio saw that Melissa was nervous when she announced Pamela. And then, when Pamela was seen into his office, she slammed down a hardback copy of *What's Wrong with America*, on his desk. It was one of the books he and Penny had seen at the mall on Black Friday.

Her face was red, and she was obviously angry. An almost sneer on her face, she said, "I expect you to do the work I have hired you to do, just as instructed, and none of the shenanigans that are in this book. You're lucky I don't fire you and hire BeLinda Nomes. She isn't like the lawyers in this book. Lawyers like you."

"And what work would that be, Pa... Mrs. Jones?" Horatio asked in an even voice.

"You know perfectly we... Oh." She closed her mouth, took a packet of papers out of her purse, and handed them to Horatio. "This. Take care of this. And I expect to be billed for actual time spent, not the padded billing you lawyers have been getting away with for years."

Melissa stuck her head in the door that she opened, Pamela having slammed it shut forcefully when she left.

"Horatio?" Melissa asked. "I heard yelling."

"Don't worry about it, Melissa." Horatio looked thoughtful, and then added, "For now. But if someone... Anyone... treats you in any way that you are uncomfortable with… Aggressively, undue anger, accusingly, anything… hang up with them immediately, if they are on the phone. If it happens out there, use your signal button to let me know."

"Okay, Horatio," Melissa said softly, worry lining her face.

Horatio sighed. "Dang it!" he muttered even as he was picking up the telephone.

Eddie and Misty showed up a few minutes later. They were smiling, at least slightly, when Melissa showed them into the office and then brought tea and coffee.

But after Melissa left and closed the door, the smiles disappeared and rather grim looks appeared. "Horatio, that stuff you were saying? It is happening again. Not as bad as before, right now, but it is happening. I take it something happened here, too?"

Horatio nodded. "Aggressive client. Had one of the new books I've seen at bookstores. One making out how lawyers and judges are all bad, and the legal system corrupt."

"Want me to hang around after I see Melissa in for work in the mornings?"

Again, Horatio sighed. He ran his hands through his hair. "I don't know, Eddie! You can't babysit us full time. You have your own lives to live, you and Misty. But I do not want Melissa getting hurt any more than she has been. I am not sure what to do right now."

Eddie nodded, exchanged a glance with Misty, and then looked back at Horatio. "Maybe you should consider a change in professions. Or maybe just a hiatus from work for a while. Leave of absence sort of thing."

Horatio was shaking his head. "I have taken off so much time lately… And I have clients that need my help… I don't want to up and let Melissa go, even for her own safety. That isn't fair to her. She needs the income for herself, and to help her folks since her mother lost her job, and her father's hours have been cut."

"Can't save the world, or everyone in it, old chum," Eddie replied. "And just because I want to, I'll be around a bit more during the days. For now. I have a feeling this situation is not going to last all that long."

Horatio looked at him in surprise. But then Eddie added, "It is going to get much worse, and what is happening now will not matter much."

Horatio could only nod unhappily as Eddie and Misty left. Patricia was the last client scheduled for an office visit for the day. Horatio checked the outside cameras and saw that Eddie and Misty were, in fact, hanging around unobtrusively.

Going out to the reception area, Horatio told Melissa, "Melissa, I have that last meeting today at the courthouse. You might as well go home. Full pay, of course. And with the way things are going, I am going to look at the books... see if I can afford to raise your pay at least some."

Trying to keep it as light as he could, he added, "Hazard pay, so to speak."

"Oh, Horatio, don't say things like that!" Melissa cried. And then did actually begin to cry.

"Hey, hey, hey..." Horatio said, taking the sobbing woman into her arms.

A few seconds later Melissa composed herself and stepped away from Horatio. "I'm sorry, Horatio. I'm just under so much pressure now, with here, and my parents, and my boyfriend..."

"Micky?" Horatio asked, surprised. "I thought you two were close to getting..."

Melissa sniffed back more tears, "He said he didn't want to get married anytime soon, just the other day. I thought he was going to propose the other night, but that is what he wanted to discuss with me."

"Oh, Melissa, I am so sorry," Horatio said softly.

Melissa wiped her eyes and blew her nose, and then looked at Horatio. "I do think I will go home and try to relax a bit." She closed her eyes, sighed, and looked at Horatio again. "Daddy wants me to quit this job and stay home with Mother and try to do something on-line to generate more income. He... uh... doesn't like me working for an attorney..."

That really surprised Horatio. "Ah..." Horatio stuttered, "Well... you know that I will help in any way I can..."

"I know, Horatio. Thank you. And... If I do leave, I will give you as much notice as I can."

"Okay, Melissa," Horatio replied, walking to the front door with her. He made sure Eddie saw her, and then turned back to get the office ready to close up before he left to go to the courthouse.

The appointment at the courthouse did not go any better than the one with Pamela Jones. Different, for sure, but not any better. Horatio was half expecting some cooperation, even a little commiseration over the situation, as his meeting was with Judge Farnsworth.

It was quite apparent that the Judge had run into some of the same attitudes as Horatio had. But in the Judge's eyes, it was the lawyers' fault, not judges fault that people were suddenly so disenchanted with the legal system.

Horatio was warned that the judge would not tolerate any of the things that were being said that lawyers were doing that was ruining society.

After the meeting, as Horatio was headed home, Eddie's words came back to him: *"Maybe you should consider a change in professions. Or maybe just a hiatus from work for a while. Leave of absence sort of thing."*

Deciding he was not quite ready to do any of those, Horatio did tentatively add them to his list of options. When he arrived home, Penny could tell he was a bit upset and coaxed an explanation from him.

She sighed. "I understand, Horatio. I have been online much of the day, on several of the forums and blogs. Preppers are being labeled survivalists, in the MSM definition, and blamed for all sorts of things. And now, unfortunately, some preppers are blaming other preppers, and just about everything other people are blaming."

"Preppers that are gamers and such?"

Penny nodded. "I think so. And some that have children that are exposed to some of those influences. For the moment, there is not much to do about it. But I have thought over what you said recently."

She smiled and brushed back a lock of Horatio's now much longer hair. "I do believe I should start reducing my footprint online. These things that are occurring in the prepping community… They had not really occurred to me. Not in the degree in which they are happening. I've always known that not all preppers are good people. But this… It is all over society."

Horatio nodded. "Yes, it is. And I am thinking it is going to get suddenly worse, just as you have said. Any further thoughts on timing?"

Penny shook her head. "No. I just cannot quite fit all the pieces together. I am missing something, too. I am sure of it."

"Well, there is nothing we can do, Sweetie. We can only be ready for whatever might happen."

Horatio took Penny into his arms and held her for long moments, each drawing comfort from the other. When they stepped apart, they went into the kitchen to prepare dinner. Their talk turned to their friends, filling one another in with more details about them that had not come out when they had met over Christmas.

After dinner, they checked their sources, to see what else might be happening. When nothing turned up, they got ready for bed.

The rest of the week was relatively calm, for Horatio and Penny. But they were still hearing about things happening all over the world, none of which was making any of the major news sources. Everything they were hearing and seeing was from independent local sources in each area.

With New Year's Eve on a Friday, and New Year's Day Saturday, Horatio and Penny decided to spend the four-day holiday weekend at Horatio's place on the lake. They invited all of their prepper friends. But like

Penny, they were worried about something happening during the four days, so those any distance away decided to stay where they were, including her parents.

But Eddie and Misty did come out to stay for the duration. Mrs. Amstead, Bunny, and Suzette were moved in to their permanent quarters. Frank and Georgie were in their permanent accommodations on the site now, as well.

Penny was able to hide her concerns well, and the others, except for Horatio, were able to get into the spirit of the holiday, even to the point of toasting the new year positively, ringing in the start of the year with hope it would be a better one.

When nothing of any import occurred by the end of New Year's Day, Penny relaxed in Horatio's arms after everyone else had gone to bed. "I don't know, Horatio, perhaps I have been wrong about this… But there are so many signs…"

Horatio shook his head. "Penny, you are not wrong about this. Perhaps your initial thoughts on timing turned out not to be exact. That does not mean that something is not going to happen at some point. Sooner or later."

"Perhaps. I wish I was totally wrong about the entire thing."

"Don't we all? Don't we all?" Horatio squeezed her tightly, kissed her, and then they relaxed and fell asleep.

The next morning, Sunday, everyone was relaxed, and in good spirits. After a leisurely breakfast, Eddie and Misty made ready to go back to town. And Penny was headed for her place for two weeks. Horatio would join her for the second week. But they would be back for two weeks after that.

Since they would be at Horatio's place, everyone agreed to meet there for a Super Bowl party. Feeling better about things, Penny, Horatio, and the Mercers headed out, with even Penny deciding that perhaps things were not quite as bad at the moment that she had come to believe.

Every once in a while, during the following week, Penny did have recurring thoughts that she still might be correct. But when Horatio arrived the next weekend, she found herself diverted, rather pleasantly.

Horatio helped Mr. Arcade with some work on farm equipment in the equipment barn, while Penny helped her mother with some major household work they had been planning for some time.

But there was plenty of time for them to spend together, not only working around Penny's place, to accommodate Horatio's presence, now that they were married and he would be there on a regular basis, but with continuing to get better acquainted with each other, in all the ways newlyweds always did.

It was not until the Saturday before the Super Bowl Sunday, with everyone back at Horatio's place outside of town, settled in for the Saturday Night Movie, which had been advertised as a repeat of a popular classic, that Penny became very concerned. As did all the others.

Just before the movie was to start, there was an announcement that the scheduled movie would not be shown. In its place would be run a new movie, especially produced to be part of this year's Super Bowl extravaganza.

Penny was curled up next to Horatio when the announcement came. She sat up suddenly, leaning forward to stare at the television.

"Penny?" asked Horatio. The others all looked over at her, with questions in their eyes. When Horatio put his hand on her shoulder, it broke her concentration and she looked over at him.

"Oh!" she said. Her eyes went back to the TV, but she continued to talk. "This could be it," she said. "Another movie like the first one. One to stir up more trouble. With the Super Bowl being played tomorrow, tensions are going to be very high, just like they always are for it.

"It could really turn ugly, really quickly, if this movie in some way plays on those tensions."

Everyone looked back to the television, all eyes having been on Penny. They watched in fascination as the movie began, with no lead in credits, right after the commercial break that came after the announcement.

Hardly a word was said during the movie by anyone at Horatio's. "OMG!" exclaimed Misty when the final scene concluded, and the screen faded to black, again with no credits of any kind.

In a rather awed voice, Georgie added her comment. "It is going to stir up every hate group in the US!"

"And much of the rest of the world," added Frank.

"And they were so subtle about it," Eddie whispered, drawing Misty into his side even closer than she already was.

"Will people really react the way you are saying?" asked Mrs. Amstead. "I mean... there really wasn't much violence, at all. And the language... not nearly as bad as I hear on regular tv shows..."

Penny looked over at her, and Bunny, who was shaking her head in agreement. Suzette, on the other hand, looked as worried as the rest of them.

"Mrs. Amstead... Bunny... This is only the setup, so to speak. This movie, by itself, probably will not trigger much. Although some, I am sure, in those that are already at the point of doing something violent, anyway. I am not sure what else they have planned. But my guess is it will be right after the Super Bowl.

"As far as I know, there are no computer game releases scheduled, or other movies, but with the way they did this one, there might be something like that. It may even depend on which team wins the Super Bowl. They may have different plans for each case. I just don't know. But I do now believe the Super Bowl is part of it."

Mrs. Amstead nodded. "Well. You were certainly right about that other movie, and what happened after it and all those electronic games and such."

She paused for a moment, then asked, "Do you think I would have time to gather up a few additional supplies and such tomorrow? Before anything too terrible happens? Before the game starts?"

Penny and Horatio exchanged quick glances. "We really do have pretty much anything you might need, Mrs. Amstead," Penny assured her.

"Oh, I know that, Dear. These things… they are just some things I would like to have with me. In case it is too dangerous to go after them later."

Horatio looked over at Eddie. At his slight nod, Horatio looked back at Mrs. Amstead. "Of course, Mrs. Amstead. Eddie and I will go with you to make sure nothing happens."

"And I will be right there, as well," Suzette said softly, one hand going to Mrs. Amstead's, to grip it gently.

"Well, then," Mrs. Amstead said, her hand going to her wheelchair control when Suzette released it. "I do believe I will turn in now. Bunny, would you mind helping me with my bath?"

"Of course, Alice. I will say good night, then, too." With that, Bunny followed Alice out of the entertainment room. The others shared good nights after that and headed for their own rooms, each person and couple thinking thoughts of their own.

Horatio could tell that Penny was in her 'deep thinking mode' when they went to bed, so he simply held her until they fell asleep. She was still somewhat pensive the next morning when they rose.

Mrs. Amstead was an early riser, so after a quick breakfast, Suzette, driving the van, and Horatio and Eddie in the Suburban, they left to get done everything Mrs. Amstead wanted, so they could get back before the game started. Or anything else, for that matter.

Eddie and Horatio exchanged glances several times when they stopped at the places to which Mrs. Amstead directed Suzette. They had been expecting stops at stores. And they did stop at a couple of those that were open on that Sunday.

But most of the stops were at private residences. Both in town and out in the country. A couple of times Mrs. Amstead went inside the places where they stopped, met people at their front door at a couple more, with Suzette going inside several of the places by herself.

Suzette did go with Mrs. Amstead each of the other times, too. Mrs. Amstead had 'suggested' that Horatio and Eddie simply keep an eye out. If she needed one of them to carry something at some point she would say so.

Which she did twice. The last two stops, that were outside of town on the far side from Horatio's place. Both times Mrs. Amstead stayed inside the van, and someone came out to talk to her. Then Suzette signaled Horatio and Eddie, and they followed her out to a garden shed in one case, and a horse barn in another.

The first time, Horatio and Eddie carried several boxes of home canned goods from the garden shed to the Suburban, and the second time, they rolled out a large, old style, upright, wheeled, wood and leather steamer trunk. After a bit of a struggle, and only with Suzette's help, due to its weight, was the trunk lifted up into the back of the van and tied down securely, since the van had more clearance for it.

Picking up the steamer trunk was the last stop, so they headed for home. Before they left town, though, Suzette called Horatio on one of the radios that Frank and Eddie had installed in the van and told him and Eddie that they were making one more, unscheduled, stop. Mrs. Amstead insisted on getting some extra snacks and things for the Super Bowl party that they were having later on.

So, with several grocery sacks of goodies in the back of the Suburban, they headed for home. While Horatio had thought it might take a while, they had actually accomplished everything rather quickly and were back well before noon.

Horatio saw the relief in Penny's eyes when they came inside, and the humor, as well, at Mrs. Amstead's purchases for the Super Bowl party.

Though Penny was careful not to show her on-going concerns, Horatio was well aware of them, seeing her tension from time to time. But Mrs. Amstead had the others in stitches most of the time, during and after lunch, telling humorous stories from her life.

And when everyone gathered again after a break to watch the pregame show, Mrs. Amstead continued with more stories, involving each of the various snacks she had purchased, as they were passed around. Even Penny was laughing when the game started.

Though none of them were fanatical football fans, all but Penny and Horatio did enjoy football, and especially the Super Bowl. Even Penny admitted to having watched a few times in the past, just to see some of the commercials. This year she was as engrossed in the game as the others, simply due to the potential for some type of trouble.

By the end of the first quarter, everyone was quite caught up in the game, for the game. It was an exciting one. As the teams switched goals, everyone took a quick bathroom break, got another drink, and added more snacks to the tables.

Just before play was to resume, Mrs. Amstead asked Penny, "Penny, honey, do you have some eye drops? My eyes are bothering me just a bit. Might have been the cold air this morning."

"Of course," Penny replied. She had not yet joined Horatio on the sofa, so headed toward the room set aside for medical gear.

"Actually," Frank said, "I could use something, as well."

Georgie put her hand on Frank's shoulder. "I noticed you rub your eyes a couple of times. I thought it was just the new glasses."

"I'm sure it is," Frank said with a shrug. "I'm not having trouble seeing, just my eyes are a bit... I don't know... Tired. A bit dry feeling, as Mrs. Amstead said."

"Hm..." they all heard Suzette say, as she touched her temples with her fingers. She rubbed her temples for a moment and looked around at the others. "I didn't really think about it until you all brought it up, but my eyes are hurting a bit, too. Enough for a headache to be trying to start."

Penny had stopped and turned to look at the others. Her smartphone buzzed annoyingly. She looked at it after pulling it from its holster. "Horatio, would you get the eye drops? That notification bypassed the regular filter. I should probably see what it is. There aren't too many..." Her words faded as she walked down the hall to the study absently, her fingers working on the screen of the phone.

Horatio hurriedly got up, retrieved the eyedrops, and handed them to Mrs. Amstead to use and then pass on. He ignored the game, which was in play again, and joined Penny in the study.

Her phone was on the desk, beside one of the computers. She was glancing from the phone to the computer monitor, typing slowly, and then rapidly, watching the screen, and then she would do it over again, in various sequences.

"Penny?" Horatio asked, standing at the end of the desk.

Penny look over at him. She shook her head. "It's a text from Adam. But it is encrypted. Which isn't that unusual for him. But the text is also encoded, once I unencrypted the message. And now that I have put in the key for the code, the resulting text is another of our message codes. And part of it seems to be missing."

Again, she shook her head, her attention going right back to the computer screen as she typed something else. "It's... it seems to be just another key to an encryption code for an e-mail. It is missing the last element, but I know what that is. I'll have to find the e-mail, and then unencrypt it."

Penny looked up again. "Sweetie, go on back to the game. This could take me several minutes. Even Adam is not usually this obtuse. He must think whatever it is to be important. I do not want to wait to check it."

"But..." Horatio said, intending to object and tell Penny he would stay with her. But her attention was already back on the computer screen, and her fingers were flying over the keys.

Horatio did not understand all the communications protocols Penny used with some of her prepper friends, especially those that believed various government, as well as non-government, agencies were monitoring their communications.

He did know that some of them required the recipient to be interactive with the software for it to code and decode some of them. Deciding to give her the space and time that would make things easiest for her, and give the quickest outcome, Horatio went back to the game.

At the looks he received when he sat back down he just shrugged and said, "Something she needs to do."

The others nodded and turned their attention back to the game. Horatio did, as well, but he often found himself looking toward the end of the hallway, hoping he would see a smiling Penny every time he looked.

When Penny had still not appeared when the second quarter of the game ended, and the half-time show was starting, as the others got up to do another bathroom break and refresh the snacks, Horatio joined Penny in the study.

"Penny?" Horatio asked quietly. He started to say her name again when she did not respond.

But Penny looked around at him, obviously still distracted. "Almost ready," she said, looking back at the computer monitor. "It was much more than I thought. A fairly large program. And Adam had even encrypted the code for it." Penny shook her head. "I do not like this, Horatio."

"Honey, it is half-time. Can you take a break? Or I can bring something in here for you."

A soft smile accompanied the look that Penny gave Horatio. "That would be nice, Horatio. Thank you." Turning back to the monitor, she did not add anything as to what she might want.

Horatio smiled. That did not matter. He knew her likes and wants fairly well now. He headed off to the kitchen to prepare a tray for her. The others were back in front of the television after Horatio had dropped of the tray and received another smile.

Frank could never remember exactly what it was he was going to say when he opened his mouth to speak, just as the television screen went blank for a second, and then the network national news set appeared. One of the news anchors was just sitting down, plugging in her earpiece.

There was no preliminary report or information. The anchor just started talking. And from the looks of it, and the occasional hesitation, the teleprompter she was reading was being updated even as she spoke.

"Both teams in the Super Bowl have refused to take the field for the second half of the Super Bowl game," were the first words she spoke.

"Player representatives from both teams announced that they were now on strike, until new contracts could be negotiated for higher salaries across the board.

"Team owners have responded with counter demands, indicating that there would be no negotiations, and threatening to disband the teams completely."

An image box appeared to one side of the anchor. It was showing a full-scale riot occurring at the stadium. It was only on for a few seconds, and then the anchor began reading the teleprompter again.

"As you just saw, the announcement has triggered violent reactions at the stadium."

There was a pause, as the anchor touched her earpiece and listened intently, her eyes losing focus for a moment. When her eyes went back to the camera, she looked shaken.

"We are receiving reports that riots are breaking out all over the country." Before she could continue, the screen went blank, a notice stating that there were technical difficulties and to please stand by. And then then there was only white noise on the screen as the satellite signal was lost.

Everyone was looking around at each other, in shock, when Penny hurried into the room. She had her laptop with her. Horatio noticed immediately how pale her face was.

"Penny?" Horatio asked, rising to go to her.

"This is very bad," she said. Going to the entertainment center, she connected her laptop to the system, and brought up her laptop screen on the television screen.

There were murmurs, but Penny ignored them. "Adam sent me this. And just before I finished unencrypting everything I got another text from him. His front door was being hit with a battering ram."

There were tears in Penny's eyes when she spoke again. "He just said, *"Been nice knowing you, kid. I think my days are over."*

"It seems that the powers that be have developed some new techniques for adding subliminal messages to a wide variety of video and audio media."

"That's illegal!" protested Georgie.

Penny nodded. "In commercial advertising, and for advertising in general. But there are no real laws against using subliminal messages that are not geared toward selling.

"Besides, these new techniques are much more subtle, and much more... invasive. They have been in use for well over two years now. Remember that movie here while back?"

When everyone nodded, Penny touched a few keys on her laptop and a recording of the movie began to play. "Adam managed to decode the software that they are using to add the subliminal messages to the various media. Watch..."

Everyone watched entranced as words and images appeared, overlaid on the video, though very faint.

"Oh, my God!" exclaimed Misty. "No wonder people got so angry."

"Yes," Penny replied. "Not only was the movie itself geared to generate hatred between various groups, but the subliminal messages added to that in much more insidious ways, and much more strongly."

Horatio looked at Penny. "And this has been going on for two years?"

"At least that long," Penny replied. "Adam believes... believed... that early forms of it have been being tested for somewhat longer. And it has been used in every audio visual medium that the powers that be had any type of access to and were able to get the messages added.

"Computer games, internet games, sports broadcasts, movies, television shows, even news broadcasts. They have been spreading unmitigated hate messages for years, including in things like sporting event broadcasts from the majors to things like golf, gymnastics, everything.

"Always targeting the audience, to direct hatred against another group."

There were tears in her eyes, Horatio saw. He went to her and took her in his arms. "Poor Adam," she sobbed. "He will never survive, if he isn't already dead. He has too many health issues."

Horatio guided her over to a chair, and helped her sit, kneeling in front of her. Someone turned the television off, and silence, except for Penny's slowing sobs.

In only a few more moments, she had herself under control. She wiped her eyes with the handkerchief Horatio handed her. She met Horatio's eyes. "We need to see what was being broadcast during the game."

"But..." objected Horatio.

"It is important, Horatio. It never occurred to me... Adam... any of us that were working on the problem that they would use the Super Bowl. This could be the Black Swan event that will trigger... something..."

Horatio moved when Penny got up. The others were still silent as they watched her connect to one of the off-the-air recorders that were part of the entertainment system.

When she started the playback, running it through the computer, and then back to the television screen, back on now, the shimmery background of the subliminal messages was visible, as were the words being scrolled on the screen.

Penny made an adjustment on the computer and suddenly a very angry sounding, but very low voice was reading the words as they scrolled.

"That is absolutely hideous!" Mrs. Amstead said loudly, the obnoxious and inflammatory words that were seldom heard in modern society until just recently, when they had started to be used by some of the hate groups.

After only a few moments of the horrific tirade, this one about people that would not share food and water with others in time of need, Penny stopped the playback and disconnected her laptop.

The others were whispering to each other when Penny turned around and spoke. "Adam said in his e-mail that this is the worst. All the samples he checked after he got the software working gradually led up to this point."

"Do you think it will really trigger anything... really big?" asked Eddie. "I mean, what will just even those words do?"

"You heard the comments about the players, and then their owners, and finally the lawyers, before it switched to preppers," Penny said calmly. "I am sure that there was something like we just saw and heard aimed at every group of like-minded people that were watching the game."

Though he seldom played, Horatio did have a gaming system connected to the entertainment equipment. "Help me here, Penny," he said.

Penny routed the gaming console through the computer. The internet was still up, and Horatio was able to log into one of the games he had played a few times against one of the people that played regularly.

Horatio barely had the game screen on the television when the subliminal messages started. Penny did a few more adjustments to the software and everything became more clear, though none of the images were crystal clear, just visible enough to be made out easily. It was the same with the sound. Barely audible, but very understandable.

Penny and Horatio turned to look at the others, after Horatio turned off the system. "I suspect that pretty much everything on the internet is also being targeted. And has been for a long time," Penny said.

"My eyes!" Frank suddenly exclaimed. "They did not feel so bad during the break, when I was away from the TV. Just now, as we watched again, they started to get that dry feeling."

Three of the others muttered similar feelings.

"It is those subliminal messages causing it, isn't it Penny?" asked Misty.

Penny nodded. "I don't know for sure, but I think Frank is correct. And if what I suspect is also true, they probably upped the intensity for the movie and other stuff last night, and the game today, and that is why people are having the eye problems. It would not surprise me if people with sensitive eyes have been having problems all along."

"What do we do?" asked Bunny.

"We find out what is going on elsewhere," Horatio replied. "Frank, Eddie, would you lock us down? I do not want to take any chances."

Horatio went to the study and turned on his radio monitoring equipment as Penny fired up the various internet sources they often checked for news on the extra monitors grouped around the large TV screen.

Horatio was listening to the radios with a headset, but the main TV sound was on, with the internet monitors silent, showing only the various talking heads or scrolling text.

The others had all joined Horatio and Penny in the study and were watching along with them. Penny's left hand suddenly went to Horatio's right shoulder.

He looked up just as Penny, the monitor remote in her hand, turned up the volume of the TV just slightly. They all saw the primary newscaster for that network suddenly start yelling. The man yanked his mike and earpiece out and threw them on the desk.

Seconds later, three men approached the screaming man and as two tried to tackle the newscaster, the third man began fighting with them, alongside the newscaster.

Eyes went to another screen and Penny put it up on the large screen.

The graphic indicated the scene was in New York City. Despite the cold, there were thousands of people in Times Square. And they all seemed to be fighting one another. It seemed every possible dispute between two opposing views was being addressed with violence of one sort or another. Mostly fighting or wrestling. But occasionally some type of club would flash into view.

It was mostly one-on-one, but they saw two-on-one, and even a couple of what appeared to be violence between two groups of three or more each.

"I can't believe no one is doing anything..." Misty said quietly.

"No," Penny said, studying the video. "It looks as though each... dispute... is totally independent and isolated. The ones involved do not seem to even be aware of the others around them."

"I think you are right," Frank said. "Even when it looks like the same type of disagreement, once an altercation starts, they lose interest in everything else."

Suddenly Georgie muttered, "Or not..."

They all saw one woman, knife in hand, her face bloody, turn from what certainly seemed to be a body now, rather than a living person, lying on the pavement, blood seeping from her side.

The woman suddenly lurched toward another pair of people fighting, and joined in. None of those watching could tell exactly which side she seemed to be on.

Suddenly they heard a loud crack, and the image zoomed into two men, armed with handguns. They seemed to be firing into the crowd at random. The screen went blank.

Penny saw something on another of the monitors and brought it up on the big screen. Someone had started to ask where the images were coming from, but a scrolling graphic at the bottom of the screen indicated that the images were from Moscow.

The Kremlin was being attacked by people with everything from brooms to hunting rifles and AK-47s. And the Kremlin guards, though many were down, were firing back into the mob with their own weapons.

Penny quickly switched to another scene, almost identical. Except this one was Tieniman Square in Beijing. After several more switches, Penny finally turned everything off. Horatio took off the headset.

The two turned toward their friends and fellow preppers. "I think this is it," Horatio said.

The others looked to Penny. "I am afraid he might be right," Penny replied. It is going to depend on just how far TPTB tried to set this up for, and what actually winds up happening. If what some of us have theorized, it will get well beyond what those that set it up and started it believe it will go. We just do not believe that people will stop these activities when TPTB think they will."

"And if they don't?" Frank asked.

"It could be the end of civilization as we know it. If it gets bad enough to have a negative impact on much of the infrastructure, here in the US, and in some other parts of the world, it will almost be certain. Modern societies cannot function without large amounts of electricity over a very wide area."

Misty was not the only one that gasped when the lights went out suddenly. But they were back on in less than ten seconds.

"Power went off, and a generator picked up the load," Horatio calmly said. He reached over and flipped a switch on one of the control panels next to the communications equipment, silencing the commercial electrical power failure annunciator.

"If anyone has any calls to make," Penny announced, "you better make them now. I do not expect the cell system to last long, and I am not too confident of the land line system."

Only Bunny pulled out her cell phone, besides Penny. Bunny apparently made a connection, for she talked softly, but intently for nearly a minute before she sighed and turned off the phone.

Penny had moved out into the hallway when she dialed her cellular phone. She had just enough time to confirm that her parents had gone to lock-down in their shelter already before the cell phone squealed slightly and Penny lost the signal.

Mrs. Amstead had rolled over to the second desk in the study, the one Penny used most often, and picked up the regular telephone receiver. "Dead," she said, hanging it back up. "No dial tone. And not even any background noise like there usually is on the lines out this way."

Chapter Nine

-

"I never thought the effects would begin to occur this fast," Penny said. She was standing beside Horatio now, and felt comforted by his arm going around her shoulders.

"Much less the effects that are occurring. At least locally," Penny continued. "We... Or at least I always thought that when the violence started, the government, or those in it that are part of this, would immediately declare martial law, and start a crackdown on those they want to control.

"I honestly do not think it ever occurred to them that people would react the way they seem to be. I believe they thought they would be able to take over and set things up the way they want. With them in total control."

"Seems they might have miscalculated," Mrs. Amstead said dryly.

"Definitely," commented Suzette.

Suddenly Penny realized all eyes were on her, with an expectant look in them. She blushed. "I..."

Mrs. Amstead smiled. "It is alright, child. We do look to you for guidance, but we are not your responsibility." She looked at Horatio. "Nor yours. But I, for one, will gladly accept any suggestions and recommendations as to what we should do now."

Penny smiled. "Thank you, Mrs. Amstead." She looked up at Horatio. When he nodded, Penny spoke again. "Well, I believe the best course of action at the moment is simply to hunker down and use our communications devices to find out everything we can about what is happening elsewhere."

"Your parents..." Horatio gently asked.

"They will be fine," Penny said, though her concern was evident in her eyes. "They know what to do and do have some good people with them. When we can, I do want to go and check on them, and my place there, as well. But that will have to wait unless we hear from them and they need us."

Horatio nodded. He looked at the group. "Well, since the Super Bowl party is a bust, what say we find something else to occupy us. Any suggestions?"

Eddie grinned. "I brought a basic tattoo kit with me. Anyone want a tat?"

The others laughed, but all declined.

Suzette spoke up a bit hesitatingly. "Horatio, would you mind if I do some monitoring with the radio gear?"

"No, of course I don't mind. I was going to myself, but there are some other things I can be doing. It would be a help if you could take a shift on the radios."

Suzette grinned. "You got it." She moved over to the chair in front of the communications console and put on the headset, one hand reaching out to select a frequency on the broadband receiver.

"I think, if you don't mind helping, Horatio, I would like to get some of the things we picked up this morning put away."

"I'd be glad to help," Bunny said.

"You will be, my dear. But some of this is of direct interest to Horatio. Once we take care of that, I would dearly appreciate your help with the rest."

Bunny smiled. "Of course, Alice. Just let me know. I think I will be in the kitchen, seeing what we might have to prepare for supper." She looked over at Penny, who nodded.

The others all seemed to have decided on what they wanted to do, and the group dispersed, Horatio following Mrs. Amstead to her room.

"Well now," Mrs. Amstead said, surveying the items they had set out of the way in her room. "If you would be so kind as to gather up those small parcels…"

Horatio moved to do so. Mrs. Amstead maneuvered her wheelchair over beside the bed. "Please open each one and place everything on the bed. I need to sort out some things."

When Horatio opened the first item, a large padded manila envelope, and poured the contents out into his hand, he shot Mrs. Amstead a sharp look.

The papers he was expecting did slide out, but they were not anything like the papers he was expecting. No. These were Gemological Institute of America certificates, each with a small Zip-lock bag attached. And inside each of the Zip-lock bags was a diamond.

And there were many of them. Of several different sizes. But all the same shape. When Horatio's eyes went back to Mrs. Amstead, she was grinning.

"Surprised? I thought you might be. And I do expect you to tell your lovely wife all about what we are now doing, but I would ask that you not mention it to any of the others."

"Yes, of course," Horatio hurriedly said when Mrs. Amstead looked at him expectantly.

"Very good. Now, as to what we have here, is one of the less traditional investments Bernie I have made with some of our disposable income over the years.

"These are all round brilliant cut diamonds, IF clarity or better, and D color or better. Sizes range from one caret to ten carets, all up to zero point zero two carets over. Never less than the even caret weight. And as you can see, all have GIA certificates."

Mrs. Amstead leaned forward and selected three of the diamonds and set them aside. "Now, if you would put those back in the envelope, I would ask you to put those away in your safest safe for future use. By me, of course, or once I am gone, on behalf of my friends, and everyone here."

She raised her hand when Horatio opened his mouth to protest. "No, Horatio. Do not try to talk me out of this. This is my home now, and all of you are my family. I have made provisions for my biological family, as you well know, if they do manage to survive this, and things return to any semblance of normal.

"I do not think they will, at least in my lifetime, and I plan to help insure the survival of the human species, in some semblance of good society. My best chance to do that is through you and Penny. So, no arguments. Please just do it. You can even consider it as part of your duties as my attorney. Can even take a fee out, if you want."

When Horatio went red, again ready to protest, Mrs. Amstead grinned. "Don't blow a gasket. I was kidding. I know you and Penny will do what is best when it comes time to use those."

Horatio calmed down. He slid the certificates and diamonds into the envelope and put it on the corner of the dresser, to pick up when they left.

"Next one," Mrs. Amstead said, indicating a small cardboard box.

When Horatio opened it, he cut another quick look at Mrs. Amstead. "Before we learned what we did about diamonds, we made a few bad choices. Not in these particular choices, but in choosing any of them.

"These may or may not have much real value until far in the future, if then. Investment grade diamonds are one thing. Colored gems, quite another, when it comes to their value as trade items. But we did get good deals on all of them, and Bernie did dearly love the colored stones, much more than the diamonds we decided on later. So, I kept them. Just put them away, for just in case."

Horatio took a good look at the stones in the box. Each, like the diamonds, was in a Zip-lock bag. But none had a certificate. Though each bag was stapled to a 3" by 5" note card with the details of the stone.

There were emeralds, rubies, and blue sapphires. Various sizes, as with the diamonds. Also, like the diamonds, each type was a specific cut. All the rubies were cushion cut, the emeralds the traditional emerald cut, and the deep blue sapphires were all oval cut.

"May or may not ever be a market for them, financial wise," Mrs. Amstead said. "But they will make some nice jewelry at some point, perhaps. Into safe keeping in your safe."

Horatio closed up the box and put it with the envelope.

"Probably the same with these," Mrs. Amstead said, handing Horatio another stout cardboard box. When Horatio opened it, there were more gems, he thought at first. On closer look, he realized there were dozens, if not more, of pearls. Many different sizes, but even in the light from the LED fixtures in the bedroom, they showed their luster.

"Black pearls?" Horatio asked, turning his head toward Mrs. Amstead after he had shifted some of the Zip-lock bags around to see below them.

"Yes," Mrs. Amstead replied. "Bernie was rather enamored of them. Bought all he could, along with the white ones, whenever he ran across a deal when he was over in southeast Asia and environs."

When Horatio dug a bit deeper in the box, and gave Mrs. Amstead another quick look, she chuckled. "On the other hand, I had Bernie looking for quality amber when he was in and around the Mediterranean area. And points north, if you get my drift." The last was added rather softly.

"Ah," Horatio said. He would not mention Bernie's actions in certain parts of the world that were not on good terms with the US at the time.

"These are all beautiful," he continued, taking out a few of the packets of amber. Some were pieces of raw amber, and some were finished, ready to be mounted. "Wait. Green? Red?"

Mrs. Amstead rolled over and took the two packets that Horatio was holding up. "Why yes," she replied. "Vegetation is what causes the green amber for the most part. And the red... Well, that is like me. Very, very old. As in 200 million years and more. At least for the red amber. Not me."

Horatio chuckled and put the amber back in the box. "Are you sure you do not want some of this out? You obviously love it."

Mrs. Amstead sighed. "I have several pieces in my jewelry. These are just... keepers... I guess I would say. We never really thought they would have great value, but with the gemstones... well, they were just two more possibilities that might generate some income at some point. Not to mention Bernie loved pearls, and I do love amber." She waved her hand, to emphasize the two amber mounted rings on her fingers.

Powering back, and over to the bed again, Mrs. Amstead waved a hand. "Store them, please."

When Horatio joined Mrs. Amstead again at the bed, she had managed to pull a much larger box to the edge. It was the biggest item, other than the steamer trunk, they had brought in.

It was not nearly as heavy as Horatio was expecting when he shifted it enough to open it up. Again, his eyes widened when he opened the box and moved the top layer of packing. "Your jewelry?"

Shaking her head, Mrs. Amstead replied. "Nope. Another of Bernie's and my future possibilities. A friend of Bernie's... actually, the friend's father and grandfather, owned a jewelry business. They made almost everything they sold.

"When both decided to retire, Bernie's friend, who had no interest in the business, offered to sell it to Bernie. We talked about it, and with both our interests in gems, though not all that great, we decided to purchase everything, but to store it in order to open up a business later, somewhere else."

Mrs. Amstead sighed. "Sadly, we never really got around to it. But that box contains the pieces that had not sold. In the bottom of this box, and in the box... right there..." Mrs. Amstead indicated another box, a bit smaller than they one Horatio had open, "are the various tools for jewelry making, minus a furnace, of course. And careful of that second box. It is heavier than it looks."

Closing up the first box, Horatio added it to the growing stack at the dresser. He grunted a bit when he picked up the other box. It was heavier.

When he turned to Mrs. Amstead, she had moved her wheelchair slightly. Picking up another box, larger, but still fairly light from the way she was handling it.

When she handed it to Horatio he decided Mrs. Amstead was a bit stronger than he had given her credit for, since the box was somewhat heavier than he expected. When he opened up the box, there was a stack of old manila envelopes inside.

After a glance at Mrs. Amstead, Horatio opened the top envelope and slid the contents out far enough to read the documents it contained. His eyes widened and he cut a quick look at Mrs. Amstead.

"Now don't you be thinking there is anything nefarious about those bearer bonds, young man. They were an investment, a good one, way back in the day. And are still valid, I'll have you know, despite the law changes in 1982.

"Each of those envelopes contain bearer bonds in various amounts from various banks and governments. I seriously doubt they will ever be redeemed for anything near their original value. But you never know. Some of those outfits might just make it through all this. Pack them away."

"Should I ask how much is in here?" Horatio did ask, sliding the bonds back into the envelope and securing it in the box. He added it to the other things he would be taking to the financial safe in the vault in the shelter.

"Not quite a million. Never did hit that goal we set. But they were always there, if we needed them," Mrs. Amstead replied. She indicated another box, this one much larger, and if Horatio remembered correctly, quite heavy.

"No need to open it up right now. Just be aware that it is cash, almost all of it with print dates of 1999, 2000, and 2001. All denominations, and quite a few of each."

Mrs. Amstead cut a look toward Horatio. "Well, are you going to ask?"

Horatio shook his head. But he was smiling.

"Oh well. You'll know eventually, I am sure. Bit over a million. I think the count is one million, two hundred-thousand, and some additional bills all under fifty dollars."

"Vault?" Horatio asked.

"Yes," Mrs. Amstead replied, her attention now on the old steamer trunk. Horatio slid the box over by the dresser. He decided he would get a set of hand trucks to move it.

Mrs. Amstead powered her chair over to the steamer trunk. She pulled a key from some type of pouch on her belt, leaned forward, and unlocked the three locks on the front of the trunk.

She powered the chair backwards so Horatio could pivot the two halves of the tall, upright trunk apart. Once Horatio had struggled the two halves open, he could see why the thing weighed as much as it did.

"US mint coin bags?" Horatio asked, looking at the several canvas bags on the floor of the hanging clothing half of the steamer trunk.

"'fraid so, Horatio," Mrs. Amstead said with a grin. "And not bags of... I think preppers call it 'junk' silver. Those are all $1,000 face value bags of uncirculated dimes and quarters. Pretty as the day they were each minted."

"Actually, Penny and I don't refer to it as junk silver. Penny has me using the term she does. Pre-1965 circulated 90% silver US dimes, quarters, and halves."

"No halves there," Mrs. Amstead cautioned Horatio.

"Why am I not surprised?" Horatio asked softly. "Penny does not like half dollars, either. I will go get the dolly and take these down."

"Not so fast, Horatio," Mrs. Amstead. "Open the top drawer."

Horatio shook his head. Inside the top drawer were clear coin tubes, carefully racked in trays. There were two trays, which only took up a third of the drawer space. But when Horatio lifted the first tray out of the drawer, it was heavy. When he checked a few of the tubes, he saw US silver dollars in every one of them.

"The top tray is silver dollars from the late mid-1800s through 1899. The second tray is 1900 through 1934," Mrs. Amstead informed Horatio as he stacked the trays next to the bags of dimes and quarters.

Rather gingerly, thought Mrs. Amstead, Horatio closed the top drawer and opened the second of the five drawers. "One tray," Horatio said, seemingly relieved.

"Yes. Just one. Those were rather difficult to acquire. A few were from circulation. The rest were all from collectors. And, I am ashamed to say, some of those were from desperate people that had to use them to try and save their farms and businesses during the depression that a collector managed to acquire from one of the bankers at the time."

Mrs. Amstead shook her head. "Didn't know it at the time. I think we would have passed on them if we'd known. I like to think so, anyway."

Horatio did not even try to count the various denominations. They ranged from gold dollars to double eagles, in several patterns. He added that tray to the others and went back to close the second drawer and open the third.

"You've been collecting all the way up until just recently, haven't you, Mrs. Amstead?" Horatio asked when he saw the clear tubes of US Mint one-ounce Silver Eagles. A very heavy tray full of them.

"Sure have," Mrs. Amstead replied. "Bernie and I agreed when we got married to always put away a portion of our earnings in safe ways. My last purchase was a bit over a month ago. Those items I will keep with me." She grinned at Horatio again when he groaned carrying the tray over to the others.

And then again when he opened the fourth drawer and found an identical tray of Silver Eagles. With that tray on top of the other one, Horatio, rather reluctantly, went back to the open steamer trunk. There was one drawer left.

Horatio had a feeling he knew what would be in it before he slid it open. And he was right. More gold, this time US Mint Gold Eagles. Several tubes each of one-ounce, one-half-ounce, one-quarter-ounce, and one-tenth ounce coins. Probably two-thirds were the one-tenth-ounce Gold Eagles. But there were plenty of the others, too.

"I don't know why I removed the bags and the trays," Horatio suddenly said, when he started to pick up that last tray. "I can just wheel the trunk down. I won't need to get the dolly."

"Well, actually Horatio, I was planning to use the steamer trunk in here for a few of my things, including some of the other items you helped bring in today."

"Oh," Horatio said. "Okay. That is not a problem. I will get the dolly when we are finished."

"Finished," Mrs. Amstead said, giving Horatio yet another grin. "Move them at your leisure, of course."

Horatio rolled his eyes and Mrs. Amstead laughed. "You are such a good boy, Horatio. Thank you." The last was added rather softly, Mrs. Amstead's left hand going to touch Horatio's sleeve as she powered the wheelchair past him.

Horatio shook his head and headed to get one of the moving dollies. He did carefully make sure the door was closed behind him. He did not lack trust in any of those in the house, but all that wealth just lying about had him on edge. He hurried a bit to get the dolly and get the job finished.

Since it was Mrs. Amstead's business, Horatio did cover the load when he took it down to the basement, and then on into the shelter, and finally into the walk-in vault beyond the generator room. He carefully labeled everything, and then stowed the dolly before joining Penny to see what she was doing.

When he found Penny, she was in the kitchen, taking over for Bunny, who was now following Mrs. Amstead to her room to put away the other things.

After a hug and quick kiss, Penny put Horatio to work helping her. "What are the others doing?" Horatio asked her. "Do you know?"

Penny shook her head. "Not really. Frank and Eddie put their heads together and then took off into the garage. Misty and Georgie are doing something in the sewing room."

They were silent for a few more minutes, but when they came to a point where they did not need to pay close attention to anything, Penny turned to Horatio and put her head on his chest, her arms going around his waist.

Horatio wrapped his arms around her and held her tightly. "I wish I had been wrong. About the addictive entertainment, and all the other aspects of it."

"Sweetie, the blame goes on the people that orchestrated this. While the general population may be to blame for getting to the point where the powers that be could take advantage of the situation and set all of this up. They and they alone are the ones that must bear the brunt of guilt this is going to cause. I hope they get what they deserve."

"I know, Horatio," Penny said softly. "It is just hard for me. I always seem to think I can prevent things from happening, if I just figure them out in time. I know I can't, of course. There are just things that are so far outside of my control and influence."

Penny chuckled. "Kind of think of myself as having much more ability than I really do."

Horatio leaned back, his arms still around her, to look at her face. She looked up and met his eyes. There was humor in them. "Well, I think you have just the right amount of abilities. Pretty perfect to me."

Penny smiled, put her head back on Horatio's chest. But only for a moment. She slipped from his arms and turned back to the stove. "You are pretty perfect for me, too," she said. "Now go find something else to do. You distract me."

Horatio laughed. "Very well. I will go see what other mischief I can get into."

Penny waved a hand, and Horatio had a sudden thought. So, he grabbed a heavy coat, his winter gloves, and a warm hat, and went out one of the back doors. His destination was the boathouse, and he could have taken the tunnel, but Horatio wanted to get a really good look at the finger of the lake at its furthest point, where it came into the property.

He kept looking around, just to stay in practice with his situational awareness, as he walked. When he reached the far end of the water, he looked around and found a handful of small sticks. He pushed one into the nearly frozen mud right at the edge of the water, in several different places around the shore.

That done, Horatio walked more quickly toward the boathouse. The temperature was dropping, and the wind was picking up somewhat. He was glad to get inside, out of the wind.

Horatio took a few minutes to check the exact level of the water inside the boathouse. He made marks on walls, right at the water level, in several places.

At first, Horatio had really only considered the lake a possible source of fish as food, and of course, as a water supply. There were three intake pipes run out, with protected pickups, in different places.

They fed the firefighting, irrigation, and wash down pump systems primarily, though all were connected to the potable water system, through a pre-filter unit that would take anything that might be too large for the regular purification system to handle.

Though not all that much of a fisherman, he did fish occasionally, usually when his buddy Andy wanted someone to go with him. So, he had purchased a small boat quite well equipped for several types of fishing on the lake, after having studied up on it.

It was only somewhat later that Horatio decided there were many more useful aspects to the lake than just water and fish. It could be used for transportation in several ways, and through that, a way to communicate. There were defensive aspects to it, though it did require instituting defensive measures on the property in case of attacks coming from the lake.

Horatio did a great deal more research, and finally decided to add a few boats to his then one boat navy. And to build the boathouse, which included many additional features to its primary one of housing the boats in out of the weather.

Not only was there a significant workshop incorporated, but a warehouse area for repair parts and spare parts for not only the boats and their motors, but for the electronics, as well. And since fishing was a part of the plan, the boat house boasted a fish and water animal processing area, so all the messy work involved in turning the animals and fish into food could be done away from the house.

As Horatio looked over the small fleet, he wondered about the possibilities that had prompted him to come out here. The lake was not a natural lake. It had formed as the result of a significantly sized dam. If anything major happened to the dam, the lake could very well disappear.

He wanted to know as soon as possible about anything happening to the dam and any water level change. He had found a way to monitor the lake, but he was not sure he would be able to get it now. That was the reason he had come out to make water level markings after things had occurred.

Satisfied he had done all he could for the moment, Horatio left his coat loose, and took the tunnel back to the house, to stay out of the cold. He was tempted to try to sneak up on Penny and put his still very cold hands on her just to startle her but decided that was not a good idea.

Not only was it not very nice, he probably could not accomplish it anyway, since she was so attuned to her surroundings, but it could be a bit dangerous. To him. She had the quickest reflexes of anyone he had ever met, and despite her diminutive size, she could do major damage in a fight, and if he did startle her, she was likely to respond like that.

So, he was whistling softly when he joined her in the kitchen again, after depositing his outdoor gear back where it belonged. "Man, that is smelling good!" he said, giving her a quick kiss. And got a tiny bit of satisfaction when she jumped a bit when his cold lips touched hers.

Suzette had not had any luck to speak of finding out anything on the radios, so joined the others when the supper was ready. There was not much discussion of the event, though there were lively ones about several other things.

Everyone was ready for bed early, however, the stress having been tiring, on top of the fact that everyone had been up early. When Horatio mentioned setting up a radio watch rotation, Penny talked him and the others out of it. "We may have to have something like that at some point. But we are not likely to find out anything tonight. Let's save the effort for when we really need it."

The next morning, there was a serious discussion about whether to stay locked down at Horatio and Penny's or go into town to see what might be going on.

It was primarily the concern that some of them had for other people they cared about that swung the decision to going into town. Since she did not really have anyone else in town, Penny played devil's advocate for the group, which was fairly easy for her, since she was against the idea, at the moment, anyway.

Since Suzette had no one she wanted to check on, she said she would stay and monitor the radios again, as well as be available for defense, if needed.

Frank and Georgie said they would stay, as well. Frank wanted to work on a few projects, and since Bunny was going in to check on a couple of people for herself and for Mrs. Amstead, Georgie would stay and help her do some food prep for the next few days that Penny wanted to do.

Eddie and Misty had a discussion of their own, away from the others, resulting in Misty going along despite Eddie's protests. So, near midmorning, Horatio, Eddie, Misty, and Bunny headed out. Horatio was driving the Suburban, with a well-armed Misty riding the front passenger seat and Bunny in the seat behind Misty.

Eddie was on his bike, despite the cold. But having seen Penny's heated inner layer that plugged into a power jack on her modified Harley, Eddie and Misty had obtained the heated clothing to wear under their cold weather leathers and added the power jacks to their bikes. It extended their cold weather riding ability significantly. At least for cold.

None knew exactly what to expect. One of the things they did not expect was to see several cars abandoned on the shoulders of the road, and others headed away from town at high speed, as well as several that came up fast behind them, and went around, also at high speed.

"Careful up there, Honey," Misty cautioned Eddie. "People are driving crazy."

"Yeah," Eddie replied. "And what is with all these vehicles stopped on the road? I mean, there wasn't an EMP, was there? I didn't think so."

"No," Horatio replied thoughtfully.

"Uh-oh," Eddie suddenly radioed. "I think I know why. Look at the vehicles at the station. The sign says..." Eddie was slowly down. "No Power So No Gas."

"And they do not have a generator," Horatio commented. "Guess that means power is out in the whole area, then." After another moment, Horatio continued. "Eddie, head for my office. It isn't too far, and that mall will tell us as much as anywhere else. And be careful. I... well... I kind of have a hinky feeling about this."

"You aren't the only one, buddy."

Cautiously, meeting or being passed by the occasional vehicle, the two rigs worked their way through the edge of town and pulled into the mall.

Misty and Bunny both gasped when they saw the destruction. It was far worse than the riot the previous time. The only business that was not totally destroyed by fire was Horatio's building. And there were scorch marks and smoke marks on in several places where things had been piled up against it and set afire.

Bunny stayed in the Suburban, and while Eddie and Misty stood guard, Horatio took a closer look at the building, walking around it slowly. When he got back around to where Eddie and Misty were standing back to back, he told them, "They tried to get in. There is some minor damage on two of the security shutters, but they weren't able to breach them.

"If they had used a chain or cable, and a bigger truck, they might have ripped something off. I saw tire burn marks where someone was spinning tires, trying."

When Horatio indicated with a head nod, the two followed him over to the Suburban, approaching the second seat row door. Bunny rolled the window down.

"Guys... Look... If someone really wants in, they will be able to with a big enough truck and cable. Now, all of my electronic files are safe. Backed up. But I really would not like to lose some of the things inside. If you 'all don't mind staying a bit, I would like to load some things up."

Horatio looked at Eddie. "We can do the same at your place."

"You got it, Horatio," Eddie said after Misty nodded. They looked at Bunny.

"Yes, of course," she said. "Will we still be able to check on people?"

"Yes," replied Horatio immediately. "We can do that first and stop here on the way back." When Bunny looked relieved, Horatio was glad he made the offer.

Their first stop for Bunny and Mrs. Amstead was one of the places they had picked up some of the home canned food. It was a worrisome couple of minutes before anyone answered the door when Bunny knocked, Horatio at her side.

But the two people assured Bunny, after profusely apologizing for the worry the delay caused, that they were okay. They were being very careful about coming up out of their basement, as they had already run into a situation that had scared them badly.

Bunny had strict orders from Mrs. Amstead not to offer any real help, and definitely no invitation to join them at Horatio and Penny's, no matter what. Only Horatio could make that decision, and the offer had to come from him first, was the instruction.

The next stop was a disappointment. There was no one around, and from the looks of things, someone had tried to gain entry to the house, though without success. The door was open, but it appeared that the attempt had been made, and then the people inside had left on their own.

"Their things are gone," Bunny told Horatio and Eddie. "So are both of their vehicles."

Horatio nodded. "Anyone else on your list?"

Bunny shook her head and returned to the Suburban, where Misty was standing guard once again. "You sure?" Eddie quietly asked Horatio.

Horatio nodded, understanding Eddie's question about whether or not he was willing to go check on the person Eddie and Misty were concerned about.

This time there was major disappointment. Eddie held Misty for several minutes as she cried, when they found their friend dead, spent cartridges all around him, though no gun. He was inside the house, where he had obviously made a stand against whoever had attacked.

When Misty dried her eyes and got back into the Suburban, a hard-eyed Eddie told Horatio, "John was convinced there would not be any problems. And if there were, he could handle things. I could never get him to understand the danger he was in, knowing the people he did, and them knowing him."

At Horatio's questioning look, Eddie added, "He was a dealer. Small time, light stuff. Mary Jane mostly, but he had a tendency to talk about his gun collection. As you saw, they were all gone, too."

Horatio nodded. "What do you want to do about his body?"

Eddie sighed. "I would like to bury him. But, as hard as it is, I am not going to spare the time and effort. He made his choices, a long time ago. He paid for them. I do not aim to let him cost me any more than he already has. Let's go."

Eddie turned and went to his bike. Horatio got back into the driver's seat of the Suburban and pulled out after Eddie. Since it was on the way for him to check on Andy, Horatio radioed Eddie to swing by Mrs. Amstead's former place.

It turned out to almost be a major disaster on Horatio's part. They had barely turned off the road, onto the long driveway when several people rushed Eddie.

Eddie gunned the bike, driving right through the group, in order to keep them from taking him down, but immediately spun the bike around and headed back.

Misty, her carbine out the window, fired several rounds close to the group, that was again trying to force Eddie to stop. She was not shooting to hit, but it was a near thing when two of the faster men almost got to Eddie before he could get his speed up.

Horatio had reversed the Suburban, and spun the steering wheel, putting them back on the road, and giving Misty a better chance to control the situation.

"Go!" Horatio yelled into the mike, following Eddie as soon as he got on the road and gunned the bike again, headed back the way they had come.

"Criminy!" Eddie said, his breath coming fast and deep.

"Those were Alice's people," Bunny whispered. "Terrible! She is going to be so mad!"

Horatio took a look in the rearview mirror and saw how upset Bunny was. Almost as much as Misty was, in fear for her husband. Eddie slowed, but voiced his willingness to keep going to check on Andy, when Horatio suggested they just go back to the property.

Much more cautious, on general principles, even though they had yet to see more than a couple of people out and about in the area. And those had disappeared from sight as soon as they could when they saw the two vehicles approaching.

Horatio had Eddie stop well before they reached Andy's small property. "You and Misty stay with Bunny here. I am going ahead on foot."

Eddie could not talk him out of it. A few minutes later Horatio reached the junction of Andy's driveway and the road. Staying near the fence that ran along the highway, Horatio crouched down and looked over the place carefully.

No one was stirring that he could see. All the drapes were closed, which was unusual, as Andy loved the outdoors. More than a bit worried, Horatio slipped around the end of the fence and onto the property. But he moved over to the hedge that separated Andy's place from the vacant lot next to him.

Keeping a watch all around, Horatio moved along the hedge until he reached a point where he could look into the back yard. What he saw there relieved him slightly. There were good indications that the grill had been used very recently, and there were several items on the patio that indicated that Andy and his family were doing their cooking and cleanup outside.

Thinking about it long and hard, Horatio finally decided to call out. "Yo! Andy! It's Horatio! You okay in there?"

Still crouched down, Horatio was vulnerable, he knew, if someone else was there, or Andy came out shooting. Which Horatio did not think would happen, but with everything the way it was, there was that possibility.

Horatio saw Andy quickly stick his head out the back door and do a quick survey around. He jerked back when he saw Horatio, but again leaned out slightly to check again.

"That is you, Horatio… Right?"

Horatio slowly stood up, keeping his hands out from his body. He had his rifle slung, barrel down, but where he could bring it up quickly if needed.

"Yeah. It is me, Andy. I wanted to check and see if you guys were okay after what happened?"

Gun in hand, but pointed to the ground, Andy stepped outside, but stayed by the door. He looked around occasionally, but motioned Horatio to come toward him. "Yeah. We are okay. For now. But, what did happen? Do you know? Things went crazy when the game was stopped yesterday.

"Vicky and I were in town watching the game at the country club. It wasn't more than twenty minutes when people started showing up there, as a bunch of us were leaving. Man! They were crazy! Started attacking members. I just barely got Vicky into the Land Rover before they got to us."

Horatio nodded. "Yeah. Things have gone bad, Andy. You know how I suggested you kind of put by a few things here while back…"

Andy nodded. "Yeah. I wasn't going to. But there was something about you… the way you said it… something. So, I did. Vicky thought I was nuts. But she is glad now that I did. We have food and water for a while. And, of course, all our camping equipment. But I don't know how long we can get by. How long do you think this will last?"

Horatio dreaded the question. "Andy…" Horatio shook his head. "Andy, it could be a long time. A very long time. And people are turning on each other all over the place. They tried to burn my office. And I had death threats before, after those first riots. Eddie and Misty, too."

"What? Death threats? Why didn't you tell me, man? At the wedding or something."

Horatio shook his head again. "I didn't know how, Andy. I wasn't even sure if something like this would really happen."

"What should I do, Horatio? You know I can take care of myself. But… Vicky… She's pregnant. We just found out a few days ago. We were planning on getting together next weekend with you guys. Vicky really likes Penny… And so do I, too… and we wanted to get to know her. We wanted to tell you about the baby… and… all…"

Horatio ached at the look on Andy's face. Before he could speak, Andy spoke again. "Look… Horatio, I need you to be straight with me. You've changed. A couple of the guys have mentioned it. Not just getting married. You just seem different. Can you help me figure out something? I am afraid I won't be able to protect Vicky and when the baby comes… if this is long term like you say… It really can't be that long, can it? Nine months?"

Seeing the hopeful look on Andy's face, Horatio hated to tell him. "I think it will, Andy. And so does Penny."

Andy looked crestfallen. And scared. Horatio hesitated. He and Andy had been friends a long time. They had drifted apart after Andy got married, but they were still good friends. He made the decision.

"I tell you what, Andy. Sometimes we butt heads, you know…"

Andy managed a small smile. That was a truth they both knew well.

"But, if you can assure me, because of Vicky's condition, that if you will follow my lead, and Penny's, you can come out to our place. You will be safe there.

"And Vicky will get the care she needs. Penny has the kind of training that unless there is some kind of really major problem with Vicky or the baby, Penny will be able to take care of both of them, including delivering the baby. She has delivered one before."

"Horatio, you place isn't big enough for…"

Horatio interrupted Andy. "Not my house here in town, Andy. Though it would work better than you might think. Penny and I have a place out on the lake. Believe me, it is adequate to have you and Vicky there, with absolutely no problems."

Andy's eyes widened for a moment in surprise. Then he squeezed them shut for a long moment. "Lord... you know I hate being beholden..."

"Andy," Horatio assured his friend, "You will not be beholden. In fact, you might be doing some of the most difficult work you have ever done in the coming months, if this plays out like we think. We all will be working our tails off to survive this. It might even come to violence. Major violence, to protect ourselves. I need to know you will be all in. And not be worrying about owing us."

Andy looked at the door of his house. Horatio knew he was thinking about Vicky and not himself. "I'll have to convince Vicky," Andy said. "She is scared out of her mind. I can't get her to come out of the master bedroom's bathroom."

"Do what you have to," Horatio said. "Wait." Horatio keyed his radio. "I'm coming back on foot. Things are okay, but we will be taking some people back with us. I need to leave my radio with Andy, so will be out of communication until I get back to you.

"Contact Penny and tell her to expect a radio call from Andy's wife."

He nodded at Eddie's radio acknowledgement. And then smiled when Penny's voice sounded. "Okay Horatio. I heard. I will be waiting."

Horatio took the radio off his belt, and the headset off his head after removing his hat. He handed it to Andy. "Have Vicky talk to Penny while you start getting things ready. Take what you need right now, and then try to secure everything else you want to come back and get.

"Things may or may not still be here when we come back to get the rest if it isn't well hidden."

A determined look on Andy's face, he took the radio and headed into the house. Horatio headed back to the Suburban.

Almost two hours later Eddie left Andy's place, with the Suburban right behind him, with Andy and Vicky, and a load of their things inside.

It was well they left when they did, for when they arrived at the strip mall, just as Horatio had feared, there were six people at his office, with two vehicles, one of which was a four-wheel drive pickup truck. And a chain was being readied to connect the pickup to the front door security shutter.

Caught totally by surprise, the five men and one woman froze when Eddie, Horatio, Misty, and Andy all suddenly had weapons trained on them. They had their own weapons, but it was far too late for them to even reach for them, much less use them.

"Go," Horatio shouted. "I catch you around here again it will be shoot first and ask questions later!"

Andy gave him a concerned look, but kept his handgun aimed at one of the men.

It was with obvious reluctance, and a great deal of hate being shown, that the six entered the two vehicles and sped away.

Horatio had seen the look Andy had given him. "Andy... look... I would never do what I told them. But I had to make an impression. Right now. I might not ever even be back here, but I want some things from here that are important."

Andy looked relieved. "Okay. I kinda figured that..."

Horatio took a look around. He turned to the others and spoke. "Andy, Eddie, Misty, and I have on body armor. You don't. I want you inside the Suburban, with the doors closed.

"Bunny, you and Vicky stay below the level of the open windows. Andy, keep your head on a swivel, and call out if you see anyone. Anyone at all. After I show Misty what I want to take, she will be bringing it out to Eddie, and he will be handing it up to me on the roof rack to secure."

There were four almost identical, 'Buts'. Horatio waved them away. "I am not putting anyone else up top. It is too dangerous. It is my risk to take."

With that, Horatio opened the security shutter, with a bit of difficulty, as it had been hammered on severely. But he got the door open and quickly showed Misty the items he wanted.

As he carried out one file drawer, Misty was bringing another. Horatio handed the drawer to Eddie, and then climbed the ladder to the roof rack of the Suburban. It took only seconds to release the tarp and flip it back. With the fold down steps on the rear bumper deployed, Eddie stepped up and handed the file drawer to Horatio, who set it where he wanted it.

It did not take too long to get everything from inside the office that Horatio wanted. Eddie did have to go inside to help Misty disconnect some of the electronics, but that did not add too much time.

Since it had gone as quickly as it had, Horatio decided to take a bit more time to take down the outside cameras. But when he heard the sound of brakes squealing, and then engines being gunned, Horatio abandoned the thought, secured the tarp, and was on the ground quickly.

Eddie already had the security shutter down and was on his bike, the engine started. Just as Horatio closed the driver's side door, right after Misty did the passenger door, four vehicles came screaming around the corner down the street. Two of them were the ones they had run off earlier.

Eddie took off, with the Suburban right behind him. Three of the vehicles pulled in next to the office building, smoke coming from their tires as their brakes were slammed on. One vehicle gave chase, accelerating after the Suburban.

Three quick rounds from Misty had them slowing, and then stopping. The vehicle was turning around when Horatio took the Suburban around a street corner behind Eddie.

Andy and Bunny were comforting a very scared Vicky. She was fairly calm by the time they got to the property. She, and especially Andy, looked around, rather in awe, at the place Horatio had created on the lake.

Cutting wide eyes at Horatio when they exited the Suburban, Andy softly said, "I had no idea… Man… And I have a feeling there is a lot more to this than it appears…"

"You got that right," Horatio replied.

Penny was running out to him and he caught her as she leaped into his arms. "We saw what happened. Is everyone okay?" she asked, after the two shared a kiss and tight, long hug.

Horatio answered as Penny moved over to Vicky. "Yes. We're fine. But I do think it would be a good idea to check Vicky over so Andy will not be so worried." Horatio smiled a bit at his friend as he hovered over his wife as she talked to Penny.

"Wait," Andy suddenly said, turning back to Horatio for a moment. "Penny said she saw…"

Horatio nodded. "Internet is down, but I have a data link from the office to the Suburban, my house, and out here. And one from the Suburban to the house and out here, and from the hou…"

"I get it. I get it," Andy said. "You always were a thorough SOB." Andy hesitated a moment. "And I sure am glad of it. Thank you, Horatio."

Horatio nodded, seeing the gratefulness in his friend's eyes and posture. Horatio was very glad he had been able to maintain the friendship and was able to be there for Andy and Vicky. He smiled slightly. All thanks to Penny, of course.

Once Penny had Vicky settled, and Frank had shown Andy around a bit, Penny motioned to Horatio. He followed her into the study. Suzette was on the radios, headphones on her head. She acknowledged them but turned back to her monitoring.

Quietly, Penny told Horatio, "It is much worse than I… any of us… expected. We know why it has turned out the way it has. You remember Bradley? From the Prepper convention?"

When Horatio nodded, Penny continued. "Bradley was another of the ones working with Adam and I, along with a couple of others. When Adam sent him the information he did me, Bradley tied it in to something he was working on.

"It seems… No. Not seems. Is very obvious… that THE Powers That Be are not the ONLY Powers That Be. Some group, within the main group, without the main group's knowledge, was using the subliminal technology to add their own agenda messages to all the rest of the messages the main group authorized.

"These are much more… intense… much more provocative in what they are suggesting. More violent, against more groups. Without any type of moderator… No goal, so to speak. Something that would stop the activities… Like an end point."

Penny closed her eyes. She shook her head. "These… people… had… have no idea what they have created. Set loose on society. Civilization."

Cutting her eyes up to Horatio, she added, even more softly, "They have turned a large number of human beings into… Lord… Zombies of a sort.

"Not movie zombies. Oh, no. These are living, breathing, fast acting, angry zombies, with only one drive. To destroy. Whatever their pet peeve is. They will seek out those they connect with it and do everything they can to destroy them.

"And with all the different, mixed messages, once they have done what they can to destroy whatever is their primary focus, another one will suddenly become just as important. Just as necessary to destroy."

Once more Penny looked away. And then back at Horatio. "The ones that orchestrated this, thinking they will be able to control it, will wind up being the targets at some point.

"But it may be too late for real justice to be done. If the wrong people wind up influenced… If they are in the right position… with the right authority… Anything could happen. Anything. Even nuclear war, Horatio."

When she fell silent, Horatio took her in his arms and held her. For a long time. She was not sobbing, or even crying, but she held on as if for dear life.

She relaxed a bit, and Horatio released her, stepping back, his hands going to her upper arms. "We will persevere, Penny. You know we will."

"I know," she said sadly. "But millions… Billions of innocent people are going to die in this process, along with the guilty. I just hope that the society that comes out of it in the end will be a better one than the one going into it."

Horatio could only nod. Time would tell. He had done what he could, for the moment. The next days, weeks, months, and years would not be easy ones. But Horatio knew that he was willing to, and would, do what was necessary to bring about that better society. With Penny, and the others, he was confident they would succeed.

THE END

THANK YOU
FOR READING!

If you enjoyed this book, we would appreciate your customer review on your book seller's website or on Goodreads.

Also, we would like for you to know that you can find more great books like this one at
www.CreativeTexts.com